a Tenacity romance

The Proper Choice

ANITA BLOUNT

Printed in the United States of America by
Kindle Direct Publishing, an Amazon
company.

Cover art by Artist,
Bobby Walters of Hattiesburg, MS

ISBN 978-1-63821-716-9

**FOR MY DAUGHTERS,
WENDY AND MEGAN,**

who make my life complete.

ANITA BLOUNT

CHAPTER ONE

The night virtually sparkled with merriment, oblivious
to the misfortune that shadowed Samantha's world.
Pasting a smile on her face, the maid of honor
surveyed the scene. Snow white linens covered tables
brimming with platters of roast beef, fried chicken,
and a smorgasbord of delectable southern dishes.
Sweet tea sat at the end of a buffet, soft drinks and
bottled water chilled in galvanized tubs on the ground,
and alternate libations flowed from car trunks and
truck beds positioned around Mill Village Park. The
guests, as well as the band, were well fed and
pleasantly lubricated.

A hundred years before, in the same exact spot,
local mill workers picnicked, played baseball, and
challenged one another to games of horseshoes. Their
simple, solid homes, with banistered front porches,
still bordered the park. The turn-of-the-century
homes, with their exterior gas-lights, blossoming
azalea bushes, and flowering dogwoods, created a
dream-like backdrop for Max and Anna's much
anticipated wedding reception.

Even though Samantha longed to join the revelry,
she forced herself away from the portable dance floor.
Her body begged to move with the music, but dancing
involved touching, and Samantha didn't know how
she'd react. The party guests were friends, many of
whom she'd known all her life, but she didn't trust

herself not to panic and wouldn't risk causing a scene. She'd avoided a man's touch for two years, and her friend's wedding reception was no place to launch a recovery program.

Convinced people would see her in a different light if they knew what had happened, Samantha tried to erase the reprehensible event that changed her world. She was content now. Her life was pleasant. But if her secret was discovered, she might never escape the despised memory.

Despite her personal difficulties, Samantha was pleased with the success of the evening. Practically everyone in Tenacity, Mississippi had turned out for Anna and Max's wedding reception.

Guests laughed at stories they'd heard for years. Folks sang along with the band, whether they could carry a tune or not, and dancers of all ages cavorted on the platforms.

Everything glittered and swayed. Strings of lights, looped from tree to tree, stirred in the breeze, competing with bright stars in a dark sky. A current of gentle air blew across the Tanakbi River, cooling the April evening. The night felt magical. Samantha smiled at the thought, for when Tenacity friends gathered on quiet evenings, conversations often turned to stories of their town's abundant mystical occurrences.

A surprising number of locals believed the corridor, the gateway to their community, held some kind of magical power. The three-quarters-of-a-mile tunnel of old oaks, with limbs reaching across the road to block out the sun, was given credit for all manner of miracles: curing illnesses, calling wayward children home, casting love spells, even granting women the ability to conceive.

Samantha's friend, Anna, was one of many who believed the old oaks were enchanted. On that dazzling night in the park, Samantha thought the notion of magic almost seemed possible, for the air shimmered with an uncommon brand of excitement.

If magic really did reside in that mystical green corridor, she'd wish for it to make her whole again. Samantha didn't truly believe it was possible, but just in case she was wrong, she turned her face skyward, closed her eyes, and willed her world to right itself.

When a gust of wind blew across her face, she opened her eyes and saw Conner Wilmington weaving his way through the crowd. Oh dear. He was moving her direction, his gorgeous blond head towering over the other guests.

Pretending not to see him, Samantha steadily inched away. Conner was a friend, who shouldn't make her heart beat faster, but he did. She made the mistake of glancing his direction. Their eyes met, and she couldn't look away. When Conner reached her, he took her hand in his, nodded toward the band, and gently tugged her toward the dance floor. Samantha shook her head, her strawberry blond curls bouncing. Trying to be heard over the music, she said, "I'm not dancing tonight."

"Come on," he coaxed. "You have to dance at our best friend's wedding."

"Our best friend?"

"You were Anna's friend and confidant growing up," Conner explained. "I took over when she was in

3

college. Now that she's back in Tenacity and I'm just down the road in Clarkston, we'll have to share."

"Okay, but you have a long-row-to-hoe to get Max to accept you," Samantha chided, "and he's her husband now." Standing on her toes, she moved close to his ear. "He may never forgive you for sleeping with Anna."

"You know about that?"

Smiling, she sing-songed, "I do now."

"That was a long time ago," he assured her. "Come dance with me. Anna told me you like country swing."

"I do, but I'm surprised you even know what that is? You don't seem the type."

Conner didn't ask what she meant. He knew. He was a prep-school kid who graduated with honors from a top university, and his parents were influential Savannah socialites.

Sometimes he wondered if that information was printed on his forehead. For no matter where he went, new acquaintances made surprisingly accurate assumptions about his background. But when it came to guessing who he was inside, their suppositions often went awry.

"I love it," Conner insisted, "much to my mother's chagrin. She sent me to dance school for ballroom lessons and I discovered country swing."

"What's wrong with that?"

"To her, dancing should be reserved for cotillion balls and formal events, not country bars."

"No fun, huh?"

"Not so much."

When the music sounded louder, Samantha realized Conner had led her through the crowd to the dance floor. As "Boot Scootin' Boogie" rang out, a line dance formed, and he pulled her onto the wooden platform.

I'm okay, she told herself. Line dancing doesn't require being held. I can handle this. The music lured her, and before she knew it, she was having fun. So was Conner. The man had moves. She hadn't expected that, although it made sense that a former basketball star would be agile.

When the band's front man began singing Lady in Red, Conner spun Samantha into a slow dance before she had a chance to protest. She pulled away, but because Conner looked so disappointed and confused, she pasted a smile on her face and let him pull her back in. Trying to relax, she reminded herself that Conner was one of the good guys, but she was all too aware of his long slender hand on her bare back.

When he spoke, Samantha had to look up, even though her heels helped even out the difference between her five-foot seven frame and Conner's six-foot five one. He leaned back so he could see her face as they discussed swing dance moves. The distance helped reduce her tension, but when their discussion subsided, Conner pulled her close again.

Samantha surprised herself by resting her head against his firm chest. She marveled at how comfortable she was beginning to feel in his arms. Fear of being close to a man had done more than keep her off the dance floor. It had governed her life for the past two years. Strangely, in Conner's arms, she almost relaxed.

She thought about how handsome he was. He could easily be a model or a movie star instead of an attorney. He wouldn't even have to be talented. Women would pay just to sit and look at him for an hour and a half.

Conner wasn't a celebrity, not in the normal sense, but he definitely had a following. She'd never admit it, but she'd googled him and found an online group dedicated to Conner McArthur Wilmington. She joined, using an alternate e-mail address, just to see what it was all about.

The members seemed young, based on their posts, and most lived on the east coast where Conner grew up and attended college. They reported sightings of him, extolled his hotness, and posted photographs, most of which were from his college basketball years. Others were from debutant balls, newspapers, and yearbooks. After perusing the posts, Samantha left the online group, hoping no one would discover she'd been there.

When the song was over, rather than loosen his hold on her, he tugged Samantha toward the band. He spoke to the lead singer and grinned as the man announced, "We have a request, folks, for 'Honky Tonk Bedonka Donk.' "

The announcement was followed by whoops and hollers and a stampede of dancers to the wooden platform. But it didn't take long for Conner and Samantha to dominate the space.

Guests moved aside to watch, giving the couple the boisterous appreciation they deserved. They looked as if they'd been dancing together for years. When

Conner flashed a huge smile, Samantha thought that even the man's teeth were perfect.

When the dance was over, Conner said, "We have to do that again. Know any good places around here?"

"A few."

"Pick one and we'll go."

"Us? Together?"

"Sure. We were good out there, and I don't know when I've had so much fun."

"We'll talk about it," Samantha said, knowing it was something she'd never seriously consider. She used to love going to country bars with big dance floors, but that was before.

Her phone lit up with a text. "I have to do a favor for Max," she explained.

That's what Conner liked about this little, out-of-the-way town; people took care of one another.

"I need transportation," she reluctantly told Conner. "Anna insisted I ride with her to the ceremony, since I was her bridesmaid and she dressed at my house. Now I'm without wheels. Wanna help?"

"Sure. What are we doing?"

"You'll see. Where did you park that fancy little car of yours?"

Just for fun, Samantha didn't tell him where they were going. When she directed him to turn his shiny, black Porsche onto a gravel road, he said, "If you wanted to park, you should've just said so. I'm up for it."

She gave him a side-long glance. "I didn't bring you here to park."

"Then why are we in the middle of nowhere?"

7

"We're not in the middle of nowhere, Mr. Big-city-lawyer."

"Hey, I work down the road in Clarkston and grew up in Savannah, Georgia. Neither of those are big cities."

"They are compared to Tenacity. We're going to my house to get my truck. Max asked me to do a few things at his cabin before Anna sees it."

"Where's the cabin?"

"Down that little road we just passed." Instead of doing as she asked, Conner backed up until he found the dirt-packed passageway.

"But I need my truck. Or just let me out. I can walk the rest of the way."

Conner's eyebrows furrowed. "What's wrong? Why don't you want me to go with you?"

"Nothing's wrong. I just figured you'd rather be at the party," she lied.

A few minutes later, they pulled up to a beautiful cabin on a hill. "Max and his crew built this as a surprise for Anna," Samantha explained. "He's bringing her here for their honeymoon."

"It's great. Can we go in?"

When Samantha hesitated, Conner hurried around the front of the car to open her door. She got out, and seeing no choice, reluctantly allowed him to follow. She removed a key from under a stone and used it to enter the cabin.

Inside, she took flowers from the refrigerator and replaced them with containers of food from the reception. After promptly arranging the blossoms in vases, she situated them around the cabin, sprinkling rose petals on the master bedroom bed as well as on the screened porch.

Watching her bustle about in the knee-length, flared skirt, Conner thought she couldn't be any cuter. He liked the way her dress dipped almost to the waist in the back, but, mostly, he liked the girl wearing it. Samantha had a pretty face, a great smile, and a killer body. It didn't hurt that those spike heels made her legs look fantastic. And the way her strawberry blond curls bounced when she walked was downright fascinating.

"Did I tell you how pretty you look tonight?" Conner asked.

"I don't think you did."

"Well, I'm telling you now. You look beautiful. Now what can I do to help?"

"You could start the fire," Samantha said, after thanking him for his compliment. "The wood is already stacked in the fireplace. You just need to take some kindling from the copper pot and..."

"I know how to start a fire," Conner said.

"You mean your staff lets you do those sorts of things?"

"I don't have a staff."

"But Mama and Daddy do," she teased.

"They do," he admitted, "and I won't apologize for it."

After turning on flicker candles and mini lights in the cabin and on the porch, Samantha turned off the overhead ones. "Wow," she said, appreciating the ambience.

"Wow," Conner agreed. "It's beautiful. You know," he said, wrapping a long arm around her, pulling her close, "this is very romantic." Leaning down, he gave her a light kiss, and before she regained enough composure to stop him, his mouth returned with a swoon-inducing one.

Another wow, Samantha thought. He's really good at that. Then she remembered what Anna told her about Conner. "He's a gentleman and a loyal friend, a sweetheart of a guy, but he's also something of a tomcat. I don't mean he's a skirt chaser. He doesn't have to be. He just picks and chooses from his bevy of admirers."

Still reeling from the kiss, Samantha reminded him the romantic atmosphere was for Max and Anna—not them. She couldn't believe she'd let him kiss her that way, especially when they were alone in a cabin in the woods. But glory hallelujah, she hadn't freaked out.

"I need to text Max," Samantha said. "Let him know the cabin's ready."

Conner reluctantly released her. "Do you want to go back to the party?"

"No, I need you to take me home. It's just over there," Samantha said, pointing to the trees behind the cabin. "But to get there, you'll need to head back down the dirt path that brought us here and then take a right. My house sits at the end of the road."

Gravel crunched under the sports car's tires as Conner pulled in front of Samantha's two-story farmhouse. Chickens clucked and hunting dogs barked. "Nature's security alarm," he observed.

"They are. But I have the other kind, too."

"Good. You're pretty isolated out here. You stay in this big house alone?"

"I do. But I love it. The farm is the only home I've ever known. Mama and my biological father renovated it early in their marriage. He died before I was born," she said matter-of-factly, "but he left Mama and me this beautiful old place. It's a lot to keep up, but I love it," she repeated.

"Situated at the end of the road like it is, it looks like we've stepped back in time," Conner said.

"It does, and I like it that way. Max says it reminds him of an old black and white television series. The one where everyone tells John Boy good-night."

"Even your truck is from another era. What year is it?"

"It's a 1950 Ford," she said proudly. "You know Doug McKinnon. Before he started buying quick-stop stores, he refurbished old vehicles. I saw that truck after he finished it and fell in love with it. So my parents gave it to me on my sixteenth birthday."

After opening the Porsche door to help Samantha out, Conner kissed her again. Still shocked she could accept his advances, she remembered what her therapist had said. "You can heal, but it won't happen until you give yourself the opportunity." And for the first time, Sam believed it might be possible.

If anyone could make her feel like a woman again, it would be Conner. According to Anna, he'd been with a lot of women—which was no surprise. He was male perfection, and Samantha was smitten the first time she laid eyes on the elegant man. Elegant isn't a word often used to describe men, but Conner Wilmington was elegant.

Because both were in Anna and Max's circle of friends, Samantha knew Conner well. He flirted with

11

her at social gatherings, and occasionally, she'd slip and flirt back. It was hard to hide her infatuation in those situations, but she'd managed until now.

Initially, his looks attracted her. But once she knew him, the attraction grew, making him even harder to resist. She genuinely liked Conner, but she'd always feared he'd make a move on her that she couldn't handle. Well, she was handling it now.

Samantha debated the decision she was about to make. Maybe Conner could perform a miracle and bring intimacy back to her life, but trusting was hard after what had happened. She'd trusted another man, and that had been a huge mistake. If she turned Conner away, she might miss the opportunity to become whole again. And she'd never recover if she didn't take a risk.

She could rationalize all day, but the truth was, once she knew how it felt to be in his arms and feel his lips against hers, she simply couldn't resist the man. She could trust him, she told herself. He wasn't anything like Hal. She knew Conner, they were friends, and Anna had known him even longer. He was steady, reliable, and the sexiest man she'd ever met.

Samantha pulled back from Conner long enough to tell Hot Shot and Queenie to hush. "That's enough," she told the bird dogs. They obeyed, but stayed close and on alert.

As Samantha continued to accept Conner's advances, their kisses became more passionate. His tongue teased her mouth, they pressed tightly against one another, and Conner's hands roamed seductively over her body. When they couldn't get any closer, he lifted her hips, bringing their most intimate parts temptingly close.

This is really happening, Samantha thought, amazed. Coming up for air, she joked, "Wanna come in for coffee?"

"Coffee sounds delicious," he said, a little breathlessly.

Okay then. She couldn't quite believe she was about to do what she was about to do. Hot Shot and Queenie followed them to the front door, wagging their tails, watching.

Samantha and Conner's approach to the front porch activated a motion-sensitive light, overpowering the single-bulb fixture hanging above the front door. One was a glaring symbol of the modern world, the other a gentle reminder of a simpler past.

Samantha removed a key from her purse and opened what must have been the original door of the turn-of-the century farmhouse. She wasn't kidding about having security. Inside, she re-activated the alarm and set three separate locks.

They resumed kissing the minute she completed the task, the brief intermission doing nothing to cool their passion.

"Bedroom?" Conner asked, his lips still on hers.

"That way," she answered, pointing down the hall. Their lips and tongues never slowed as they inched toward the downstairs bedroom, They lay on the bed, fully dressed, embracing, kissing, fondling.

This might be their only time together, Samantha realized, but she wanted him enough to dismiss the thought. Then it happened. Conner's body moved over hers and she went rigid.

"What's wrong?"

Samantha looked away, tears forming in her eyes. "Nothing. I'm fine." Turning her face toward him, she said, "Just kiss me." He did, but she clearly wasn't fine.

"Talk to me. What did I do?"

"Nothing. I'm sorry. It's not you. It's me. I'm just broken."

"What happened, Samantha? You're sure I didn't do anything wrong?"

"You didn't. Like I said, I'm broken."

"Did someone hurt you?" It's the only thing he could think of that might cause such a reaction.

She nodded.

"Do you want to talk about it?"

Samantha shook her head. "Don't tell anyone. It's something I don't share. I wish you didn't know."

"Then let me hold you. That's all. Can you do that?" She nodded, and Conner held her until she relaxed. Once his eyes adjusted to the dark, he looked around. "I can tell this isn't your bedroom. Do you sleep upstairs?" She nodded again. "Do you trust me?" he asked.

"Yes. I think so."

"Then I want you to go upstairs, take a bath, put on your coziest pajamas, and get into bed. I'm going to sleep beside you. Sleep. That's all. Nothing else— unless you want more. That's completely up to you. But I've had a drink or two and shouldn't drive back to Clarkston. The firm frowns on its attorneys getting DUIs."

"You never drink too much," Samantha said. "That's one reason I feel I can trust you."

"So maybe I just don't want to leave. Go on up. I'll give you some time before I join you."

"Okay," Sam said, surprising herself yet again. He might witness one of her nightmares, but he already knew she had a problem.

Conner wasn't sure what he was doing, but he had to do something. He couldn't leave her alone after what just transpired. She'd obviously gone through something traumatic. She was hurting, and he wanted to help. Since the situation was new territory for him, he'd have to wing it. He'd do whatever made her comfortable.

The following morning, Conner woke to the smell of coffee and sausage. After a quick shower, he donned his pants and the shirt he'd left on the chair the night before. He'd go commando. If he kept seeing Samantha, maybe he should keep sleep pants and extra underwear in his car.

Smiling, he threw the boxer briefs he'd worn to bed into the clothes hamper and pictured Samantha finding his surprise. Conner had been true to his word, only cuddling the woman lying beside him. It was sweet torture, but it was the right thing to do.

He found Samantha downstairs in the kitchen, taking sausage from an iron skillet as if nothing out of the ordinary had occurred. Before last night, Conner thought he knew Samantha. Now, he realized he'd only seen what she wanted him to see. She was truly a beautiful, generous, woman, but she was also a puzzle. Never would he have guessed that her usual cheerful demeanor hid a painful secret.

As she stood at the stove, with a smile on her face, Conner thought he was beginning to understand how she coped. She seemed to pretend the traumatic event never happened, and she'd convinced everyone she was completely carefree. He wasn't sure that was the right approach, but he wasn't a therapist. If that's what she needed, he could play along.

After telling Samantha good morning and kissing her cheek, Conner poured coffee into the flowered cups he found sitting next to the coffee maker. He placed them on the kitchen table next to Samantha's mixed-patterned, vintage china and eyed the steaming biscuits, butter, and jar of home-made jam. Pulling out a ladder back chair, he sat down at the painted wooden table and picked up his coffee.

He was about to take a sip when Samantha asked, with feigned indifference, "Did I have a nightmare last night?"

"No, not that I could tell," he said, mimicking her lack of emotion. "Do you have them often?"

She nodded.

"But you don't want to talk about it," he guessed.

"Nope."

Looking around, he changed the subject. "I like this room. It has character, not only because of the throwback style. There's just something about it."

"I think so, too," Samantha said. "Mama and I refurbished it. We stripped and painted the cabinets, bought new appliances, that sort of thing. But it seemed wrong to change too much. By keeping it close to the original, I like to think we're paying tribute to the families who came before us. Sometimes, I feel as if they're still here."

Conner raised his eyebrows. "Do you see apparitions or feel cold spots?"

16

"No. Nothing that startling. It's more of an awareness, an appreciation of all the families who've loved this house and worked this farm. I can almost see an overall-clad boy running through the kitchen, grabbing a cookie, and a sweet-faced woman, wearing a flowered apron, making biscuits. And right over there," she said, pointing to a door leading to the outside, "is a man taking off his boots and hanging his coat on a hook by the door. Who knows? Maybe those families still exist in a way we can't understand. You know, sort of like an echo."

"Maybe. That's a pretty detailed vision you described," Conner said. "Have you always had a vivid imagination?"

"I suppose so. I had an imaginary playmate when I was young. I don't remember, but according to Mama, he was quite real to me."

"Have you thought about researching the house's history?"

"I have. I just haven't gotten around to it. There always seems to be something more important than wading through legal documents at city hall."

"Let me help. We can do much of it online— maybe all of it. Most agencies and newspapers have digitized their files."

When he swallowed the first bite of biscuit, his eyes widened. "Are these homemade?"

"Only the best for you."

"They're fantastic."

"But you owe me for breakfast."

"And how do you suggest I pay?" It took all Conner's self-control to say that without sounding suggestive.

"You can feed the chickens while I feed the cows and dogs."

"You have cows?"

Samantha laughed at the expression on his face. "What did you expect? This is a farm."

"Do you milk them?"

"We used to milk Lazy Maisie, but now she's just a pet. Daddy bought Maynard when he was a bull calf, planning to butcher him when he was older. A word of advice—never let your child name something you plan to eat. I fell in love with the massive baby. So now I have a two-thousand-pound pet whose name is Maynard."

"I've never known anyone with pet cows. You said you feed them. Don't they eat grass?"

"They do, but they need hay in winter, and I give them feed pellets—treats with added nutrients," she explained. "Have you ever had a pet?"

"No. I used to want a dog or a cat, but my mother doesn't allow animals in the house. And in town, letting them roam outside isn't an option. Now, I'm not home often enough. It wouldn't be fair to the animal."

"Then feeding mine will be a new experience." That would be Conner's second new experience since leaving the reception with Samantha. The first was sleeping with a woman without having sex.

A couple of days later, Conner phoned Samantha. "Thought of a place to go dancing?"

"That's not a good idea."

"Why? We were great together."

Until we weren't, she thought, wishing she could say yes. But Samantha knew, with their chemistry, things were bound to get passionate, and her problem would raise its ugly head. Conner deserved better. "You're right. We were good together. And it was fun. But I'm broken. Remember?"

"I'm not asking you to have sex, although I certainly wouldn't be averse to that. We'll just go dancing."

Samantha couldn't, or wouldn't, explain why she was turning him down. She simply said no.

Sex or no sex, Conner liked Samantha; so he phoned often. Sometimes they'd talk for hours. On the nights he didn't call, she wondered where he was and what he was doing.

He certainly wasn't sitting alone in his apartment pining for her. He probably had a long list of beautiful women waiting to go out with him or, more likely, stay in with him. On the few occasions she nonchalantly asked what he did on a night he didn't call, he always had a breezy, vague answer.

Samantha chided herself for letting thoughts of a man occupy her mind. What Conner did was none of her business, and there was no reason to torture herself over something that couldn't be.

But it was hard not to obsess over a man who was kind, gorgeous, and intelligent, with a smile that made her forget the rest of the world existed. A romantic relationship wasn't in her future, and grieving the fact accomplished nothing. As hard as it was, she might as well resign herself to a life alone.

Every now and then, Conner would sneak a date invitation into one of their conversations, but Samantha always refused. Over the next few months, as mutual friends of Anna Anderson's, Conner and Samantha were thrown together. They joined her for lunch a couple of times in Clarkston and had Sunday dinner with Max and Anna at Max's parents' house.

Despite what happened the night of the reception, they never felt awkward around one another. They joked, flirted a little, and, in general, enjoyed one another's company. Samantha discovered she'd have to add the word fun to Conner's long list of attributes. He was her idea of the perfect man, but a relationship with him was a foolish dream.

CHAPTER TWO

Samantha hurried to the ringing phone, hoping to hear Conner's voice, but it was Anna.

"How are you, Sam? How's teaching going?"

"Good. I like second grade, and my kids are great. They've already grasped the basics, so we're able to do some fun things."

"They're lucky to have you."

"Thank you, my kind friend. How are you and the little peanut doing?"

"I'm ready for this baby to be born. But first, I want to see that matinee in Clarkston on Saturday. Will you go with me? Max isn't interested, and Conner wants to meet us there. And you know how Max is about Conner. I'll drive. Please come."

What could she say? "Sure. Sounds like fun."

Saturday afternoon, Anna picked Samantha up, arriving at the theatre parking lot forty-five minutes later. Conner was waiting. Leaning against his shiny, black sports car, his legs crossed at the ankles, he was every woman's fantasy—tall, slender, fit, with thick blond hair and piercing blue eyes. He had it all.

Samantha's heart raced as she helplessly moved toward him. She shouldn't have come. Conner Wilmington was too much of a temptation.

Pushing away from the Porsche, he flashed his killer smile, strolled toward the women with his loose-limbed gait, and kissed them on the cheek.

"Looks like it won't be much longer," Conner said, eyeing Anna's extended belly. "Or is that the wrong thing to say to a pregnant woman?"

"I don't know. I just hope you're right."

"Glad you could both make it," he said, wrapping an arm around each of them as they walked to the theatre. "Today is my treat—tickets, drinks, and all the popcorn you can eat."

When they found an unoccupied row of seats, Anna entered first, and then Samantha. Conner sat last, folding his long legs into the confined space. As his spicy scent wafted Samantha's direction, she almost groaned, thinking she should have sat where Anna was sitting. Now, she'd have to absorb Conner's warmth and inhale his delicious scent for an hour and a half, when mere minutes near him made her edgy. Everything about the man was seductive.

To make matters worse, he kept leaning close to comment on the movie. Did he realize his warm breath felt like caresses on her neck? Probably. He had to know how he affected women.

Samantha tried, without much success, to concentrate on the plot. She wasn't even sure how the movie ended. On the way to the parking lot, Conner invited Anna and Samantha to dinner. "Come on, I'll take you anywhere you want to go. How about it, Anna?"

"I wish I could, but I need to get home to Max and Gracie. Thanks for the idea, Conner. This could be the last time I go out to a movie for a while," she said, patting her belly.

"Samantha, will you stay?" Conner asked. "I'll drive you home."

"Yes, stay, Samantha," Anna said. "There's no reason for you to rush back to Tenacity. Stay and have a nice dinner. We'll talk, later." She hurried away, leaving Sam with an unspoken protest on her lips.

Conner kept his hand on Samantha's lower back as they walked to the car and then to the restaurant. Unable to ignore the warm tingles his light touch sent through her body, she did her best to hide her reaction.

Over an excellent meal at a corner table of a nice restaurant, they chatted easily. "I've never asked you," Samantha said, "what area of law you prefer."

"I'm still deciding. Don't tell my father, but I'm glad he got me this job in Clarkston. Since the law firm I'm with represents several specialties, I'm being allowed to work in each area for a while, to get an overview of what it encompasses. I usually balk when Dad interferes in my life, but this time, I appreciate it. He's hoping I'll choose corporate law, but I don't think I'll go that direction."

On the surface, dinner was just a friendly date. But the longing Samantha felt when she arrived at the theatre parking lot and saw Conner leaning against his car had escalated as the evening progressed. It was his voice, his scent, the way he walked, the way he looked at her, his touch. All six-foot-five-inches of Conner Wilmington oozed magic pheromones.

Attraction aside, he was an honest, caring person. He'd been right when he said they were good together. As far as Samantha could see, they were well suited in every way, except one very important one.

So far, the evening had gone exactly as Conner planned, but all through dinner he'd thought about kissing Samantha. He didn't expect anything more, but maybe, if he played his cards right, he'd get a kiss and she'd agree to another date.

At the farmhouse, Conner hurried around the front of the Porsche and helped Samantha from the low, road hugging car. He wrapped an arm around her waist and peered into her wide, blue eyes, his intense expression holding her captive. Pulling Samantha close, Conner cupped her head in his long hand, and without taking his eyes from hers, inched toward her lips.

Samantha's skin warmed and her lower body clenched before he even kissed her. She wanted to tell him to just do it, but she couldn't speak, couldn't move, couldn't breathe. She just waited, hoping she wouldn't pass out.

When his lips finally met hers, the kiss was soft and gentle. His tongue moved tenderly in her sweet mouth until her body molded to his, and he felt willingness give way to wanting. Deepening the kiss, Conner's tongue became insistent, and Samantha's arms tightened around his neck. When she pulled his head down, he moaned.

Lost in the moment, Samantha wanted to devour him. Abruptly, one of the dogs nudged her leg with his wet nose, interrupting the passionate kiss, hurtling Samantha and Conner back to reality. After their brief flirt with ecstasy, they held one another, breathing hard, reluctant to part.

"You know I can't invite you in," Samantha whispered, wishing more than anything that she could.

"I understand," Conner said, not sure that he did. They walked to the door, shielding their eyes from the glaring, motion-sensing light. "I had a great time, Samantha. I'd like to do this again. Only next time, I'll pick you up. No expectations. I just enjoy being with you."

Sam nodded. She enjoyed it too much. Being with him made her yearn for what she couldn't have, and it hurt. "Good-night, Conner. Thank you for a lovely evening."

He could tell she'd had a good time, but that didn't mean she'd agree to another date. He'd tricked her into this one. Well, they had phone calls. He'd just have to find a way to make the most of them.

On one of their late-night phone conversations, Samantha told Conner she planned to give Anna a baby shower.

"Are guys invited?"

"I hadn't thought of it, but I like the idea."

"And Gracie will want to come," he added.

"Of course. We couldn't have a shower without the big sister. She's so excited. She wants the baby to hurry and come so she can take it to show-and-tell. I like your suggestion, Conner. I think I'll call it a friends and family shower."

"So, what has to be done before the occasion?" Conner asked. "Mom always has a long 'to do' list before a party. Polishing silver, waxing floors, pruning hedges, that sort of thing."

"I'll have to declutter my office and clean the house. Daddy had the exterior painted before he and Mama moved. So it looks good. But I'm sure you noticed the front door needs sanding and refinishing. The dogs scratched it."

"Your dogs did that?"

"They wouldn't normally. There were extenuating circumstances. Even though the shower is planned for early December," she said, as if she hadn't left her previous comment hanging, "I'd like to put up the Christmas tree and hang a garland on the staircase. And I'll put a wreath on the door and the windows. The house is so pretty when it's decked out for the holidays. It looks like a Currier and Ives print."

"Does your family get together to decorate?"

"Not anymore. It'll just be me."

"I can help," Conner offered. "When I lived at home, Mom always commandeered me to help trim the tree. I can reach the high branches."

"You'd help decorate? You'd do that for me?"

"Sure. I'd enjoy it. And I can help with the door, too. Just tell me when."

"No funny business?" Samantha asked.

Conner chuckled. "No funny business."

"Okay then. How about next Saturday morning? I'll make a pot of stew for lunch."

"Conner McArthur Wilmington, reporting for duty, Ma'am," Conner said the following Saturday morning.

"Come in Sgt. Wilmington," Samantha said. "Or is it Lieutenant?"

"Whatever you need me to be. You're the boss today. Hey," he said, looking back at the road leading to her house. "Do you realize you have a mini-corridor?"

"I do. Some of the tree limbs almost meet above the road. Maybe they'll have magical powers like some say the corridor has."

Conner came dressed for work in jeans, plaid shirt, jean-jacket, and slightly worn boots. Samantha playfully scanned his body. "You could almost pass for a Mississippi boy today."

"Why, thank you Ma'am," Conner said, accentuating his southern accent. "I appreciate the compliment." In the normal masculine voice Samantha loved, he asked, "What are we doing first?"

"I thought we'd have coffee and muffins. I know you're always hungry."

"What can I say? I'm a growing boy."

"I think you can stop now," she said, looking up. "Let's eat. Then we can get the Christmas boxes down from the attic. When the day warms up, we'll work on the doors."

After their morning snack, Samantha led Conner upstairs to her bedroom. When he lifted his eyebrows in question, she said, "Don't get any ideas. That's not what we're here for." Then she slid open a wall panel, revealing a secret staircase to the attic.

"You're kidding! That's so cool," he said, sounding like the thirteen-year-old boy he once was. "Do you know the story behind this?"

"I do, and it's not that interesting. I suppose I should make up something more dramatic. The stairs are original to the house, but this probably wasn't a bedroom at the time. My biological father built the fake wall. He told Mama every old house needed a secret. So he gave the farmhouse one. If he had another reason, I don't know what it was."

Following Samantha up the stairs to the attic, Conner mused, "I guess when this place was built, people didn't use pull-down ladders."

"With the lofty ceilings," Samantha said, "no one could reach high enough to pull one down. Well, maybe you could."

"Unbelievable," Conner said, when they reached the top. "This looks like the set of an old movie or something from a dream. Where did all these things come from?"

"Who knows? A lot of it has been up here for generations. Besides the furniture, there are lockers full of clothes, hats, pictures, all sorts of things. That area in front of the window was my childhood playhouse.

When Anna and I were eleven or twelve, we'd come up here and rummage around. Mama called it meddling. We'd dress up in old clothes we found and pose in front of that standing mirror in the corner."

"So you and Anna were good friends way back then?"

"We were always friends, but Max was her best friend until he discovered girls."

Conner nodded. "Anna told me about that. She said he broke her heart."

"Yeah. That happened more than once, although I don't think he even realized it. But his marriage to Janine was the worst. I guess he'll spend the rest of his life making up for that."

Conner couldn't stop looking around. "This place is amazing. But I guess we should get to work. Tell me what I can lift for you."

"That box over there," she said, gesturing. "I just need to put away these toppled things." A minute later Samantha looked up to see Conner holding a heavy wooden chest. "Oh, no. I'm sorry. Not that. It's the cardboard box next to it."

Conner sat the locked chest down, picked up something from the floor behind it, and slid the trunk back where it belonged. Handing his find to Samantha, he said, "Look at this."

She took the stack of envelopes, turned one over, and withdrew a piece of plain, almost-white stationary. "They're letters, without stamps. They must have been hand delivered or left in a secret place," Samantha said dramatically, her eyes lighting up. "There's no telling how old these are. We assume the house was built in the early 1900s, like the ones in Mill Village. These letters could have been written during the Great Depression or the Second World War."

The envelopes were dusty and worn, as if they'd been read often, but the paper was only slightly yellowed, and Conner didn't think they were that old.

29

"Let's go downstairs and read them," Samantha said. Conner carried the Christmas box through the bedroom and then down to the large living area. There had once been a hallway through the middle of the house, extending from the front door to the back. But Samantha's parents had taken down the hall walls at the front of the house to connect the living room, hallway, and dining room. The result was one spacious living area.

As soon as Conner joined Samantha on the sofa, she opened a letter. "Did you notice the numbers on the back of the envelopes? I think the recipient numbered them because the numbers are in blue ink and the letters are written in black. And the slant is different from the letter writer's. Shucks. No date."

Conner smiled. "It wouldn't be a good mystery if you knew all the answers from the start. Is that number one?" he asked, nodding toward the letter Samantha held.

"It is. Ready?" After glancing at the page, she looked back at Conner, her eyes wide and sparkly. "It's a love letter." Smiling at her excitement, he urged her to read.

> *Sweetheart, staying away from you is the hardest thing I've ever done. I physically ache to be near you. But I'm keeping my distance because you asked me to and because I know it's for the best. I can't give you and the little one what you need. Heaven knows, I've tried. I understand your decision. You're doing what you have*

to, just like I am, but that doesn't
make this any easier. I miss you both
terribly. My heart will always be
yours.

Samantha looked at Conner with big, sorrowful eyes. "How sad. This must have been a clandestine romance. The writer is careful not to divulge any identifying information. We don't have names or even know the genders of the people involved."

"I assume the little one belongs to the recipient of the letter," Conner said. "I wonder what the writer's relationship is to the child. Is he or she a parent?"

Sitting up straight, Samantha's eyes widened. "I know. The receiver was a widow with a child." She stopped to think. "And her parents arranged a second marriage. But she fell in love with the writer of the letters, and her parents considered him unsuitable. Or maybe she was just honor-bound to keep a previous commitment."

"You've been reading too many historical romance novels."

"Maybe. But do you have a better explanation?"

"Not yet," Conner said, giving her a peck on the lips. "I'll read the next one." After taking the letter from the aged envelope, he unfolded it and read.

Sweetheart, I've been staying
away like you asked. Now, I'm asking
you for something. I miss you and the
little one so much; I feel I've lost a
piece of my heart. I know we can't be
together but think about letting me

visit the child, please. Knowing
you're with another man hurts like
hell, but seeing the child from time to
time would ease my pain. My heart
will always be yours.

"I can't believe how sad this is," Samantha said, wiping away a tear.

Conner cocked his head to look at her. "You're too cute. Now I know what a softy you are." He kissed her again. It was more than a peck but stopped short of being passionate. "We learned a couple of things from this one," he said, holding up the letter. "Since he mentions another man, we know for sure the writer is male. And I think we can deduce the letter is fairly recent."

"Why do you say that?"

"Because he said, 'it hurts like hell.' A few generations back, a man would never use a curse word in a letter to a woman. Just a theory."

Samantha got an excited look on her face. "I bet you're right. Do you think these people could still be alive?"

"It's possible."

"I wonder if the man was ever happy again," Samantha mused. "We don't know how the woman felt or even if she answered his letters. I can't wait to read the next one."

Sweetheart, thank you for letting
me see the child. It was good to see
you too, even though it was only for a
moment. As I knew it would, it hurt to

see you with someone else, but it also relieved an ache I hadn't understood. I needed to know you were all right. I'm grateful he came out of the house and shook my hand. He seems like a good man. He promised to take care of you both, and I believe him. Surprisingly, he didn't seem to resent that I came to the farmhouse.

I guess it seems odd that I only refer to him as he. Calling him by name makes him sound like a friend, and I can't think of him that way. Not yet. And I can't bring myself to call him your husband either. In my dreams, that's my role.

Sweetheart, the child is lovely, even if she doesn't have your dark hair and eyes. Thank God she remembered me. Getting to see her and knowing you'll let me play a part in her life is a tremendous gift. Thank you. My heart will always be yours.

Samantha wiped her eyes, feeling a little foolish. "Damned allergies."

Conner only smiled.

Samantha thought about what she'd read, looking for clues to solve the mystery. "The writer used the word 'she' several times. He must be less concerned about someone seeing the letter, or maybe he was emotional when he wrote it and simply made a mistake. He was dealing with some heavy issues."

"We still don't know the man's relationship to the child," Conner said, "although it's sounding more and more like he's the biological father. The writer mentioned that the child didn't have her mother's hair and eyes. Was he insinuating she inherited those characteristics from him?"

"Maybe. And we know he visited the farmhouse. I guess it could have been another farmhouse, but since we found these in the attic…" Samantha handed a letter to Conner. "You read the last one."

"Here's hoping for answers."

> *Sweetheart, we've experienced a lot of changes since the last time I wrote. I still miss you like crazy, but I've accepted that you have a good life with someone else. At least I get to see you and our child on Sundays. That's made me into a regular church goer. Our girl is growing up, and I'm so proud of her. She's smart, sweet, beautiful, and talented. I see all her performances and take every opportunity to interact with her. She'll never know how much I love her. I'm putting money aside to help with college when the time comes. Let me know if there's anything I can do for either of you. I'm enclosing a photograph of us in front of our Christmas tree. I hope that's all right. It would be a better picture if my arm were longer, but it's a*

reminder of a happy moment. My
heart will always be yours.

"Okay. We have confirmation the child is his," Conner said.

Samantha nodded. "I wonder what kind of performances he's referring to."

"Probably school plays—that sort of thing. Think we should get to work?"

"We should. But you know what I'd rather do, don't you?"

"Look for the picture?"

"Yep. But there's no telling where it might be. Maybe we should work on the front door now. I can manage the decorating by myself."

"No. I'd like to stay until it's finished. That is, if you don't mind. I want to see the house lit up after dark."

Refinishing the door was a big job. Conner took it off the hinges and laid it across saw horses he found in the barn. While in there, he noticed a man's shirt hanging on a hook and wondered who it belonged to.

Samantha was surprised when Conner took an electric sander from the trunk in the front of his car.

"Where's the motor in that thing?" Samantha asked, nodding toward the vehicle.

"It's a Porsche. The motor is in the back."

"Well I'll be... What are you doing with a sander? I wouldn't think an attorney who lives in an apartment, would need one."

"Don't all guys have a sander?" he said. But Samantha could tell it was brand new.

Working in the front yard, Conner sanded the scratches out of the door. Samantha stained it and varnished the parts that would be unreachable after it was hung. "I'll do the rest when it's back on its hinges. I want to allow plenty of drying time between applications. Let's stop and eat. It's past time for lunch. You must be starving. We can tackle the decorations when we've finished."

The afternoon of the baby shower, the women and six-year-old Gracie gathered around Anna in the large living room. The men watched the proceedings from a spot near the kitchen, close to a tub of iced-down beer.

From time to time, the women heard laughter from the men. They were making wise-cracks about how an infant would change Max's life— lack of sleep, dirty diapers, no sex, and breasts reserved for baby. Nothing was off limits. Max let them have their fun, resisting the temptation to remind them he'd done it all before, and with little help from anyone. Not even from his ex-wife Janine, Gracie's mother.

Eventually, all the guests left the farmhouse except Conner who used the excuse he was staying to help clean up.

"It's all done," Samantha told him. "The dishes were disposable, which made things easy. And I had more help in the kitchen than I knew what to do with."

"Don't you have some chickens or dogs, or something that needs to be fed?"

"You don't want to go home, do you?"

"Not really. It's lonely there," he said, making puppy-dog eyes.

"Humph. I'm sure there are plenty of beautiful women who would be glad to keep you company."

"But I'd rather be here," he admitted, "with the beautiful woman I'm looking at. Can't we have a drink, put our feet up, and relax a while?"

"We could do that," Samantha said. "I am tired."

"Then sit down. I'll get the drinks. Beer, wine, or something stronger?"

"I could use a glass of tea," Samantha said. "There's a pitcher in the refrigerator, unless someone drank it during the shower."

Moments later, Conner appeared with two glasses of sweet tea and sat beside Samantha on the sofa. Slipping off his loafers, he put his long sock-clad feet on the coffee table next to Samantha's.

"I don't think I've ever seen you tired. I was starting to think you had an endless supply of energy."

"Good grief, no," Samantha said, "you should see me when I get home from school. Dealing with second graders is exhausting. Don't get me wrong. I enjoy it. But I'm spent at the end of the day."

Changing the subject, she said, "Didn't you love watching Gracie tonight? She had so much fun. And Max's parents enjoyed it, too. I think this was the best baby shower I've ever attended, even if I was the hostess. Thanks for your help, Conner. I should have put your name on the invitation as a host."

"Hell, no. There are enough people wondering which team I play for."

"Really? You mean people think you're gay?"

"I'm approached from time to time."

"That's just wishful thinking on their part, 'cause you're so pretty," she teased. "What do you do when that happens?"

"It's usually easier than letting down a woman I have no interest in. I just shake my head. Normally that's all it takes. No one should be made to feel awkward because of a sexual preference."

"Conner Wilmington, you're just so dang sweet," Samantha said, playfully pinching his cheeks.

"Take that back. I'm not pretty and I'm not sweet. I'm tough, rough, and dangerous," he said, moving closer to Samantha, feigning aggression.

She shrank away, and her arm flew to her face for protection before she realized she was over-reacting.

"What the…" Conner said. "Did you think I would hit you?"

"No," Samantha assured him. "It was just a reflex." Before he could question her further, she changed the subject again. "I got some good pictures tonight."

All right, Conner thought, she doesn't want to explain. But he knew the sweet woman sitting beside him had been on the receiving end of violence, and it made him feel sick. "Good," Conner said, in response to Samantha's picture comment. "Anna will love that."

They sat quietly until Conner broke the silence. "Sam, I have a question to ask, and I'd like an honest answer." When she looked away, Conner gently turned her face his direction. "Please."

"What do you want to know?"

"We get along well," he said. "I think it's safe to say we like each other, that we're friends."

"We are."

"So," he asked. "Why won't you go dancing with me? I've been asking for months." He looked toward the ceiling, thinking. "Approximately eight months. What's keeping you from saying yes?"

Samantha was relieved he'd asked something she could answer without revealing too much, but she still took her time formulating an answer. "When we danced at the reception, we were surrounded by friends. So I felt relatively safe. When I go to a bar, guys ask me to dance, and sometimes, especially if they've had too much to drink, they don't want to take no for an answer." Looking down at her hands, she sighed. "I can't dance with strange men. Not anymore. It's the broken thing."

"Then we'll tell them I'm your jealous fiancé, who won't let you dance with anyone else."

Samantha shook her head. "I don't think that'll work."

"Sure it will. I'll get you a ring. Sorry, it'll have to be fake. Come on," Conner urged. "I'm a pretty big guy. I promise to take care of you. In two weeks, I'll be twenty-eight. Help me celebrate my birthday. Go dancing with me."

Samantha sighed, giving in. "Okay. But at the first sign of trouble, we're out of there. Agreed?"

"Agreed."

"And no shenanigans."

"Shenanigans?"

"You know what I mean."

"Whatever you say. No shenanigans—unless you change your mind," he said, with a sly grin.

When Samantha walked Conner to the door, he put an arm around her and kissed her, intending it to be a small good-night kiss. But holding himself back with Samantha wasn't easy. He pulled her close before he realized he was doing it, and his tongue insisted on exploring her mouth.

She kissed him back, her arms wrapping around his firm abs. His body felt so good against hers and his mouth—his delicious, wet mouth... Conner Wilmington pushed all her buttons.

Sam finally forced herself to pull away. "See, that's why we shouldn't go out. We're too attracted to one another."

Conner flashed a flirtatious smile. "Or maybe that's why we should."

CHAPTER THREE

"How do you feel about having a poker game here Friday night?" Max asked Anna.

"Sure. I'm up for it."

"I thought I'd ask Jeff and Scott to come over. Does that sound okay?"

"If I can invite Samantha and Conner."

Max sighed. "I guess I have to accept Conner as part of the family."

"He's part of mine."

"I want to ask you something," Max said. "How many people do you think adopt an old boyfriend as a member of their family?"

"I don't know. But there was a time he was the closest thing to family I had."

"I know all that," Max said. "It's just that…"

"That I had sex with him."

"Yeah. That."

"It was a long time ago. You know you're the only man for me," she said, giving him a kiss.

"I believe you. I'll try not to think about your previous relationship with the golden boy, but I'm not sure it'll work."

"So it's all right with you if I invite Samantha and Conner."

"Whatever makes you happy, my dear wife, but they have to know how to play."

Friday night, while Max readied the table for the poker game, Anna helped her stepdaughter bathe and dress for bed. Gracie's daddy joined them for her bedtime ritual, knowing she'd try to stay awake to see their guests.

Everyone arrived about the same time. Max got the drinks. "Want a beer, Scott?"

The sheriff nodded. "Definitely, I'm off duty tonight."

When Anna walked toward the kitchen, Max took her by the shoulders and led her to a chair at the table. "You, lovely lady, need to sit and rest. We can't have you giving birth during our poker game."

"If she does," Samantha joked, "we could call him Ace."

"Or Jack," Conner chimed in.

"What if it's a girl?" Anna asked, since they hadn't found out the sex of the baby.

"Queen?" Samantha tried.

"Nah," they all said.

Changing the subject, Conner jested, "Is gambling legal in Tenacity? Can we do it with the sheriff present?"

"If he plays," Max said.

Scott leaned back in his chair. "I'm in. And I'll start the betting off with a quarter."

"Whoa," Samantha said, "high stakes right off the bat. You must have a good hand."

"Maybe. But I might be bluffing." He was bluffing, but he pulled in the pot anyway.

About that time, a pretty, dark-haired six-year-old padded down the stairs wearing Disney Princess pajamas. "I'm thirsty."

Max smiled, not surprised by the request. "You know it's too late for you to have a drink."

Conner smiled at the little girl. "How about a book instead?" Then he looked at Max. "Sorry, I should have asked first."

"That's fine. Go for it."

Gracie grinned up at Conner. "Will you throw me over your shoulder like you did the other time?"

"I think it's too late for roughhousing. It's quiet time for little girls with curls."

"You made a rhyme, Uncle Conner," Gracie said, putting her hand in his.

"Uncle Conner, huh?"

"I can make you an uncle if I want to. Aunt Samantha wasn't born my aunt, but we made her one."

"I'd love to be your Uncle Conner, Miss Gracie." The group at the table laughed at the smug look Conner threw over his shoulder.

A few minutes later, they heard him burst into laughter. When he returned, Anna asked what he'd found so funny. Shaking his head, he grinned. "Gracie is one-of-a-kind. She picked a book called *Don't Eat Your Classmates*. Penelope Rex, a dinosaur, is the main character who has to fight the urge to eat her classmates. I'm not sure whether the author is clever or a little insane. Gracie assured me she has no desire to eat her classmates, and I commend her for that. But I'm a little concerned that she's willing to let

Penelope have Liam Ladner—because he's gross and likes to eat worms."

They all chuckled. Anna said, "You never know what's going to come out of that child's mouth."

"Liam's my cousin's kid," Scott said. "I'll have to ask him about the worm-eating thing."

Later in the evening, when Anna's stack of poker chips was getting low, she warned, "Samantha Suzanna, you'd better not raise the stakes."

Jeff, who hadn't had much to say that evening, burst into a chorus of "Oh Suzanna." Looking at Samantha, he said, "I didn't know your middle name was Suzanna. You don't hear that much anymore. It was my grandmother's name, my dad's mother. My grandfather used to sing that song to her all the time."

"I hate to leave good company," Samantha said a little later, "but I'm going to have to say good-night. It's been a long day and I'm bone tired. Thanks for inviting me. I had a good time."

"I need to go, too," Jeff said, "It's been fun. But I have cows ready to calve, and tonight's a full moon. I could have a long night ahead of me. I'll follow you home, Sammy. Make sure you get there okay."

"Good idea," Scott said. "You packing, Samantha?"

"Under my car seat."

"Good. You take care of yourself and call me if you need me, anytime night or day."

"I can see Sam home," Conner said. He wasn't happy about Jeff's offer and wished he wouldn't call her Sammy. It sounded too affectionate.

"No need, I'm going right past there," Jeff insisted. He could tell he was getting under Conner's skin. A guy like that, he thought, probably needed a taste of jealousy.

When they arrived at the farmhouse, Jeff walked Samantha to the door. "Is something going on between you and Conner?"

"Why do you ask?"

"Vibes, I guess. And the fact that he couldn't keep his eyes off you all night."

"I agreed to go dancing with him next week-end, but I'm not sure I'm ready for that." She shrugged.

"You need to get back in the game, Sammy, and I think Conner's a good guy. The two of you are certainly great on the dance floor. Pops videoed ya'll at Max and Anna's reception and shows it to anybody who'll watch."

"Do me a favor, Jeff," Samantha said. "Don't say anything about Conner and me. We're just friends, but there are folks in town who would love something new to talk about. I'd rather not be the latest gossip."

"Mum's the word. Good-night, Sammy," Jeff said, kissing her cheek.

Friday night, Conner pulled into the gravel parking area at the farmhouse and patted Hot Shot and Queenie. Samantha met him at the door wearing jeans, a western shirt, and fancy boots. She filled out the clothes perfectly. He was going to have trouble keeping his hands to himself. Easy boy, he told himself. If you're not careful, she'll bolt.

45

"You're wearing cowboy boots," Samantha noticed, raising her eyebrows, "and they're not brand new."

"Of course not. I wouldn't embarrass you." Conner scanned her body from head to foot. "You're looking mighty good tonight, Ma'am," he said, in his best cowhand voice.

Samantha mimicked his body perusal. "You'll do," she teased, admiring his long, powerful legs. Conner didn't have an inflated ego, but he had to know how good he looked. "And happy birthday. Is it actually today?"

"Yesterday, but tonight is my celebration."

Stepping onto the porch, Samantha locked the door behind her. "We can take my truck if you like. I don't think there'll be other sports cars in the parking lot."

"That's okay. They'll just be jealous."

"That's what you think."

Reaching the car, Conner opened Samantha's door, made his way to the other side, and slid behind the steering wheel. "Where are we going?"

Samantha chose a bar about thirty miles from Tenacity in the opposite direction from the town of Clarkston. "The music is loud and the dance floor large," she explained. On the drive, she admired Conner's long hands on the steering wheel and the tall, perfect body he managed to fold into the Porsche. "What made you get such a small car?" she asked. "The fancy factor?"

"The fancy factor. I've never heard it put that way. But yes. I guess. What guy doesn't want a sports car?"

"But you're so tall."

"I fit."

"Barely. Are your parents tall?"

"They are. But my mom's stick thin and Dad's a big man."

"You said you have a sister."

"A younger sister—Kendall. She's a junior in high school. I can't decide whether she's immature or spoiled. She and her best friend are always up to no good."

"Is your sister tall, too?"

"Five-ten, I think. Why all the questions?"

"Just curious. As often as we talk on the phone, we never say much about our families. Does your mother work?"

"Mom's a professional fund raiser. Well, not really professional. But she could be. She just doesn't get paid for what she does." He sent her a crooked smile. "That would be gauche, you know."

"So undignified," Samantha said with a straight face. "I completely understand. Your dad's a lawyer, isn't he?"

"He is. But mostly, he's his own client. He manages his inheritance and investments, his stocks, and properties. Among other things, he's a venture capitalist."

"What exactly does that mean?"

"He loans money to companies with high growth potential in exchange for an equity stake."

"Okay. So, you don't have to worry about money."

"If I worked for my dad, I wouldn't have to worry about money. But I don't. So I live on what I earn as a junior attorney."

"Your turn," Conner said, glancing toward Samantha. "Tell me about your family."

"Well, I'm an only child. I always wanted to be one of those kids from a big noisy family, but it was just the three of us. And you already know my biological father died before I was born. I don't know much about him. I only have pictures."

"Do you look like him?"

"Not really. I don't look like either of my parents. My coloring must have come from some latent gene, compliments of one of my ancestors. Mama married Daddy when I was three. He's twenty years older than she is, and he retired from the Army before they ever met. He says his first wife divorced him because she didn't like military life. His marriage to Mama was sort of an arranged thing, almost a business deal. But it worked out. They care about each other, and he's a good dad."

"Arranged? How did that come about?"

"Mama spent years taking care of my biological father. He was an invalid. They squeaked by on Social Security Disability, which disappeared when he died. Mama didn't have the skills to work outside the home, at least nothing that would pay both day care and the bills. So she stayed home, took care of the animals, worked her garden, and got by on welfare. My grandparents introduced her to Daddy, and they married soon after. He got a ranch out of the deal, and Mama got a good man who could support us. Like I said, it worked out."

"Interesting. How did you end up in that big house by yourself?"

"When I was in college, my parents moved to Smokey Creek to help my aging grandparents. Although no one has ever said so, I think farming was getting to be too much for Daddy. He has some problems with his heart."

"It's hard to believe your parents left you alone in that big house."

Looking a little sheepish, Samantha said, "I wasn't exactly alone at the time, but I'm not ready to talk about that."

For such an intelligent, vital woman, Conner thought, she sure had a lot of secrets. Was the person who lived with her the one who hurt her? Conner wanted to know more but didn't ask. He'd find out in time.

"Did either of your parents go to college? You said your mother didn't have the skills to work outside the home. That's what made me wonder."

"Mama didn't. Daddy completed two years before joining the Army. But they made sure I went. I started at community college and then finished at Southern Miss."

"And now you teach second grade. Did you always want to be a teacher?"

"Ever since I can remember."

"So you were a good student."

"Yes, I was conscientious about school and my piano lessons."

"I noticed the piano in your living room and wondered if you played."

"I used to love to play."

"But not anymore?"

Samantha shook her head. "I haven't wanted to for the past couple of years."

Fearing they'd touched on Samantha's big secret, he changed the subject. "Did you date a lot in high school?"

"What made you ask that?"

"I want to know everything about you."

"I didn't date a lot, but I wasn't a wallflower." Sending him a flirty smile, Samantha said, with feigned pride, "Anna and I were Gator Girls."

Conner smiled. "And just what do Gator Girls do?"

"Perform synchronized dance moves at football games and prance around in short sparkly outfits."

"You and Anna did that?"

"Yep, with about fifteen other girls."

"I would like to have seen that."

"Oh, there are videos. If you're a good boy, I might let you see them one day."

"I can be good," Conner said suggestively. "I can be very good."

Samantha turned to stare out the side window and went quiet.

Damn, he silently cursed. I guess that was too much. After finding a space among the pick-up trucks in the bar's parking lot, Conner opened Samantha's door, took her hand, and they walked across the packed dirt to the bar's entryway. "Ready?"

She nodded, and they entered a world of loud music, clanking glasses, and raucous laughter. Finding an available booth, they ordered beers. While they waited, Conner told Sam what he'd discovered. "I hope you don't mind," he said, "but I did some research on your farm."

"Of course not. Did you find anything?"

"I did."

"Tell me. I can't wait."

"The house was built in 1920," Conner began, "by Jonathan Shoemaker. Upon his death, in 1949, the title transferred to Harold Shoemaker."

"Probably his son," Samantha said.

"More than likely. That part was easy to find. It's public record. I found the rest of the information in an old newspaper article, and it's interesting," he said, emphasizing the word *interesting*.

"What did you find?"

An attractive waitress, dressed in jean shorts and a shirt tied in a knot above her waist, brought their drinks. "Want to run a tab?"

"No," Conner said, remembering Samantha's concerns. He didn't want a tab to deal with if they needed to make a quick exit. The waitress looked Conner over as he pulled out his wallet. Appreciating the view, she winked when he told her to keep the change, wiggled her butt as she walked away, and glanced back at him over her shoulder. Conner didn't seem to notice.

"What else did you find?" Samantha asked when the waitress was out of hearing distance.

"Harold was married to a woman named Daisy, and they had a son named William."

"Billy. Wow."

"Who's Billy."

"Remember when I told you I had an imaginary playmate? Mama said I called him Billy. That's a little spooky. Maybe he wasn't as imaginary as she thought."

"Who knows," Conner said. "Want to hear more? It's sad."

"Okay."

"In 1952 the whole family died in their sleep—most likely from carbon monoxide poisoning. But the newspaper sensationalized their deaths, referring to them as mysterious. That may be why your parents got such a deal. The house, alone, should have fetched a pretty penny. People may have been superstitious about living in a place where three people died the same night. There's no record of anyone else owning the property until your parents bought it."

"Surely Mama would have heard about such a tragedy."

"Maybe she did but never thought to tell you."

With his finger, Conner smoothed away the furrow between Samantha's eyes. "What's wrong?"

"I was just thinking about that poor family, hoping they didn't suffer." Then Samantha's eyes widened. "The letters! If only two families lived in the house, the letters must have been for Billy's mother or grandmother."

"They could have belonged to someone else. Around the time the house was built, it was common for several generations to share a home."

When they finished their beers, Conner asked Samantha if she was ready to hit the floor. Nodding, she stepped from the booth, took Conner's waiting hand, and relinquished thoughts of Billy's family.

For a while, they did the two-step like everyone else. But when the band played Alan Jackson's "Chattahoochee" and Conner and Samantha cut loose with a country swing dance, couples around them stepped back to cheer them on.

They danced the night away. Just as Samantha predicted, men tried to coax her away from Conner, and he was approached by just as many women. But sticking to their plan, they smiled and shook their heads, and Samantha flashed her fake ring. When a guy persisted, Conner pulled Samantha close. "Sorry. She's all mine. You'll have to find your own girl." Then he'd give her a brief proprietary kiss.

Dancing with Conner amounted to foreplay, especially when they moved back and forth to the rhythm of slow, belly-rubbing tunes. His strong arms pulled her close, and their bodies molded deliciously together. With their faces practically joined, they were tempted to lock lips in the middle of the dance floor.

On the ride home, in the enclosed space of the small car, Samantha felt enveloped in Conner's warm spicy scent. Her need for him was so strong and powerful it was almost painful. He was too much temptation. How could she resign herself to a life without passion when he made her ache for what she couldn't have?

As they arrived at the farmhouse, Samantha became anxious about how the night would end. When Conner opened the car door and helped her out, she saw the desire in his eyes. I'll allow myself one last kiss, she thought, rising on her toes, reaching for his shoulders. Conner's arms tightened around Sam, and he kissed her the way he'd wanted to all evening.

Sighing with regret, she pulled back. "We shouldn't be doing this."

"And why is that?"

"It's not fair."

"Not fair to whom?" Conner asked.

Samantha shook her head. "Is your grammar always correct?"

"Usually. You didn't answer my question."

"It's not fair to you."

"Why would you say that?"

"You know why. Nothing will come of it."

"Let me ask you a question. Do you enjoy kissing me?"

"You know I do."

"How about when I hold you close? Do you enjoy that?"

"I do. But I might freeze."

"Don't worry about it. Think of it this way," Conner said, searching for an appropriate analogy. "People don't necessarily have a destination when they go for a swim or walk along a beach. They do it because it makes them feel good, because they enjoy it."

"You know that's different."

"What I'm trying to say is that we don't have to deprive ourselves of the pleasure of kissing and holding one another."

"We don't?" she said, looking at him hopefully.

"We don't." He kissed her again, while the dogs jumped around them, wanting attention. "Let's go in. They're not going to leave us alone."

"What are you thinking we'll do inside?" Samantha asked uncertainly.

"That's up to you. We can sit on the sofa and kiss—maybe grope each other a little," he said with a cocky smile.

"Are you sure?"

"I am." They began kissing before they reached the sofa, and it wasn't long before they both wanted more. "We could take this upstairs," Conner suggested, "and see where it leads. If you decide you only want to sleep, so be it. You know I won't push for more than you're ready to give."

"That's the problem. I want it all. I want you, but…"

"I know. You think you're broken. We can work on that. Not all at once but a little at a time."

Samantha hesitated.

"You can trust me," Conner said. "You know you can."

"Promise?"

"I promise. You know me. Have you ever known me to lie?" He kissed her to remind her what she'd be missing if she sent him home.

She sighed. "Okay. Wait a little while to come upstairs? I need to freshen up. You can use the downstairs bathroom if you like."

Smiling through his sexual haze, he said, "I like that just fine. I have an overnight bag in the car."

Samantha playfully batted his chest. "Pretty sure of yourself, aren't you?"

Standing, he pulled her up from the sofa, held her close, and whispered in her ear, "Just being prepared. I was a Boy Scout."

"Of course, you were," she said breathlessly, as he planted kisses down her neck. "I bet you were an Eagle Scout."

"What makes you think that?" he said, pulling back to look at her.

"You were, weren't you?"

"I was."

"I knew it," Samantha said. "Go get your things." She turned off the house alarm and showed him how to reset it. "Don't forget," she warned. Conner assured her he wouldn't.

Samantha's body fluttered with excitement as she climbed the stairs. She hadn't forgotten how it felt to have Conner's warm body lying beside her.

Was she right to trust him a second time? She'd trusted another man completely, and that had been the worst mistake of her life. But Conner wasn't Hal, and so far, he'd proven himself to be a man of his word.

Samantha was sitting on her bed in panties and a long t-shirt, when Conner appeared in her doorway wearing only low-slung drawstring pants. Looking at the woman in front of him, he smiled, appreciating the view. "Very sexy."

"Sexy? You didn't say I should try to look sexy."

"I didn't," he said, leaning against the door jamb. "That's what's so enticing. You don't have to try. You just are."

Samantha unabashedly gazed back, appreciating his fit, long-limbed body. "I guess you're okay too," she teased.

Conner ambled toward the bed, looking smug. He knew women liked his looks. Fighting the instinct to possess, he sat beside Samantha and said, "Kiss me."

She moved closer, doing as he asked, her hands exploring his admirable torso. Taking over the kiss,

Conner found himself in unchartered territory, unsure how to progress with a woman who might bolt at any moment. He eased her down on the bed, trying not to overpower her or seem aggressive, which was hard considering the difference in their sizes.

Remembering her previous reaction to his advances, he didn't hover or lower himself onto her. He lay beside her and tenderly kissed her lips. Then he slipped a hand under her t-shirt and inched his way up her body. Hoping for the best, he took the next step. Slowly, lovingly, he caressed her full breasts, imagining how they must look. When she arched toward his hand, he felt like a kid who'd reached second base for the first time.

Samantha's skin was smooth and soft, and she instantly responded to his touch. Conner wanted her, and she obviously wanted him right back. But he knew their lovemaking could be halted at any moment, that arousing touches might be all they would get.

He wanted to ease her shirt up and replace his hands with his mouth but wouldn't take a chance on breaking the spell. Instead, he slowly, gently moved his hand downward. Recognizing her need for more, he took a chance and cupped his long hand over her most intimate place. Initially, when she drew in a quick breath and tensed, he thought it was a normal, sensual reaction. When he realized that it wasn't and removed his hand, Samantha turned and buried her head in her pillow.

Conner rubbed her back, simultaneously trying to soothe Samantha and calm his lust. When his breathing slowed, he said softly. "It's all right, Sam. Don't cry."

"It's not all right," she said, turning to face him. "It's awful, and I'm afraid I'll never get any better. Dammit, why won't my body do what I tell it to do?"

Samantha snuggled close to Conner, needing his arms around her, and then realized he was still aroused.

"Sorry," Conner said. "It seems you're not the only one with a disobedient body. I told it there'll be no sex, tonight, but so far, it hasn't listened."

"Wanna trade problems?" Samantha quipped.

Conner chuckled. No, we're going to fix this. It's a journey. Remember? And on this trip, we went farther than we've gone before."

"Do you really believe that hog wash?" Samantha asked.

When their laughter calmed, Conner gave her a sweet kiss. "Yes, I really believe that hog wash."

"But look what I'm doing to you," Samantha said, gesturing toward his disobedient body part. It's not fair."

"I can handle it," he said with a sly grin, knowing a shower was in his near future.

Despite the events of the evening, and without the comfort of the cuddling they wanted, they both fell into an uneasy slumber. Later, Conner woke to find Samantha babbling and thrashing in her sleep. She was kicking as if trying to push someone away. "No, no," were the only words Conner could make out.

"It's all right," he soothed, afraid that touching would be the wrong approach. "You're having a nightmare. That's all. You're all right."

She calmed at the sound of his voice, and Conner rolled away. He lay on his back with his hands behind his head and stared at the dark ceiling, wondering, for about the millionth time, what had happened to her. Whatever it was, had really messed her up. But he admired her. She had a problem, but she was trying to work through it, even making jokes in the middle of her pain. She'd said she was afraid it wouldn't go away. Well, she had him, now, and he was going to help her through this if it killed him. And it just might.

Before the night of the wedding reception, he would never have dreamed she had issues. Every time he saw her, she had a smile on her face. She hid her problem well. Maybe too well. Was she carrying her burden completely alone?

CHAPTER FOUR

When Samantha woke the next morning, Conner wasn't lying next to her. Surely he wouldn't have left without so much as a good-bye. No, he wouldn't have done that.

She threw on her robe, ran downstairs, and found Conner standing at her stove dressed in pajama pants and a t-shirt, his long feet bare.

"You can't stand on a cold floor like that," she said, leaving the room. When she returned holding his socks, Conner was touched. He'd never dated a woman who worried about his feet being cold.

"Put these on," Samantha ordered.

"Yes, Ma'am," he said, smiling, and then thanked her with a kiss.

Looking somber, she asked the same question she'd asked before. "Did I have a nightmare last night?"

"You mumbled something," he said, with a slight shrug. "That's all."

She nodded.

Conner slid an omelet onto her plate. "Go ahead. Eat while it's hot."

Samantha brightened. "I can't believe you made this for me,"

"Why not? It's my turn. You cooked last time."

"Smells good. Who taught you to cook?"

"Miss Emma. She's been the cook at Mom and Dad's ever since I can remember."

"Tell me about her."

"She's one of my favorite people. I think she gave me more attention than anyone when I was a child. She swears I'm this tall because I ate so many of her magic cookies. Mom recently hired an assistant cook since Miss Emma is getting up in years. Now, she mostly sits and tells someone else what to do.

"I write her almost every week. It's often more of a note than a letter, but I keep in touch. She doesn't like computers. So I actually put pen to paper and mail real letters. She knows more about me than my mother."

Conner feigned a disgusted look when Samantha said, "That's so sweet," but it was. The more she found out about Conner, the more she admired him. Samantha took a bite of her omelet. "This is delicious," she said, covering her mouth. When she finished chewing, she added, "I want to know exactly how you make this—every step. Don't leave out a thing. And put it on paper like you do for Miss Emma, so I won't forget."

"You have a pen and paper?" Conner asked.

"On the desk in my office. I'll get it."

"No, you finish eating," Conner said. "I'll get it. Where's the office?"

"Behind the living room."

After a while, Samantha left the table to see what was taking Conner so long. When she walked into the room, she found him standing behind the desk with a stunned look on his face, holding a letter.

No, he didn't, Samantha screamed in her head.

Conner looked at her, accusingly. "You're married?"

Samantha was shaking. "I can't believe you read my letter."

Conner had been looking in a desk drawer for a piece of paper when he saw an open letter with a prison logo at the top of the page. He scanned it out of curiosity and then picked it up to read again. He was having trouble believing what it said. "You're married?"

"No, I'm not. You invaded my privacy."

"Try to get over that," Conner said. "Explain this to me. Please." He wasn't sure why he was so upset. He and Samantha weren't a couple. Not really. But they had a relationship even if it was presently undefined. Why had no one mentioned that Samantha was married?

"You came by that information dishonestly. I don't have to tell you anything."

"That's something a guilty person would say. You may not owe me an explanation, but I'd like to hear one. Whoever this guy is," Conner said, waving the letter, "he thinks he's your husband, and he says he'll see you when he gets out of prison."

Clutching her own arms, Samantha turned her back on the confused man and walked to the living room. Conner followed, hoping for some answers.

"All right," she said, shaking her head. She couldn't believe he was pushing her into this admission. "I made a mistake. A huge one. I married someone I thought was a great guy. Turned out he wasn't. I divorced him, but he says I promised him forever, and he won't let me go."

"Is this the guy who traumatized you?"

Sliding down the wall she'd been leaning against, Samantha sat on the floor, her hands covering her face. The incredulity and exasperation Conner felt only moments before dissolved, replaced by unease and the desire to comfort.

Sitting beside the distraught woman, he took her hands in his and looked into her eyes. "Are you ever going to trust me with your secret, or do you plan to hide it from me forever?"

Samantha looked so upset Conner didn't press for an answer. Instead, he asked a question he'd asked before, "Is it okay if I hold you?"

Wiping away tears, she nodded. Samantha wanted his arms around her—needed them.

Conner pulled her tense body between his splayed legs, her back to his front. Leaning against the wall, he kissed the top of her head and asked, "Is this guy dangerous?" Sam nodded again.

"Damn," was all he said. He didn't know the whole story, but he knew enough for now. Samantha felt enveloped in his arms, warm and protected. They sat that way for what seemed like a long time.

When Conner's phone rang, he said, "Don't worry about it. I'll check it later."

"No," Samantha insisted. "Go ahead. Get it. Really."

"You're sure? Are you okay?"

"As okay as I'm ever going to be. Go ahead."

Conner retrieved his phone from the kitchen table, where he'd left it, as it began ringing again. Samantha heard him say, "Hi, Mom," followed by lots of "yes ma'am's" and "I will's." He ended the call by telling her he was with a friend and would call back later.

When Conner returned to the living room, Samantha was still sitting on the floor. So, he put out a hand, pulled her up, and led her to the sofa. "Let's sit somewhere more comfortable." For a while, they sat companionably, shoulder to shoulder, holding hands, lost in their own thoughts.

Samantha broke the silence. "Conner?"

"Yes."

"I'm going to ask you something, and I hope you won't be offended."

"Go ahead."

"When you talk about your mother, it sounds as if she's demanding, impossible to please, and short on affection."

Conner nodded, confirming the allegations.

"Yet you treat her with respect that seems genuine. I guess I'm wondering how you manage that?"

"Hmm," he mused. "Mom has some good qualities as well as the ones you mentioned. And she's my mother," he said with a shrug. "Like a lot of mothers, she struggles with me being an adult with a mind of my own. I know I can't change her. So I accept her as she is, the bad with the good."

Samantha contemplated what he said. "You see the world in such a positive light. I don't mean you're a

Pollyanna or anything. But nothing seems to rile you."

"I believe," Conner began, "that each person establishes his own expectations of how others should act, who they should be. But people won't always behave the way we want them to. So when they disappoint us, we have to decide if their behavior falls within acceptable parameters. I guess you could say my parameters are fairly broad."

"You mean you accept behavior you don't really approve of."

"When I can," Conner admitted.

"So rather than forgive someone after the fact, you just refuse to condemn them in the first place."

"Something like that." He cocked his head and looked at Samantha. "I think you do the same thing."

"Maybe. But that hasn't always worked out for me," she admitted. "And some behavior is unacceptable."

"Of course it is. I see it in my line of work all the time."

Samantha stared at her hands. "It's one thing to be tolerant of people's faults; it's another to be totally blind to them."

"Now I think you're talking about someone in particular."

"Him," she said, motioning toward the letter Conner left on the floor. "Because of him I can't trust my own judgment."

"What happened, Sam? What did he do to you?"

"I can't talk about it."

"I don't want to harp on this, but I need to know so we can get past this issue. You can trust me."

"You'd see me differently if you knew. You'd see me as a victim."

"I'm an attorney, honey. A lot of people are victims at some point in their lives, but they don't have to remain that way. It takes courage and a lot of work, but people can move forward. I've seen it happen."

Samantha looked up and glared at him. "Oh, I faced it all right. I took him to court. It was the hardest thing I've ever done. But it's over and I'd like to forget it."

"You took him to trial? Did you win?"

"I don't know if I won anything, but he's in prison. That's all I have to say about it."

"Tell me one thing. When did all this happen?"

"Two years ago. I've tried to keep it quiet, but it's probably a well-known secret. The prosecutor on my case was a woman who had experienced violence. I don't know how she did it, but she managed to get a closed courtroom and have my personal identifying information redacted from the records. Blessedly, there was only a blip in the papers minus my name." Samantha dropped her head then raised her eyes, "You're going to look it up, aren't you? I know you can get the trial records."

"How would you feel if I did?"

"I'd rather you didn't. You wouldn't think of me the same way."

"Give me some credit, Sam. I care about you. Maybe I can help. Who else knows what happened?"

"Only a few people. Uncle Russ is the one I called for help. He's Jeff's dad. So Jeff knows."

"Jeff is your cousin?"

"No. I've just always called his dad Uncle Russ. He's close to the family and owns the land adjoining ours. Well, he and Jeff do. Doc knows, and my parents, of course, and Scott because he's the sheriff. They all know I want it kept quiet, and I believe they've honored my request. I'm learning to live with what happened, but if others know it'll be harder to put behind me."

"Max and Anna don't know?"

"Anna doesn't. She would have said something if she did. I told her Hal hit me, and I divorced him. But that's all. I don't know what Max knows."

When Samantha's phone rang, she found it in the kitchen and then returned to the living room. "Did I hear you say you're at the hospital in Clarkston?" When Conner looked concerned, she let him know with a shake of her head it was nothing serious. At least she didn't think so. Switching the call to speaker mode, Samantha put a finger to her lips. Conner got it. She didn't want to explain why he was at the farmhouse so early in the morning.

"We came to the hospital last night. I hope I didn't wake you," Max said. "I should have waited to call, but I wanted to tell somebody." Conner and Samantha could hear the excitement in his voice. "Anna had the baby about two this morning. A boy. Eight pounds, three ounces. We named him Rex."

"Congratulations," Samantha said. "Why didn't you call last night? Who's taking care of Gracie?"

"We dropped her off at Mom and Dad's on the way to the hospital. Anna didn't want me to call anyone in case it was only those Braxton Hicks things. The doctor said he might let them go home today, although I think I'll push for tomorrow. She needs time to rest. I know you're anxious to see the baby but give us a little time to settle in first. Will you call Conner? Anna wants to make sure he knows."

"How about that?" Conner said, when Samantha put down the phone. "Anna is a mother and Gracie has a little brother. Did I hear right? Did they really name him Rex?"

Samantha laughed. "They really did. Now there's granddaddy Alex, daddy Max, and baby Rex. Maybe they misinterpreted the concept of generation X."

Conner had only been back at his apartment a few hours when he received a call from the new mom. "I'm home," she told him.

"I thought you planned to stay another day."

"I was anxious to leave. I can't wait for you to see Rex. Can you come over tomorrow afternoon? Samantha's coming."

Seeing an opportunity to spend more time with Sam, he phoned. "Are you feeling okay?"

"Sure, I'm fine," she said, as if none of the morning's drama had occurred.

"Good. I've been worried about you."

"Don't. I'm fine."

Conner didn't believe her but let the subject slide. "Anna just called to invite me over tomorrow afternoon. I thought maybe I could pick you up. We could see Anna and the baby and then go to Lucky's for an early supper."

"Sure, as long as I get to ride in that cute little black car of yours."

"You're not referring to my turbo charged beast, I hope."

"Oh, right. That's what I meant to say."

Max opened the door to his and Anna's recently renovated home to greet Conner and Samantha. "I suppose those flowers are for me," he joked, taking them from Conner. "I'll put them in a vase." They were lilies, Anna's favorite, and it bothered Max that Conner was privy to that information.

Samantha hugged the new mother and sat on the sofa beside her. Conner kissed Anna's cheek, settling on her other side. They'd only been admiring the baby in Anna's lap a few minutes when Samantha reached for him. "I'll take him while you open the gift I brought."

Samantha gazed at the baby in her arms, unsuccessfully trying not to cry. "He's just so beautiful," she explained, but Conner saw the sadness in her expression and wondered if the tears were about something more.

"You shouldn't have brought me anything else," Anna said. "You've already given me a gift. And a shower."

"I made this one," Sam said.

Seeing the tucked and embroidered receiving blanket, Anna's hand flew to her chest. "I can't believe you made this," she said, hugging her friend. "When did you have time?"

Another tear ran down Samantha's face. "I started it a while ago."

Samantha was cooing to baby Rex when a maroon pick-up truck stopped in front of the house. Jeff Windom, in his customary jeans, plaid shirt, and boots, stepped out holding three gift bags. "Come in, Jeff," Max said, glad to see his friend.

Anna looked up and smiled. "What a nice surprise!"

"I had to come see my favorite riding student's baby brother, didn't I? Hi there, little guy," Jeff said, looking at Rex. "Who does he look like, Gracie?"

She shrugged. "Mama says he looks like Daddy, but he just looks like a baby to me."

Jeff handed a blue bag to Anna. "This one is for the Wild Gators' future quarterback. You'll think one of the items is strange." Jeff sat in a near-by chair putting the other bags on the floor beside it.

Weighing the bag in her hand, Anna looked at Jeff questioningly. "It's heavy." First, she pulled out two Dr. Seuss books.

"The gray-haired sales-lady at the store told me she used to read that one to her kids," Jeff said, gesturing to *Hand, Hand, Finger, Thumb*. She said they liked the rhythm of the words. As Anna pulled a horseshoe out of the tissue-paper stuffed bag, Jeff said, "That's the one you'll think is strange."

He was about to explain when Samantha said, "Oh, it's a good-luck horseshoe. I've had one above my bedroom door all my life."

"I remember," Anna said.

Samantha smiled, thinking of how they used to play in the farmhouse. "When I took my parents' room, Mama made sure the horseshoe moved with me."

Jeff looked surprised. "I didn't think anyone did that but my family. When I moved into the old cabin on our property, I declared I'd outgrown horseshoes over my bedroom door. So Pops promptly nailed one above the cabin's entryway. There's one in the bag for Gracie, too."

Jeff looked around. "But I didn't know you'd turned your house into such a showplace. You might not want horseshoes hanging above your doors. Maybe you could paint them or something."

"Maybe. I love them, Jeff, especially the sentiment behind them. Thank you for thinking of us. How about a cup of coffee?"

"No thanks. I just came by to get a look at the little guy and congratulate this rascal on being a big sister," he said, ruffling Gracie's curls." Ever since he'd sat down, Gracie had been leaning against his chair.

Jeff noticed his young friend eyeing the bags on the floor. Grinning, he said, "Oh yeah, I almost forgot. I have a couple of things for the big sister." When he set the bags in front of Gracie, she jumped into his lap to hug him."

Max winced in sympathy. "You all right, man? Those knees are deadly."

"I'm okay, but it was a close call." He nodded toward the pink bags. "Go ahead. Open them."

Pulling something from the first bag, Gracie let out a shrill yell. "Mama! It's a book about horses!" Ever since Jeff had given Gracie riding lessons, she'd been fascinated by the large, graceful animals.

Samantha looked at the baby she swayed on her knees. "It's hard to believe, but Rex barely flinched when Gracie squealed."

Max chuckled. "He does really well with that. Must have gotten used to it in the womb."

Enjoying Gracie's excitement, one of the adults urged, "Open the other one."

"Aww," Samantha and Anna said, when Gracie pulled out a framed picture of herself. She was sitting atop a wooden fence, a beautiful chestnut horse beside her.

"It's Topaz! Look, Mama, it's Topaz. She's the horse Jeff let me ride."

"Thank you so much," Anna said. "I love it. Who took the photo?"

"I did. I've been photographing animals since I was about twelve."

"It looks professional," Samantha said. "You could go into business."

"Thanks, but I think I'm more suited to ranching."

While the adults were talking, Gracie ran to the kitchen. "Oh, no," they heard her say. Then she walked to where they sat, an open can of cola spewing over her small hands. "I was getting a cola for Jeff, and it jumped out all over the floor." Max got up to help. "Did you drop the can?"

"Uh huh. But it didn't come open."

Jeff gave Gracie a sympathetic smile. "My dad always says, 'When you make a mistake, admit it.' "

Samantha joined in to finish the saying. "Then hold up your head and keep going."

"Did my dad say that to you?" Jeff asked.

"I don't think so. It's something my mother always said when I was little."

"Huh." They both mused.

After Jeff left, Conner asked, "Are you going to hold that baby all day, or are you going to share?" Everyone looked at Conner with amusement.

"Do you even know how to hold a baby?" Samantha asked.

"Not exactly. But it doesn't look that hard."

After getting advice from everyone in the room, Conner held Rex in his arms looking like a child with a new toy. "He's great. Look at him. I think he's smiling at me."

Samantha thought, wistfully, that he would be a great dad someday. If only it could be with her.

❧

As Conner drove down the narrow gravel road toward Lucky's, he asked Samantha if she was all right.

"Yes. Why?"

"I don't know. You just seem a little sad."

"Not at all," she lied. "Just hungry. I plan on eating a bait of catfish."

"A bait?"

"A lot, city boy."

"Don't forget about the redneck hors d'oeuvres," Conner said.

"Never. I love Lucky's turnip greens and hushpuppies."

After pulling into the dirt parking lot, they carefully zig-zagged through the menagerie of dogs, cats, and chickens, to join the line of people waiting to get inside. "This place is one of a kind," Conner said, looking at the vintage signs and car tags nailed to the side of the unpainted building. "At first, I thought the owners may have collected a tag from each state, but now I see they're all from Mississippi."

"But from different counties," Samantha noted.

While enjoying their catfish supper, they talked about the new baby, Jeff's thoughtful gifts, and Gracie. "I think Gracie may have a little crush on Jeff," Samantha said.

Conner clutched his chest dramatically. "Say it isn't so. My heart may be broken."

"You can take comfort in the knowledge that she hasn't made him an honorary uncle." Then a faraway expression overtook Samantha's face.

"What are you thinking?" Conner asked.

"Isn't it funny that Jeff's dad and my mom use the same phrase about making mistakes? I've never heard it anywhere else. I always thought Mama made it up."

Conner shrugged. "Just a coincidence, I suppose, like the horseshoes."

"I guess so. But it makes me think Uncle Russ and Mama were siblings or something in another life."

CHAPTER FIVE

Conner and Samantha returned to the farmhouse to find Russ and the sheriff waiting on the front porch. Leaping from the car the moment it stopped, Samantha ran toward them. "What happened? Did something trigger the alarm?"

"No," Russ said. "Scott asked me to meet him here. He has some news and didn't want you to be alone when you heard it."

"He's not getting out," she stated, as if saying it made it so.

"Sorry," Scott said. "I just found out. He was released yesterday."

Russ took a step toward Sam, with the intention of comforting her, when he realized she was clinging to Conner.

"I'm not ready," she said. "He got five years and it's only been two. How could that happen? I'll have to leave my home and my job. They were supposed to let us know before he was released, not the day after. Now he can follow me."

Scott was sympathetic. "I know. I'm sorry. Somebody dropped the ball. Let's go inside where we can sit and talk."

Russ and Conner accompanied them, standing while Scott ushered Samantha toward the sofa.

"Sammy," Russ said, "you shouldn't be alone tonight. You can stay at my place."

"I don't know, Uncle Russ. I guess I should, but there's so much to do to get ready to leave town. Maybe I'd better stay here. At least this house has an alarm and the hiding place you built."

"I know you'd prefer that, but you shouldn't be alone."

"I'll stay with you," Conner said, looking at Samantha.

"Would you? This is happening so fast I can't get my mind around it. I'm not ready to leave. I have so much to do, and I need to say good-bye to my house and the animals."

"Sure," Conner said. "I'll take off work tomorrow if you need me."

"That shouldn't be necessary," the sheriff said, "at least not for safety reasons. Either Deputy Garret or I will be here all day. And Samantha, stay two or three nights if you need to. We won't leave you unguarded."

"Thank you, Scott. I appreciate that. Conner, you go on to work tomorrow. I'll be fine. But if you can stay another night or two, that would be great. Once it gets dark, I'm afraid all sorts of scenarios will occur to me—none of them good."

"Whatever you need," Conner said. "If you think you'll be all right here tomorrow, I'll leave early in the morning, grab a few things from my apartment, and drive back as soon as I leave the office."

"That should work," Scott said. "Like I said, either Deputy Garret or I will be here. We won't leave Samantha alone."

"You could stay in the house where it's warm," she suggested.

"Thanks, but we'll be fine. We'll be in our cars most of the time."

While Scott asked Samantha questions and reviewed safety procedures, Russ nodded for Conner to follow him onto the porch. Standing in the cool night air, he asked the younger man, "How much do you know about what happened?"

"Very little."

Russ pressed his lips together. "You need to know how dangerous Hal is. When Sammy married him, everyone thought he was a good guy. Then one night, he snapped and put her through hell. Nearly killed her. I feel sure he would have, or worse, if she hadn't managed to call me. I'm telling you this, so you'll know what we're dealing with."

He hesitated, looked down, and then continued. "When I got here, she was lying naked in the middle of the living room floor with blood pooling at both ends of her body. I was surprised to find her still breathing. He'd raped her and beaten her half to death."

Russ shook his head, remembering the worst night of his life. "It was bad. Real bad." He closed his eyes and swallowed hard. When he opened them, he saw that Conner was white as a ghost, and his eyes were wet.

With a quivering voice, Russ forced himself to continue. "I try not to think about what we found on the floor beside her. But if you're staying here, you need to know. For reasons I don't even want to consider, he had masking tape, scissors, a butcher knife and a paring knife."

While Russ looked down at the floor, Conner stood suspended, unsure which emotion to give in to first. Then he jumped off the porch, stalked to the barn, and sank to the straw-covered ground. He had to be strong, but he needed a minute alone to absorb the shock of Russ's revelation. Burying his head in his hands, he allowed the gut-wrenching emotions to wash over him. Then he dragged his hands down his face, stood, and strode back to the porch where Russ waited. There was no need to explain his abrupt departure.

"Do you know how to shoot, son?" the older man asked. "Ever been hunting?"

Conner looked around for a chair and dropped into it. He still wasn't feeling too steady. After taking a few moments to collect himself, he found his voice. "I've been skeet shooting."

"That's better than nothing. Before I leave, I'll show you where the guns are and make sure you know how to use them. You need to keep one with you at all times and have a second one nearby. And they need to be loaded. Make sure you have a charged phone, too. Don't leave Sammy's side. Stay in the bedroom with her, and remember what you're there for. You're to make her feel safe and protect her if necessary. Nothing else. Her door is solid and has three locks on it. Use all of them."

"Of course," Conner said, finally realizing the magnitude of what he'd volunteered for.

"If you hear anyone inside the house," Russ said, "use the secret door to the attic. Hal knows about it, but there's a hiding spot up there I built after the attack. Have Sammy show it to you. And if that son-of-a-bitch somehow manages to get to you, shoot to kill before he kills you or Sammy. The guy is insanely jealous. Literally. If he sees you with her, it definitely won't sit well. And don't mistake those of us keeping guard for intruders."

"Got it," Conner managed to say.

"You should be fine. But you need to be prepared, just in case. I almost hope the demented bastard shows up so we can wipe him off the face of the earth. One more thing," Russ said. "Even though Sammy's a crackerjack shot, she'll be too jumpy to have a gun tonight. But in a pinch... Well, I'm just saying, she's a good shot."

When Russ and Conner walked back inside, Scott noticed that the younger man looked shaken. "Conner," the sheriff said, "don't feel like you have to stay awake all night. Sleep if you need to. We'll be outside. But leave a light on so you can see as soon as you wake up. If you hear a gunshot or the alarm, head for the attic, and be sure to take the guns and phones with you. No heroics. That hiding place is the best way to protect Samantha. When you get upstairs, you should have a practice run, go through the motions."

"Russ," the sheriff said, "let's check the windows and doors to make sure they're locked."

"Why don't you do that while I show Conner the gun cabinet?" Samantha accompanied Scott, while Russ acquainted Conner with a pistol and a shotgun. "Keep them loaded. They go wherever you go."

"Everything's locked up tight," Scott said when they all returned to the living room. "When we leave,

Samantha, you need to show Conner how to silence and arm the alarm."

Scott gave Samantha a side hug. "You're going to be fine. We don't expect any trouble," he lied. "We're just preparing for the possibility."

Russ hugged Samantha and kissed her on the cheek. "Don't worry, Sammy. Conner will be inside with you, and there'll be someone outside all night. Scott and I will take the first watch. Deputy Garrett and Jeff will take the second one. Try to get some sleep. And don't lie there worrying about the future. Everything will work out. A lot of people love you, and we'll make sure you're okay. Want me to call your mom and let her know what's going on, or would you rather do it?"

"No. You call. And please ask her not to contact me tonight. I'm having a hard enough time holding it together. If I hear her voice, I'll lose it. And Uncle Russ..."

"Yeah?"

"Thanks for everything. You know I love you, don't you?"

Russ nodded and mumbled, "Me, too," as he turned to leave, and Conner saw tears in the robust man's eyes.

Once Russ and Scott left the house and the alarm was set, Conner asked, "What do you want to do now?"

"Throw up," Samantha answered.

"Try to hold off on that. Why don't you go on upstairs?"

She grabbed Conner's hand and tugged. "Come with me. I don't want to be alone."

Inside the bedroom, Conner fastened all the locks on the door. "You want to show me the hiding spot in the attic before you get ready for bed?"

"I guess I should."

Conner helped Samantha open the hidden door, and they ascended the staircase. Looking around, he saw nothing that hinted of a secret panel. Then Sam reached behind a locker and pressed a recessed button at the bottom of a stud. Like magic, a section of wall slid away, leaving an opening wide enough for a person to slip through. It could be opened manually if the electricity was off.

Conner was amazed. It was a panic room, hidden so well anyone would have trouble finding it. Russ had even attached studs to the fake wall, making it look exactly like the rest of the attic.

After briefing Conner on the operation of the hiding place, Samantha followed him back to the bedroom. "I should have gone home with Uncle Russ," she said. "Staying here is a lot of trouble for everyone."

"I'm sure someone would stand guard at Russ's, if you were there, and you wouldn't have a secret hiding place or three locks on your door."

"I guess so. I just hate that people I care about will be out in the cold all night."

"They'll do whatever is needed to keep you safe. And Scott said they'll be in their cars most of the time." Conner sat in a chair, upholstered in large white flowers, and slipped off his loafers. "I know it's early, Sam, but why don't you go ahead and take your bath and get ready for bed? I don't see how anyone could get to us tonight. Russ and Scott seem to have thought of everything."

"I won't take a bath. I can't be naked—not when Hal could be close. I know it makes no sense. It's just how I feel."

He waited while Samantha dressed for bed in the adjoining bathroom, thinking about something she once said. After finding out what had happened, he did see her as a victim.

Normally, he'd be having sexual thoughts about the beautiful woman he was about to share a bed with. Instead, he was picturing her lying in a pool of blood, battered and broken, and it shook him to the core. No one deserved that, especially not the sweet, lively woman in the next room.

Samantha, dressed in drawstring pants and a long sleeve t-shirt, sat on the closed toilet. She had a lot of difficult decisions to make in the next few days, but one of them needed to be made immediately.

Since she'd gotten Conner involved in her messy drama, he deserved an explanation. It was time to face facts and stop pretending there could be something between them. They couldn't do that until she found the courage to tell him the truth. Hurrying from the bathroom, she jumped into bed, leaned against the headboard, and pulled the blanket up for warmth.

Fully dressed, with the guns and his phone resting on the night table, Conner sat in the bed next to Samantha. It was too early for sleep. But the sun had gone down, and the bed was inviting, especially with Sam in it.

"I'm ready to tell you what happened," she said without emotion. "You know some of it. You might as well know the rest. I've put you smack dab in the middle of this chaos."

Sitting beside her, Conner shook his head. "Sam, I know I asked you to tell me what happened, but I've changed my mind. I know enough. You don't have to say any more."

"Yes, I do. I need to. I've done it before. I told my lawyer, and then I had to tell it in court. Just let me get this over with."

"Okay, but first let's get you warm. You're shivering." He put an arm around Samantha's unyielding body, pulling her close, finding it hard to believe she'd only shared her story twice. He was no therapist, but maybe she should talk about it.

Samantha longed to melt into him, to feel cherished one last time before he knew her vile story, but yielding to his embrace would shatter her resolve. Vowing to remain strong, she straightened, mentally preparing to reveal the events of the most terrifying night of her life. She needed to tell Conner what happened without allowing the psychological trauma to regain its hold.

Her physical mending had been slow, but that process was a run-away train compared to the pace of her emotional healing. Until Conner, she couldn't even let a man touch her. The advancements she'd made in her recovery had taken counseling, self-talk, a determined "fake it until you make it" attitude, and Conner's ceaseless patience.

To explain what happened without shattering her tenuous progress, she'd have to insulate herself from the emotions of the experience. She'd deceive herself, she decided, by pretending she was relating a scene from a book or television. If she could trick her mind into thinking it didn't really happen, she might survive the telling.

Girding herself with the fabricated armor, she mustered the courage to share the events that plagued her dreams and burdened her days. Conner could almost see her emotionally distancing from the surroundings.

Looking down at her hands, Samantha began. "I was in the kitchen cooking supper, grateful that Hal would be home for a while. He'd been out on the oil rig two weeks. I hoped he and his buddies wouldn't stop by the Bar None. They sometimes did that at the end of a rotation—to blow off a little steam, Hal said. I didn't like it because he tended to drink too much, and when he drank, he changed into someone I didn't know.

"He'd hit me twice before that night, and both times it was after he'd been out with the guys." Her hands began twisting the sheet, and she glanced at Conner, half expecting to see accusation in his eyes. Seeing only concern, she continued. "Like an idiot, I forgave him. I figured it was the result of alcohol and a bunch of macho drivel. Now, I believe he suffered from a mental disorder, and those were triggers.

"When I heard a truck pull up out front, I took off my apron, glanced in the dining room mirror to make sure I looked okay, and opened the screen door with a smile on my face." She shrugged, feeling the need to defend her behavior. "He was my husband. You know? I loved him. Then I saw Hal's wobbly gait. I was disappointed, but it didn't occur to me to be afraid."

Conner watched as she fisted the sheet in both hands. When he placed a hand over hers, she shook her head. "Don't try to comfort me. I want to do this without breaking down."

Conner frowned. "I'm getting the feeling this isn't a good idea. You don't have to tell me anything."

"No. Let me finish. I want to get it over with." She took a deep breath and continued. "I was about to go help him into the house when he looked up, and I saw his angry expression. Before I knew what was happening, he'd balled up his fist and hit me in the face. Then he grabbed my arm and pulled me in the house. At first, he left the door open. But when the dogs came onto the porch and started barking, he kicked it closed. But I'm getting ahead of myself. Like I said, he dragged me inside.

"When I could focus, I was lying on the living room floor, and Hal was squatting down looking at me. The anger on his face made him almost unrecognizable. I'd never seen him like that. Then he asked who I'd been screwing around with while he was out on the rig. I was flabbergasted. I couldn't imagine where he got such an idea. He kept asking the same question, getting louder and louder. 'Who have you been screwing around with?' He said my truck was seen almost every night at the Bar None. He just kept asking the same thing.

"I told him I never went there without him. Not even with girlfriends. And that was the truth. I never did." She glanced at Conner to gauge whether or not he believed her. Satisfied, she continued. "He called me a liar and kept saying that people saw my truck in the parking lot. When I told him it wasn't mine, he slapped me."

"That's enough," Conner said. "You don't have to do this."

"But I do." She swallowed hard and continued telling her story, almost in a monotone. "Then Hal said, in the meanest voice I've ever heard, 'You couldn't wait until I got home to get fucked?' He didn't usually talk like that, at least not around me. It was like he was someone else. Then he said, 'I was out on the rig with a bunch of men, knowing I had a sweet thing waiting at home for me, and I came back to find you've been fucking around. Well, I'll give it to you now.' Then he jerked off my trousers and ripped off my panties."

"Don't," Conner said, "you don't have to tell me."

Resembling someone in a trance, Samantha seemed not to hear. "I told him I would never run around on him and begged him to stop. Then he pulled his pants down, and I could see he was aroused. I don't understand how he could have been aroused," she said, looking at Conner. "That doesn't make sense to me."

Tears ran down Samantha's face. Conner wanted to comfort her, but she was staring straight ahead as if watching it happening. He took her hand in his, but she didn't seem to notice.

"I screamed for him to stop. I told him he was hurting me. If my screaming had any effect, it further aroused him. 'Why the tears?' he asked. 'You don't like it rough? Aww. Was your lover gentle?' "

Then Samantha's voice became very small. "I finally stopped talking and just endured the pain. I

knew he was tearing me, but I couldn't stop him.
Finally, he pulled his pants up. I thought he'd go
away after that, but he wasn't through with me. He
wanted to humiliate me. He stripped off the rest of my
clothes and kicked me with those hard shoes he wore
on the rig. That's when he broke my ribs."

Samantha stifled a sob, and then let out a ragged
breath. "Then he pulled me up by my hair, and I
thought my body was ripping apart. He was yelling
and I had trouble understanding what he was saying.
When I was able to focus, I heard him growl, 'Are
you ready to tell me who you've been with?' When I
didn't say anything, he cursed, slapped me, and threw
me down again. I tried to tell him I hadn't been with
anyone, but the pain was so bad, I couldn't get out the
words. So, he kicked me in the stomach. I curled my
naked body into a ball and…"

"Stop," Conner said. "That's enough, Samantha.
You're shaking." He didn't want to hear any more.

She finally looked at him and in a small, defeated
voice, said, "No. You should hear the rest. Then
maybe you'll understand why I'm so broken, why I'll
never be fit for any man."

Conner tried to pull her into his arms, but she
resisted. So he moved as close as he could and kissed
the top of her head.

"The prosecuting attorney at Hal's trial was
surprised I remembered so much," Samantha said.
"But, unfortunately, I remember every agonizing
minute."

Conner watched her swallow hard before
continuing. "When I curled into a ball, he said…" She
paused, hugging herself tightly, and took a deep,

87

ragged breath. "He said, 'So you want it that way? I'm not quite ready to go again.' Then he proceeded to get himself ready."

"God no!" Conner exclaimed, running a hand through his hair, and then clasping her arm to show his support.

Samantha kept talking. "The torture went on for some time."

Then, for the first time since her story began, she laid her head on Conner's shoulder and allowed herself to cry. Grateful to finally be able to hold her, Conner hoped she'd finished. But she managed to speak through her sobs. "He'd already broken my body. Then he broke my heart.

"I still hear that sarcastic voice in my nightmares. 'Oh, sweetie, you've started your period. You're bleeding on the floor.' He knew I was pregnant, Conner. He knew it."

"Dear God!" Conner said, at a loss as to what to do or say. So he just held her, smoothing her hair, which reminded Samantha that Russ had done the same thing on that terrible night. After hearing what happened, Conner understood why she'd been reluctant to explain. It was a horror story.

No more, Conner thought. No more.

But she continued recounting the gruesome details. "He left the room and as he walked away, he muttered, 'Wouldn't know whose kid it was, anyway.' Then I heard him rummaging around in the kitchen, talking to himself. He'd gone bat-shit crazy, and I was terrified of what else he might do. So I crawled to my pants where he'd thrown them on the floor, hoping my phone was still in the pocket. It wasn't. Then I saw it across the room.

"I prayed, with every excruciating inch I crawled, that he wouldn't come back before I got to it. I was having trouble breathing. I don't know how I did it, but I got the phone.

"Long ago, Uncle Russ insisted I program his number into my cell, so all I had to do was touch number one to reach him. He said if I had an emergency, he could get to me faster than anyone else. He repeated it so often that it was the first thing that came to mind.

"Thank God he answered. All I said was 'help me.' Then Hal kicked my arm and I screamed. I felt a lot of pain that night, but that was the worst. Later, I found out he'd broken my arm.

"I think I passed out for a minute, but the noise from the dogs brought me back. They'd howled and scratched at the door throughout the whole ordeal, but their barking got louder, more urgent."

Conner remembered Samantha's cryptic comment when he expressed surprise that her dogs had scarred the door. Now he knew the extenuating circumstances she'd mentioned.

"I thought I heard a vehicle, but I was too far gone to care," Samantha said. "I was fading fast when the front door burst open and Uncle Russ said something like, 'Oh God no.' I heard the back door slam a few times, and then I heard gunshots.

"I don't know how he knew where it was, but Uncle Russ went right to the gun we keep loaded with birdshot and peppered Hal's backside. I found out later that after Hal was arrested, Doc refused to give him pain medicine while removing the pellets.

"Uncle Russ thought I was dead until I moaned. After covering me with an afghan he found draped over the sofa, he called Doc and Scott. Poor Uncle Russ was beside himself, stroking my head, trying to soothe me. I remember him saying, over and over, 'He's gone, baby. He's gone. You're going to be all right.' Doc gave me something for pain, and I only know what happened after that because I was told. Scott took pictures of the crime scene. He probably should have photographed me without the afghan, since that's the way Uncle Russ found me. Instead, he moved it just enough to show I was naked beneath.

"The prosecuting attorney enlarged the pictures for display at the trial. It was bad enough, seeing the horror on the juror's faces when they saw what he did to me, I don't think I could have endured the shame if I'd been naked in those photos.

"They tell me it took thirty minutes for the ambulance to arrive from Clarkston. I was hemorrhaging and doc was afraid I'd bleed to death, but he wouldn't take me in his car. He was concerned about internal damage and broken bones. Turned out my husband broke my nose, three ribs and my arm. And he killed my baby, as well as the chance to live the life I've always wanted."

"You mean a life with him?"

"Heavens, no!"

Samantha closed her eyes and took a deep breath before answering. "I've always wanted a big family. I dreamed of filling this old farmhouse with children."

"You can still do that, Sam," Conner said.

She shook her head, tears running down her face. "No, I can't. The doctor said it's unlikely that I'll ever be able to conceive after the trauma my body experienced."

"I'm sorry, Sam. But there are other ways to have a family."

She kept shaking her head. "No. A man deserves a wife who can give him his own children."

Conner interrupted. "Bullshit. A man doesn't have to contribute sperm to have his own children. Adopted kids are loved just as much as children raised by their biological parents—sometimes more. You're beautiful, smart, and the strongest woman I know. Any man would be lucky to have you."

He realized it was true. Samantha was extraordinary. Wondering how she'd come through the ordeal as well as she had, Conner held her close, rubbing her back. Exhausted, Samantha welcomed his comfort and cried herself to sleep.

CHAPTER SIX

The following morning, after Conner left for work, Samantha spent the day packing. Having no idea where to go when she left Tenacity, she gathered basic items needed anywhere. Her mother could mail more things later.

Sam hated the idea of leaving Tenacity. It was hard to imagine life without her beloved farmhouse, her school children, her family, and friends. But the prospect of a horrible, pre-mature death made leaving the only rational option. She certainly didn't want to die, but that wasn't what she feared most. The torture that would likely precede it terrified her. She couldn't go through that again. She just couldn't.

After fighting her fears all day, Samantha was more than relieved to hear the distinctive sound of Conner's car returning for the evening. As soon as he walked through the door, she fastened her arms around the man who'd become her lifeline. She hated being needy, but fear and indecisiveness threatened to overwhelm her. It was unfair to make him her ballast, but he was strong and steady, and at the moment, she wasn't.

Forcing herself to release him, hoping to hide how close she was to falling apart, Samantha tried to act casual. "Are you hungry? I'm not sure what's in the kitchen."

"I should have picked something up," Conner said. "I was only thinking about getting back as quickly as possible."

Following Samantha into the kitchen, Conner watched her competently prepare an appetizing meal. She fried chicken, boiled field peas from the freezer, added chopped green onions to mashed potatoes, and baked cornbread in a large iron skillet. Conner was impressed. His mother and Miss Emma planned menus at least a week in advance, and meal preparation often took hours.

Jeff and Deputy Garret refused to abandon their post to join Conner and Samantha at the kitchen table. They did, however, accept the proffered supper plates, happily devouring them from the comfort of the front porch rocking chairs.

Conner waited until Samantha finished eating to address the decision she had to make. Feigning a nonchalant attitude, he asked, "So where do you think you'll go when you leave here?"

Samantha shrugged. "Maybe I'll waitress at one of the gulf coast casinos, at least until I have a feasible plan. It's too close to home, but I can probably find a job there."

"You don't have any idea where you want to settle?"

"No. Maybe I'll just move from town to town for a while. I can always clean hotel rooms. I'm not afraid of hard work." Conner hated the idea of her roaming the countryside alone, taking any kind of job she could get. So he resolved to give the situation serious thought once Samantha fell asleep.

The tall, kind man, with movie-star good looks, spent the night in Samantha's bed once more, reminding himself he was only there for support and protection. Expecting anything else would make him the worst sort of cad.

He was almost getting used to the torture of lying beside a desirable woman without making a move on her. He told himself he was just offering support to a friend. But it was more than that, and deep down, he knew it. He had feelings for Samantha and couldn't abide the thought of her being hurt again.

Snuggling close to Conner, Samantha was more than grateful for his strong, calming presence. He distracted her from the danger she faced, and she was becoming increasingly dependent on him. Every minute they spent together made it harder to imagine life without him. How had he become such an important fixture in her life so quickly?

Conner offered to make the morning meal, but Samantha insisted on staying busy. After breakfast, as they sat at the kitchen table with a second cup of coffee, she confided in him.

"I'm so conflicted. My mind bounces from one thought to the opposite one. I try not to think of Hal, but it's stupid to ignore the danger he poses. The idea of leaving my home devastates me, but I have to prepare to do just that. I've spent two years trying to forget what Hal did to me, but I can't, can I? And I don't see how this nightmare will ever end."

Samantha shook her head, attempting to dislodge the destructive thoughts. "I'm sorry. It's not fair to dump my problems on you. You don't know how much I appreciate you being here. I'm just feeling sorry for myself because I don't know what to do and can't decide where to go."

"I've been thinking about that, and I have an idea," Conner said. "It won't solve your problems. It's more of a reprieve, but it would give you time to make your decisions."

"What?"

"Go home with me for Christmas. That lunatic won't find you there, and I'd love to spend the holidays with you. I'll show you around Savannah," he said, sounding upbeat. "We'll wander through the historic district, experience River Street, tour some old mansions. In fact, my family lives in one of those old mansions. And we can eat in some of the best restaurants in the South. You'll be safe, and we'll have a good time. Please say yes."

Samantha surprised herself by doing just that, mostly because she had no idea what else to do. "Will you show me where Anna's relatives live?"

"Of course. We can even invite them to lunch if you like." Then Conner laughed quietly.

"What is it?"

"I was thinking about how confused Anna will be when she finds out you're spending Christmas with me. She doesn't even know we're seeing one another, except for the dinner we shared after the movie the three of us saw together." Conner held up a hand. "I know what you're going to say. But you can't deny that we're seeing one another. Maybe not in the typical fashion but…"

Samantha gave Conner a small smile. "Well, we did go dancing once."

"And we decorated your house for Christmas," Conner added. "Surely, that can be considered a date."

"If that counts," Samantha said, "so does finding the letters in the attic. But that was the same day, wasn't it?"

"It was. If we're looking for evidence that we're dating," Conner began...

"Seeing one another," Samantha corrected.

"All right. If we're looking for evidence that we're seeing one another, we're overlooking an important detail."

"And what's that?" Samantha said, knowingly.

"The fact that we're sleeping in the same bed."

"Yeah," Samantha said slowly. "That definitely counts. Okay. You're right. You can say we're seeing one another."

Samantha's phone rang. When she answered, her eyes widened and she mouthed, "It's Anna."

Oblivious to what was happening in her friend's life, Anna said, "Gracie's playing out back and Rex is asleep. So I have a few free minutes. I want to thank you again for the lovely receiving blanket. It means so much to me that you made it yourself."

"You're very welcome. I'm happy for you and Max. Rex is adorable. Just a minute, Anna." Covering the phone, she whispered, "I'm not sure what to do. Anna doesn't even know what Hal did to me. What can I say? I don't think I can bear telling the story again."

"Want me to explain?"

96

"Would you?"

"I will," Conner said. "But how much do you want me to reveal?"

"Say whatever you want, but ask her not to tell anyone but Max. And don't tell her I lost the baby," she whispered. "It'll make her feel bad because she has little Rex."

Conner wondered how Samantha could think of someone else's feelings when she was in such turmoil. Picking up the phone, he said, "Anna, this is Conner."

"Conner? Why are you at the farmhouse?"

"I have a lot to tell you. Samantha wants you to know what's happening in her life, but she isn't up to explaining right now. I volunteered to fill you in."

"What do you mean she's not up to it?"

Not wanting to listen to the conversation, Samantha pointed a finger toward the ceiling and mouthed, "I'll be upstairs." Then she left the room.

"If you'll be patient," Conner told Anna, "I'll explain. First, I should tell you that Samantha and I have become good friends, and we're sort of seeing one another."

"Really? How did that come about?"

"It began at your wedding reception."

"That long ago? And neither of you thought to tell me?"

"What can I say? It took me a while to win her over."

"Don't hurt her," Anna said, concern in her voice.

"I'm not going to hurt her," Conner said indignantly. "I'm trying to protect her."

"Protect her from what?"

97

"Do you want to know what's going on or not?"

"Of course, I do."

"Then stop asking questions and listen."

"Okay. Go ahead."

Conner took a deep breath and began. "Sam told me she explained that she was married, and her ex hit her."

"She did," Anna said, sounding confused.

"Well, you don't know the whole story. It was worse than she led you to believe." Sparing Anna the grisly details, Conner told her what happened the night their friend almost died. "She took the bastard to trial, and he was sentenced to five years in prison. But because of an early release, he got out a couple of days ago, and there's a chance he'll come after her."

"No," Anna cried. "No."

"I'm staying with her so that she won't be alone. The sheriff, Russ, Deputy Garret, and Jeff are taking turns patrolling the exterior of the house. We're taking good care of her. She'll call when she can, but she doesn't want to talk about what her ex did to her. Right now, she's upstairs packing a few things."

"Where's she going?"

"I'm taking some vacation time to visit my family for the holidays, and she's going with me. We're leaving tomorrow. That'll remove her from immediate danger and give her time to think about what comes next."

"What's she going to do after that?"

"I don't know. She doesn't know. But Sam's strong and will be okay. She just has a few things to work out." Anna knew he was trying to lessen her apprehension, but he might as well be telling a passenger on a sinking ship not to worry.

When Conner joined Samantha upstairs, she thanked him for helping her out of an uncomfortable situation. "I just wasn't up to telling her. I know it wasn't easy. What did she say?"

"She's upset. You should call her when you can, or she'll worry herself half to death."

"You're right. And she'll have a million questions," Samantha said, "that I won't know how to answer."

At the airport, they checked their bags curbside, returned the rented vehicle, and walked the short distance back to the terminal. Conner would have suggested that Sam wait inside while he drove to the rental place, but he didn't want to take the chance of leaving her alone.

Samantha removed her shoes, placed her belongings on the conveyor belt, and looked back at Conner. "Don't you just love airports?"

He didn't tell her he found air travel barely tolerable unless he was flying first class. His legs were too long to be comfortable in economy. But he was paying for this trip and exit row seats would have to suffice.

Instead of answering, he sent her an affectionate look and asked, "What is it you like so much about airports?"

"The possibilities. Just think about it. We could get on a plane and go anywhere in the world."

Conner smiled. She was so cute. "From this airport," he explained, "you can get to nine or ten cities in the United States, "but from Atlanta, where we're changing planes, your choices are almost limitless."

One day, he promised himself, he'd take Samantha on a first-class trip complete with champagne and sleeping pods. And they'd go someplace like Paris or London. He enjoyed London, with its pubs and historic theatre district, but he'd take Samantha wherever she wanted to go.

Once they cleared security and found seats in the proper concourse, Conner asked, "Where would you go if you could choose any place in the world?"

"I've been thinking about that a lot since I can't stay on the farm or anywhere else in the area. But I don't know where I'd like to go."

"We'll have time on this trip to talk through your options. You might want to try another country for a while. Maybe I'll go with you. It would be an adventure."

"You can't do that."

"Why not? You can't go alone. I mean, of course, you could, but you shouldn't have to."

"That's crazy. You have your job and family and friends. You can't just up and leave."

"Of course, I can. I'm an able-bodied man. I can find work, my family is always a plane ride away, and I'd be with a friend, wouldn't I?" He hadn't really thought it through, but he couldn't let Samantha travel to some strange place alone.

"Conner, I appreciate all you're doing for me, but I can't let you give up your career. You're an attorney. That's who you are."

"No. That's my profession, and I wouldn't be giving it up. I'd be taking a sabbatical."

Not knowing where to go or what to do filled Samantha with dread. Having Conner at her side would provide an immense sense of security, but as much as she wanted and needed him, she couldn't let him make that sacrifice.

Upon hearing an announcement for another gate, Conner checked the arrival and departure board. "Looks like our plane is on time. The flight to Atlanta is an hour and fifteen minutes. After a ninety-minute layover, it's a one-hour jaunt to Savannah."

"I'm nervous about meeting your family," Samantha admitted. "They won't think you're bringing me home because we're serious or anything, will they?"

"I told Mom we're friends and will need separate bedrooms, even though that isn't my preference."

"Thank you. Did you tell her about my situation?"

"No. I assumed that's what you'd prefer."

Once they reached the Atlanta airport, Conner explained that they were looking for Terminal C.

"I think they should stop using the word terminal," Samantha said. "It sounds ominous, as if getting on a plane is the end of something. They should change it to expedition area, or launching pad, or transport area. I think I like that one. Doesn't Transport C sound better than Terminal C?"

"I have to admit it does," Conner said. "The things that come from that pretty head of yours never fail to surprise me."

Conner took Samantha to a restaurant which was also a bookstore. Looking around, she smiled. "This place has such a tranquil ambience. It's hard to believe it's in a busy airport."

"I thought you'd like it." With his hand on her lower back, he guided her to a cozy booth. After Samantha chose something from the menu, Conner encouraged her to browse the selection of books. "You might see something you want. Go ahead. I'll give the waitress your order." It felt good to put a smile on Samantha's beautiful face. Then he imagined that sweet face, bruised and swollen, and couldn't fathom how anyone could do that to her.

It wasn't long before she returned, holding a copy of a recently published novel. "I've been wanting to read this. The setting is in your neck of the woods."

"Then that'll be your first souvenir from our trip," Conner said. Once Samantha slid into the booth opposite him, his outstretched legs purposefully cocooned hers. Conner met her surprised expression with a cocky grin, sending warmth throughout Samantha's entire body.

Riding down streets lined with moss-laden live oaks, Samantha peered at the statuesque old Savannah homes through the window of a cab. She wished she knew the stories of the venerable structures. They must have witnessed multitudes of romances and backstairs intrigue. "Except for modern-day cars," Samantha said, "Savannah must look like it did in the eighteen hundreds."

Before Conner could reply, the taxi stopped in front of a grand old mansion. The architecture, Samantha guessed, was Regency or maybe Greek Revival.

"We're here," he said. "This is home."

While she stood beside the cab, admiring the imposing structure, Conner paid the driver and helped take the luggage to the front door. Returning to Sam's side, he held out his hand. "Coming?"

"Of course," she said, realizing how much she would miss having Conner to herself.

Opening the heavy front door, he unceremoniously yelled, "We're here." A plump older woman hurried to greet them. When Conner bent down to her level, she clasped his face in her soft hands and kissed him on the forehead.

Smiling, he kissed her cheek. "Samantha, I want you to meet someone very special to me. This is Emma Martin, Miss Emma."

"I'm so glad to meet you, Miss Emma. Conner speaks very highly of you. And I understand your cookies are responsible for his height."

She laughed and hugged Samantha, hurrying away when a slender, dignified woman descended the staircase and sedately crossed the foyer. "Hello, Son," she said, exposing both cheeks for Conner to kiss.

Turning to greet the woman at his side, she extended her hand. "You must be Samantha. Welcome, dear. We're glad you're joining us for the holidays."

"Thank you for allowing me to visit. You have a beautiful home, Mrs. Wilmington."

"You're kind. I'm sorry Conner's father and sister aren't here to greet you. Kendall has a previous engagement, but Mr. Wilmington will be joining us for dinner. So will the Pattersons," she said, glancing at Conner.

"Mom, couldn't you have given us time to unpack before bombarding us with guests."

"I'm hardly bombarding. Ralph Patterson is a business associate of your father's, and their daughter is home from school. Since you're old friends, I thought you'd want to see her."

Conner sighed. Damn. She was matchmaking again and doing it while Samantha was visiting. He was well aware of his parents' plans for him. He was supposed to move home, marry a girl with the proper social status, eventually take over his father's law firm, and become a pillar of the community. If not for Samantha's dangerous situation, he'd be tempted to turn around and go right back to Mississippi.

Conner picked up both suitcases. "Come on, Sam. You can choose your room."

"We've prepared the pink room for Samantha," Mrs. Wilmington said, "on the third floor. It's pretty and feminine and has a nice view of the square. She should be comfortable there."

"No, Mom. I'm not putting Sam on the third floor alone." He didn't like disagreeing with his mother, but sometimes it was unavoidable.

Mrs. Wilmington stuck out her chin. "That's the room that's ready for her."

"Then I'll stay up there, too," Conner said, wearing a rare stubborn expression.

Samantha felt uncomfortable. "I don't want to be any trouble."

"It's no trouble," Conner said, looking directly at his mother. "The rooms are always ready. Come on. We can put our things away and relax before dinner."

Knowing she'd lost the battle and not wanting the two of them on the top floor alone, Mrs. Wilmington finally consented. "All right. I'll have the room next to yours made up. I just thought Samantha would enjoy the pink room."

Sure you did, Mom, Conner thought.

In her bedroom, Samantha said, "What was all that about the pink room?"

"Oh, Mom's afraid we'll sleep together."

"You're kidding. If she worries about you having sex, she must have a cabinet full of anti-anxiety meds."

"And how would you know that?"

Ignoring the question, she asked one of her own. "How should I dress for dinner?"

"Since we're having guests, I'll wear a sports coat. Does that help?"

"It does." Not knowing what to expect, Samantha had filled a huge suitcase with a variety of outfits. The boutique that employed her every summer didn't pay much, but her closet was full of lovely clothes, thanks to a generous year-round discount.

When Conner and Samantha returned to the first floor, his father stood and smiled. After introductions were made, he greeted Sam warmly and welcomed her to his home. "Have you met Kendall?"

"No," Mrs. Wilmington said, gliding into the room. "Kendall already had plans with Reagan." For the next little while, the woman alternated between feigning interest in their conversation and overseeing dinner preparations.

Samantha hung back when the Wilmingtons greeted their guests with hugs and kisses. After a servant took the Pattersons' coats, Mrs. Wilmington hurriedly introduced 'our friend Samantha.' Then she invited them into the living room for drinks and hors d'oeuvres.

Samantha would have preferred spending the evening in a casual setting, getting to know the Wilmington family. Instead, Conner's mother expected them to immediately dress for an elaborate dinner and entertain guests.

Conner, bless his heart, made the situation tolerable. Mindful of Samantha's feelings, he did everything he could to make her comfortable: sitting beside her, pulling her into the conversation, and explaining unfamiliar references. In return, she did her best to participate in the conversation and pretend to enjoy the evening.

When they entered the dining room, Samantha was disappointed to find a place card seating her between Mr. Wilmington and Mr. Patterson. Not only was she separated from Conner, but she'd been seated between two older gentlemen with whom she had nothing in common. Beginning to understand the situation, Samantha wasn't surprised to find Conner placed between Mrs. Patterson and her daughter.

It didn't take long for Conner's mother to lead the conversation to a long-ago Easter egg hunt at their club. "Remember how cute Serena and Conner were? Where you saw one of them, you saw the other."

Serena laughed. "I remember that day. Someone roped Conner into hiding eggs for the younger kids. He was probably fifteen, and I was about nine. I followed him around all day because he had a 'tell.' Every time someone was close to an egg, he got this encouraging look on his face. So I watched closely and found more eggs than anyone."

"Serena!" Mrs. Patterson scolded.

At the same moment, Mr. Patterson said, "Smart girl."

Samantha thought she liked Serena, despite the fact that Mrs. Wilmington was trying to pair her with Conner.

Once again, the evening's hostess tried to guide Conner and Serena down memory lane. "You certainly weren't a child when Conner escorted you to the debutant ball. You looked so beautiful that night. You still do, doesn't she, Conner?"

"She does," he said. Afraid the conversation might be making Samantha uncomfortable, he leaned forward, sending her a wink. But instead of seeing the annoyed look he half expected, he saw amusement.

Hoping to lead the conversation a different direction, Serena asked Samantha if they had debutant balls in her hometown. At that, Samantha and Conner both laughed.

"I'm sorry," Sam said, reining in her amusement. "If you saw Tenacity, you'd understand the humor in that question. It's a small, rural community of hardworking people who would never be interested in a ball. They'll dress up for weddings and funerals, and that's about it. Clarkston, a larger town near us, has a formal Mardi Gras ball every year, with a king and queen. That's the Deep South's version of a debutant ball. The king is a respected member of the community, and the queen is one of the debutants being introduced to society that year. But I'm not sure what kind of society actually exists in Clarkston.

"My little town of Tenacity has a diner, a hardware store, a grocery market, a flower shop that can't make ends meet, and a City Hall. We used to have a family-operated drugstore, but they couldn't compete with the nearby chains. And oh, yes, we have an old jailhouse that doubles as a library and a sheriff's office. That's about it."

Serena asked, "What do you do in Tenacity?"

"I teach second grade at the county elementary school. The majority of our students are from local farms and ranches, like I am."

"You mean you live on a farm?"

"It's no longer a working farm, since my parents moved to be near my grandparents, but I still live in the house."

"Do you have animals?"

"A few. I have a cow and a very large bull left from our farm days. I also have chickens, Daddy's two hunting dogs, and four barn cats, at last count. A neighbor is looking after them while I'm away."

Conner chuckled. "The cow's name is Lazy Maisie, and the bull is Maynard. Sam considers them pets. And one of the hens follows her around like a dog."

Smiling, Samantha added, "That's Henrietta. She's smarter than the average hen."

Serena was charmed. "That lifestyle sounds peaceful. I think I'd like having animals around, but maybe not the bull."

Mrs. Wilmington sent her son a disapproving look. "I, for one, am glad to be right where I am." She turned to Serena. "Tell us about university life, dear. You're a senior this year, aren't you?"

As soon as the guests left, Conner announced that he and Samantha were going upstairs. "We've had a long day." When they were out of his parents' earshot, Conner apologized for his mother. "I'm sorry she behaved the way she did. She thinks if I become interested in someone from Savannah, I'll move home. I've told her I have no such intention, but I see she hasn't given up."

"It's all right. She's so obvious, it's kind of funny."

"Maybe," Conner said. "But it needs to stop. I'll talk to her. Thanks for being such a good sport."

He pulled Samantha close and tenderly kissed her, his tongue teasing her lips before entering her sweet mouth. When her tongue joined his, Conner's kisses became hungrier.

"Right now," he said, his mouth still touching hers, "I wish we were anywhere but in this house." Reluctantly pulling away, he told her good-night and went downstairs to speak to his mother.

CHAPTER SEVEN

Conner knocked lightly on Samantha's door and eased it slightly open. "You up?"

"Come in," she said, drowsily.

Finding Samantha still under the cover, half asleep, Conner sat on the edge of her bed and stroked her hair. "Are you ready to get up, sleepy head, or do you want to sleep in?"

"I'm ready,"

"You sure?"

"Uh huh."

"Okay then," he said, pulling off her cover. "Up you go." He picked up the half-awake woman and set her on the floor, holding her to make sure she didn't fall. "You're really out of it this morning."

"Yesterday was a long day. I slept hard." She didn't tell him she'd stayed awake half the night, trying to decide what direction her life should take.

"Get dressed and I'll take you out for breakfast. I told Mom and Miss Emma not to expect us in the dining room."

"What should I wear?"

"Something comfortable. And good walking shoes. I have a lot to show you."

Samantha was glad not to interface with Conner's family, especially his mother. But as they left the house, they crossed paths with Kendall and her friend Reagan. Introductions were made, and Samantha could tell right away that the friend had more than a passing interest in Conner. "We're thinking about going horseback riding today," Reagan said sweetly. "Want to join us?"

"Not today," Conner said, tugging Samantha toward the garage behind the house.

"Tomorrow?" Reagan yelled to their backs.

"We'll see," Conner answered over his shoulder.

Taking a key fob from his pocket, Conner unlocked his family's navy Mercedes and opened Samantha's door. When he slid behind the steering wheel Sam said, "This car suits you. It's more your size, and it's your color."

"My color? What do you mean?"

"Sometimes I associate people with a color. It's just an impression I get. And you're navy blue."

"I'm not sure that's a good thing."

"Oh, but it is. Navy is a stately, elegant color—confident, dependable."

"What color are you?"

"I don't know, but I'd like to be yellow. It's such a happy color."

"How about Max and Anna?"

"Anna is serious and introspective. I see her as deep purple. I'm not sure about Max. Maybe red. It's just something fun to think about."

Conner drove the short distance to the river district and parked on a narrow, quiet street. Escaping the brisk morning breeze, they entered a cozy, understated basement bistro. It was the kind of place where students might gather to discuss classic films and art theory over a cup of coffee.

Conner and Samantha hung their coats on wooden pegs, seated themselves at a table beneath a small window, and gave their order to a waiter with a man-bun. Lingering over coffee and warm pastries, Conner answered Samantha's questions about growing up in Savannah. While caressing her hand and fingers, his mellow voice blended with the background music from classical greats.

"I love this one," Samantha cooed, when strains of 'Greensleeves' floated through the intimate, underground café. "Ralph Vaughn Williams is my favorite twentieth century composer."

"I didn't know you are a classical music fan."

"I enjoy classical, country, and everything in between. Good music is good music, no matter the genre. I used to play the pieces we're listening to."

"When are you going to take 'used to' out of that sentence and play for me?"

"I don't know. It's been a long time since I've sat at a piano. But I'm feeling more inclined lately."

Donning their jackets, they left the comfort of the cozy bistro and walked hand-in-hand through the quiet streets of Savannah. They wandered the manicured public squares and watched the city steadily come to life. Under the giant old oaks, in view of the stately homes of the historic district, they shared sweet, soft kisses when no one was looking.

From a bench on one of the carefully tended squares, they watched their surroundings shift from a near-perfect impression of the past to a contemporary city of active people. Early morning runners jogged on the sidewalk, and leashed dogs sniffed the ground, exploring the world with their gifted noses. Professional men and women rushed to their offices, and students from Savannah College of Art and Design headed home for the holidays.

"I like the city best this time of year. It's not so crowded. Fewer tourists," Conner said, holding out his hand to Samantha. "Come on, there's more to see."

While strolling past historic homes and churches, Samantha noticed Conner consulting his watch. "Are we late for something?"

"Not late, but there's someplace I'd like to be at ten thirty, and it's time to move that direction."

Conner parked on a cobblestone street flanked by moss-laden trees. Taking Samantha's hand, he led her to a queue of people waiting to enter Mrs. Wilkes Dining Room.

"There's always a line," he told her, "but we got here in time. The door opens at eleven, but if you arrive after ten thirty, you might not get in. You're about to learn that Mississippi isn't the only place that has good southern food."

Inside, locals and tourists sat together at long tables to enjoy an old-style boarding house meal. Dishes of fried chicken, country fried steak, sweet potato casserole, squash, rice and gravy, and more, were passed up and down the long table from patron to patron. It was good, basic southern food. The meat was either fried or smothered in gravy, and the vegetables were seasoned with ham or bacon. Biscuits and cornbread rounded out the meal.

Watching Conner interact with the people at their table, Samantha noted how naturally he fitted into any situation. Remarkably unselfconscious and comfortable in his own skin, he captivated her.

After lunch, they meandered toward Forsyth Park, the home of Savannah's famous fountain. They'd spent most of the morning holding hands, and Samantha was surprised at how right it felt. On rare moments, when they walked without touching, she felt deprived.

Conner must have experienced the same urge to connect, for he possessively claimed her hand as they strolled down the wide path leading to the fountain. Surrounded by overhanging oaks, Samantha absorbed the essence of the man beside her. He filled her with an almost forgotten sense of well-being. When she was with him, thoughts of her problems all but disappeared.

"Take a picture of me in front of the fountain," she said.

Instead, Conner handed his phone to a passerby, and asked if he'd photograph Sam and him together.

"Wait," she said, tugging Conner to a nearby bench. Then she climbed onto it, peered over his shoulder, and smiled.

After the stranger returned the phone, Conner stood in place to prevent Sam from falling. Carefully turning, he wrapped his fingers around her waist, intending to help her down. But when the contours of their bodies aligned in an unfamiliar, provocative way, they were overcome with need. Their eyes met, and ever so slowly, his lips closed over hers, taking them to a place too sweet to abandon. So they lingered, aware only of one another, until people around them began to applaud. Breaking apart, they laughed and took a little bow, garnering more applause.

Lifting Samantha off the bench, Conner let her slide down his body. Then they strolled away, hand-in-hand, feeling alive and illogically optimistic about life.

Returning to the Mercedes, they drove to the waterfront area. Strolling along the ballast stone street paralleling the Savannah River, they admired extravagant yachts, left tips for colorful street performers, and wandered through tourist shops brimming with souvenirs.

Samantha wished she could block out the rest of the world and make this time with Conner last forever. They'd always been attracted to one another, but while wandering the streets of Savannah, their attraction moved closer to yearning, and they experienced the age-old, gravitational pull toward intimacy. Their relationship was changing, and it threw them in the middle of an irrational, ridiculously euphoric predicament.

Being with Conner made Samantha happier than she'd been in years. Maybe ever. He was everything she wanted in the body of one man, but they faced too many unsolvable problems for a relationship to survive. She had a perplexing problem with sex, she couldn't give him children, and a man from her past was probably trying to kill her.

Nevertheless, she was falling hard, and there was no help for it. She should have held her ground and refused to go out with him, but he'd patiently charmed her excuses away. Once she'd experienced his tenderness and knew how it felt to be held by him, her will to resist faded like a puff of smoke.

She almost hoped Conner felt less for her than she did for him, for at some point, their time together would end. She would be hurt. That much was clear. But maybe he could escape with his heart mostly intact.

When the delightful day came to an end, Samantha and Conner returned to the grand home he grew up in and endured another evening with Mrs. Wilmington's guests. Mr. and Mrs. Vandenberg and their eligible daughter, Corinne, were the night's dinner guests, while Conner's sister, Kendall, and the ever-present Reagan rounded out the group.

Conner had asked his mom not to have more dinner guests while he was home, but she'd insisted it was too late to change plans. At least she promised to be nicer to Samantha.

Thanks to Kendall and Reagan, the conversation was lively, but Samantha might as well have been invisible. At first, Conner tried to include her in the conversation, but he finally gave up. Even though they had to lean forward to see one another, they exchanged glances throughout dinner, smiling like children with a secret.

After the guests left, Conner walked Sam to her room, apologized for his family, again, and went downstairs to confront his mother. He'd attempted to reason with her the night before, to no avail. So this time, he didn't even try. Hoping to avoid an argument, he simply informed her that he and

Samantha would eat out the remainder of their time in Savannah.

"But I've already invited the Halversons for tomorrow, and they're bringing Andrea.

"All the more reason not to be here," Conner said.

Mrs. Wilmington tried to cajole him into changing his mind. When that didn't work, she tried guilting him. When that was unsuccessful, she tried exerting her authority, which was absurd, considering he was a grown man. "I insist," she said. "It would be rude for you not to be here."

"Do you really want to talk about being rude? Mom, you have to stop trying to set me up. I'm perfectly capable of finding my own dates."

"I'm aware of that, but you need to start dating proper young ladies."

"And what, exactly, is your definition of proper?" Conner asked, getting heated. They were having the conversation he'd hoped to avoid because he knew how it would end. Nothing would be accomplished, he'd be angry, and his mother would be hurt.

"Don't pretend you're unaware of my meaning," she retorted.

"No, really. I'd like to know."

"You have a position in this town, Conner, and so will the woman you marry. You need to find someone who can fill that role, someone prepared to move in our circles."

"Who said anything about marriage?"

"I did," Mrs. Wilmington readily admitted. "It's not too early to start thinking about it. I know young men are expected to sow their wild oats, or whatever you call it these days, but the time for that will soon be over. You need to start developing relationships with the right kind of girls. Life is about more than fun and excitement. It's about duty and responsibility."

Tired of arguing, he curbed his anger. "In case you haven't noticed, I'm dating someone."

"You said she was a friend."

"She is a friend, but she's more than that." When he'd kissed her in front of the fountain, earlier that day, his feelings had become absolutely clear.

"I'm sure she's perfectly nice, Conner. But a farm girl from some rural town in Mississippi isn't right for you."

"What's not right, Mom? She's smart, educated, polite, beautiful, and doesn't have a lazy bone in her body. Plus, she's the most courageous woman I've ever met. What do you find so unacceptable?"

"She's just not our sort of people."

Unable to hide the sarcasm in his voice, he asked, "And just what kind of people are we?"

"We're respected members of society. And you need to find a woman suitable for that role."

"So that's what you want for me—suitable? I'm overwhelmed." There was no sense arguing anymore. So he didn't. "Don't expect us for dinner tomorrow night," he told her, "or any night while we're here. We'll eat out. I promised to take Samantha to some of our best restaurants."

"You have to come to the Christmas party," Mrs. Wilmington said, becoming more upset.

"Don't worry. We'll be here for your party."

Mr. Wilmington sat in his favorite chair during the exchange, quietly sipping a glass of single malt scotch, pretending to read the *Savannah Morning News*. When he appeared from behind the paper, he gave his son a small nod. Conner didn't know if his father was sanctioning what he'd said, approving his agreement to attend the party, or something else.

After he left the room, Mrs. Wilmington turned to her husband. "We have to do something. He's falling in love with that girl. I can see it. Maybe he already has."

"And just what do you propose we do about it? Throw her in the Chattahoochee?"

"I don't know, but we need to do something."

Kendall, listening from the hallway, silently agreed with her mother. Sam, or whatever that woman called herself, was all wrong for Conner. Her best friend, Reagan, would be perfect, and she was crazy about him.

"We have to show him," Kendall said to her friend when they spoke on the phone, "that the woman he brought home doesn't belong in our world."

A couple of mornings later, Samantha answered the knock on her bedroom door, wearing a robe and holding a hairbrush. Conner stood in the hallway, dressed for the day, looking ready for a photo shoot.

"Hey," he cooed. "What do you want to do, today?"

Absently brushing her hair, Samantha stood back, inviting him in. "You don't have to entertain me, Conner. You must have friends you'd like to visit. I'll be fine curled up with my book."

119

"I'd rather spend the day with you," he said, nuzzling her neck, "and Mom wants everyone out of the house while the staff prepares for tonight's party. Kendall still wants us to go riding. Interested?"

She was more interested in what he was doing to her neck. "Sounds like fun," she said, "but I probably don't have the appropriate riding attire for your club."

"Some of the women wear riding breeches, but jeans are fine. If you don't have boots, I can borrow a pair from someone."

"I have a pair that should do."

Kendall and Reagan waited near the entrance of the equestrian club, having already chosen four horses. As soon as Conner and Samantha arrived, an old friend of Conner's engaged him in conversation.

"Come on, Samantha," Kendall said, leading the way to a large brick equestrian barn. "We picked a beautiful horse for you. His name is Thunder. If you need help saddling him, the club has people for that."

Samantha admired the clean, orderly interior of the dignified, old stable. A brass plaque graced each stall door, displaying the name of its equine occupant. Like much of Savannah's existing architecture, the building was reminiscent of a past era, when even horse barns were meticulously crafted.

"You probably don't have stables like this where you live," Reagan commented.

"Not usually," Sam said. "This is beautiful." But she'd seen barns like this before.

Thunder was a sleek, spirited black stallion that Reagan incorrectly described as gentle. It took only a moment for Samantha to see what was happening. The girls, assuming she was a novice rider, were setting her up for failure by giving her a hard-to-manage horse. She wondered if they understood how dangerous that could be.

"Don't wait for me," Samantha said to Kendall and Reagan. "I'd like to have a talk with Thunder before saddling him." The girls eyed one another with amusement.

"Maybe you should wear a helmet," Kendall suggested, handing her one with a polo visor.

Sam was relieved. At least they weren't trying to kill her. She didn't normally wear a helmet, but since the animal and terrain were unfamiliar, she accepted it gratefully.

Stroking the horse's muzzle, she looked into his wary eyes and spoke softly. After telling him how beautiful he was and promising to handle him carefully, she expertly saddled the spirited animal.

Conner strode to the stall where Samantha waited with the black stallion. "Sorry that took so long. It's been a while since I've seen Blake, and I didn't want to brush him off." Then he noticed the horse. "What a beautiful animal."

"He is. I'm surprised to see a stallion like this in a club stable. Horses for loan tend to be mares or geldings. The castrated males are more docile than guys like this," she said, patting the horse's neck.

Watching Thunder prance like a racehorse at a starting gate, Conner asked, "Don't you want a calmer horse? This one looks a bit anxious."

Samantha smiled. "Thunder has a lot of spunk, but we've had a talk, and we'll be fine. Don't worry, Conner, I know how to ride."

When they walked their horses out of the barn, Kendall and Reagan were waiting. Samantha easily mounted Thunder and looked around. "I need to know about the terrain before we begin. Are there obstacles I should know about? I'm not a jumper."

Reagan was the first to speak. "It's pretty straightforward. Flat and slightly rolling pastureland to the right, a mile of oval track to the left."

Samantha rode off as Conner was saying, "I remember a ditch out there somewhere." Fearing she didn't hear, he kicked his horse into gear and rushed to catch her. Kendall and Reagan followed, grinning at one another.

But Samantha was in complete control of her mount, hunkering down, loving every minute of the exhilarating ride. Uh-oh, she thought, spying a ditch ahead. So she settled herself securely in the saddle, looked forward, gave Thunder his head, and let him sail over the ditch. When she looked back and saw her companions' faces, she couldn't help feeling a little smug.

Slowing Thunder, Samantha patted the horse's neck and waited for the others to catch up.

Conner was frowning. "You said you couldn't jump."

"I said I'm not a jumper, but I know the basics."

"Thank God for that. You told me you could ride, but you didn't say you were a pro. Warn me next time. You just took years off my life."

"I'll race you on the track," she said, urging Thunder into action. Leaning into curves, Samantha rode as though she'd been born in the saddle. When she thought the horses needed a rest, she brought Thunder to a stop.

"Where did you learn to ride like that?" Conner asked.

"I always had a horse growing up. I don't have one now because they require more time than I have to give, but Uncle Russ had me on a horse by the time I was three." When Sam explained that she was once the first runner-up in the State Barrel Racing competition, Reagan and Kendall exchanged displeased glances.

CHAPTER EIGHT

Gardeners, designers, and florists worked for days before the Wilmingtons' big event. The interior of the spacious home featured five professionally decorated Christmas trees, stair-rail garlands intertwined with velvet ribbons, and fresh floral arrangements on every available surface.

Outside, lights twinkled from perfectly trimmed shrubs. An elaborate, silver-bedecked wreath adorned the front door, and generous garlands graced the entryway handrails.

Mrs. Wilmington inspected the preparations, making sure every detail was perfect. Crystal sparkled, silver shone, and candles were arranged to be lit at the last moment. A tuxedo-clad doorman stood ready for guests to arrive. Uniformed attendants were available to take coats and purses, and servers awaited the signal to circulate silver trays of enticing delicacies. The kitchen staff bustled about, attending to last minute tasks. No detail was left to chance. Satisfied that everything was in order, the lady of the house went upstairs to dress for the festivities.

Wanting to make Conner proud, Samantha strived to look her best, taming her curls and dressing in a velvet dress she'd paid too much for. When Conner knocked on her door to accompany her downstairs, she wasn't prepared for the sight of him.

He was the epitome of handsome, elegant in his tuxedo. Samantha's eyes lingered in appreciation. Conner was a beautiful man, but he was more than just his appearance. He was kind, giving, and generally wonderful, and Sam knew he deserved more than she could give.

The sky was the limit for Conner, as his mother was well aware. Samantha didn't like the way Mrs. Wilmington treated her or the way she tried to manipulate her son, but she thought she understood. If I had a son, Samantha mused, I'd want the best for him, and I'd care who he dated. But she'd never have a son—nor a daughter, and if Conner stayed with her, neither would he.

"Wow," he said, giving Samantha the once-over. "You look especially beautiful tonight. Don't forget who you came with," he teased.

As they descended the garland-laden staircase, Samantha noticed Kendall and Reagan whispering. She decided to speak up about what occurred that day. "Conner, I guess you realize your sister and Reagan attempted to undermine me today."

"What do you mean?"

"Assuming I was a novice rider, they purposefully gave me a spirited horse they thought I couldn't handle. There would have been a very different outcome if I hadn't known what I was doing."

"Are you sure that was their intention? Maybe they just made a bad decision. But you're a great rider, and thank God, you're all right."

Surely, Samantha thought to herself, Conner didn't really believe the horse incident was an accident. He was avoiding a confrontation, and Samantha didn't understand why. He was an attorney, and attorneys argue for a living. Yet, he was choosing not to address the situation. Then she remembered a conversation they'd had. He said he often accepted behavior he didn't agree with. Is that what he was doing? Whatever the reason, it looked as if she'd have to handle this herself.

As soon as Conner's feet left the bottom step, Mrs. Wilmington pulled him away. Samantha took the opportunity to approach Kendall and Reagan. After exchanging niceties, Samantha said what she'd walked over to say.

"I enjoyed my ride on Thunder this morning, but I want to make sure you understand what a disaster that could have been. A novice rider on that horse could have been badly injured or killed. And the same could be said for an experienced rider with the wrong terrain information. If I hadn't seen that ditch in time and hadn't known what to do, that beautiful animal and I would both have been in serious trouble.

"If you ever have the misfortune of seeing a horse with a broken leg, you'll never forget it. Did you know a horse can scream? The pain is excruciating, and it marks the end of the horse's life. Everything turned out fine today, but I want you to understand what could have happened."

Samantha walked away from Kendall and Reagan, who seemed speechless. Whether it was because of what she said or surprise it was mentioned at all, she didn't know, but when a waiter offered her a glass of wine, she gladly accepted it. Samantha didn't enjoy confrontations, but that needed to be said.

Kendall joined the rest of her family at the front door. Conner had explained to Sam, before they went downstairs, that it was tradition for the entire family to greet guests as they arrived for the party. He offered to abandon the task, if she felt uncomfortable without him, but Samantha assured him she'd be fine.

Watching Conner welcome friends and acquaintances, she admired his easy manner. The social scene was obviously second nature to him. Far from being an introvert, Samantha enjoyed gatherings with friends, but she didn't know these people and would probably never see them again. Without Conner, she'd rather be upstairs reading her book. But she took a deep breath, introduced herself to someone, and joined the party.

Whenever anyone asked what she was doing in Savannah, her answer was vague. "I couldn't miss the Wilmington's Christmas party, could I?" Every now and then, Conner scanned the room until he located Samantha, pleased she appeared to be having a good time.

Just as he was about to leave his post at the door, Reagan moved rapidly toward the woman she considered an intruder. Pretending to lose her balance, she crashed into Samantha, spilling wine down the front of Sam's beautiful, expensive dress.

"Oops," Reagan said, holding back a smile. "I'm so sorry."

Samantha wasn't fooled. The trick at the stables hadn't been enough. The hateful girl ruined the dress on purpose. Sam glared at Reagan before swiftly climbing the stairs to her room.

Conner was winding his way through the crowd, looking for Sam, when Reagan appeared and slipped her hand through the crook of his arm. "I see you're finally off door duty. You need a drink," she said, intending to tug him toward the bar.

Not moving an inch, Conner's eyes continued searching the room. Politely loosening his arm from Reagan's hold, he said, "Excuse me, I need to go find Samantha."

Reagan seized the opportunity to influence the story he was bound to hear. "I saw her go upstairs a few minutes ago. She bumped into me and spilled her drink. She got a little on my dress, but it's not too bad. Maybe she went up to change."

Without a word, Conner strode across the room, nodding politely to guests wanting to engage him in conversation. He hurried up the stairs, knocked lightly on Sam's door, and then opened it a bit. "Samantha? Is everything all right?"

"No. It's not. I'm thoroughly disgusted."

Conner walked in, wrapped his hands around Sam's upper arms, and cocked his head, giving her a little smile. "And what has you so upset?"

"My dress, among other things."

Releasing her, he stepped back and looked. "I see what you mean. It's kind of messed up, isn't it?"

"You could say that," she agreed, gesturing to the soggy, velvet dress. "Reagan did this—on purpose. She and your sister have made it clear that no one wants me here. And so has your mother. I'm ready to go home. But I can't, can I?" Slumping onto a near-by stool, Sam took a deep breath and looked up at Conner. "I may be feeling a little sorry for myself."

Conner stroked her hair. "You've earned the right. But are you sure Reagan did that on purpose?"

Samantha glared at him. "I know she did. I'm beginning to think you believe everybody but me."

"No, Sam. I'm sorry if I make you feel that way. And you're wrong about no one wanting you here. I want you here. Don't be sad." He kissed her until her anger subsided.

"Will you come back downstairs?"

"In this?" she said, looking down at her dress. This is what I brought for the party."

"It doesn't matter what you're wearing."

"What a ridiculous, guy-thing to say. Go back downstairs. I'll find something to wear." Conner thanked her, kissed her sweetly, and left the room. Samantha took her time changing, emerging about twenty minutes later.

From the top of the stairs, she saw Conner in the corner of the room talking to a stunning brunette. The woman was wearing a tight-fitting sheath that must have cost a fortune. Noticing how comfortable she and Conner were together, Sam wondered if they'd dated. Then she realized he could have been with half the girls at the party, and she wouldn't know.

Heads turned as Samantha descended the stairs, including Conner's, whose attention was no longer on the brunette. When she reached the bottom of the staircase, he was waiting with an outstretched hand.

Samantha looked gorgeous in a cream-colored crepe pantsuit that showed off her figure. The bodice fitted like a wrap dress, drawing attention to her ample breasts. The pants portion fell over a perfectly flat stomach and draped loosely over her long legs. Conner was sure every man in the room watched her descend the staircase like a queen in spiked heels, and he was proud to be the one holding her hand.

Strolling across the room with Conner, Samantha saw Reagan. Making sure the girl wasn't holding a drink, she stopped and whispered in her ear. "No more tricks. We country girls will only tolerate so much, and I've reached my limit. I have twelve guns in my gun cabinet and I'm a crack shot with every one of them. Just saying."

"What was that about?" Conner asked.

"I just warned her not to play any more tricks."

Conner stayed by Samantha's side most of the evening. They were talking with a group of guests when Mrs. Wilmington joined them to introduce Judge Jay Harrison. Before she had the chance, Samantha said, "Mr. Jay?"

"Yes?"

"I'm Samantha Lindsey."

"Samantha! The last time I saw you, you must have been about fifteen or sixteen. Give me a hug. Forgive us," Judge Harrison said to the others. "Samantha's dad is an old friend. He saved my life when we were in the Army. I've visited his family in Tenacity, and they've joined mine in Hyannis Port." When Conner saw his mother's surprised expression, he suppressed a smug smile.

Mrs. Wilmington excused herself, walked toward a grand piano, and rang a small silver bell to attract everyone's attention. "Excuse me," she said to her guests. "Our young friend, Reagan, who is an excellent pianist, has agreed to perform a few songs for us this evening." Polite applause ensued as Reagan situated herself on the piano bench. When she began playing, Samantha had to admit the hateful girl was an accomplished pianist.

When she ended her performance, Judge Harrison said, loudly enough for those near him to hear, "Samantha plays and does it quite well." Putting her on the spot, he said, "Play for us, dear. I'd love to hear you, again."

Guests applauded, urging her on, but she shook her head. "I'd rather not. I haven't played in years."

She looked at Conner, silently asking for his support. Instead, he said, "Show them. Play for us. I know you can." He'd never heard her perform, but he believed in her.

Samantha couldn't remember when she'd started playing the piano. It seemed as though she'd been born knowing how. Even before she started to school, she performed in recitals, her little legs dangling from the piano bench, not nearly long enough to reach the pedals.

Through the years she'd played and sung for church services, weddings, funerals, school productions, and talent shows. Sometimes she sang with a popular band when they performed in the area. They asked her to join them permanently, but she had no desire to travel around the country with a bunch of men on a tour bus.

An accomplished pianist, Samantha added cords and flourishes to her music as easily as most people breathe. Combined with her sense of rhythm and instinctive knowledge of how to strike or press the keys, her musical renditions were memorable. Still, because she hadn't touched a piano for the past two years, she was hesitant.

Then she saw the smirk on Reagan's face. The smug girl didn't believe she could play. Bolstered by Conner's encouraging words, she settled on the piano bench, put her fingers on the keys, and began playing Christmas carols. Guests crowded around the piano and sang. It felt good. Soon people began making requests.

When someone asked if she could play "Just the Way You Look Tonight," she smiled and nodded. "That's one of my favorite classics." As her fingers lingered above the piano keys, she took a deep, cleansing breath, allowed her passion for music to flood her body, and relished its escape through her fingers and voice.

Already astonished at Samantha's piano skills, Conner was mesmerized when she began singing. Her voice was clear, full, and rich, with a tenderness that pulled everyone in. She was amazing, and until that moment, he hadn't even known she could sing.

Conner realized he was watching more than a performance. A transformation was occurring before his eyes. He was glimpsing the enthusiastic, vital person Samantha Lindsey was meant to be, the person she had been before that demented man stole her joy.

"Sing something else—something you like," someone shouted.

So she did. "You may not know this song," she told the appreciative group, "but it's fun and I love it. It's called 'Valentino.' She reveled in the lively tune, her fingers moving over the piano keys like racehorses, demanding everything the instrument had to give.

The music was happy and upbeat, but the words were not. Conner's eyes became moist as he saw the correlation between the song, with its conflicting music and lyrics, and the beautiful woman performing it.

A truth manifested itself he hadn't fully understood until that moment. Samantha must struggle with heartache every day, trying to forget what happened, searching for reasons to smile. How she managed to move forward after experiencing such a violent betrayal by the man she loved, Conner didn't know. It had to require a Herculean effort.

He could envision her climbing from a pit of pain, reaching for the good-humored person she was meant to be. How had she risen as far as she had, with such soul-deep hurt and the threat of a deranged man tugging at her like a sack of stones? At the moment, with her fingers on the piano keys and a melody flowing from her lips, Conner could almost see her worries floating away.

Wishing Samantha would stay in that unburdened place, he had another epiphany. Not only did he want to protect Samantha, he also wanted to reach into that pit, cut away the bag of stones, pull her out, and make her happy again. Therapists would probably say she had to do that for herself, but that wouldn't stop him from trying.

When Samantha tore herself from the piano, amid appreciative applause, Conner wrapped his arm around her waist and kissed her cheek. "You're wonderful. I knew you'd be good, but wow! I had no idea."

"I'm glad you enjoyed it. It was fun. I hope I didn't offend your mother. She didn't ask me to play, and I can get carried away when I perform."

"Everyone loved it. And you shouldn't worry about my mother. If Judge Harrison approves, Mom will too."

The judge approached. "Samantha, you're even better than the last time I heard you. Conner, you'd better watch out or some record company will scoop her up and take her away from you."

Toward the end of the party, Conner leaned close to Samantha and whispered in her ear, his warm breath tickling her neck. "Leave your door unlocked for me tonight."

"We'll see," she said, her grin giving away her intent. Samantha's heart raced. Ever since their kiss in front of the fountain, she'd felt an intense desire to feel Conner's body against hers. She prayed, with everything in her, that she would be able to stay in the moment. She couldn't flash back to the worst night of her life. She just couldn't.

After the last guest left, Mrs. Wilmington announced she was turning in for the night, leaving the clean-up to a well-compensated caterer and her housekeeper.

The house finally quieted, and Conner slipped from his room, hoping the evening would end the way he intended. He breathed a sigh of relief when the handle of Sam's door turned. Locking the door behind him, he pulled off his t-shirt, found his way to the bed in the darkened room, and reached for Samantha.

He smiled. If the short, silky lingerie was any indication, she wanted the same thing he did. When he kissed her, his body begged for more. "I'm going to make love to you," he told her, "if you'll let me— really, truly make love to you."

"I want that, more than you can imagine, but this might not turn out the way we hope," Samantha said.

"I know. But are you willing to try?"

"I'm willing, all right. I want you, Conner. I really do."

They kissed, softly at first, then passionately, their tongues mimicking the movement they craved. With warm hands and wet mouths, they explored one another's bodies, until Conner said, "I don't think I can wait any longer."

"Same here," came a breathless reply.

Thinking he'd never been more grateful for anything, Conner held his body over Samantha's. He forced himself to give her time to change her mind. Then, resting on his elbows, he said, "What happens next is up to you." So she reached for him and guided him to her most intimate place.

For a moment, he didn't move. "All right?"

"Mmm hum," she said.

So Conner carefully began to move, watching her face for signs of distress. When all he saw was exhilaration, his movements became more rhythmic, but he still watched. She moaned, and Conner couldn't suppress a guttural response. He found himself in the unfamiliar position of fighting for control.

He'd been with his share of women, more than his share if he was honest, but he'd never wanted to please anyone more. When she started making uncontrollable sounds of ecstasy, he covered her mouth with his and came with her.

Breathing hard, overwhelmed by the power and significance of what just happened, they tried to muffle their relieved, happy laughter. "That didn't take long," he whispered.

"I know. It was wonderful. We did it, Conner. I didn't freeze." With intertwined limbs and full hearts, they smiled broadly between tender kisses. Tears of joy dampened Sam's pillow. "I was afraid that part of my life was over."

"It's just beginning. We're beginning. That is, if you'll have me."

Samantha wasn't sure what he was asking. He probably didn't know either, but she nodded.

Cradling her jaw, Conner wiped a tear away with his thumb. "Let's go to sleep."

"You're staying in my room?"

"If you don't mind."

"What about your family?"

"I'll slip out in the morning. If someone sees me, they'll get over it."

"It'll give them another reason to disapprove of me, but I want you to stay," she said, snuggling against him.

He wanted to make love to her again but warned himself not to be greedy. They'd taken a huge step. It was definitely progress, but he wouldn't push his luck.

Conner eased the door open the next morning and quietly left without notice. After giving Sam time to dress, he returned to her room. She was sitting on the edge of the bed, staring at her phone, looking worried.

"I got a message from Scott," she said. "My parents and Uncle Russ hired an investigator to keep an eye on Hal, and he's been seen at the Jackson airport twice. Both times, a plane from Savannah was landing."

"I got that message, too. Who knows you're here?"

"Only my parents, Uncle Russ, Jeff, and Anna—and I suppose Max. Scott asked if I posted anything on social media. I did, but it was only a picture of a sunset over the river. I commented that I was out of town and wished everyone a Merry Christmas. That's all."

"Pull up the picture." Conner said, sitting next to her. "What's that in the distance?"

"A hotel, I think," Sam said. She enlarged it until it was so fuzzy it was hard to make out the name. "Even so, how would anyone know where it is?"

"I'm not sure, but I do know we can't fly into Jackson."

"No, we can't. Hal is definitely looking for me. Mama called to make sure I wouldn't try to come home. When a car like the one Hal's been driving parked near their house, the Smokey Creek sheriff ran a check on the license plate. It belongs to the woman Hal is staying with."

"Should we be worried about your parents?"

"I don't think so. Their sheriff seems to be on top of the situation, and Mama knows how to shoot. Believe me, if Hal threatens them, she won't hesitate. In fact, I think she'd welcome an excuse to kill him. He probably knows that."

Sam looked down at her hands. "I've never missed Mama's Christmas dinner before, and I'm sorry I can't be there to help her cook and clean-up. My grandparents will join them, as well as friends, so at least they won't be alone. But Mama has traditions she looks forward to. She always makes my favorite pie, sweet potato with whipped cream on top, and she still fills my Christmas stocking with gifts every year. I know they're missing me. And with Daddy's heart being bad..."

"He's all right, isn't he? He hasn't had another attack?"

"No. The last one was about a month ago. It was minor, but I worry... Nevertheless, Mama made me promise not to show up."

Samantha stood, turned away from him, and began pacing. He thought she was worrying about her parents. But she turned to him with watery eyes and said, "We need to talk."

"That doesn't sound good."

"It's not." Disheartened, Samantha forced the dreaded words from her mouth. "Conner, I think you should go back to work and let me fend for myself."

"What? I thought we were doing great."

"We are, but I've been thinking. You can't simply give up your job to watch over me. It's not fair. I'm a big girl. I can take care of myself."

"What changed your mind? What did I do wrong?"

"Nothing. Heaven knows, I don't know what I would have done without you. But right now, Hal doesn't know who you are. Just because I have to look over my shoulder for the rest of my life doesn't mean you should suffer the same fate. This is my problem. You don't have to be involved in this mess."

"But I am involved. I care about you, Sam. And you need me. You know you do. I'm not leaving you alone and that's that."

Samantha knew she should stand her ground, refuse to let Conner sacrifice what he'd worked hard for, but she looked into his eyes and gave in. Releasing a sob, she threw her arms around him and squeezed.

When Samantha's phone dinged with a text, she sniffed, wiped away tears, and read. "It's from Anna. She wants us to know we're invited to Christmas dinner at Max's parents' house, on the off chance we decide not to stay here. I'll let her know we'll be in Savannah."

"You don't have to," Conner said.

"What do you mean?"

"If you'd like to spend Christmas day with Anna and Max, that's what we'll do—unless you think Hal might look for you there."

"He'd never consider Max's parents' house. I don't think he even knows where they live. But what would your mother think if we just up and left?"

"It doesn't matter. Her behavior this trip doesn't warrant our consideration. We can go back to Mississippi and stay at my apartment." With a wicked grin, he said, "We can fool around without sneaking, have loud sex, laugh, do whatever the hell we want."

"Conner," Samantha said with mock amazement, "what a bad boy you're getting to be."

He sent her a crooked smile. "Are you objecting?" When she shook her head, he picked her up, swung her around, and kissed her resolutely.

Conner had planned to spend Christmas Eve and Christmas Day with his family, but the Wilmingtons hadn't given Samantha the warm welcome he'd expected. She deserved to spend Christmas with people who cared for her. And after their passionate night together, he wanted her to himself without the disapproving eyes of his family.

Still in his arms, Samantha cupped Conner's face in her hands and kissed him. "If you keep that up," he said, "we might never leave this room."

Conner sat Samantha on the bed, settled beside her, and pulled out his phone to find another airport. "There's a plane leaving for New Orleans this morning at ten-thirty with two seats left. They're not together, but if we want to get out of here..."

"Let's do it. It won't take me long to get ready."

After making the reservation, a slow smile came over Conner's face.

"What are you thinking?"

"I'm thinking we should stay a couple of nights in the Big Easy, if we can find a room. Then we'll drive back to Clarkston, spend Christmas Eve at my apartment, and still make it to Max's parents' for Christmas day. How does that sound?"

"I love it." Samantha said, her eyes sparkling

Mission accomplished, Conner thought, pleased he'd put a smile on her face. After kissing the delighted woman, Conner went downstairs to break the news. Sam hoped his mother wouldn't guilt him into staying, but she needn't have worried. Conner was more than ready to leave, especially when he discovered his mother had extended a Christmas dinner invitation to the guests he'd dodged a couple of nights before.

After watching his son leave the room, Will Wilmington looked disapprovingly at his wife. "Are you happy now that you've chased him away? You know he's leaving because of how you've treated that sweet girl he brought home."

"But she's not right for him."

"That's not your decision to make. I need to tell you something," he said, using his most serious tone. "In case you haven't realized it, our son is not intimidated by you. He just doesn't want to hurt you."

"Well, he hurt me just now."

"I don't think he did. I think you're just sorry you didn't get your way. Our boy is one of the kindest people I know. I'm proud of him for that, but sometimes he's too nice for his own good. Don't confuse kindness with weakness. If you're not careful, you'll push him too far. One of these days he might leave and not come back." Mrs. Wilmington huffed and left the room, but not before her husband noticed her watery eyes.

The last-minute plane tickets were expensive, but Conner would have paid almost anything to spend time alone with Samantha, especially with their future so uncertain. He had meant it when he said he'd quit his job and leave with her, but she was hesitant to accept his offer. He intended to make their time together so sensational she couldn't imagine leaving without him.

On the trip from Savannah to New Orleans, Conner squeezed into the seat next to Samantha, which he'd obtained by convincing the flight attendant they were on their honeymoon. They played the part well, holding hands and stealing kisses, which was easy considering their status as new lovers.

Wishing she had the fake engagement ring from their night at the Western bar, Sam switched her sapphire ring to her left hand and turned it so that the gold band was showing. Conner asked the flight attendant to keep the knowledge of their nuptials to herself. He said they'd eloped and were going home to tell their families. When he smiled and turned on the charm, the man was impossible to resist.

"You're a good liar," Samantha whispered. "I'm not sure how to feel about that."

"Think of it as acting," he whispered. "Admit it. This is fun." It was, but Sam would have to keep reminding herself it was only a game.

If she was honest with herself, she'd have to admit it was too late for caution. She'd been enamored by him from the moment she first looked up into his deep, blue eyes. Of course, that was simply attraction. When they became friends and she discovered what a beautiful soul Conner had, her feelings grew. The more time she spent with him, the more intense her feelings became. And making love was the point of no return.

Loving Conner was a bad idea for many reasons. He wasn't a one-woman man if Anna's assessment was correct. But despite the warning, Samantha trusted him, and she worried he'd be hurt when their time together ended. Then she reflected on a possibility she hadn't allowed herself to seriously consider. If Hal found out she was with him, Conner could become a target.

Samantha reprimanded herself for giving in to her attraction in the first place. But Conner had been persistent, and she'd let her guard down. Now she loved him, and that was that. Even if they parted ways and never saw one another again, the ache of losing him would remain.

CHAPTER NINE

Four hours after leaving Savannah, Conner and Samantha reached their hotel in New Orleans's famous French Quarter. When Conner had called about a room, the desk clerk said, "Man are you lucky! We've been fully booked for six weeks, and I just got a call from a family cancelling a five-night reservation for two rooms. They won't last long."

"Great," Conner said. "We'll take one of them for two nights."

When they checked in, the receptionist asked if they were there for Jackson Square caroling.

Samantha's eyes lit up. "That's not tonight, is it? Tell me it's tonight."

He nodded. "You're in luck. It's tonight. The program begins at seven, but I suggest you be there at six-thirty when the gate opens. The square fills up pretty fast."

"What's this about caroling?" Conner asked.

"You'll see. I've always wanted to do this." Sam looked around, admiring the lobby. "This place is great, and it's right in the middle of the Quarter."

Beginning the trek to their room, they followed a porter from the lobby into the secluded courtyard. Samantha was enthralled the minute her feet touched the worn, uneven brick floor. Surrounded by multistoried old buildings, the courtyard featured two ornate fountains, an ivy-covered wall, and low-growing palms. It was the epitome of old New Orleans

As they traveled through the maze of hallways connecting multi-level buildings, Samantha and Conner exchanged bewildered glances. "What happened there?" Conner asked, gesturing to the staircase leading to a blank wall.

The Porter shrugged. "This place has been added to and re-arranged so many times, nobody knows. The inn is a conglomerate of once-private buildings— seven, we think. And their courtyards were merged to make the large one we passed through."

"That's why it has so many nooks and crannies," Samantha said.

"That's right. Next time you're out there, if you'll look down at the courtyard floor, you'll see where walls once existed."

Sam was even more excited when they reached their room. While Conner thanked the Porter and tipped him for his trouble, Samantha twirled, her arms outstretched. "I can't believe they gave us this huge room," she said when they were alone. "And that ceiling! It's towering. And look. We have a balcony." Rushing onto it, she turned to look back at Conner. "You can see the river from here!"

About that time, a calliope from one of the Mississippi River paddleboats began playing "Birth of the Blues." Samantha threw open her arms and belted out the words. No one seemed to think twice about someone singing from a balcony. Maybe they didn't notice over the bustle of the city.

But Conner noticed everything about Samantha. She was extraordinary. He'd do anything to keep her safe and make her happy. The problem was that it was hard to do both at the same time.

Joining Samantha on the breezy balcony, he smiled. Her reaction was exactly what he'd hoped for. With their arms wrapped around one another, they watched ships travel up and down the Mississippi and surveyed the busy sidewalk below. The passersby ranged from young to old. Some were tattooed non-conformists, their hair dyed an array of colors. Others were professionals, hurrying to a bar to meet friends after work. Most were tourists, from places near and far, enjoying the unique personality of the city. The New Orleans French Quarter was a people-watcher's paradise.

Feeling a little grungy from the trip, Samantha showered before their big night on the town. Relishing the warm cascade of water in the roomy shower, she was surprised when Conner joined her. Together, they washed away the travel fatigue, replacing it with pure, sensual pleasure.

They were tempted to crawl into the luxurious bed to continue what they'd started in the shower, but it would be shameful not to take advantage of what New Orleans had to offer. They'd both visited the city before, but not with one another, and everything was more exciting when they were together.

Conner reached for Samantha's hand as they left the unconventional inn. "There's something I'd like to do before caroling. Café Du Monde is across from the square, and if the wait isn't too long, we'll have time for coffee and beignets. That'll hold us until the caroling is over. Be thinking about what you want to eat later."

The line of people waiting to enter the green-and-white-striped, canopy-covered coffeehouse extended almost a block down the sidewalk. "Should we join the queue?" asked Conner. "It's moving quickly."

"Sure. The square is right across the street. If it looks like it's filling up, we can hurry over." An outdoor jazz band entertained the waiting customers, until it moved down the street in search of more tips.

Inside, sheets of heavy plastic hung from the ceiling to keep out winter breezes, giving the impression they were inside a building rather than on a covered patio. A bevy of waiters hustled, efficiently serving three to four hundred people under the roof of the famous cafe.

"Mmm," Samantha hummed, as some of the warm beignet's powdered sugar trickled onto her coat. "This is delicious."

"The chicory coffee is good, too," Conner said.

Samantha nodded. "Did you know that chicory comes from the root of a plant in the dandelion family?"

"I've heard that. But not the yellow kind that grows in our yards."

"No, the flowers are blue, I think. But surely no self-respecting dandelion has ever dared pop up in your mother's perfectly groomed yard?"

Conner laughed, reaching across the small table to fondle her hand. "Oh, heavens no."

Samantha cocked her head and gave him a flirty smile. "Do you know how this coffee got to be such a staple in New Orleans?"

"That I don't know," Conner said, enjoying her enthusiasm

"Well, during the Civil War, because the New Orleans port was blockaded, coffee was scarce. So, they added chicory to make it go further."

"Of course you'd know that. I'm going to start calling you the trivia queen."

"I appreciate the honor, kind sir." Standing, Sam brushed the sweet white powder from her clothes and wondered how the sugar affected the small bodies of the wrens pecking it from the floor.

"You have a little speck. I'll get it," Conner said, before kissing her, licking the white powder from her mouth. They were still grinning when they crossed the street.

As Conner and Samantha approached Jackson Square, street performers and vendors packed their belongings for another day. Artists stacked paintings on carts, jugglers stuffed colorful balls into canvas bags, and a silver-painted man poured the day's earnings from a tin can into a velvet pouch.

Samantha stopped to pet a bored-looking mule hitched to a fringed tourist carriage. "How are you, sweet boy?" she said, rubbing the mule's nose. "You're a handsome fellow."

"Want a buggy ride?" the weather-worn driver asked. "I'm about to leave for the night, but I have time for one more quick spin around the Quarter."

"Thanks. But we're on our way to the gate," Samantha said, gesturing. "I just wanted to pet this guy. I like mules. One day, I'm going to have one of my own." If I ever return to the farm, she thought.

Sitting on the carriage driver's box, the reigns in his hands, the man nodded. "They're good animals all right. Stronger, smarter, and more sure-footed than horses."

Listening to Samantha discuss mules with the stranger made Conner smile. She was so cute, so sweet and guileless. That made Conner wonder if her ex had truly snapped, as she believed, or had he exploited her? Her honesty and faith in others would have made her a perfect target. Had he simply taken advantage of her innocence?

When they reached Jackson Square's wrought-iron gate, they were each given a leaflet of song lyrics and a small, white candle. It didn't take long for the square to fill with carolers of different ages, races, and nationalities. Early arrivals lit candles for more recent ones, and strangers wished one another a Merry Christmas.

Admiring the illuminated Saint Louis Cathedral looming over the candle-lit park, Sam sighed. "Isn't this beautiful?"

Conner agreed. The idea of a stop-over in New Orleans was inspired. Samantha had been smiling ever since they'd arrived. He was enjoying the visit, too, but that didn't keep him from behaving like a secret service agent.

So far, Hal had limited his travels to Tenacity, Clarkston, and Smokey Creek, with an occasional trip to the Jackson airport. It was highly unlikely he'd show up in New Orleans, but the slim possibility kept Conner alert.

He noticed a young man pulling a cart, selling beer in the clear, plastic cups people were using to protect their flames from the breeze. So Conner and Sam drank a beer, cut a slit in the bottom of the cups, and pushed their flickering candles to safety.

Hearing a microphone come to life, they focused their attention on the temporary stage. After a few preliminary statements, the singing began.

The experience was lovely, with hundreds of candles glowing in the dark, the cathedral looming in the background, and strangers lifting their voices in song.

When the music stopped, someone at the microphone yelled, "Who dat say who dat." The chant was echoed by carolers, followed by, "Go Saints." Only in New Orleans, Conner thought, would beer and football be included in a Christmas celebration.

When the caroling concluded, Conner pulled Sam close, rubbing her arms to ward off the chill. "This was a unique experience. I'm glad we came. Now, what do you want to eat? New Orleans is known for its fine restaurants. We'll go anywhere you want. Just name it."

"You know what I'd really like?"

"What's that?"

"An oyster po-boy."

"You're sure?"

"I am, unless you want something different."

"Your wish is my command," he said, nuzzling her neck.

"Why Conner," she exclaimed, feigning embarrassment. "You're getting pretty comfortable with public displays of affection."

"Don't you know? PDA is not only acceptable in New Orleans, it's expected. In fact, it's a requirement for couples staying in the Quarter. I thought everyone knew that."

After asking several clueless tourists where they could get a good oyster po-boy, a local gave them directions to a nearby café. "It's a small place, and you may have to wait," he said, "but it has the best po-boys in the city."

Sitting at a table covered with a red-and-white-checkered tablecloth, they ate fried oysters slathered in remoulade sauce, sandwiched between slices of French bread. Conner was so impressed by his po-boy that he ordered a second one.

They paid the bill, thanked the proprietor for an outstanding meal, and then wandered the area, making sure to stay on brightly lit, crowded streets for safety.

With their arms around one another, Conner and Samantha joined throngs of people meandering down the center of Bourbon Street. Occasionally, the crowd grudgingly moved aside for an out-of-town car to crawl past. The locals knew better than to drive through the area, especially at night.

Music poured from open bar doors, inebriated young people yelled from crowded balconies, and strangers extended friendly greetings. It was one huge party, and everyone was welcome.

"Zydeco!" Samantha shouted, seeing a banner hanging outside an establishment.

"What's Zydeco?"

"South Louisiana music. Let's go in," Samantha said, tugging her companion toward the open door. Inside, they found a blend of people, many with local accents Conner had never heard.

His eyes widened when he surveyed the band. "Is that a washboard?" he asked, watching a band member rub the handle of a wooden spoon up and down the metal ribbing.

"It is. That's common in Zydeco music." There was also an accordion, a harmonica, a guitar and a drum.

Conner and Samantha smiled big smiles as they joined the dancers swirling to the irregular rhythm of the fast and furious music. It didn't take long for them to look like experts. After a couple of dances, they decided to see what else the street had to offer. They were walking out the door when an elderly man with a strong Cajun accent said, "Did you enjoy the fais-do-do?"

"Fais-do-do?" Samantha asked.

"This," he said, which sounded a little like 'dis.' He gestured around the room and translated. "The dance party."

They assured him they had, waved good-by, and rejoined the throngs in the street. When they heard authentic New Orleans jazz pouring from a club's open doors, they went inside, sat at the only empty table, and ordered a drink. Conner covered Samantha's hand with his, realizing he'd never experienced such a constant need to touch a woman. "Having a good time?" he asked.

"The best." And it was true. She didn't remember when she'd had more fun. Maybe never. New Orleans was a boisterous, entertaining place, but Samantha knew her exhilaration was due to Conner. She'd be happy with him anywhere.

They sipped their drinks, listening to the edgy, improvised jazz. "Tell me when you're ready to go back to the room," Conner said, anxious to have Samantha to himself.

"Before we go, I'd like to find a blues bar." It didn't take long to locate one. The slow, sexy music poured through the doors and open windows. Conner immediately led Samantha onto the dance floor and pulled her into his strong arms. When Sam twirled away, put her hands in the air, and swayed her hips, Conner was mesmerized by her seductive moves.

As the band began playing Norah Jones' "Turn Me On," Samantha said, "I know this one. Put me on the stage." Conner did as asked, wrapping his hands around her waist and lifting. When she walked to the microphone and began singing, people stopped talking, dishes stopped clinking, and everyone listened to her sultry rendition of the song.

Conner stood to the side of the bandstand, looking like a smitten bodyguard. When a woman asked him to dance, he nodded toward Samantha. "Thanks for asking, but I'm with her, and she's the jealous type."

When the song was over, Samantha thanked the audience for their applause and readily agreed to their request for another song. After conferring with the band's leader, Samantha spoke. "I'm about to sing a country song," she explained, "but we're going to throw in some good old-fashioned blues, the kind that stirs the soul and speaks to the rhythm that resides in us all."

The band's church-style comments conveyed their agreement. "That's right. Ah-huh. Tell 'em about it, sister."

Samantha was laying it on a little thick, but she was having fun. "This tune is about a good woman who rescued a broken man from the evils of whiskey."

"Here's to whiskey," someone bellowed. The audience held up their glasses and yelled, "To whiskey."

"I know you know this one," Samantha told the rambunctious crowd. "Feel free to join in." Then she sang a slow, bluesy version of "Tennessee Whiskey," which stirred the patrons' souls just as she said it would.

When the song was over, Conner caught her as she jumped from the bandstand. She grabbed his hand and shouted above the cheers and applause. "Let's go."

One of the female patrons cupped her hands around her mouth and yelled, "You go honey! I'd take him home, too!"

A man in the crowd bellowed, "You can have him, I'll take the songbird."

Samantha and Conner laughed, waved good-by, and hurried back to the eccentric inn, stopping for a few preliminary kisses along the way. The minute their door locked behind them, they kissed their way to the bed, and it wasn't long before they experienced the delicious feel of warm skin on warm skin. Entwined in one another's arms, an already extraordinary evening became one they'd never forget.

Sam woke to find Conner watching her. The minute she opened her eyes he pulled her naked body on top of his and kissed her.

"Morning breath," Sam mumbled when he released her.

"Mine?"

"No, mine."

"You always taste delicious," Conner said, pulling her in for another kiss.

After spending a leisurely, sensual morning in bed, Conner took Sam to an upscale restaurant, where the waiters dressed formally, crystal chandeliers hung above the tables, and eggs Benedict came with a side of fried oysters. After completing the delicious brunch, they wandered around the Quarter, hand in hand, until they heard a jazz band and saw a procession of people dancing down the middle of the street waving handkerchiefs.

"It's a second line!" Samantha exclaimed, giving a little jump. Seeing the question on Conner's face, she explained. "After a French Quarter wedding, the bride and groom hold umbrellas above their heads and march through the Quarter, their wedding guests trailing behind. It's a New Orleans tradition."

"What's the significance of the umbrellas, and why is it called a second line?"

"The umbrellas signify the couple's new life together. I've never heard a more specific explanation than that, but personally, I think they symbolize protection from the storms of life. The band is considered the first line, and the people behind them the second line. I'm not sure they're supposed to, but strangers sometimes fall in step behind the wedding guests."

Conner took Sam's hand. "What are we waiting for?" Tugging her onto Royal Street, they joined the procession of parading revelers. They were strutting to the beat of the music, grinning like Cheshire cats, when the color drained from Samantha's face.

"What's wrong, Sam?" At first, she didn't seem to hear. But when he repeated the words, she reacted frantically.

"We have to get out of here!" she said, dodging frolicking wedding guests. When her feet hit the sidewalk, she had to stop herself from breaking into a run

"What are we escaping?"

"Ralph. We can't let him follow us."

"What are you talking about?" Conner asked, pulling her to a stop.

Scanning the area behind her, she fought to escape his hold.

"Talk to me," he insisted. "Tell me what's wrong!"

"It's one of the men Hal works with. He saw us, and now he's talking on the phone."

"Damn. Come on," he said, his eyes searching the area. Spying an antique store, he pulled her inside. "Someone's following us," he told the salesperson. "Is there another way out of here?" Acting as if that sort of thing happened all the time, the antique dealer opened a door at the back of the store, pointed down a hallway to an exterior exit, and locked it behind them.

At the end of the alley, Samantha peeked around the corner of the building. "It's okay. I don't see him."

They walked briskly, zigzagging from one alley to another. They'd only gone about two blocks when Sam stepped on a jutting stone and fell. It happened too quickly for Conner to catch her, but he kept her head from hitting the street. It bruised and scraped the back of his hand, but the action limited Sam's injuries to a scraped arm, sore shoulder, and a sprained ankle.

"Can you walk?"

"I think so. I'll have to."

She tried but was clearly in pain. "How about a piggy-back ride?" With her arms encircling his neck and his hands behind her knees, Conner carefully traversed the streets and uneven alleys of the French Quarter. As soon as they arrived at the hotel lobby, Conner told the desk clerk they had an emergency and needed their car as soon as possible.

They hurriedly packed and left the room. Since the old inn lacked the convenience of an elevator, Conner heaved both suitcases down steep stairs and the oddly connected hallways. Waiting in the lobby for their rental car, Samantha repeatedly peeked out the front door to assure herself Ralph hadn't followed.

Before the car arrived, they left suitcases with the front desk clerk and made a quick trip to the tourist shop next door. To lessen the possibility of being recognized and followed, they bought a dark wig for Samantha and a cap for Conner.

As they drove away from the inn, Sam tried to recall every moment of the last twenty-four hours. She didn't want to forget a thing, except, of course, that one unfortunate incident. And Conner had even taken the sting out of that. No matter what happened in the future, she'd always treasure this amazing trip with the most incredible man she'd ever known.

CHAPTER TEN

Leaving New Orleans, they drove along raised roadbeds overlooking uninhabitable swamplands. As the scenery changed from cypress trees and palmettos to native azaleas and pines, Conner and Samantha silently contemplated their futures.

Samantha was all too aware she had to leave Tenacity, but accepting it was another matter. Time spent in Savannah and New Orleans, as well as her growing feelings for Conner, had distracted her from her dire circumstances. But as they crossed the state line from Louisiana to Mississippi, Sam's dark reality began catching up to her.

Conner's thoughts centered around Samantha's hesitancy to include him in her plans. She was certainly able to care for herself under normal circumstances, but her present situation called for back-up. If she insisted on leaving him behind, how would he protect her?

Samantha's concerns eventually became too heavy to bear silently; so she gathered her courage and admitted she didn't know what to do. "Since we left Tenacity, I've been living in an alternate universe where Hal doesn't exist. I've denied what my life has become, ignoring the changes that have to be made.

But after seeing Ralph this morning, reality is following me around, tapping me on the shoulder."

"It's obviously time for you to make some decisions, but I want you to enjoy Christmas," Conner said. "You should be safe at my apartment for now. When the holidays are over, we'll sit down and talk seriously about what comes next. How does that sound?"

"It sounds like a good excuse for delaying a while longer, and I'll gladly use it. But there's one thing I have to do. I need to let my principal know I'm not coming back. Maybe the substitute who took my class while I was in Savannah will be available. That way, the children won't have to get used to another teacher."

Samantha hugged herself for comfort. "I have no idea where to go, but there's one thing I do know. I won't sell the farm. Someday, somehow, maybe this situation will come to an end, and I can go home."

Conner was relieved she was finally addressing the issue. He normally decided things quickly, identified what needed to be done, and got to work. He didn't like putting things off, and if he left with Samantha, he'd have to give notice at work. But he wanted her to enjoy the holidays. Even though she couldn't be with family, at least she could celebrate with friends.

Sam covered her face with her hands, overwhelmed with what she was facing. Looking up, she said, "Deciding where to go isn't even the hardest part. What will I do for money? I'm afraid I'll be too easy to find if I take a teaching position."

"Are you sure he'll come after you? Maybe he'll give up."

"I'm not willing to take the chance," she said, unable to keep her hands still. "I have to assume he'll look for me. I could get a job playing the piano and singing, but at some point, someone would expose me on social media. It's almost impossible to hide these days."

"We'll figure it out together. I've given this some thought."

"You have?"

"Maybe you won't need to work, at least for a while. You could lay low until he gives up, and we could live off what I make."

"You're really planning to go with me?"

"If you'll let me. You shouldn't have to do this alone, Sam. Besides, who would I dance with if you left?" She pictured him holding another woman and didn't like how it made her feel.

The following morning, as Samantha slept in Conner's apartment, he ran a few errands. When she woke, he was putting up a Christmas tree.

"Don't you think it's a little late for that?" she said, sleepily.

"Tonight is Christmas Eve. We have to have a tree." Conner knew Samantha would rather be in her beautifully decorated home. Putting up a tree was the least he could do. "All this was on sale," he said, gesturing to the live fir, the lights, and the ornaments.

After drinking a cup of coffee, they removed the items from their packaging and proceeded with the last-minute decorating. When it was finished, they sat on the sofa to admire their handiwork.

Conner put his arm around Sam and kissed her, which led to more kisses, which eventually led to the bedroom. Once they were naked, one of Conner's long legs moved over Sam's. His instinct was to pull her body under his. Instead, he held her close, still trying to avoid anything that might trigger bad memories.

Sam's words were a surprise, as well as a relief. "I'm okay now, Conner. I'm not going to break. You don't have to hold back anymore."

"You're sure?" he asked.

When her response was, "I am," his smile was big and a little wicked.

Searching the kitchen, Samantha looked for ingredients to make a decent Christmas Eve supper. Conner had gone to the trouble of buying a tree to make the evening special, and she wanted to do her part.

He obviously hadn't been grocery shopping recently, but Sam found a good bottle of red wine, an unopened box of crackers, and the necessary ingredients for a pot of chili. It wasn't exactly a gourmet meal, but she set the dining room table with wine glasses, candles, and the flowers Conner had brought home that morning.

Relaxing across the table from one another on Christmas Eve, they listened to Kenny G, drank wine, and ate chili. "This is nice," Sam said. But then everything was nice when she was with Conner.

After dinner, he pulled a movie from a bag. "I found this when I was out this morning. Want to watch?"

"*White Christmas*. I like that one. A lot of people think the song 'White Christmas' was written for this movie, but it was actually the third movie to feature the song."

"How do you even know things like that? That reminds me of a question I've been meaning to ask since New Orleans. You can consider this a test," he teased.

"Okay, shoot."

"Mules are produced by mating a horse and a donkey. Right?" Conner asked.

"Right."

"Which is the father, and which is the mother? Or does it matter?"

"I know this one," Sam said with a smile. "The donkey is the dad, and the horse is the mom."

"Always?"

"Yep. If it happens the other way around, the offspring is a hinny. They're usually smaller, and their appearance isn't consistent. Sometimes they're more like a horse, and sometimes they're more like a donkey."

"That's what I mean," Conner said. "How do you even know that?"

She shrugged. "I'm curious. I look things up."

"Do you really want a mule?"

She chuckled. "I really do. There's just something about them I like."

Cuddling up on Conner's steel-gray, upholstered sofa, they watched Bing Crosby and Rosemary Clooney sing and dance their hearts out. The movie was interrupted by Christmas Eve phone calls from

Samantha's parents, Uncle Russ, Anna, and Conner's family.

Noticing how quiet Sam became after the calls, Conner pulled her closer. "Are you missing your parents?"

"A little. But I'm happy to be here with you."

"That goes for me too."

When the movie was over, Conner walked to the tree and picked up a small package. "Do you want to open this tonight or tomorrow?"

"Tonight please," she said coyly.

"Then tonight it is. I hope you like it." Sitting down beside her, Conner handed her the store-wrapped package.

Samantha untied the bow, carefully removed the foil paper, and took out a silver charm bracelet.

"This one represents us swing dancing," Conner said, fingering one of the small figures. "And this one is for Lazy Mazie and Maynard. After I heard you play, I found the piano charm, and the fleur de lis, of course, is from New Orleans. I'll add more charms as we make new memories."

"Conner, this is so thoughtful. I love it." After admiring the bracelet a while, she went to the bedroom for Conner's gift. "It's not nearly as wonderful as yours, but I hope you'll like it."

A big smile covered his face when he opened the package. "A belt buckle. You must have known I felt underdressed the night we went dancing. I think I was the only guy in the place without a Western belt buckle."

"Well, this isn't exactly Western."

"It's perfect," he said, kissing her. "I wore that Tar Heels symbol on my jersey for four years. It's perfect," he said again, giving her another kiss.

When his tongue slipped into her mouth, the kisses became more passionate, and their hands began to roam. Conner unbuttoned Sam's blouse, and unzipped her pants. Samantha unbuttoned his shirt and slipped it off his shoulders. Eventually, all their clothes disappeared, and Christmas Eve ended the same delicious way as the last couple of nights. Making love to Samantha seemed so natural, so right, Conner thought. It was hard to believe their first time had been only two nights before.

The next morning Samantha woke to the smell of bacon. Wearing her t-shirt, panties, and socks, she rinsed her mouth, brushed her hair, and padded to the kitchen to see Conner standing at the stove.

"Good morning, beautiful," he said, giving Samantha a sweet kiss. "Merry Christmas."

Once they finished breakfast and Samantha could think of something other than how Conner made her feel, she got excited about seeing Anna and her family. It was Christmas Day, and Sam was happier than she'd been in a long time.

Conner looked perfect in gray slacks and a Christmas-plaid dress shirt. As he stood in front of a full-length mirror to tuck in his shirt tail, Samantha grinned.

"What are you grinning about?"

"I was just thinking of Max's nick-name for you."

"I'm afraid to ask."

"Well, now he just calls you Conner, but for a while he referred to you as the GQ model." He chuckled, knowing how Max felt about him when they first met.

Conner's eyes roamed over Sam, who was dressed in a kelly-green sweater and fitted off-white pants. "You're the one who looks like a model. No, I take that back. I've known a lot of models, and not one of them competes with you in the looks department." Samantha had always been beautiful to him, but the last three amazing nights had sailed her to the top of his hotness scale.

Samantha was standing in front of the bathroom mirror, putting the finishing touches on her hair, when Conner walked up behind her and put a chain around her neck. "When I was buying the piano charm, I saw this and couldn't resist."

"Conner, you shouldn't have. You've already given me a gift." After admiring it in the mirror, she turned and kissed him. "I love it, Conner."

"The guy at the store said it was a treble cleft—the sheet-music symbol indicating what a pianist's right hand should do. The diamonds are miniscule, but I like the shape of the piece. You could wear it on your bracelet if you prefer."

"No. It's beautiful as a necklace. Thank you."

Samantha and Conner arrived at the Anderson home bearing amaryllis blossoms for the ladies and gifts for the children.

Hugs, cheek kisses, and handshakes were exchanged, and Merry Christmas rang from every voice. Gracie ran from a back room to hug her Uncle

Conner and Aunt Samantha, and Anna's dog, Classy, leaned against the newcomers for a pat.

Grabbing the new arrivals' hands, Gracie excitedly tugged them toward the Christmas tree. "Grandpa brought me this," she said, hugging a red-haired ragdoll. "That's my new grandpa," she said, pointing to Anna's father, "because he's Mama's daddy. Now I have a Paw-paw, a Granddaddy, and a Grandpa."

Sam was pleasantly surprised to find Charles Fairchild spending the holidays with his daughter, Anna, and her family. When Anna was a baby, her mother disappeared with her during a difficult divorce. Father and daughter had only recently reunited.

Anna had made it very clear that her father was to make no difference between his biological grandson, Rex, and Max's daughter, Gracie, which didn't seem to be a problem for him. In fact, Charles Fairchild appeared quite smitten with baby Rex's big sister.

As Conner and Samantha sat on the floor next to the tree, Anna noticed how comfortable they were in close proximity to one another. She knew they'd spent time together at the farm, as well as in Savannah, and Conner had said they were 'sort of seeing one another.' But watching them together made Anna think the relationship was more serious than he'd led her to believe.

After admiring Gracie's new treasures, Samantha handed her a gift bag. The child dived in, tissue paper flying into the air.

"Mama, look!" Gracie yelled to Anna. "It's a…"

When she hesitated, Samantha jumped in to help. "It's a fairy costume."

"A fairy costume!" Gracie echoed. "I'll go put it on."

Anna smiled at Savannah, knowing her friend remembered her childhood fixation with fairies. "Wait, Gracie," Anna said. "We want to see you in your Christmas clothes a while. You can change later."

Samantha scanned the room. "Is Rex sleeping? I can't wait to see how he's grown. Babies change so quickly."

"More than likely, he'll wake up when we sit down to eat. The smell of food must stimulate his appetite, even though all he gets is milk. You'll find out about that one day," she told her friend.

When Conner put his hand over Samantha's, Anna thought, "Something's going on between those two. I'm sure of it."

While Sam followed the other women into the kitchen to tend to last minute details, Conner joined the men in front of the television. "First down!" someone yelled, as they all cheered for their chosen team.

The Saints game, the one everyone was waiting for, would take place later in the day. Since moving to the area, Conner discovered that South Mississippians thought of the New Orleans Saints as their home team. They had no problem overlooking a little thing like a state line.

Sitting at the dining table, covered with traditional, southern Christmas dishes, Gracie said, "There he goes." Just as Anna predicted, they'd only been eating a few minutes when Rex demanded attention. "He's been asleep a while," Anna said. "He'll be hungry."

"May I hold him when you finish feeding him?" Samantha asked, before anyone else had the chance. She couldn't wait to get her hands on the soft, sweet baby. When Anna returned, Samantha pushed her chair back from the table and reached for Rex. Touching the baby's face, her eyes softened. Conner watched as she placed her finger in the infant's tiny hand and carefully kissed his sweet-smelling head. He wondered if her longing was as obvious to others as it was to him.

Samantha knew the desire for motherhood varied from woman to woman, and some didn't have it at all. Life would be easier, she thought, if she fell into that latter category. But, unfortunately, she felt the need for a child deep in her bones. Her yearning was intense. Sometimes her arms actually ached to hold a non-existent infant. She'd tried to suppress the feeling. She really had, but it refused to disappear.

"Hello, little guy. Remember me? I'm your Aunt Samantha. You're getting to be such a big boy. Uncle Conner and I brought you a toy alligator from New Orleans." The baby stared at Sam's pretty face, listening intently to her words, rewarding her adoration with sweet cooing sounds.

"Okay," Samantha told the group, holding Rex up for everyone to see, "I know men have to be all macho, but even you guys have to see how adorable this baby is." Chuckling, they agreed, and it wasn't long before Rex was passed from person to person.

With full stomachs and grateful hearts, the group lingered at the table after the hearty, seasonal meal. Looking from Sam to Conner, Anna asked, "So when did you two go to New Orleans?"

Conner answered. "Our flight from Savannah landed there; so we stayed overnight. It was a short trip, but we crammed a lot into it. We just got back yesterday."

Samantha jumped into the conversation. "We were there for the Jackson Square caroling. I've always wanted to do that. It was beautiful with the Saint Charles Cathedral all lit up in the background. Afterward, we ate oyster po-boys at a great little place on St. Louis Street. And we danced to a Zydeco band."

Conner asked, "What did that Cajun guy call it? A fais-do-do?"

"Yes. And then we went to a jazz club and a blues bar."

"On Bourbon Street?" Max asked. When they both nodded, he added, "Did you go in the strip clubs?"

Conner laughed. "Sam wouldn't let me."

"That's not true. You didn't say a word about that."

"You should have seen Sam in the blues bar," Conner said. "She sang with the band. The audience loved her."

Samantha's eyes sparkled as she rushed to add to the story. "And the next morning we followed a 'second line.' That's a wedding parade," she explained to those with questioning faces. "It's a French Quarter thing."

Max was still thinking about the blues bar. "What did you sing, Sam?"

" 'Turn Me On' by Norah Roberts and then 'Tennessee Whiskey.' "

"That's one of my favorites," he said. "Sing it for us."

"I'd need a piano or string instrument to do it justice."

Conner wondered if Samantha would ever stop surprising him. How many instruments did she play?

"Mom," Max said, "do you still have my old guitar?"

"You mean the one you never learned to play? It's in the back bedroom upstairs."

"Shall I get it?" Max asked Sam.

When he returned with the neglected instrument, Samantha tuned it as well as the old strings would allow. "This would sound a lot better with a band behind me, but I'll give it a try."

Everyone applauded when the song was over, but Gracie's compliment was the one Sam appreciated most. "Will you teach me to sing like that?"

"I certainly will. The first thing you have to do is listen to lots of music and try to sing the notes like the singer does. I'll show you what I mean."

She played the guitar and sang off key. "Does that sound right?" Gracie shook her head. When Sam sang it correctly, the child agreed that it sounded better.

"Now, you do it." When she sang on key, Samantha complimented her and stroked her pretty face. "You're on your way. You just need to practice."

"I will. I'll practice every day."

"Oh boy," Max said, wearing a crooked smile.

After enjoying the impromptu lesson, everyone stood, complimented the cook, complained they ate too much, and helped clear the table. Max and Conner dutifully offered to help in the kitchen but were grateful to be shooed away.

Gracie, who finally received permission to try on her fairy costume, danced between the men and the television. Waving her new fairy wand over Alex, she giggled. "Paw-Paw, you're a elephant. And Daddy, you call me a monkey. Now you're a monkey," she said, waving the wand toward Max.

He rose from his chair, grabbed her, and swung her around. "Who's a monkey?"

When he let her down, she backed away and giggled, "You are!"

Then she dubbed Conner a zebra. "Not a giraffe?" he joked.

Waving her wand once more, she said, "Grandpa, you're a..." She stopped to think. "You're a Tiger." Unfamiliar with little-girl-play, he, nevertheless, showed his claws and growled. Gracie giggled and ran to perform her magic on the women in the kitchen.

"Will she take a nap?" Max's grandmother asked.

"Probably not," Anna answered. "I'll put her in pajamas before we head home, and she'll zonk out as soon as we pull out of the driveway." When Max's mother and grandmother left the kitchen to join the men, Anna caught Samantha's eye and nodded toward the guest bedroom.

"Let's talk," she said, patting the edge of the bed. When Samantha sat, she asked what she'd been wondering all day. "What's going on between you and Conner?"

"What do you think? We've been living in the same house, he's beautiful, he's fantastic, things happen."

"You're trivializing something that isn't trivial—at least not to you. I know you too well. Have you fallen for him?"

"Anna, how could I not? He's completely loveable. And did I say he's beautiful?"

"So you're in love with him?"

"Head over heels."

"That's what I thought. Does he feel the same?"

"It seems like it, but a piece of me wonders if he might have a damsel-in-distress disorder. I mean, he helped you when you needed a friend, and the two of you got involved. Do you think he has a weakness for needy women? You've known him a lot longer than I have."

Anna thought a moment before answering. "He tries to help his friends, but a weakness, no. Definitely not. I can tell he cares about you. In fact, I've never seen him like he is today. He's always so smooth, so polished. But today, he seems almost giddy. You both do, despite the problems you're facing."

"He says if I have to disappear, he'll go with me. He even offered to support me financially. We're afraid Hal will trace me if I teach."

Anna took Samantha's hands in hers. "Do you really have to leave?"

"Looks like it. Hal's been hanging around my parents' house, watching for me."

"Could he want to apologize or something? Maybe he doesn't want to hurt you."

"Anna, I left the room when Conner told you what's going on in my life, so I don't know exactly what he said. But Hal almost killed me. That's why he was in prison. If Uncle Russ hadn't rescued me, I'm sure I'd be dead, or worse. Hal's dangerous and I'm profoundly afraid of him."

Maybe one day, Samantha thought, I'll tell her about the baby, but not when Rex is so new, and not on Christmas Day.

When Anna returned to Tenacity, after being away for four years, Sam had explained that she'd married Hal Jacobs and then divorced him because he'd hit her. Now, Anna realized that Sam downplayed the incident and hadn't told her everything. Anna might never know all that happened, but she was beginning to grasp the gravity of the situation. It must have been an extremely violent assault to land Hal in prison.

Anna was amazed at her friend's resiliency. "I'm so sorry, Sam. Why didn't you tell me before?"

"I don't like to think about it. Maybe it's impossible, but I keep trying to put that horrible night behind me."

"I can understand that. How can I help?"

"It'll help to know you're in Tenacity, living a normal life, taking care of your family. Don't worry about me. I'll be all right. Conner is keeping me sane, as well as safe. And my parents, Uncle Russ, and Scott are all looking out for me."

"That's good," she said, unsuccessfully trying to erase the concerned frown on her face. "Will you be able to get in touch with me?"

"I hope so. If you get a letter from someone you've never heard of, you should probably read between the lines. I don't know how, but I'll try to let you know I'm all right. Or that we're both all right, if Conner really does go with me."

Still holding Sam's hands, Anna absently fingered one of the charms on her bracelet.

"That's my Christmas present from Conner," Sam said, relieved to find an excuse to change the subject. Showing Anna each charm, she explained its significance. "This morning, he gave me this," she said, gesturing to her necklace.

"He put a lot of thought into your gifts, and that necklace is gorgeous." Anna heard Rex crying. "Thanks for confiding in me," she said, glancing toward the door. "I'm glad you have Conner. You can depend on him. If he tells you something, you can believe him. It's a blessing to have a man like that in your life."

Rex's crying got louder, and someone called for her again. "I'm sorry. I have to see what the little guy needs. Just remember I love you, and above all, I want you to be safe and happy. Let me know how I can help. I'll do whatever you need." Anna meant what she said, but it was impossible for either of them to know what an important role she would play in Samantha's future.

CHAPTER ELEVEN

When Samantha picked up her phone a few days later, she heard Jeff Windom's voice. "Are you still at Conner's place?"

"I am. Are the animals all right? I really appreciate you feeding them while I'm away."

"They're good." Most of them anyway, he thought. "I'm going to be in Clarkston later this morning. I'd like to stop by. I want to see, with my own eyes, that you're doing all right."

"I assure you I'm fine, but we'd love to see you. Conner's here too. I'll text you the address."

Jeff knocked on the door about an hour later. After hugging Samantha and shaking Conner's hand, he settled on a living room chair and accepted a Cola. Setting it on a coaster, he glanced down, but then looked up and said what he came to say. "I wanted to check on you, Sammy, but there's another reason I'm here. I have bad news. All the animals are good except Henrietta. I'm sorry to have to tell you she's dead. I know she was special to you; so I buried her in your pet cemetery."

"Aww. Poor Henrietta," Samantha said. "She was a good hen. Thanks for burying her instead of having her for supper." Everyone chuckled.

"I'll have a little tombstone made for her," Sam said, "like I've done for other pets. Could you tell what happened to her?"

Jeff sat straighter and looked her in the eye. "That's the worst of the news, and I hate to be the one to tell you. When I went to feed the animals, I found her…" He paused, took a deep breath, and gave Samantha the news. "She was hanging by her neck from the ceiling of your porch." He didn't tell her the Christmas garland was used as rope. Somehow, it made the macabre act even grimmer. "I'm sorry, Sammy. It's a clear warning."

Samantha buried her face against Conner's chest. Enfolding her in his arms, he looked over her head and asked, "What should we do?"

"I called Scott when I found her. He took photographs, checked for fingerprints, shoe prints, tire prints. No hen's death has ever been better investigated."

When Jeff noticed Conner's mouth twitching, he regressed to a freckled-faced boy, sitting in church, covering his mouth to keep the silliness inside. He also remembered his dad taking him by the arm, walking him outside, and spelling out the consequences of a repeated offense. Jeff was a man now; so he pressed his lips together and looked away.

But when Samantha snickered, he lost control, Conner followed suit, and the laughter of the three friends eased the tension in the room.

"Sorry," Jeff said. "I wasn't trying to be funny. Henrietta was a very clever hen." For some reason, that flung them into another fit of laughter.

"That sounds like an opening line in a children's book," Sam said.

Once they'd purged themselves of laughter, Jeff returned to his mission. "I told Scott I'd relay what happened, and I didn't want to tell you over the phone. He realizes you might need another trip to the house and wants to make sure you don't go without him."

"And after that? After I get what I need from the house, then what do I do?"

Jeff shrugged. "Pops may have an idea. He's been doing some research on the Internet. He wants to come by tomorrow, if that's all right.

He's been talking to your mom. She doesn't want your dad to know what happened to Henrietta. He's already worried about you, and the doctor told him to avoid stress. So Pops offered to help."

The following morning, Russ visited Conner's apartment. "How are you handling all this, Sammy?"

"I'm worried, but thanks to Conner, I'm doing as well as can be expected."

With his elbows on his legs and his hands clasped, he looked up at Samantha. "After the hen incident, I think we can assume Hal intends to come after you. I'm convinced you should make plans based on that assumption."

Samantha nodded. "I agree."

"What are you going to do about teaching?"

"I called Mr. Carson this morning, apologized for waiting so long, and told him I'd be out the rest of the year—for personal reasons. He was nice about it and didn't ask questions. He probably knows what's going on. I wouldn't be surprised if the whole town does."

"That might not be a bad thing," Russ said. "The more eyes watching out for him, the better. I assume you'll need to go back to the house to get more of your things."

"I will, since it looks like I'll be leaving for good."

Russ didn't like the sound of that, but there was no help for it. "Scott has some suggestions about your trip back to the house. That's the main reason I'm here."

Conner joined the conversation. "Tell us what to do."

"First of all, let Scott and me know when you plan to come. Don't return on your own. And you should disguise yourselves. We won't let Hal get close, but he could watch from a distance. He'll suspect any car taking the road to Sammy's, but we could get lucky and confuse him. That means you too, Conner. He doesn't know who you are, and we have to keep it that way. Wear sunglasses and a hat that covers your hair.

"If he's watching, he'll try to follow when you leave. So Scott suggests a vehicle switch. You'll travel to Tenacity in a rented vehicle. Just to be safe, I'll list it in my name. Scott will have a second rental waiting behind his office, and some of us will be there to help transfer Sam's things. We'll need to be quick."

Samantha slowly nodded, the danger suddenly seeming real and imminent. "Any ideas about what I should do after that—where I should go?"

"If this turns out to be a long-term situation, heaven forbid, Scott knows people who can set you up with a new identity. But that's a last resort. As messed up as Hal is, he's bound to run into a problem that'll land him back in prison. If ya'll are happy with this arrangement," he said, gesturing to the room they were in, "and Hal doesn't find out about Conner, you should be safe here for a while. But you need to decide where you'll go if you have to leave quickly. It should be a place where people are transient, where everyone doesn't know everyone else. Choose someplace Hal would never guess you'd go."

"This is hard," Samantha admitted. "Why does Hal get to ruin my life?"

"I can't answer that. We can only hope it's temporary.

Hal is still staying with his cell mate's sister on the far side of town, and we have someone watching him. Jeff and I will take care of your place and the animals. And don't worry about money. Your parents and I will support you."

"I hope that won't be necessary," Samantha told him, "but it's good to know you have my back."

Standing to walk Russ to the door, Samantha asked, "Why are you so good to me, Uncle Russ?"

He briefly looked away, then pulled her to his side and kissed the top of her head.

After Russ left, Sam and Conner sat in silence for what seemed like a long time. Finally, Conner said, "You should be comforted knowing so many capable people are looking out for you. Let's do our best not to worry."

Changing the subject, he said, "I called my boss this morning and told him about our situation."

"You told him?"

"Only a little. And in vague terms. He agreed to let me work from home, for now, but I have to go to the office to pick up some files and get briefed on a case. A fellow attorney is meeting me at two-thirty this afternoon. Come with me," he said, not wanting to leave her alone. "You can see where I work."

Every time they left the house together, they took a chance that Hal would see them. But the chance seemed so slim, they ignored it. Arriving at the law office, Conner unlocked the front door and invited Samantha in with a sweep of his arm.

They walked through a large, desk-filled outer room, where support staff for the junior attorneys worked. Conner was showing Samantha the room he shared with another attorney when they heard the front door open.

"That'll be Denise," he said, taking Sam's hand. "Come with me. I want to introduce you." Walking back through the large room, they saw Conner's co-worker unlocking her office door. She was tall and slender, and from the back, Sam guessed her to be thirty-something.

When the attorney turned around, Samantha's face went ashen. She backed away, bumped against a chair, and abruptly sat.

Conner crouched beside her. "What's wrong, Sam? You're white as a ghost."

The other attorney asked. "Who is this, Conner?"

"My girl," he answered quickly, more concerned about Samantha's sudden vulnerability than making introductions."

Fellow attorney Denise Graham narrowed her eyes. "She looks familiar. What's her name?"

"Samantha Lindsey," Conner replied, his attention still on Sam.

"She's not from Tenacity, is she?"

"Yes. Why?"

"Oh, crap," Denise said. "Samantha Jacobs."

That got Conner's attention. That was the name on the envelope from Samantha's ex. That was her married name.

Conner finally turned toward Denise. "What's going on?"

"I'm afraid I represented her husband when she took him to trial."

Before she could say anything else, Conner gave her a glare that could melt stone.

"I'm sorry," she said, showing him the palms of her hands. "I was court appointed. I had no choice. Ms. Jacobs," she said, looking directly at Samantha, "I understand why you're upset, but I'm legally bound to represent a client to the best of my ability, whether he's a paying client or a court-mandated one."

This time, it was Samantha who glared. "My name is Samantha Lindsey," she said, emphasizing her last name. "And I don't care about your reason. How do you sleep at night after demeaning a victim or getting some lowlife released to kill or maim again?"

"It's not easy, and I assure you I had no part in getting your husband released. If it makes you feel any better, I almost hoped I'd lose his case."

"Almost," she laughed, without humor. "And don't refer to your client as my husband."

Logically, Conner understood the other attorney's position, but that didn't change the way he felt. "Come on, Samantha, I'll take you home."

She shook her head. "No. Do what you came here to do. I'm okay."

"Before you go," Denise said to Conner. "I need to see you in my office." When he hesitated, she said, "Just for a minute."

"Go ahead," Samantha encouraged. "Really, I'll be all right. Seeing her was just a shock."

"I don't want to leave you here by yourself."

"Go," she said, raising her voice. "Just do it."

Reluctantly, Conner walked into the office behind Denise, who closed the door behind them.

"Do you know what you've gotten yourself into?" she asked, her tone intense. "I was told you were helping a girl whose husband just got out of prison. Did she tell you what he did to her?"

"She did."

"She probably didn't tell you the half of it. Her husband is a dangerous man."

"Stop calling him her husband."

"Okay. Her ex-husband is a dangerous man. And he's out of prison?" Conner nodded.

Denise walked to her file cabinet and pulled out two folders. Throwing them on her desk, one at a time, she said, "Here's the file you came for, and here's the transcript of your girlfriend's trial. Look at it before you leave. You need to know what you've gotten yourself into. I'm going to talk to your girl. I'll tell her you have documents to read. Don't worry. I'll play nice. You just look at that file."

After a brief hesitation, Conner sat down at Denise's desk and opened the folder. He thought he'd heard the whole story, but reading the exact words Samantha uttered at the trial, her blow-by-blow description of the attack, was more disturbing than he expected. She'd been pretty graphic when she related the incident to him, but the details that came out in the trial made him want to retch.

Denise's cross examinations made him furious. At least she hadn't attacked Sam's character. But she would have if she'd found anything damaging.

Conner understood why every American had the right to representation, and in theory, he agreed, but as he read Denise's cross examination, he realized something. Experienced attorneys had told him he had the makings of a crackerjack defense attorney. He had the expertise, but at that moment, he realized he didn't have the appetite for that aspect of law.

Toward the back of the file, Conner found Samantha's hospital records. It was a wonder she was still alive. If Russ hadn't found her when he had, she wouldn't be. She'd been tortured to the point of death—and at the hands of someone who professed to love her. How could she trust anyone after that? How could she trust him? But she did, he thought, amazed and humbled by the gift.

Conner's hand shook as he picked up the photographs of his beautiful, funny Samantha, bloody and beaten beyond recognition. His eyes filled with tears, and for the first time since he was a child, he truly cried. He folded his arms on the desk, rested his head on them, and cried.

Needing to hold Samantha, he wiped his eyes, closed the evidence of her horror, and left it on the desk. He'd started for the door when he remembered why he came to the office in the first place. He had a job to do, so he went back for the other folder. He'd call Denise later to discuss the case, but at the moment, he didn't even want to look at her.

Samantha noticed Conner's red eyes and suspected she knew the reason, but she waited until they entered the apartment to ask about it. When he admitted he'd read the trial transcript, Sam silently walked into the extra bedroom and locked the door. Conner wasn't sure what to do, but she obviously wanted time alone. So he gave it to her.

Over breakfast, neither of them mentioned the visit to the law office or their separate sleeping arrangement the previous night. When Conner saw her red, puffy eyes, he started to reach for her but sensed his embrace might not be welcome.

As they lingered over coffee at the dining room table, Samantha announced, her eyes watery, that it was time to make the trip to the farm. "I dread leaving Tenacity, but since I have to, I'd like to get it over with. I've made a list of things to pack."

Conner took out his phone. "Want me to call Scott?"

"Sure," Sam said, using a napkin to dry her damp eyes.

Conner put the sheriff on speaker, and the three of them scheduled the trip for the following afternoon. "Russ wants to help," Scott said. "I'll give him a call."

The doorbell rang for the third morning in a row.

"You expecting anyone?" Conner asked.

When she shook her head, he motioned for her to stay where she was, walked to the door, and cautiously peered through the peep hole.

"Surprise!" Kendall and Reagan sing-songed when he opened the door.

He was surprised all right, but invited them in. "You know Samantha," he said, when she appeared from the dining room.

"What's she doing here?" Reagan asked.

"That's what I should be asking you," Conner said, irritated by her question.

"We came for a visit," Kendall chimed in. "We wanted to surprise you."

"Well, you certainly did that." He eyed the two big suitcases. "I see you came to stay," "I'll put your things in one of the extra bedrooms."

"Can I get you something to drink?" Samantha asked. "You must be thirsty after your trip."

"I'll get it," Kendall said, denying Samantha the right to serve as hostess. Returning with a Cola for Reagan and one for herself, she said, "Oh, Samantha, did you want anything?"

"No thank you." Uncomfortable with the cold shoulder she was getting from the girls, Sam escaped to the bedroom she'd been sharing with Conner. He could deal with his sister and her rude friend alone. She seemed to bring out the worst in the teen-agers.

They ordered pizza for dinner, and Samantha retired to Conner's room shortly thereafter. She'd tried to engage the girls in conversation, but it was clear they were uninterested in anything she had to say.

Russ and Jeff showed up early the next morning with a hatchback full of empty cardboard boxes and packing tape. After handing the rental's keys to Conner and going over the day's plans, Russ and Jeff returned home in Jeff's truck.

As Conner and Samantha drove through Tenacity's corridor of overhanging limbs, she felt a sense of unease rather than the peace the place normally engendered. It seemed to be sending a warning, making her wonder if the corridor really did possess some kind of supernatural power. Or maybe the imposing, green tunnel simply had a way of intensifying a person's emotions.

Willing herself to dismiss the illogical notions, Samantha pushed her fears aside, gathered her courage, and focused on the task at hand. She had things to do but readily admitted the trip was about more than packing.

Russ and Jeff would take care of the farm while she was away, but she needed to see it one last time. The thought of saying good-bye to the animals and locking the farmhouse doors felt almost like a death. In a way it was. It was the death of the life she loved, and the drive to the farm was a one-car funeral procession.

Mazie, Maynard, and the hens would be fine, as long as they were being fed. Even the barn cats could manage. But she worried about her loyal, protective Hot Shot and Queenie. They'd miss her and wouldn't understand why she'd abandoned them.

She consoled herself with the knowledge that Russ or Jeff would adopt her dogs permanently if her absence turned out to be an extended one. And they would either keep the other animals or find good homes for them.

"Drive past Anna's house and down Main Street," Sam instructed. "I want to see the town one more time and take a few pictures." Conner understood. This could be Samantha's last trip to Tenacity for a long time.

"Since we're incognito, I don't see how that would hurt." Conner wore a western hat, which looked great on him, Sam covered her hair with the dark wig they'd purchased in New Orleans, and both wore sunglasses.

As they approached the road to Samantha's farmhouse, Scott stepped out from the trees. "Go on in," he told them. "Russ, Max, and Jeff are waiting. They'll check out the house before you go inside and keep watch while you get what you need. I'll position my car about a quarter of a mile down this road. No sense advertising your visit."

When Conner pulled the Porsche up to the house, Sam removed her wig, stepped from the hatchback, and managed a weak smile for her friends. Giving each of them a grateful hug, she thanked them for taking the time to help, while Hot Shot and Queenie bounced around them, vying for Samantha's attention.

Stooping down, she hugged the loyal bird dogs. "Yes, I've missed you too. I'm leaving for a while," she told them, "but Uncle Russ and Jeff will take good care of you. They might even take you hunting." She stood, blinking tears from her eyes.

"Okay," Sam said. "I'm ready. Let's do this." The visit to the farm was like getting a tiny taste of her mother's banana pudding when she craved the entire dish. How could she say farewell to the one place on earth that truly fed her soul?

Sam looked around. She'd spent her whole life on the farm, except for her time at Southern Miss. Even then, she came home most weekends. Growing up in the country had been the best kind of childhood, playing in the barn, helping with the animals, and running free in the pasture.

And the house, which seemed like a mansion when she was little, meant so much to her. She recalled playing board games with her parents at the kitchen table, hiding on the secret staircase when she wanted to be alone, playing make-believe in the attic with Anna.

Samantha didn't understand how she could dissociate Hal from the farm, but miraculously, she could. It was as if the house had performed an exorcism to expunge him from the premises.

Something else made the farm extraordinary— something mysterious and hard to define. It had to do with its history and the people who previously lived there, like Billy, Harold, and Daisy. She knew they weren't alive, at least not in the normal sense of the word, but they existed, in some form, in the cherished old house they all called home.

After checking the house for unwelcome surprises, Max and Russ stood guard outdoors while Conner and Jeff went inside with Samantha. She'd given a lot of thought to what she'd need, but with an uncertain future, the decisions were difficult. She chose to take pictures, jewelry, some of her favorite grooming products, a few pairs of shoes, and clothing for various climates.

She also packed her sapphire blue formal and spike heels to wear to an event the following evening. Before Sam's ex-husband was released from prison, Conner's boss had asked him and Denise Graham to represent the firm at a client's function on New Year's Eve. Conner had asked Samantha to be his date, but after discovering that Denise was the defense attorney at Hal's trial, Conner didn't think she'd want to attend. Surprising him, Sam insisted on going. She could never repay him for his kindness and understanding, but at least she could show her appreciation. She would put away her resentment for one evening and be the woman Conner deserved to have at his side.

CHAPTER TWELVE

Jeff, Conner, and Samantha climbed the attic stairs to retrieve Sam's suitcases. "I came up here with Pops when he was building the panic room," Jeff said, looking around. "This place amazes me. Where did all this stuff come from?"

"Most of it was here before I was born, but my family added to the stash. My old stereo's here, somewhere, and my Star Wars Mandalorian figures. Also a box of Mama's cassette tapes."

Jeff couldn't stop looking. "I'd love to know what's in these boxes."

Conner nodded. "That's what I said."

"Someday," Samantha said wistfully, "when all this is over, we'll do that. We'll pick a nice cool day, I'll make soup and cornbread, and we'll come up here and meddle to our hearts' content." They bumped fists, in a pretense of solidifying the tenuous date.

Back in the master bedroom, Samantha began packing. For most of her life, the room and its adjoining bath had belonged to her parents, but when they moved out, Sam moved in.

"It's stuck," she said, tugging at the bottom drawer of an old chest of drawers.

"I'll get it," Jeff said. When he gave it a hefty pull, the drawer came completely out.

"Don't put it back yet," Samantha said. "I can't get under that chest to vacuum, and it's filthy. Let me clean it while the drawer is out."

When she returned with cleaning supplies, Jeff was brushing the dust from a photograph. "This was stuck to the back of the drawer," he said, showing Samantha the picture. "It's Pops, holding me when I was a baby."

"I've never seen that before. That used to be my mom's chest of drawers." Taking the picture from him, Samantha looked more closely. "But that's not you he's holding. It's me." She flipped the photo over. "See, it says two months, and that's my mother's handwriting."

"That doesn't mean it's not me," Jeff insisted. "Why would there be a professionally taken picture of my pops holding you? Besides, he keeps a framed copy of that on the chest of drawers in his bedroom with other family pictures. You know, school pictures of Brian and me, photos of us with dad when we were kids. There's a family picture with Mom in it, and one of you and me riding horses when we were kids."

"Do you ever see your mom?" Samantha asked, unconcerned about the photo.

"Not too much anymore. Brian visits more than I do. The cattle keep me busy. Mom married a nice guy, and they occasionally come to Tenacity for a visit. He's a city boy but likes the ranch. When they come, they stay in my cabin, and I bunk in my old room at Pops' place. We cook out together, go to Lucky's. Sometimes Mom cooks at my cabin. Everybody gets along. It's all very cordial."

Samantha left the room and came back with a baby picture of herself. "This is me. Doesn't that look like the baby your dad's holding in the picture?" Jeff shrugged. "I guess bald babies all look alike."

"I think it looks like me," Conner joked.

Jeff smiled, "Were you a bald baby?"

"Bald as a basketball."

Samantha continued packing while the men talked.

"Yeah," Jeff said. "You played for the Tar Heels, didn't you?"

"Four years."

"Can you palm a basketball?"

Conner wondered why people always asked that. "I can."

"Cool."

When Sam announced she'd finished packing, Conner asked, "Anything else you want to do before we leave?"

"Yes, there is." While Conner and Jeff carried her things to the hatchback, Sam wandered out to the barn, sat on the hay-strewn floor, and petted the barn cats.

Conner watched as she walked through the pasture, a beautiful Pied Piper with enchanted cats and dogs trailing behind. She'd become important to him, Conner admitted to himself, more important than he'd intended.

Lazy Maizie and Maynard, who'd been grazing side-by-side, looked up and ambled toward her, hoping for treats. She fed the huge animals, stroked their necks, and told them good-bye. By the time she reached the front yard, most of the cats had wandered off, but the dogs remained at her side.

While Samantha was telling her animals good-bye, Conner and Russ reviewed the exit plan. Conner was to drive the packed vehicle to Scott's office and transfer boxes and suitcases to a rented SUV.

In Clarkston, Conner would unload Sam's things at his apartment, return the rented vehicle, and take a taxi home. Russ and Jeff offered to follow, to help unload, but Conner insisted he could do it alone. He would, however, need help moving Sam's things from the hatchback to the rented SUV parked behind Scott's office. That needed to be done quickly.

"All this may seem like overkill," Russ said, "especially since Hal doesn't appear to be around, but it can't hurt to be cautious." When Samantha joined them, Russ asked if she'd like him to lock up with the key he kept for emergencies.

Sam wanted to take a last look, but lingering would only prolong the pain. "Thank you," she said. "I'd appreciate that."

She petted the dogs one last time. "Okay. We can go now." On her way to the car, she looked at the ground. Then Sam remembered the kind men watching her leave.

With glossy eyes, she walked back to Russ, Jeff, and Max. "Thank you for being my guardian angels and taking such good care of me. I'll never forget all you've done. And Uncle Russ, there isn't a word big enough or strong enough to express my gratitude for you." Sam didn't try to stop her tears.

"Hey, hey," Russ said, pulling her into his arms. "You're not going away yet. You'll be close by for a while. And when you do go, it won't be forever. Just think of it as an extended vacation." His voice sounded upbeat, but Conner saw tears well up in the man's eyes.

Scott pulled his squad car to the side of the road he'd been blocking, allowing the hatchback to pass. He followed at a distance, and Jeff wasn't far behind. When they reached the sheriff's office, behind the library and out of sight, Scott, Jeff, and Conner transferred Sam's things to the SUV in record time. Hopefully, anyone watching would think Samantha and Conner were in the sheriff's office while they were really driving away in the SUV.

Once the task was complete, Conner sat behind the steering wheel of the vehicle, breathed a sigh of relief, and leaned over to kiss Sam. It had been an emotional day, but they'd done what they needed to. Now, he just wanted to go back to the apartment and hold Samantha.

They'd only traveled a few miles from town when Conner noticed that the same car had been behind them since they'd left Tenacity. He was probably being paranoid, but as Russ said, it didn't hurt to be cautious. So he exited the highway, and immediately took the ramp leading back to the road they'd just left. The car followed.

Samantha was on the phone with the sheriff when the car following them moved alongside the SUV. She'd just gotten out the words, "We're being followed," when the driver of the other car smiled a wicked smile, pointed a finger-gun at them, and began easing them off the road.

"The bridge!" Samantha yelled, staring at the concrete railing looming ahead. If Conner continued on the same trajectory, he'd hit it head on. If he swerved off the road, they'd hit a stand of trees or slide down an embankment into a creek. He cursed the rented vehicle for not maneuvering like his Porsche, but at least it was bigger than the mid-sized car next to them. Then he remembered that SUVs were prone to tipping and did the only thing he could.

"Hold on," he told Samantha as he poured on the gas. Moving toward the front of the other car, Conner rammed its right front fender and sped away, narrowly missing the bridge. The other car went into a spin.

Conner was sweating as if he'd played back-to-back games in a basketball tournament. If his timing had been off, just a little, he could have killed Samantha. Coming down from an adrenaline rush, he needed to stop and gain his equilibrium. But he didn't dare.

Glancing in the rear-view mirror, Conner said, "Looks like he ricocheted off the other side of the bridge, but it might not have stopped him."

Samantha found her phone on the floor, redialed Scott, and put him on speaker. After filling him in on what had happened, she described the vehicle and verified that it was Hal.

"There's a car behind us, pretty far back," Conner yelled loudly enough for Scott to hear, "but it's traveling fast. Does it look like the same car, Sam?"

She looked over her shoulder. "Maybe. I can't tell."

"Just keep driving," Scott advised. "I'm hanging up, but keep your phone handy. I'll get back to you."

Driving as fast as he dared, Conner tried to stay ahead of the approaching car. Now he really missed the Porsche. The mid-sized sedan was gradually closing the distance, and he had no desire to play bumper car roulette again. "We could use a little help," Conner said, just before hearing a siren and seeing flashing red and blue lights behind him.

When Samantha's phone rang, she put it on speaker. "Scott here," the caller said. "I'm on the radio with the highway patrol, and they're attempting to pull over a speeding, dark sedan. Just keep driving. I'll keep you posted."

"We see the lights," Conner said, glancing in the rear-view mirror. Sam turned in her seat, "He's not pulling over. Looks like he's trying to outrun the patrol car."

They could hear the squawking of the sheriff's radio over the phone. "Gotta go," Scott said.

The scene behind them kept repeating itself. Almost as soon as the highway patrol car pulled up next to Hal, they'd have to fall back to let an oncoming vehicle pass. Eventually, Conner and Sam lost sight of the flashing lights.

With their heartbeats coming too fast, they were desperate to know what was happening. Maybe the highway patrol had pulled Hal over, or maybe he'd run the patrol car off the road. Samantha phoned Scott but got no answer.

Finally, Deputy Garret called. "You can relax. We got him. I caught up to the sheriff and the highway patrol, and between the three of us, we pulled him over. It's Hal all right. He's in the back of the sheriff's cruiser now. Highway patrol wrote him a ticket for speeding and reckless driving, and we're taking him in for evading a police officer. He broke his probation, but I can't say what the punishment will be. That's at the discretion of the court. We'll hold him as long as possible. At least you'll be able to get where you're going without being followed. Are y'all all right? Do you need anything?"

"No, we're all right, thanks to you guys," Conner said.

"Just scared out of our ever-loving minds," Samantha added.

"I spoke with someone at the rental place," the deputy said. "They know what happened, and they'll deal directly with our department concerning any damage to the vehicle. If anyone gives you any trouble, ask for Rudy Johnson. He'll take care of you."

Conner pulled up to his apartment, rested his head on the steering wheel, and took deep, slow breaths. Watching over Samantha was more treacherous than he could have dreamed. He was a big, strong guy, but that didn't help in this situation. He'd unintentionally gotten into a bar fight, once, protecting a girl from unwanted attention, and he'd held his own. But Conner had never been up against a maniac like Hal.

Samantha and Conner made trip after trip from the SUV to the apartment. When Conner signed the rental agreement, the only unit available was a three-bedroom. That was proving fortuitous. Kendall and Reagan were staying in the room with the twin-beds, Sam's things were stacked in the other guestroom, and he and Samantha were sleeping in the master.

"Is she moving in?" Kendall and Reagan asked incredulously.

"For now," was all Conner said.

Physically and emotionally drained, he wanted to crawl into bed and wake up three days later. But the vehicle had to be returned. He couldn't take a chance, however unlikely, that Hal might discover the banged-up SUV.

Just as the deputy promised, they had no trouble returning the vehicle. After calling an Uber, they silently rode home, leaning against one another, holding hands. Kendall and Reagan, unaware of what had happened, bombarded them with chatter the moment they returned to the apartment.

Conner was still too shaken to deal with the teenagers. "Not now, please. This isn't a good time, girls."

"If you're staying home, may we borrow your car?" Kendall asked excitedly. "We'll drive carefully."

"No. You're not driving my car. I'm sorry, but you'll have to find something to do here at the apartment. Watch television. This was a bad time to visit, Kendall. You should have called."

In the master suite, Conner and Samantha slipped off their shoes and sat on the edge of the bed. Sam stared ahead while Conner phoned Scott, letting him know they'd arrived safely and thanking him for his help.

"Are you all right?" Conner finally asked Sam.

"No. My life is upside down. I want to live in my house, take care of my animals, teach my class, go to Big Mama's for breakfast, and eat catfish at Lucky's without being afraid someone will kill me. My life used to be simple, and I liked it that way. Now I have to move God knows where. I'm gonna miss everybody—Mama and Daddy, Uncle Russ, Max and

Anna, and sweet Gracie. And I won't get to watch little Rex grow up."

"I know," Conner said, smoothing her hair. "I'm sorry. I know it's not the same, but we'll find a way to stay in touch with them." Sam crumpled onto the bed. Conner lay behind her and held her close. Exhausted and grateful to be alive, they fell asleep.

Hoping to talk Conner into taking them somewhere, Kendall and Reagan knocked on his door. When no one answered, they opened it a crack and were surprised to see Conner and Samantha asleep on the bedspread. Shrugging, they returned to their room, seriously disappointed at how their visit was turning out.

"Please take us to the party," Kendall and Reagan begged the next day. "We brought dresses for it."

"Why would you do that? And it isn't exactly a party. I'll be representing my law firm and Samantha is my date. It's not a function for teen-agers."

Conner was pretty sure Sam wasn't looking forward to the obligatory New Year's Eve party. For that matter, neither was he. They'd both prefer some alone time. But his boss had asked him to attend, and Sam insisted she wanted to go. Besides, he didn't want to leave her unguarded, and wouldn't saddle her with babysitting two ill-mannered teen-aged girls.

Kendall whined, "But it's New Year's Eve and we don't have any place to go."

"You should have thought of that before you came without an invitation. How do you even know about the event?"

"You told Mom"

He chastised himself for his loose tongue. When his mom phoned, she asked how he was bringing in the new year. Unfortunately, he'd told her. She probably guessed he was taking Samantha and sent the girls to disrupt his plans.

After lunch, Conner announced he was going to the office for a couple of hours. "The boss wants to talk with Denise and me about the event tonight." The thought of Denise made Samantha feel ill. Not only did she remember the woman's venomous cross examinations, she'd bet good money the attorney had designs on Conner. She might be a little older, but she was beautiful, and most likely cunning.

"I'll call for a car," Conner said. "I'm leaving my keys with you, Samantha, in case of an emergency." She understood. He was leaving her a means of escape if the need arose. "The gas gauge isn't working properly. I haven't had time to get it repaired. But there should be enough gas in the tank to get you out of town if necessary. Kendall, Reagan, you are not to drive my car under any circumstances. And if Samantha tells you to do something, you do it. Understood?"

"Understood," they said, rolling their eyes. When Conner looked away, Reagan whispered something to Kendall, who responded with a nod.

"You're kinda bossy today," Kendall said to her brother, "but I guess I love you anyway." She hugged him and gave Reagan a knowing look before heading to their room.

The teens ironed out the details of a plan that had already begun taking shape in Reagan's mind. "If Samantha isn't here when it's time for Conner to leave for the party," the devious girl told Kendall, "he'll have to take us—or, at least, me. That'll give him a chance to see me as more than his sister's friend."

Reagan and Kendall accomplished step one of their plan before Conner left the house. When Kendall hugged her brother and apologized for dropping in unexpectedly, she was actually slipping his phone from its holster.

"Now we have to find a water hose," Reagan said. Covertly roaming the neighborhood, they located one, dragged it behind Conner's apartment, cut a long piece from it, and nonchalantly walked to Conner's car at the end of the building. After siphoning out all the gas, they put a small amount back in. Step two of their plan was complete, except for washing the gasoline smell off their bodies and out of their clothes.

They waited to execute the last step. When they felt the time was right, they did some research on the Internet, locked themselves in their room, and texted Samantha using Conner's phone.

I'm at Gus's Place on Old Timber Road. Come get me. I'll explain later. Please hurry

Patting herself on the back for her cleverness, Reagan hid the phone in the closet.

Samantha immediately phoned Conner. She thought she heard a phone ring in the house, but assumed it was for one of the girls. When Conner didn't answer, she surmised he was in some kind of trouble. He'd never ask her to venture out alone unless he had to—not with Hal on the loose. What was Conner even doing at a place called Gus's? He was supposed to be at the office.

Sam had been standing in the master bathroom, getting ready for the party, when she received the text. So she'd pulled the curlers from her hair, thrown on jeans and a sweater, and slipped her feet into a pair of loafers.

While Samantha located Gus's Place on her laptop, Kendall stood at her side, purposefully blocking her view. Out of her line of sight, Reagan carefully reached into Sam's purse and retrieved her phone. Samantha told the girls she was running an errand and hurried to the Porsche, grateful she knew how to drive a stick shift. She reached into her purse, intending to use her phone for directions, but it wasn't there. Good thing she'd googled the place.

When Denise Graham dropped Conner off at his apartment, he noticed his car wasn't in its parking place. "Denise, I hate to ask you this. I know you need to get ready for the party, but will you wait here while I check on something. It shouldn't take long."

He took the steps two at a time, an easy accomplishment for him, and rushed into the apartment. Seeing his sister, he asked, "Where's Samantha?"

Reagan answered. "I think someone called to tell her she was needed at home. You're supposed to go to the party without her and not worry. She'll return the car tomorrow. Oh, and her phone's not working."

It wouldn't have been a good lie under any circumstances, but there was no way Sam would have returned to the farm alone. When he reached for his phone and discovered it wasn't there, he asked the girls if they'd seen it. Looking as innocent as possible, they shook their heads and shrugged.

Conner heard a faint ring. The girls heard it, too, and froze. They hadn't turned off the ringer. Conner might simply have thought the sound came from Kendall's or Reagan's phone, but their wide-eyed expressions said something wasn't on the up and up.

He followed the sound to the bedroom the girls were occupying. Then it stopped. When it began again, he followed the sound and found his phone in the closet—next to Samantha's. Denise was calling to find out if he still wanted her to wait. "I need you in the apartment," he said, "I may need back up." Conner wanted to lash out at Kendall and her scheming friend, but first, he had to find out where Samantha was.

Denise was amused when she saw two teen-age girls sitting on Conner's sofa, looking as if they'd been caught smoking a joint or sneaking a boy into their room. She soon discovered it was worse than that.

The ability to cross examine a witness was a skill every attorney learns, and Conner had mastered it. Bit by bit he dragged the story from the girls. They'd found a map on the Internet and sent Samantha to Gus's Place on the other side of town. To get there, Sam would have to go through the area where Hal was staying. With clinched jaws and fisted hands, Conner glared at the girls.

"We're sorry," Kendall said, seeing how angry her brother was.

Conner glowered, shaking his head in disbelief. "I'll deal with you later," he said, rushing from the room.

Denise was two steps ahead of him. "Let's go get her. There are some raunchy backwater places out that way. I can be late for the party. It's a good thing you don't have a car right now," she observed. "You're too angry to drive."

She was right. Conner wasn't sure he could forgive his sister for this stunt. He suspected Reagan was the instigator, but damn it, Kendall had gone along with it.

Denise was driving on a lonely two-lane highway when they saw the Porsche on the side of the road. Samantha was sitting behind the steering wheel, and a man was peering into her window. When they pulled behind the car, they saw a second man on the opposite side. What was going on? When the strangers realized they had company, they hurried to their truck and left.

Samantha sat in the car, staring ahead, while Conner knocked on the window. "It's me, Sam." She looked at him without seeing. "Open the door, honey." He finally talked her into unlocking it, pulled her from the car, and held her close.

When he pulled back to look into her eyes, he could almost see her returning to the present from wherever her mind had retreated. "Hey, hey, you're all right," he told her. "I'm here."

Sam leaned against Conner's chest, welcoming the comfort he offered, her tears dampening his shirt. Eventually, she began to talk. "I went to Gus's, like you told me, but I couldn't find you. Some awful men dragged me to their table and tried to make me drink with them. I broke loose and ran to the car. Conner, what were you doing in a place like that?"

"I'll explain later. And the car ran out of gas?" he asked, encouraging her to move along with the story.

Samantha looked at him accusingly. "You said to hurry; so I didn't stop for gas."

Then she noticed Denise standing beside Conner. Frowning, she glanced from one to the other.

"She was nice enough to come looking for you," Conner said. "I didn't have a car. I'll explain everything, but first tell me about the men in the truck."

"They followed me from that place, and then your car stopped. They said they wanted to help and told me to get out of the car, that they couldn't hear me through the window. Anyone could tell they were lying. When they realized the tactic wouldn't work, they dropped the ruse and threatened to break the window. Conner, I didn't have a phone. I always keep my phone in my purse, but it wasn't there. And my gun is in my truck. I had no way to defend myself. And the car wouldn't start."

Because my sister and her friend siphoned out the gas, he thought. He wouldn't tell her that just yet. He was still having trouble believing it himself.

Conner tried to soothe Samantha, but she continued to shake. It was no wonder. The day before, a man who once professed to love her, had tried to kill her by running her into a bridge. And then she had to deal with his sister's perverted deception, which had almost been a disaster.

"I know what they wanted to do with me," Samantha said in a shaky voice. "I couldn't take that again. I'd rather die."

"Get in the car," Denise said to Conner. "I'll drive you wherever you want to go, and I'll tell tonight's hosts you had a family emergency. Since Sam was clinging to Conner like a barnacle, Denise started the car with the frightened woman sitting on his lap. When they stopped at the service station and Conner coaxed Sam into turning him loose, he bought a gas can and enough gas to get the Porsche back to the station.

Samantha didn't like seeing Conner with Denise, but she was grateful for the woman's help. As they left the pretty attorney's car, Samantha composed herself enough to thank Denise for coming to her rescue. "You and Conner saved me from a fate worse than death. I couldn't go through that," she repeated. "Not again."

Sam walked into Conner's apartment with a red, blotchy face, and Reagan rolled her eyes. Conner noticed, and it infuriated him. When Samantha went into the bedroom, he faced the girls and spoke through clenched teeth. "You have no idea what just happened or what would have happened if I hadn't gotten there when I did.

"Reagan, your eye-rolling is not only insensitive, it's malicious. I can't tell my sister who she can have as a friend, but don't ever come back here again. And when I'm in Savannah, stay out of my way. If you're at the house when I arrive, leave through the back door or climb out a damn window. I don't care as long as I don't have to see you. Both of you, sit on the couch," he demanded. "And don't move."

Kendall couldn't believe what she was witnessing. Conner was the most affable guy she knew. She'd only seen him angry a handful of times in her life, but she'd never seen him like this.

Conner sat at the computer in his bedroom and pulled up an airline schedule. When he returned to the living room, he explained what was going to happen. "There's a commuter plane flying out of here tomorrow at six-thirty a.m. The two of you are going to be on it. It'll take you from Jackson to Atlanta, and then to Savannah. If you miss your connections, I won't rescue you."

"But that's so early, and so many different flights," Kendall whined. "And we planned to stay a few more days."

"You're lucky I don't throw you out on the street. I don't know if I can forgive you for this, Kendall. I'll pick the two of you up at five in the morning, and you'd better be ready. If you're not dressed, I'll take you in your pajamas."

"You wouldn't," his sister said.

"Try me. I'm taking Samantha to a hotel tonight. I don't want her in the apartment with you, and honestly, I'm so angry, I can't even look at you."

"What about the party?" Reagan had the nerve to ask.

Conner cast her a look Kendall had never seen on his face. "To hell with the damn party!" Sam walked out with an overnight bag. "Did you pack anything for me?"

When she nodded, they hurried from the room, and Conner slammed the door behind them. Reagan stomped from the living room and slammed the bedroom door, while Kendall sat on the sofa and cried.

The girls were ready when Conner picked them up the next morning, and they managed to get home without missing any of their flights. When his mother phoned, he told her he was too angry to talk.

When she called again, he said, "Not yet, Mom. I'll call when I can talk calmly, and I don't know when that'll be." Then he hung up on her. By sending the girls without asking, his mother had not only inconvenienced him, she'd inadvertently set the Porsche incident into action. She had to stop interfering in his life.

CHAPTER THIRTEEN

The next few days were gloriously uneventful. Conner went into the office a few hours each morning and then worked from home in the afternoons. Listening to his side of phone conversations and watching him work confirmed what Samantha already knew. Conner was a principled, responsible, hard-working man, despite his staggering good looks and privileged upbringing. Not only did she love him, she admired him.

When their time together ended, it was going to break her heart, but at some point, that would have to happen. His family didn't accept her, and she couldn't give him children. Those were the facts, but she wasn't ready to let him go. It was selfish, but she just wasn't ready.

Once the holidays were over, Samantha had to adjust to the down time. She was accustomed to being busy and liked it that way. Besides teaching five days a week, she always had papers to grade, a house to clean, repairs to make, and animals to feed. And there were seasonal things to do, like bush-hogging the pasture, planting a garden, cleaning the chicken house.

Denied her usual activities, Sam tried to content herself with reading, conferring with her class's new teacher, and researching potential places to live.

In the evenings, she and Conner enjoyed romantic, candle-lit dinners in the dining room. Sometimes they'd cook together. Other times they'd order in. After dark, they ventured outside, hand-in-hand, for unhurried walks around the neighborhood. There was also good wine, slow dancing in the living room, and unbelievably fantastic sex. Samantha would treasure those tender moments for the rest of her life.

While Conner and Sam kept a low profile, basking in the gratification of their attraction to one another, Hal searched for the woman he still thought of as his wife. Every day that he couldn't find her, he became more frustrated.

Racking his brain, trying to think of where his wife might be, he remembered that she and Anna Robinson were once close. Someone told him Anna had moved back to town, married Max Anderson, and lived in the house she grew up in. Hal got it in his head that she was the answer to his quest. She'd know where to find his wife. He was sure of it.

On the way to Max and Anna's, he stopped at a bar he used to frequent. He'd never admit it, even to himself, but he needed a little liquid courage. Max might not take kindly to his visit, and the man could be intimidating when he wanted to be. Unfortunately, Hal drank past the false courage stage and fell headlong into foolhardy.

After walking unsteadily to his car, he drove through the corridor at the entrance to Tenacity. He hated those big old trees. Something about them gave him the heebie geebies. Maybe he'd burn them down one day.

Instead of knocking, as he should have, Hal stood on the dark sidewalk in front of Max and Anna's Mill Village home and yelled. Max opened the door, cupped a hand over his eyes, and peered into the darkness. "Who's there? I can't see you."

"Where's my wife?" Hal yelled.

"Who are you talking about?" Max asked.

"I'm talking about my damn wife. Your wife needs to tell me where she is. I can't find her."

"What's your name?"

"Hal. Hal Jacobs. Where the hell is my wife?"

"I don't know, Hal.

"You're lying."

Knowing what the excuse-for-a-man did to Samantha, Max didn't invite him to come closer. Anna stood behind the door and said, so only Max could hear, "I'm calling Scott." Glad she'd closed the curtains, she made the call and then stood on a stool to retrieve a pistol and ammunition from the locked cabinet above the refrigerator. She loaded the handgun, pointed it toward the floor, and returned to her place behind the door.

Max's eyes adjusted enough to see the dark figure gesturing wildly on the sidewalk. Hal yelled, "Some bastard took my wife and rammed his car into mine. Damn near killed me. I'll teach him. I married that woman, and she belongs to me. Nobody else. I just need to know where the hell she is."

Max didn't know whether Hal was drunk, crazy, or both, but he wished Scott would hurry. "Afraid I don't know, man."

"I think you do. How would you like it if someone took your wife?"

Max's apprehension suddenly doubled. "I wouldn't like it at all. That would be bad for everyone concerned."

Hal didn't grasp Max's implication. "Did you know my woman called the sheriff on me? Got me put in jail. But I played it cool. I was all, 'Yes, sir. Whatever you want, sir.' Those local yokels released me on good behavior. But now I can't find my damn wife."

"We haven't heard from Samantha for some time," Max told the crazed man. "I don't know where she is or what she's doing."

"Your wife knows."

Gracie opened her bedroom door and started down the stairs. "No. Go back, Gracie!" Anna whisper-yelled, motioning madly.

Max heard, glanced over his shoulder, and said in his sternest voice, "Go back to your room, Gracie. Right now. And don't come out until I say so. It's important." Hearing the dog growl, he added, "Keep Classy up there with you." Max and Anna breathed a sigh of relief when they heard her door close.

"I see you got a family in there. I thought I had a kid once, but with that whore of a wife, I couldn't know if it was mine. Had to get rid of it. She's hard headed, but I can tame her. Maybe I'll fix her so she's not so pretty. Then she won't fuck around anymore."

That was when Max and Anna realized just how deranged the man was and how dangerous their immediate situation could be.

Hal was sounding more and more agitated. "I have to find her. Tell your wife to get out here. You're the man of the house. She has to do what you say. She promised to obey you."

"Actually, we eliminated those words from our vows."

"Well, that was stupid. Get her out here anyway."

"Anna doesn't know where Samantha is," Max said, purposefully using their names. He'd noticed Hal only referred to them as wife or woman. Trying to buy time, Max asked, "Where have you looked?" He could step back and close the door, but he didn't want Hal leaving before Scott arrived. The lunatic needed to go to jail. The way he was behaving, he was bound to hurt somebody before the night was over.

"Where I've looked is none of your business. You just need to get your wife out here."

"I can't do that, Hal. She's not home."

"You're lying."

"I assure you, she can't help. I understand your dilemma. A man needs his wife. If I knew where she was, I'd tell you. But Anna and I haven't heard from her."

Hal moved closer to the house. Standing at the bottom of the steps, his face slightly illuminated by the porch light, Max saw the man's crazed expression.

"I could kill you right now," Hal said. "Then there'd be no one to protect that precious family of yours."

With effort, Max kept the anger from his voice. "What good would that do you?"

"Well let me think," the demented man said. "Your wife could help me find mine. Hey, I might marry her too. You can do that, you know. There's a guy on television with a bunch of wives. Yeah, I like that idea. Don't want your kids though."

Max was speechless.

With an evil smile on his face, Hal said, "You don't like that, do you? I don't know why I haven't thought of it before." When Max saw Hal reach behind his back, he began moving out of the doorway, but he wasn't quite fast enough. A shot rang out, and Max slumped to the floor.

"No!" Anna screamed.

Hal was standing over Max, aiming a gun at his head, when Anna appeared from behind the door. Then out of nowhere, a strong gust of wind gave the porch swing enough of a push to distract Hal. His attention was only diverted for a few seconds, but that was long enough for Anna to get into position. She stood with her feet apart, her knees slightly bent, her arms extended, and both hands on the pistol.

Seeing what she held, Hal began moving his gun upward toward her. With no hesitation, she shot him right between the eyes. When he fell onto Max, Anna shoved him out of the way, and saw that her husband was bleeding from his side.

Scott ran onto the porch, his gun drawn, and turned Hal over with a foot. The man was definitely dead.

"Good shot, my friend," he said. "How's Max?" Max opened his eyes, winced, and unsuccessfully tried to say he was all right. Anna pulled her husband's shirt out of his pants, but all she saw was blood.

"Help me move him," Scott said, after wrapping a make-shift bandage around Max's body. "I'll take him to the hospital in the patrol car." Scott and Anna attempted to lift him, but he was a big man. Max tried to stand, but his legs wouldn't cooperate. Needing help, Scott ran to the car and radioed Deputy Garret. "Get over to Max and Anna's now. Max's life depends on it."

Miss Sweet, the elderly neighbor from across the street, ran toward the house. "What happened? Did I hear gunfire?" When she reached the bottom of the steps and noticed the dead man on the porch, her hand flew to her mouth. Then she saw Max slumped in the doorway, bloodied. Shaking her hands, she cried, "No, no, not Max. What happened? Not Max."

Scott took out his phone and called his brother. "Johnny, I'm at Max and Anna's house in Mill Village. I need a hand. Can you come over right now?"

Miss Sweet was so out of control that Scott was afraid she'd have a heart attack. So he quickly escorted her back across the street and told her to go inside. She agreed to follow his instructions after he promised to keep her appraised of Max's condition.

Deputy Garret was helping his boss get Max into the squad car when the sheriff's brother arrived. After giving Scott and the deputy a hand with Max, Johnny told Anna to go with her husband. "I'll stay with your little ones. I'll call Kaye to come help. Our older kids can watch our younger ones while we're here."

"But Rex is just an infant," Anna said.

"I'm the father of six. If he wakes up, I'll take care of him."

The conflicted mother spoke rapidly. "He's breast fed, but there's formula in the cabinet for emergencies. Call Angela Bryant. If she's home, she'll come over. Use the side door and lock the front one to keep Gracie off the porch. And turn off the light in case she looks out the window. I don't want her to see the body or the blood. And thank you."

"I'll take care of everything. Just go."

When Anna sat in the back seat next to Max, he groaned, slid down, and rested his head in her lap. She checked to make sure the bandage was tightly held against the wound and willed herself to stay strong a little longer.

Once Scott reached the other side of the corridor, he turned on the cruiser's strobe lights—blue for warnings, red for emergencies. He would turn on the sirens at the first sight of another vehicle, but first, he wanted to speak to Anna.

He knew how it felt to kill a man. It's a hard cross to bear, even when a person feels there's no other choice. "When your gun went off," Scott told her, "I was attempting to line up a good shot. Sometimes, a second can mean the difference between life and death, and tonight, I'm afraid my timing was off. Thank God, yours wasn't. No one will question what happened here, Anna. I saw it all. You couldn't have handled it better, and you saved your life, as well as the lives of your family."

"What about Hal's body?" Anna asked. "Gracie shouldn't see it."

"Michael, that's Deputy Garret, will take care of it. He'll call the coroner and make sure the proper procedures are followed."

Anna stroked her husband's head, murmuring soothing words, until she noticed how still he was. "Max, Max, don't go to sleep. Stay with us. Hurry, Scott!" Wanting to scream, she told herself not to lose control. She had to stay strong.

"I'm driving as fast as I dare, but I'll call ahead so they'll be waiting for us when we get there."

Once Max was in the ER, with his wife at his side, Scott turned to Anna. "Now that you're in good hands, there are a couple of things I need to attend to. If you're all right, I'll leave and check back later."

Scott would be up much of the night. It would take hours to write his report and tie up the loose ends of the night's catastrophe. But before he could attend to any of that, he had to see Samantha.

"I'd like to come over," he said when he called. "I know it's late, but there's something you need to know, and I'd rather tell you in person."

When Scott arrived, Conner opened the door, dressed in sweatpants and a t-shirt. Samantha stood behind him, wearing a robe, slippers, and an anxious expression.

"I'm sorry to come by at this hour," Scott began, "but I thought you should know what happened as soon as possible. Let's sit." Looking sober, the sheriff sat across from Samantha and Conner, who perched expectantly on the edge of the sofa.

Seeing a red stain on Scott's clothes, Conner put his arm protectively around Sam. She noticed the spot about the same time. "Is that blood?"

"It is." He didn't beat around the bush. "Hal is dead."

"What?"

"Hal is dead," he repeated.

"He is?" Sam asked. "Are you sure?"

"I am. I saw him myself."

When Samantha buried her face in her hands, Conner pulled her close and kissed the top of her head. "Your grief is natural," he assured her. "You were married to the man.

"You don't understand," she said, with glossy eyes. "What you're seeing is relief. Does that make me a terrible person?"

"Of course not."

"The man I married," Samantha explained, "died the night he raped and beat me. I mourned him two years ago. The man who just died is a stranger—a demented, dangerous stranger. And his death is giving me back my life. Right now, I'm just relieved."

Scott leaned forward, rested his arms on his legs, and steepled his fingers. "There's more," he said, and began relating the events of the evening. "Hal got it in his mind that Anna could tell him where to find you. He was completely irrational and made some terrifying threats." When Scott got to the part about Max getting shot, Sam and Conner got to their feet as if ready to run to his aid.

"Sit back down. Please," Scott said. "There's more to tell. I feel like Max will come out of this okay. The wound is in his side where there's less chance of internal damage. Anna's being brave, keeping her feelings under control, but at some point, I expect her emotional control to break. It should, actually."

Once Sam and Conner sat back down, Scott continued. "After shooting him in the side, Hal approached Max and pointed the gun at his head. Gracie and Rex would be fatherless if Anna hadn't gotten off the first shot."

Dumbfounded, Conner asked, "Are you saying that Anna killed Hal?"

"She did. And did a right fine job of it. She held the gun correctly, lined up the sights, and squeezed the trigger. It was a perfect shot. Sorry. That must have sounded out of line. It's just that I'm so damn proud of her. If she hadn't..." Scott shook his head.

"I didn't know she could shoot," Conner said.

A hint of a smile appeared on Samantha's face. "I taught her. We used to target practice in the pasture."

"Then you taught her well," Scott said. "I was getting into position when she appeared from behind the door, but I'm afraid I wouldn't have gotten the shot off in time. It was that close. An odd thing happened, right before Anna's gun went off. The night was calm, not a leaf blowing. Then a strong wind burst out of nowhere, distracting Hal just long enough for Anna to prepare for that shot."

"She'll tell you it was magic," Samantha said. "Anna believes in that sort of thing. Did it come from the direction of the corridor?"

"I think it did."

"Anna feels a connection to that tunnel of foliage. You can add this to the list of mystical events attributed to the corridor. No matter what really happened, those old oaks will get the credit, and Tenacity will have another story to tell around the campfire."

"Hmmm," Scott said. "It could be a legitimate claim. That wind came at exactly the right time, and it may have saved Max's and Anna's lives."

Stunned by what could have happened, Samantha closed her eyes and lowered her face into her hands. Looking up, she asked, "Where are they now?"

Scott didn't have to ask who she was talking about. "At North General."

Conner thanked their friend for personally coming to explain what happened. "We'll dress and go to the hospital."

"That's good," Scott said. "Anna needs friends at her side. And it'll be good for her to see that Sam isn't devastated by Hal's death. I have no doubt she'll experience some post shooting trauma. Even people who kill in self-defense have trouble dealing with the experience. Moral beliefs conflict with the reality of the situation. Anna should see a professional, at least a few times. I'll talk to her about it."

Samantha thought about Gracie and Rex. "Who's with the kids?"

"I took Max and Anna to the hospital in the patrol car. My brother was with the kids when we left, and Anna asked him to call Angela Bryant."

Surprising Scott, Samantha walked over to him, gave him a heartfelt hug, and a kiss on the cheek. "I can never repay you for your kindness and help."

"Well, that's my job."

"No, you went beyond what your job requires. You've watched out for me through this whole ordeal, beginning two years ago, and tonight you took care of Max and Anna. I'll never forget it."

Scott was obviously uncomfortable with the praise. "I'm just glad I was around to help. Now," he said, standing up, "I need to check in with the coroner and Deputy Garret and get started on the paperwork. It's going to be a long night."

Conner shook Scott's hand, thanked him again, and walked him to the door, while Samantha gathered a few items Anna might need at the hospital.

Conner and Sam dressed quickly and then stopped at a drugstore to buy a manual breast pump for Anna. Sam was pretty sure her friend wouldn't have thought of that under the circumstances. Since there wasn't much traffic that time of night, they walked through the ER doors thirty minutes after Scott left.

When they inquired about Max, the nurse asked if they were family, and Sam admitted they weren't. "Can't you tell us something? We're friends and we're worried."

"The doctor is with him now."

"And his wife?" Conner asked.

A different nurse looked up from her paperwork. "She left me her phone number and walked outside a few minutes ago."

Illuminated by the streetlights outside the emergency room, they spotted Anna sitting on the ground beneath a tree. Her head rested on her bent knees, and she was clutching them tightly.

"Come here," Conner said, pulling a sobbing Anna off the ground. Holding her, he murmured soothing words and rubbed her back.

When Anna gained control of her emotions, she looked around and asked, "Where's Sam?"

"Right here," Samantha said, stepping forward. Anna reached out for her, and the three friends shared a group hug.

"I know you want to know what happened," Anna said, "but I can't bring myself to explain right now."

"Scott came by the apartment," Conner said, even more grateful for the sheriff's late-night visit. "He told us he saw everything. He's proud of you."

Anna's eyes jerked to Sam, searching her face. Understanding, Samantha tried to ease her friend's fears, "You did the right thing, Anna, the only thing you could. You saved your family."

"I'm sorry, Sam," Anna said, hugging her. "I didn't want to shoot him, but he was trying to kill Max."

"I understand, Anna."

Spying Conner's towering form, a couple hurried toward them. "Conner, have you seen Max?" Conner, Anna, and Samantha turned to see the worried faces of Max's parents. "There you are Anna. What's happening? Is Max all right?"

"That's the problem. I don't know. I gave a nurse my phone number so she could call when they have news, but I haven't heard a word. There was so much blood. Scott got him here quickly, but when we arrived, Max was having trouble staying conscious."

"Let's go inside," Conner suggested, "Maybe they'll know something by now."

But there was no news.

Samantha waited with Anna while Conner took Max's parents aside to relate what he knew. "Scott came by the apartment and told us what happened. I'll fill you in the best I can. Anna's not up to reliving it right now."

"Of course not," Carol said, while Alex nodded.

As Conner related the events, Max's mother couldn't suppress an occasional gasp of dismay. At one point, Anna heard her mother-in-law exclaim, "Anna?"

When a doctor finally approached, Max's friends and family moved toward him, apprehension on their faces. "Anderson family?" They all nodded. "Max is doing well." Afraid Anna's knees would give way, Conner supported her on one side, while Sam bolstered the other. Carol and Alex held one another tightly.

After giving them a moment to express their relief, the doctor conveyed the best possible news under the circumstances. "The bullet went straight through his body. The CT scan doesn't show any organ damage, but being shot is a traumatic ordeal, and he's lost a dangerous amount of blood."

"Then you're admitting him?" Anna asked.

"Yes. He needs intravenous blood transfusions and antibiotics."

"Then I'll stay, too. We need each other tonight," Anna said in a shaky voice. "We almost lost everything."

Samantha and Conner offered to spend the night with Gracie and Rex. "We'll run by the apartment," Sam said, "pick up a few things, and be there in about an hour."

Anna was grateful. "That takes a load off my mind. Gracie will be excited to have you there, and you can tell her you saw her daddy and he's going to be fine. Take our bed. Clean sheets are in the linen closet."

"What will Gracie think about that?," Sam asked. "Maybe I should sleep on the single bed in Rex's room."

"No, our room will be more comfortable. Gracie won't be concerned about your sleeping arrangements, but she will want to know about her daddy. I couldn't take the time to explain what happened. I only said Max got hurt, but I have no idea what Johnny and Angela told her. When she starts asking questions, and she will, just say that Max will tell her all about it when he gets home."

CHAPTER FOURTEEN

Lying in Max and Anna's bed that night, Samantha stared into the dark.

"I can almost hear you thinking," Conner said, "but not quite. A penny for your thoughts."

"I was just reflecting on what's happened in the last couple of months. You, Max, Anna, and so many others, have gotten caught up in my drama when it has nothing to do with you."

"But it does. We care about you, and the caring makes your concerns ours. That's just the way life is."

"But Max and Anna could have died because of me."

"No. Tonight's events were caused by a mentally ill man. Now let's get some sleep. It's been a hard day. If Rex wakes up, and I don't, shake me. I'll go feed him. I've watched Anna. I know what to do."

Conner kissed Samantha, wrapped an arm around her, and nodded off. But unsettling thoughts kept her awake. As hard as she tried to block them, memories and regrets followed the well-traveled path to her already-injured heart. Moving to the pit of her stomach, they settled there, dark and heavy.

Samantha eased out of Conners arms, left the bed, tiptoed down the hall to the living room, and opened the front door. Barefoot, wearing a white cotton

225

gown, she stepped over the bloody threshold onto the front porch. Scott's narrative of the evening's stupefying events flooded her mind as she surveyed the scene.

Staring at the second puddle of blood, Sam was all too aware that it spilled from the man who had once been her husband. She contemplated the spot where Hal took his last breath, forcing herself to dismiss the thought that she should have been with him. Samantha recognized the irony of the notion but couldn't help wishing he could have left this world in a more peaceful manner.

Reminding herself not to dwell on things that couldn't be changed, she focused on the present, and at the moment, the porch needed to be cleaned. If Gracie saw the blood, she'd ask questions, and Anna didn't need to see the stark reminder of what she'd done.

In the kitchen, Sam filled a pan with hot water and found a stiff brush. After rinsing away both puddles, she scrubbed away the blood that once flowed through her ex-husband's veins. Something about the act triggered dormant feelings, and her stoic façade gave way to regretful tears.

Samantha remembered the first few months of her marriage. Hal was different then, and she loved him. So she mourned the man he once was, or at least the one she thought he was, and grieved his wasted life.

She recalled cleaning away his blood, on another occasion, before he changed. It was a beautiful fall day on the farm. She and Hal had been working together, re-stringing a sagging barbed wire fence, when he stepped back into a coil of wire.

It was an unfortunate mistake. Steel barbs are painful and can cut a person to ribbons. "Don't move," Sam told him. "I'll get you out." When Hal used all the curse words he knew and started making up his own, it struck her as funny. Noticing his wife unsuccessfully attempting to stifle a laugh, he began laughing himself.

"Get me out of this, woman," he said, amusement tempering his frustration and pain. So Hal stood in the pasture, with steel wire cutting his legs, and laughed at himself. After Samantha freed him with wire clippers, they headed to the house where she cleaned and treated his wounds.

The man sitting in the kitchen that day, dressed in his underwear, couldn't be the same man who died on Anna's front porch. Could he? She wondered the same thing her mother had when Sam's invalid father lay in a bed at the farmhouse. Was any of the man she married still in him when he left this earth?

While Sam scrubbed, her mind manufactured questions at an alarming rate. Why had Hal's life taken such a drastic turn? What happened to change him into a monster? Could she have prevented it?

Conner found Sam in a drenched gown on her hands and knees, tears dripping from her face, her scrub brush moving in circles. He wasn't surprised. He never believed she was as indifferent to Hal's death as she pretended. For the second time that night, Conner pulled a woman into his arms to give comfort. Sitting on the porch swing, he settled Sam in his lap, held her close, and slowly, silently, rocked back and forth, his feet never leaving the floor.

After returning to bed and falling asleep, Samantha was awakened by Rex's soft cry. She was in the kitchen preparing a bottle when Gracie called out in her sleep. The only intelligible word was, "Daddy." Johnny, Johnny's wife, and Angela had all assured the child that Max was fine, but she obviously wasn't convinced. Gracie knew where her daddy was and what hospitals were for. She was worried.

Since Rex wasn't yet demanding his bottle, Sam put it in a warm pan of water and climbed the stairs leading to the pink bedroom. When she looked into the room, the sight she beheld touched her heart and brought tears to her eyes. Conner, dressed in pajama bottoms and a t-shirt, his feet bare, was sitting in the rocking chair holding Gracie and humming.

Apparently, six-year-old girls also appreciated being soothed by wonderful, handsome men. Then a truth Samantha already knew hit her hard. That lovable man was born to be somebody's daddy, and she had to let him go for that to happen.

After Gracie fell asleep in Conner's arms, he tucked her into her bed. But the next morning, Samantha and Conner turned toward one another to find the sleeping six-year-old lying between them. Smiling broadly, they eased out of bed. "I'll check on Rex," Anna whispered as Conner pulled a blanket over Gracie.

After peaking into the baby's room, Samantha found Conner in the kitchen with the refrigerator door open. "I see eggs," he said. "How about omelets?"

"Sounds wonderful. I'll fix Rex's bottle. He's stirring; so we'll hear from him any minute."

"Wait," Conner said, reaching for her. He rubbed his hands up and down her arms. "How are you feeling this morning?"

"Good. Waking up to Gracie in our bed started my day with a smile."

"No more tears?"

"No. I've had my cry. Time to buck up."

Conner leaned down and kissed her. His Sam was so brave. His Sam. That's the way he'd begun to think of her. But what would happen when she realized she no longer needed him?

Samantha changed the baby, fed him a bottle, and ate breakfast with him in her arms. When he began fussing, Conner took him from her and walked with him.

"Don't let him spit up on your clean shirt," Samantha warned. "You only brought the one. Here," she said, throwing him a clean dish towel. "Put that on your shoulder." Samantha made a mental video of Conner talking sweetly to the tiny boy. No matter what the future would bring, that memory was imprinted on her brain.

As soon as Samantha finished eating, Conner kissed the top of Rex's head and returned him to her lap. Knowing Angela was coming to help with the kids made leaving for work easier. He gave Sam a lingering kiss. "Be back as soon as I can," he said, walking out the door. The domesticity of the morning felt like an alternate reality. The problem was, he liked it, and that made him feel uneasy.

About five that evening, Max's parents pulled into the driveway with their son and daughter-in-law. Alex and Carol came prepared to stay as long as they were needed, insisting that no one should have to care for a recovering patient, an infant, and a six-year-old without help. They would stay in Max's vacated house next door, which Anna and Max kept for use as a guest house, and help however they could.

While Samantha was assuring Anna that all was well in her household, Conner returned from work. He and Sam stayed for a short visit before leaving their physically and emotionally exhausted friends to settle back into their home. Before saying good-by, just in case the injured man didn't remember her first apology, Samantha expressed her regret again. "You'll never know how sorry I am, Max, that I almost got you killed."

No matter how many times people told her it wasn't her fault, Sam seemed determined to shoulder the blame. "Oh," Sam said as they walked out the door, "I left you a casserole in the 'fridge. The baking instructions are taped to the top."

Sitting beside Conner on the drive back to his apartment, Samantha finally had a moment to consider the change in her situation. She knew all too well what ought to happen. Now that the drama with Hal was over, the logical thing to do was to stop playing house. She and Conner should return to their respective homes.

He had supported her when she'd desperately needed it, and Samantha could never convey the depth of her appreciation. But now, it was time to release him from what he must consider an overwhelming obligation. She'd monopolized him long enough. The problem was that Sam didn't want to think about a life without Conner. There was also the bothersome fact that she was madly in love with the man.

Samantha was quiet as they left Tenacity, and Conner suspected she was contemplating her future. Hal's death had totally changed her situation. His, too. They obviously wouldn't be running away together. Would they continue living under the same roof? Since the circumstances prompting the arrangement no longer existed, the answer was probably no. But surely, after all they'd been through together, Sam would still want him in her life. But in what capacity?

Conner didn't know what to wish for. He didn't want to leave Samantha. But since they were no longer in a life-or-death situation, choosing to live together indicated a degree of commitment he wasn't sure he was ready for. Unwilling to contemplate the problem any longer, he said, "How about Italian for dinner?"

"Sounds good."

Over dishes of steaming, cheesy lasagna and an inexpensive bottle of Lambrusco, they chatted about Max, Anna, and the kids, staying away from the topic utmost in their minds. Avoidance of troublesome issues, Conner realized, was a recurring theme in their relationship. It they stayed together, they'd have to work on that. Still, sensing that Sam was working something out in her head, he hesitated to push.

Back at the apartment, he urged her to watch a movie with him instead of packing. He wanted at least one more intimate night with her before she left.

Samantha eagerly agreed. No one cuddled like Conner. She loved how his long arms wrapped all the way around her. The feeling of being cherished, combined with his spicy scent and the anticipation of what would come later, made his invitation irresistible. As expected, he coaxed her into retiring early, making certain it was a night to remember

The following afternoon, Jeff drove his truck to Conner's apartment to help move Sam's things back to Tenacity. They put a few items in the Porsche, but the car clearly wasn't made for hauling. Samantha rode with Conner but didn't have much to say. He took her silence as an ominous sign.

When they arrived at the farmhouse, he carried Sam's luggage to her bedroom and looked around. He was disappointed she'd said nothing about him moving in, even though he wasn't sure that's what he wanted. He liked living at the farm and loathed the idea of parting from Samantha, but moving in would be a big step.

What he wanted, Conner told himself, wasn't important. Considering what Sam had gone through, her needs had to come first. She must still be reeling from everything that had happened. If she wanted him to leave, that's what he should do.

"There you are," Samantha said, standing at the bedroom door. "Will you come with me to say hello to the animals?"

"Of course, if you want me to."

Downstairs, Jeff came through the door with a box.

"We're going to visit the animals," Samantha said. "Join us? But then I guess you've seen more of them lately than you've wanted to."

"I haven't minded, but I'll stay here and get a drink."

"There should be soft drinks in the 'fridge," she told him. "You might even find a beer. Help yourself."

Hot Shot and Queenie celebrated Samantha's return the minute she'd stepped from the Porsche, barking, running in circles, demanding attention, but she hadn't visited the other animals.

Knowing Jeff had already fed them, Sam gave the chickens a little of their feed, took the barn cats some milk, and got pellet treats for Mazie and Maynard. Ambling toward her, the big bull and old cow almost seemed excited to see her. Conner thought maybe Sam would take the opportunity to let him know how he figured into her plans, but she said nothing, and he didn't ask.

Back at the house, they found Jeff lounging in an upholstered living room chair, drinking a Cola. After going to the kitchen for their own drinks, Conner and Samantha joined him.

"Thanks for helping me through this entire hideous situation, Jeff," Samantha said. "How are you doing these days? I've been too caught up in my own drama to ask."

Jeff spoke in his deep southern drawl. "Things are much the same for me. I feed the cows, vaccinate them, mend fences, bush hog the fields. You know, all the routine ranch tasks. I do have a pet project that's a little out of the ordinary, at least in the Deep South, but I'm proud of it. I'm building a three-sided shelter for the cows. We don't have that much severe cold around here, but when we do, this will give the cattle a break from the wind."

"I know my animals have taken a lot of your time," Samantha said. "You'll never know how much I appreciate all you and your dad have done for me."

Jeff rested one leg horizontally over the knee of the other. "I'm just glad you're safe. Can you believe what Anna did? She saved everybody."

"I can," Sam said. "She's a mama bear now. She has to protect her family. But I shudder to think what could have happened—what almost happened. If only he hadn't been looking for me..."

"It wasn't your fault, Sammy," Jeff said, "and Max and Anna are going to be fine. You're fine. Before you know it, things will be back to normal. Hey, I brought something to show you. Do you still have that picture of Pops and the baby?"

"Sure. It's right here." Sam opened the drawer of an end table, removed the picture, and handed it to Jeff. He took a photo from his wallet and held it next to Samantha's. "See. Doesn't that look like the baby in the picture with Pops?" He handed Sam both photos.

"It really does. That's curious."

"Another farmhouse mystery," Conner commented.

Samantha smiled. "That sounds like the name of a book."

"You mean this place has a mystery? Spill," Jeff said.

Samantha wiggled her fingers in front of her. "The secret letters," she said in her spookiest voice.

"Letters?"

"That's right, you haven't seen them. They're here in the drawer too. Go ahead and read them. They're interesting."

"Where did they come from?"

"Conner found them behind a locked trunk in the attic when we were getting Christmas decorations down."

Jeff took the first letter Sam handed him and stared at it, an unreadable expression on his face.

"No, wait. Give it back," Samantha said. "I'll read them aloud."

Stopping often to discuss the contents of the letters, Samantha finally finished reading.

Jeff looked pensive. "You say they were behind a locked trunk?"

"Yes. It's padlocked. One day I'm going to find a way to open it. It's not a combination lock and I have no idea where to find a key."

"Want to do it now?" Jeff asked.

"How?"

"If you have an electrical outlet in the attic, we can cut the lock off with a reciprocal saw. I have one in the truck. I used it this morning."

"All right," Sam said. "Let's do it."

Conner helped Jeff bring in his gear.

As they climbed the stairs to the attic, Jeff said, "I came up here with Pops when he built the panic room. The space has an otherworldly feel to it, starting with the staircase."

Samantha smiled. "I think so, too. I like to say it has a transcendental aura."

Jeff nodded, "Yeah. What you said." When he reached the top of the stairs, he surveyed the attic.

"Just look at the treasures left here by people who lived before we were born. Everything up here has a story."

"I'd be surprised if we found any actual treasure," Sam said.

"Maybe not. But all this," he said, gesturing, "must have been important to somebody. Otherwise, it wouldn't be here. What do you think we'll find in the locked box?"

Samantha shrugged. "Who knows. It must be something private, something the owner didn't want anyone else to see."

"Maybe it's full of old Playboys you could sell," Jeff said. "People collect them. You can buy them on eBay."

Conner chuckled. "I won't ask how you know that."

"Must have heard it somewhere," Jeff said with a straight face.

Conner made his own prediction. "I think it contains legal documents: birth certificates, marriage licenses, deeds—that kind of thing."

"That's a good guess," Samantha said. "But I think it's keepsakes of some sort: baby shoes, a wedding dress, a scrapbook."

Jeff looked skeptical. "But why would anyone lock that up?" Sam shrugged.

"If we're taking bets," Conner said. "I'm betting against the Playboys."

Jeff plugged in the saw and donned goggles, work gloves, and hearing protection. "Stand way behind me and cover your ears." It took a while, but the lock fell away, and the three friends peered into the box, looking as if they expected something to jump out.

Samantha took it upon herself to begin the exploration. The first thing she saw was a wedding veil. "I was right. Keepsakes." Samantha's cell phone rang. "It's Mama. She'll worry if I don't answer. Don't touch anything until I hang up." Sam chatted briefly, then said, "Jeff just dropped by. All right if I call you later?"

"Why didn't you tell her what we're doing?" Conner asked.

"I don't know. It just didn't feel right. When I was a kid, she was always telling me not to come up here and meddle. Of course, I did when I had a chance. I guess it still feels like I'm sneaking around."

"But now, all this belongs to you," Jeff said.

"I guess it does. So let's see what's under the veil. This is fun," she said with a mischievous grin.

Conner was pleased. After all that had happened the last few days, it was good to see her enjoying something.

Under the veil, Sam found baby clothes, a woman's printed dress, and a pair of men's blue and yellow plaid bellbottom pants.

Next, Samantha found a large manila envelope. Her eyes wide, she slowly reached in, dramatizing the moment, and then pulled out a photograph of a couple. There was also a marriage license for Viola Green and Jeremiah Johnson, dated March 1, 1921. The bride looks so young, too young for that uptight-looking fellow."

"That was often the case back then," Jeff said. "These days, he'd be arrested for being with someone that young."

"I was right, too," Conner reminded them. "A marriage license is a legal document."

"Here's another envelope," Sam said, peaking inside. "It's a stock certificate."

Conner peered over her shoulder. "What kind?"

Samantha read, "Gulf, Mobile, and Ohio Railroad Company. It probably doesn't exist anymore."

"Never heard of it," Jeff said.

Sam looked into the chest and laughed hysterically. Covering the object of her amusement, she managed to choke out a few words through her laughter. "You won't believe this." Then she held up a copy of an old *Playboy* with Marilyn Monroe on the cover.

They burst out laughing. "I was right," Jeff bragged. "And the two of you made fun of me. I bet that magazine is worth a lot of money."

Conner loved watching Sam laugh. He'd have to thank Jeff for making this attic adventure happen.

"Oh, wow," Samantha said, opening a large scrapbook. "Look at all these old pictures. And there's a program from a school play, and a graduation certificate. I could spend hours looking through this."

"See what else is in the chest," Jeff urged.

Samantha started pulling out books, some of them quite old. Among others, she found *Alice's Adventures in Wonderland*, *Charlotte's Web*, *To Kill a Mockingbird,* and *Anne of Green Gables*.

"I wonder if any of these are first editions."

"We can find out online," Conner told her. "There may be treasure here, after all."

Stacking the books behind her, Samantha pulled out a box of more recent photographs and looked at one of the pictures. When Conner saw the confused expression on her face, he took the photograph from her, looked at it without comment, and handed it to Jeff. Samantha continued pulling photos from the box and passing them to the men. No one spoke.

The box was full of photographs of Russ. There were snapshots of just him, smiling hugely at the photographer. And there were close-up shots of Russ and Martha, Samantha's mother, looking like a love-struck couple on their honeymoon.

"I don't understand," Sam said, afraid that she did. No one responded.

Near the bottom of the box, Sam found a picture of Russ rocking a baby in a chair that still sat in one of the upstairs bedrooms. And there was a photograph of Samantha, as a toddler, walking into his outstretched arms. The knockout punch was a picture of Russ and Martha in front of a Christmas tree. Could it be the one referred to in the mystery letter?

Samantha quietly gathered the photographs and put them back in the box. When she began repacking the chest, Conner broke the silence.

"We can do that later, Sam. Let's go downstairs."

Samantha and Jeff followed him into the living room, their eyebrows furrowed. Sam sat on the sofa, biting her bottom lip, staring at nothing. Jeff leaned back, in a chair facing her, a hand covering his tightly pressed lips. Conner walked briskly to the kitchen, returning with three glasses and a bottle of wine. Without asking, he poured a glass for each of them.

Uncomfortable with the tenseness of the moment, Jeff sat up straight and jested, "They could have just been very good friends."

Conner gave him an understanding smile and Samantha sighed. "I don't understand. When were the pictures taken? Was it after my real father died? But Uncle Russ was married to your mom," Samantha said, looking at Jeff.

"Yeah. There's that. If we want answers, I guess we'll have to ask our parents."

Sam wanted to deny what was happening. "I don't know if I can even talk to them. I think I'm in shock. Believe it or not, my life used to be simple. Then all hell broke loose. I thought things were getting back to normal. Now, this happens."

Jeff tried to remain levelheaded. "Let's not get upset. We'll sleep on this. Tomorrow, I'll tell Pops what we found and let you know what he says. How does that sound, Sammy?" She agreed.

After Jeff left, Conner asked, "Do you want to talk about anything?"

"No," she said, wrapping her arms around his body and looking up at him. He leaned down, placing an understanding kiss on her waiting lips.

"Since you can leave the house without worrying now, how about letting me take you to Lucky's? You need to stop thinking so hard. Let's eat some catfish, relax, and enjoy a little country music. Come on," he urged, seeing her hesitancy.

"I am hungry. And you're right. I need to stop thinking about the pictures. Okay, let's do it. Give me a minute to freshen up." Samantha wondered if Conner planned to end their living arrangement and was procrastinating. And if he wanted to stay, what was she going to do? She knew what she *should* do.

The drive to Lucky's was quiet, and the catfish house didn't hold its normal appeal. The food was good, as usual, but the mood was somber.

When the woman at the microphone began singing George Strait's "Cross My Heart," Conner held out his hand and led Sam to the dance floor. The song spoke of forever, and Samantha wished, more than anything, that she could be that for Conner. Being in his arms was heaven, and she didn't know how to let him go.

The drive back to the farmhouse was as quiet as the ride to Lucky's had been. Standing at the front door, Conner said, "May I come in. I have something to say, and I've been putting it off all day."

It was time, Sam thought. He was going to sit her down and tell her how much he enjoyed being with her, and then he was going to leave. Tears filled Samantha's eyes. She didn't think she could bear it. It was what needed to happen, but her heart felt like it would burst wide open.

Conner misinterpreted her tears. He imagined she planned to tell him to go and was sorry about hurting him. But he forged ahead. "I don't want to go home. Will you let me stay tonight?"

Sam jumped up and threw her arms around his neck. "I thought you wanted to leave," she admitted.

"I thought you were going to tell me to go," Conner said.

She knew she should, but she couldn't. "Don't you have to work tomorrow?"

"I was hoping you'd let me stay, so I put slacks and a dress shirt in the car."

"Forever the Boy Scout," she teased, "always prepared."

Pulling back to read her face, he asked, "Ready to go up?" When she nodded, Conner gathered her into his arms and began climbing the stairs.

"I'm too heavy. I can walk."

"Not this time. And you're not so heavy." The trip upstairs accomplished what he intended. When he placed her on the bed, she was smiling. Not taking his eyes away from hers, he slowly unbuttoned her blouse. A current of desire held Samantha firmly in place, and thoughts of everything but the man hovering over her tumbled into an abyss.

Conner's movements were tender and reverent. He'd never uttered the words, but that night, more than ever, his lovemaking felt like a declaration of love.

Samantha was completely enamored by the man giving her so much pleasure. Her heart told her she belonged with him, but logic said she didn't. How would she ever find the courage to do the right thing when he was such a huge part of her life?

CHAPTER FIFTEEN

At nine the next morning, unable to wait any longer, Samantha called Jeff's cell phone. "Have you talked to your dad?"

"No. I'm in the barn, feeding the horses. I'll find him as soon as I finish."

"Hurry, if you can. I've never been so anxious about anything in my whole life."

"I know what you mean. As soon as I find out something, I'll come over."

When Samantha opened the farmhouse door to Jeff, about an hour and a half later, her first words were, "What did he say?"

"Hold your horses, Sammy. You wanna let me in, first?"

"Of course. I'm sorry. Come in."

"Conner's at work?"

Samantha nodded, and then practically ran to the sofa. "Have a seat, Jeff."

He took the chair across from her. "Okay," he said, knowing Sammy was a bundle of nerves. "Pops was unloading hay when I spoke to him. I told him I was over here last night and that you, Conner, and I decided it'd be fun to go through an old trunk in the attic. When I explained what we found, he turned pale and leaned against the truck for support."

243

"Is he all right?"

"I think so. I gave him a bottle of water and offered to take him home, but he insisted on driving himself. I followed and went inside with him. Finally, he said, 'You and Sammy deserve answers, but I need some time.' He said he wasn't feeling great but would call me later. Then he went to his bedroom, and I heard him talking on the phone. I tried to listen but couldn't make out the words. So I left and came here."

Martin Lindsey had answered the phone when Russ called. "Martin. It's Russ. Sorry if I'm intruding, but I need to talk to Martha. It's important."

When she came to the phone, Russ got right to the issue. "They know, Martha."

"Who?"

"Sammy and Jeff. They've figured it out. At least some of it. They found pictures of us together."

"How? The only pictures I have of us are locked in a chest."

"Jeff said they were rummaging around in the attic, and he's perfectly capable of cutting a lock. That boy has a saw for everything. He's asking questions, and I promised him answers. I said I wasn't feeling up to it then, which was the God's truth. You could have knocked me over with a feather when he told me what they found. I had to call you before saying anything."

Suddenly feeling unsteady, Martha slid onto the nearest chair. "I haven't heard from Samantha. Heaven knows what's going through her head."

Russ sighed. "We knew this time would come. I guess
it's now. How do you want to handle it? Together?"
"I don't think so. I'd rather talk to Samantha alone,
but I can't get there until this evening. I have to take
Martin to a doctor's appointment, and I don't know
how long it'll take. He may have to have some tests
done."
"Then this evening it is. I'll tell Brian and Jeff while
you're telling Sammy. You don't know how I dread
this, Martha. Or maybe you do. But I'm about to tell
my sons I'm the biggest hypocrite they know."
"Don't beat yourself up, Russ. You've been doing
that long enough."

Jeff's phone rang while he talked to Samantha. "It's
Pops," he said, looking at the screen. He listened
briefly, thanked his father, and signed off.

"Pops called your mom," he said, his face showing
the apprehension he was trying to hide. "I guess that's
who I heard him with on the phone. She'll be here
tonight to talk to you. She can't come earlier because
your dad has a doctor's appointment. And Pops wants
to talk with Brian and me at his place this evening."

"How old is Brian now?"

"Seventeen, going on thirteen."

"I detect a little sibling rivalry."

"Nah. It's just that he's a nuisance sometimes."

"He's still pretty young," Samantha said. "If the
pictures are telling the story we think they are, this
may be hard for him. Who am I kidding? It's hard for
all of us." Samantha stood, took a few steps, then

walked back to the chair and sat down. "Why do I feel like something monumental is about to happen?"

"Maybe because it is. I gave those pictures a lot of thought last night, and there's an implication we haven't talked about."

"What do you mean?"

"I don't know why we haven't put the pieces together before. The clues are obvious. We just haven't picked up on them."

Samantha frowned, but Jeff continued. "Think about it. We both grew up with horseshoes above our bedroom doors. Martha and Pops both use that same phrase about mistakes. Your middle name is Suzanna, like my grandmother's. And you have to admit that Pops is more than just a neighbor to you—or even an uncle."

Jeff knew his words wouldn't be welcome, but Sammy needed to be prepared for the shocking announcement he believed they'd hear that night. Taking her hand and tugging her toward a mirror, he said, "You can't escape this, Sammy. Look at us. Our eyes and hair are the same color, just like Pops'. Did Martha's first husband, have hair this color?"

"No," she said, frowning. "He had dark hair and olive skin."

"And so does your mother. What color were his eyes?"

"Brown, I think."

"And your mother's?"

"Brown."

Jeff raised his eyebrows. "Think about it, Sammy. You, Pops, and I have light, curly hair and blue eyes."

She turned away, shaking her head. Jeff led her to the sofa and gave her a bottle of water he found in the refrigerator.

After taking a few sips, Samantha spoke. "If what you're imagining is true, how could they have kept that from us? Have they been lying to us all these years?"

"We don't know if it's true. And if it is, we don't know the circumstances. We do know your mom was pregnant when your father died. So if you're the result of an affair, it occurred when she was married. If she wanted to keep that under wraps, it made sense to say the baby was her husband's."

"Your dad was married, too. How could they do that?"

"It's not right," Jeff agreed, "but it happens. Where are those letters you showed me? I'd like to see them again."

"Over there," Samantha said, motioning to the coffee table where they'd left them the day before.

Jeff sat on the sofa next to Sammy, removed the first letter from the envelope and began reading aloud.

Sweetheart, staying away from you is the hardest thing I've ever done. I physically ache to be near you.

"If Pops wrote this, he had it bad for your mom."

"You don't know that he wrote it."

"No, but this sure looks like his handwriting." Jeff continued reading.

*But I'm keeping my distance
because you asked me to and because
I know it's for the best. I can't give
you and the little one what you need.
Heaven knows, I've tried.*

"The little one he refers to could be you," Jeff said. "Listen to this."

*I understand your decision. You're
doing what you have to, just like I'm
doing what I have to. But that doesn't
make this any easier. I miss you both
terribly. My heart will always be
yours.*

"The decision he's referring to could have been your mom's decision to marry Mr. Lindsey. Putting the letter down, he picked up the next one and read.

*Sweetheart, I've been staying
away, just as you asked. Now, I'm
asking for something from you. Allow
me to see the little one. Knowing
you're with another man still hurts
like hell but seeing the child from
time to time would help ease the pain.
My heart will always be yours.*

"See. The other man could be Mr. Lindsey. Pops knows he can't see your mom, but he's asking to see you." Picking up another letter, he said, "This one is longer. Wait a minute, I need something to drink."

Returning from the kitchen with a Cola, he returned to the sofa and read.

> *Sweetheart, thank you so much for letting me see the child. It was good to see you too, even for that brief time. As I knew it would, it hurt to see you with someone else, but it also relieved an ache I hadn't understood. I needed to know you were all right. I'm grateful that he came out of the house and shook my hand. I can tell he's a good man, and he promised to take care of you both. I believe him. Surprisingly, he didn't seem to resent that I came to the farmhouse. Sweetheart, the child is lovely, even if she doesn't have your dark hair and eyes. I thank God she remembered me. Getting to see her and knowing you'll let me play a part in her life is a tremendous gift. Thank you. My heart will always be yours.*

"In this one, Pops talks about meeting Mr. Lindsey and believes he'll be good to you and your mom. And he mentions that you don't have your mother's coloring."

"Stop talking as if you know these letters are from your dad to my mom. We don't know that."

249

"Okay. We don't," Jeff acquiesced. "But you have to agree they could be. Here's the last one."

> *Sweetheart, it's been a long time since I've written, and our lives have changed a lot. I still miss you like crazy, but I've accepted that you have a good life with someone else. At least I get to see you and our child on Sundays. That's made me into a regular church goer.*

"He's saying he goes to the same church as you and your mom. It fits. Listen to this.

> *Our girl is really growing up and I'm so proud of her. She's smart, sweet, beautiful, and talented. I never miss any of her performances and take every opportunity to interact with her. She'll never know how much I love her. I've been putting money aside to help with her education when the time comes. Let me know if there's anything I can do for either of you.*

"He says he saw all your performances. Sammy, Pops dragged me to every one of your piano recitals. And I always wondered why he showed up for school performances I wasn't in." Samantha looked like she was ready to stand up. "Wait," Jeff said. "There's one more thing, and it's the clincher."

*I'm enclosing a photograph of us
in front of our Christmas tree. I hope
that's all right. It would be a better
photo if my arm was longer, but it's a
reminder of a happy moment. My
heart will always be yours.*

"He's saying the picture in front of the Christmas
tree is a selfie, like the one we found. It would have
been necessary in their situation. Admit it, Sammy.
These letters could be from Pops to your mom, and
you could be the child he refers to."

"I guess it's possible."

"We should find out tonight."

"I don't think I can do this, Jeff."

"What do you mean? What is it you can't do?"

"I don't think I can sit and listen to Mom's
excuses. I'm not sure I even want to see her—or your
dad."

"Don't be that way, Sammy. They're the same
people they've always been, and no one is perfect.
Promise me you'll listen with an open mind. I'm not
happy with Pops either. I've always felt Mom was the
one who wanted the divorce, and now I see why. Pops
cheated on her and was in love with someone else.
The divorce came much later, but I guess the marriage
never recovered."

Jeff rubbed the back of his neck. "I just thought of
something. Once, when I was about fourteen, I told
my parents I was going to ask you to a dance. They
got really upset. Mom slammed the bedroom door,
and Pops sat me down and told me I shouldn't ask

you out. He said it was because you were kind of like a cousin, which I didn't really understand. Not long after that, my parents got a divorce."

Jeff saw the scared-cow look in Samantha's eyes. "This is a lot to take in," he said, "and you'll be a nervous wreck before evening. I have some fences to mend on the back side of the pasture. Come with me. It'll be better than sitting here by yourself."

"Thanks, but no thanks. This house has been sitting empty and needs a good cleaning. That'll keep me busy. Will I see you this evening?"

"I'm not sure how the night's going to turn out. Just hang on. Everything will be all right. Call me if you need something or just want to talk."

When Conner called Samantha from work, she sounded so unnerved he didn't stay late as he'd planned to. He wouldn't interfere with whatever was going to happen that night, but he'd be there if Sam needed him.

Hearing her mother's car pull into the driveway that evening, Samantha clasped Conner's arm with an iron grip. "Don't leave me."

"It's just your mother, Sam."

"I know, but don't leave."

"I'm here as long as you need me," he told her, realizing just how true that was.

Despite Samantha's distress, Conner couldn't help being amused when she pulled him to the door and said, "Open it. I can't. No, don't."

"You'll be fine, Sam," Conner said, opening the door.

Sam's life had been too full of turmoil, lately. As soon as one crisis was over, the next one appeared, and she feared her mother's visit would provoke yet another. Samantha wanted her simple life back. She didn't like drama, and she'd had enough of it to fill three lifetimes. Maybe more.

Martha hugged her daughter, but Samantha didn't hug back as warmly as usual. That was understandable, Martha told herself. Noticing the tall, blond man, who was doing his best to be unobtrusive, Sam's mother walked to him and put out her hand. "You must be Conner. Thank you for taking care of my daughter. You're a Godsend. It's been such a relief knowing you were with her."

"It was my pleasure. I'm glad to finally meet you, Mrs. Lindsey. May I take your coat?"

"Why, yes. Thank you, Conner." When he walked to the coat closet, Martha looked at her daughter and whispered, "He's gorgeous."

Samantha gestured to an overstuffed chair. "Have a seat, Mama."

"I'll wait upstairs while the two of you talk," Conner said, thinking both women looked as if they were about to face a firing squad. "Can I get anyone anything before I go up?" They both thanked him but declined.

"Don't go," Sam said. "You're part of this. Stay to hear what Mama has to say for herself."

"Your mother might not be comfortable with that."

"But you should be here," Samantha said. "You've been with me through all of this. You deserve to know the whole story."

The prospect of revealing her secret just got a little more daunting for Martha. The telling would be awkward enough without Conner present, but if her

253

daughter needed him, she could handle it. Samantha was the important one in this drama.

Conner looked at Martha, his eyes asking the question, and she nodded. As soon as he joined Samantha on the sofa, she reached for his hand, clasping it as if afraid he'd leave. Then she turned to her mother and waited.

Martha attempted to mask her apprehension. "Russ told me you found letters and photographs and want an explanation."

Samantha nodded. Martha stared at her hands, clearly uncomfortable. "I guess it's time. I've dreaded this day since before you were born, but now that it's here, I also feel a sense of relief. I'd like to tell the story from the beginning, in my own way. It'll take some time, and I'm asking you to be patient."

"However you want to do it," Samantha said, softening toward her mother a bit. Martha cleared her throat. "Let me get some water first."

"I'll get it, Mrs. Lindsey," Conner said. Martha took a sip of the proffered water and began the tale.

CHAPTER SIXTEEN

Martha

"I was eighteen when I married Thomas Dubois. He was twenty-three. Our dream was to own a farm and raise a big family; so we were thrilled when we found this place. We loved it, and the price was good. The house was a wreck, but we knew we could renovate it. It had obviously been vacant a long time, and we wondered why.

"Later, we learned that people thought it was haunted because a family died here. But we never saw any ghosts. Sometimes we'd lose things that would turn up in odd places, but we figured we'd just absent-mindedly put them there. Who knows? I did wonder about Samantha's friend Billy, but lots of children have make-believe playmates.

"Sorry. I'm babbling. That's not what you want to hear about. Three years after we married, Thomas had a stroke, and I became his caretaker. He was partially paralyzed, and his memory and cognitive ability were affected. He was bedridden, unable to feed himself or even go to the bathroom. A nurse came by twice a week with an aide who bathed him and sat him up for a while. Other than that, his care fell to me.

"Before his stroke, Thomas was a farmer. Sometimes he'd drive trucks and work on neighboring farms for extra money. When he had outside jobs, I took care of the house and farm. Tommy was a good man and a thoughtful husband, and he worked hard until he had the stroke. But once he became incapacitated, things got tough.

"A lot of what I'm going to tell you will seem like rationalization. But it's all true. I didn't have the skills to get a job that paid enough to hire a nurse and a babysitter. So I continued to farm. I tended our garden, gathered eggs from the hens, and milked our cow. I had a beef cow butchered when we needed meat, even though the butcher took half the cow as payment. We lived on what the farm provided, with the help of a welfare check.

"I had to cook and mash Thomas's food, since he couldn't chew well. I fed him, changed his clothes, including his diapers, changed his position to avoid bed sores, washed him, and made him as comfortable as possible.

"I had to make mortgage payments on the farm. We got a deal on the place but still owed quite a bit. I'd sell a cow when a payment was due, avoiding foreclosure for a while. But the herd wasn't replenishing itself fast enough, and I worried about what would happen when I had no more cattle to sell. If I lost the farm, we'd have no garden, no cows for milk, and no chickens. I didn't know how we'd survive.

"When people offered to help, I told them we were fine, but we weren't. I lost weight, and hopelessness was setting in. Then one day I heard a horse whinny and walked on the porch to see Russ tying the animal to a tree. He'd ridden over to see if I needed help."

Russ

"Jeff, Brian," Russ said to his sons. "I'm proud of you boys. I hope you know that. You're honorable, respectful, hardworking young men, just as I hoped you'd be. I couldn't be prouder." Russ combatted the emotions threatening to overcome him. Then he straightened and forged ahead. "What I have to tell you may change how you feel about me. It will expose me as the hypocrite I am. It's a long, disheartening story that I'd like to relate from the start. I hope when I've finished, you won't have lost all respect for me."

Russ explained what happened to Thomas Dubois and how Martha was carrying a load more properly borne by three or four men. "When I asked if she needed help, she thanked me for the offer, but said they were doing okay. When I asked who fed the cattle and chickens, milked the cows, and tended the garden, she explained that she did.

"I complimented her on the job she was doing but suggested it might be better if she didn't work herself to death. The farm work alone was too much for one person, and she was taking care of an invalid as well.

"I finally talked her into accepting my help, and we drove her truck into the pasture and unloaded some hay. She was too small to be doing such heavy work, but she insisted on helping. After that, Martha and I worked together most afternoons. She did everything I did, and I respected the hell out of her for that. She was the hardest working woman I've ever seen. And that includes my mother, who worked all her life.

"Together, we cleaned stalls, weeded the garden, fed the animals, herded the cows, and moved her old bull so he wouldn't kill himself servicing all the cows. Martha didn't have money for a vet; so she'd call me when one of her cows was calving. That was the one thing she admitted she couldn't do alone. Sometimes we'd stay in the barn all night delivering a calf. Then she'd be up early the next morning making breakfast for Thomas.

"With my help, Martha barely managed to make the payments on the farm. Without it, I don't know what she would have done. My intentions were good, boys. Try to remember that.

"One day I rode up to find her sitting on the front porch, her face in her hands. She was crying about her husband. Remember, Martha was only twenty and Thomas was twenty-five when he had the stroke. Very unusual. She tended to his basic needs and tried to surmise what he might want, but he couldn't express himself in any way. I still remember her unanswerable questions, 'Is there anything left of the man I married? Is he content lying in that bed all day, or is he screaming inside?' I'd wondered the same thing but didn't dare say so.

"I assured her she was doing everything anyone could. Even though she was truly worried about Thomas, her near-exhaustion must have contributed to her emotional state. So we brainstormed about what could make her life easier." Russ looked at his sons with gratitude. "Thanks for being patient, boys, for listening. I've thought about this for years but never talked about it."

Brian stood. "Mind if we stop while I get something to drink?"

"That's fine," Russ said.

Brian returned with a Cola for himself and a bottle of water for his dad. Jeff just wanted to hear the rest of the explanation.

When Brian settled back in his chair, Russ continued. "I discovered that Martha ran up and down the stairs every day to take care of her husband. There was a bedroom on the first floor, but Thomas had his stroke before he got around to remodeling it. So Martha and I went to work.

"I shaved the closet door so it would close, scraped old paint from the windowsill so it would open, and repaired the baseboards. The floors needed refinishing, but we didn't try to do that. Martha painted the trim in the room, and we both painted the wall. It looked nice. The door and trim were white, and the wall was a shade of blue-green Martha selected from paint samples I got at Cole's hardware.

"When the paint dried, I suggested we move their bed downstairs. But she chose to move twin beds from another room. When Thomas first came home from the hospital, Martha thought he'd appreciate a warm body beside him at night. But after a while, she decided he didn't care.

"If there was ever a question as to whether there was still intimacy between them, that answered it." Russ's expression turned even more somber. "Up until the day we moved him downstairs, I hadn't seen Thomas since his stroke, and I was surprised by his lack of responsiveness. He would look at us, but his eyes were vacant. Thomas and I were friends. We had helped each other with our cattle. It was hard to see him that way, a shell of his former self. Death would've been preferable to the state he was in.

"Martha was good to him. So patient. I don't think he comprehended much of anything, but in case he did, she explained that we fixed the first-floor room for him. Getting Thomas downstairs wasn't easy. Supposedly, he could move one of his feet, but I didn't see any evidence of it.

"With Martha supporting his better side and me bearing the weight of his completely paralyzed one, we managed to get him downstairs. I helped her give him a bath, put clean pajamas on him, and lay him between fresh sheets in a newly painted room. Martha beamed. It was one of her better days."

Martha

"After we moved Thomas downstairs," Martha said, continuing her story, "Russ began helping me take care of him. He helped dress my husband, put him in a chair so he could sit up a while, and several times, even helped bathe him after he soiled his diaper.

When the weather was nice, we'd put him in a chair on the porch while we worked nearby."

"Mom," Samantha said, "couldn't you have put Thomas in a nursing home?"

"Others have asked that, but I couldn't. We didn't have the money, for one thing. I was afraid I'd have to give up the farm to qualify for that much government assistance. I wouldn't do that unless there was no other choice.

"Thomas loved the farm. He'd worked so hard to get it going and renovate this old house. It was his pride and joy. He would have hated for me to give it up, and I didn't know how aware he was.

"Russ spent more and more time here. He started his ranch work early each morning so he could work here in the afternoons. Then he'd go home for supper and work in his barn after dark.

"I should have refused to accept his help. It wasn't fair for him to do so much, but he insisted. And to be perfectly honest, I was falling for him. I mean—who wouldn't? He was kind, thoughtful, hardworking, and he was young and handsome."

Martha was realizing that Conner's presence would make difficult explanations even more awkward, but he seemed to have a calming effect on her daughter. So she took a deep breath and pressed on.

"What about his wife?" Samantha asked. "Did you think about her?"

"Not really, I'm ashamed to say. I worked every minute of the day. I was so wrapped up in my own misery I didn't let my mind go there. The first time I had to face Stephanie was at church. I usually didn't go because there was no one to stay with Thomas.

"But Thomas's parents came for the weekend, and my mother-in-law insisted I go. 'Take advantage of our being here. See people,' she said. I did as I was told, wishing I could sleep instead. But once I got there, I was glad I made the effort. Everyone wanted to know how Thomas was and asked how I was holding up. I lied and told them we were fine. I don't know why it was so hard to say we were struggling, but it was.

"Outside the church, after the service, Russ came over to say hello with Stephanie on his arm. He seemed fine with the two of us being together. There was really no reason for him to be uncomfortable. I mean, nothing had happened between us. At least, nothing physical.

"He asked who was with Thomas and offered to drive to the farm and help move him so he could be in the room with everyone else. I assured him Mr. Dubois and I could handle it. We chatted a few minutes, and he asked how Thomas's mother liked his new room.

"I noticed that Stephanie, Russ's wife, seemed ill-at-ease, just standing there unable to contribute to the conversation. Unaware of her discomfort, Russ invited me to join them for lunch at Big Mama's. I was glad I had the excuse that Mother Dubois was making Sunday dinner at home."

Russ

Russ's boys listened, seeming not to judge, until Brian asked, "How did Mom feel about you spending

262

so much time with Mrs. Lindsey? But I guess she was Mrs. Dubois at the time."

Russ sighed. "You hit on my biggest regret. Your mother didn't complain until we saw Martha at church one Sunday. Staying home with Thomas normally kept her from attending services, but that day she took advantage of her in-laws being in town and got out of the house.

"Stephanie elbowed me for staring at Martha during the sermon. I was guilty as charged. She looked so pretty in her printed summer dress. Martha wasn't polished like your mother. She didn't go to the beauty shop, get her nails done, get facials, or whatever women do to make themselves beautiful. But she was pretty. She had this unique blend of sweetness and raw determination.

"I spoke to Martha after the service, and your mother didn't like it. The three of us stood together, and Stephanie heard every word of the conversation, but later, she complained about feeling like an outsider.

"Then I discovered she'd been harboring resentment on that front for some time. One day, when she was in the hardware store, Mike Cole asked if she was happy with the color she picked for our bedroom. Having no idea what he was talking about, she disguised her confusion with a nod. Later, she accused me of hiding things from her.

"When I told her it was for Thomas's room, she wanted to know why I hadn't shared that with her. I couldn't tell her why because I didn't know. I explained, again, that Thomas and Martha needed my help and assured her nothing improper was going on.

I can't deny being attracted to Martha, but I was confident I wouldn't let anything happen.

"It wasn't long until that line got blurred. We were working in the barn when Martha got something in her eye. I only meant to help, but before I knew what was happening, I'd kissed her. It was just a little kiss, and I told myself there was no harm in it. I'm telling you this, boys, to let you know how things can get started."

Brian snorted. "We've had the birds and bees talk. We know how things get started."

Jeff finally spoke. "I don't think we need to hear this."

"Hold on," Russ said. "I'm not taking that line of thought any further. I'm just saying, unless you intend for something to end a certain way, don't take that first step. Every step after that gets easier and easier.

"When I got home that evening, your mother had a question for me. After pointing out it could take as many as twenty-five years to pay off the Dubois's mortgage, she asked if I planned to run the farm, as well as the ranch, that entire length of time. Your mother felt bad for Martha, but said it wasn't my responsibility to pick up the slack and Martha shouldn't expect me to.

"She was right, of course, about it all. But when she tried to make me look at the situation objectively, I told her she was being uncharitable, that Martha relied on me to help her and Thomas. She accused me of having feelings for Martha. I couldn't deny it. Instead, I told her she had nothing to worry about. And I believed it. I convinced myself the kiss meant nothing.

"I'll tell you something else I've discovered through experience," Russ said. "Women know things. They have this creepy extra sense. They can look at a man and tell what he's thinking before he even knows he's thinking it."

"Dad," Jeff said seriously. "Are you ever going to get to the point?"

"I just want you to understand what happened," Russ said. "Bear with me a little longer. Now, I realize I was more than a little infatuated with Martha. But I wouldn't admit it—even to myself.

"That night, sleep came slowly. I kept replaying that kiss. But I was convinced it wouldn't happen again, that I could keep things under control. I looked forward to seeing Martha every day but told myself it was only because I enjoyed her company.

"Remember what I told you about a woman's sixth sense? The day after your mother confronted me, Martha asked how Stephanie felt about me spending so much time at the farm. When she saw your mother at church, Martha got the feeling your mom wasn't happy about my visits. That concerned her. She didn't want to cause problems in my marriage. I couldn't imagine how she'd manage without me, so I lied and told her everything was fine."

"But that wasn't the only reason you kept helping, was it?" Jeff accused. "How long did you split your time between our ranch and the Dubois farm?"

"At that point, it had been about a year. And you're right. I had another reason. I couldn't imagine not seeing Martha every day."

"Humph," Jeff said. "I'd say Mom was pretty patient with you."

"Yeah," Russ said, looking at the floor. He was quiet for a few minutes, remembering how drawn he'd been to Martha. And his thoughts drifted to that day long ago when everything changed.

It was a cool fall day when Russ drove over in his truck and discovered that Martha wasn't in the farmhouse.
After checking to make sure Thomas was all right, he strode to the barn and found the woman he was aching to see. He watched her slender body move with determination as she raked the clean, dry hay over the barn floor.

When Martha sensed he was there, she turned and gave him a big, welcoming smile. Her dark hair fell around her face, which was flushed from exertion, and Russ wanted her in every way.

He wanted to spend all his time with Martha: work with her, laugh with her, make love to her, and wake up with her every morning. If only they'd met before they married other people. Russ wanted what he couldn't have, and refusing to act on his impulses was bordering on tortuous.

Martha

"Mama," Samantha said, "would you like a cup of tea or coffee?"

Martha surprised her daughter by saying, "I could use something stronger."

"I have a bottle of red wine in the pantry," Sam offered.

"Or I could make you a Vodka tonic," Conner chimed in.

Martha nodded "Vodka tonic sounds perfect."

While Samantha and Conner were in the kitchen, Martha's mind wandered to a crisp fall day she'd always remember. She was raking hay in the barn when Russ walked in and took the rake from her. When his work-worn hand accidentally touched hers, her heart raced. She couldn't move.

Martha watched Russ's muscles ripple as he distributed hay on the barn floor. His days were filled with hard, physical work, and his body showed it. Everything about him was manly—his square jaw, his broad shoulders, his muscular forearms, sprinkled with reddish hair. Even the large veins in his hands were sexy to Martha.

She loved everything about him, especially the way he treated others with respect, no matter their circumstances, and the kind and gentle manner he used with Thomas. She could never repay him for all he did for her.

Martha couldn't take her eyes off her handsome neighbor. She just stood in the middle of the barn, staring, aching to feel his arms around her, grieving for what she couldn't have. Russ felt her gaze and turned. Martha hadn't moved. She was shivering, and tears were running down her pretty face.

"What's wrong?"

Unwilling to explain, she said nothing. Russ removed his jacket, wrapped it around her shoulders, and held it together in front.

Martha covered his hands with hers. They stood like that until she looked up with raw hunger in her eyes. Russ kissed her, intending it to be swift and tender like their first kiss. And it was, until his self-control crumbled, and he kissed her again. The second kiss was filled with desire, sending the indisputable message that he wanted more.

When Martha softened in his arms, Russ lowered her to the newly strewn hay, his lips never leaving hers. His hands roamed her body until his last remnant of restraint crumbled, and he made love to her as he'd wanted to for months.

Eventually, Russ rolled onto his back and stared up at the barn rafters, contemplating the gravity of what they'd done. Martha read his thoughts and kissed him. "Don't regret it," she said. "I don't."

"We didn't use protection," he said. "Are you on the pill?"

"You're a little late with that question, aren't you? And no, I'm not. But I think the timing is all right. She made a mental note to buy condoms the next time she was in Clarkston, hoping there'd be an opportunity to use them. Being with Russ made her feel like a woman again, and he was the only good thing in her life.

Martha sipped her drink before she admitted to her daughter that she'd had an affair with Russ Windom while they were both married. "I didn't think about how our actions might affect Stephanie or anyone else. I was overworked, obsessed with Russ, and feeling more than a little sorry for myself.

"I no longer thought of Thomas as my husband; so I didn't feel I was betraying him. By that time, I was convinced that very little, if any, of him remained. I cared for his body out of human kindness and because a man I loved once occupied it.

"I felt like Russ was my husband. I knew he wasn't. That's just the way it felt. We worked together, laughed together, and eventually made love together.

"Time went by, and I began to wonder about Russ's life with Stephanie. I became jealous of her time with him. When Christmas came around, Russ brought a small tree for Thomas's room and a large one for the living room. We played Christmas music and decorated the trees together. I couldn't help wondering if he decorated one with Stephanie. You probably found the picture we took in front of our tree that year.

"After the holidays, Thomas's parents came for another weekend visit. Again, his mother insisted I take the opportunity to attend church. Thinking Russ would be there, I took extra care getting ready. He usually saw me in work clothes, and I wanted to look pretty for him.

"I slipped into the sanctuary at the last minute. Russ and Stephanie were a few pews in front of me. He looked so tall, strong, and handsome.

"Again, I wondered what kind of relationship he and Stephanie had. I told myself his marriage was troubled, strained. I even imagined them sleeping in separate bedrooms. After all, if they loved each other, Russ wouldn't be with me.

"Then the choir director asked everyone to stand for a song, and my world caved in. When Stephanie stood, she turned slightly to the side, and my heart stopped. She was several months pregnant. Thankfully, I managed not to cry until I got to the truck. Then I sobbed. My heart was broken. Of course, I knew Russ was married, but most of the time, I managed to push it to the back of my mind, pretend it wasn't so.

"I was only happy when I was with him, and when that wasn't possible, I imagined I was his wife, waiting for him to come in from the fields. As unattainable as that dream was, it was the one I disappeared into when life threatened to overwhelm me. But the sight of Russ with his pregnant wife ripped that dream into pieces and punched me in the gut.

"That night, Russ knocked on my door. He'd heard I left church early and guessed why. I cried and asked why he hadn't told me. He said he felt like he'd cheated on me and couldn't find the words. He told me she was pregnant before we were intimate, but he hadn't known. Stephanie was obviously the wronged party, but it didn't feel that way to me—or to Russ."

Russ

"I never thought I was the kind of man who would cheat on his wife," Russ told his sons. "When I married your mother, I intended to love her forever.

Only her. But I put myself in a tempting situation and refused to withdraw from it.

"Martha was young and pretty, and we were alone almost every day. She desperately needed someone to lean on, and I relished her admiration and appreciation. It was a recipe for disaster, but I was sure I could control myself. I didn't. And we didn't stop with one act of infidelity, not by a long shot."

"You can stop there, Pops," Jeff said. "We don't want to hear about your sex life."

Russ stood, rubbing the back of his neck. He wanted to pace but sat down to face his boys. "I'm ashamed to say the affair continued. I even bought two heart-shaped boxes of chocolates on Valentine's Day. Remembering what happened with Mike Cole and the paint samples from his hardware store, I bought Stephanie's chocolates from O'Neal's Drugstore, and Martha's from a place in Clarkston. I knew I was playing with fire, but I couldn't let Martha go, and Stephanie was carrying Jeff. They both depended on me.

"When Jeff was born, Martha was the first person I phoned. She congratulated me and was relieved everyone was all right. We'd reached a new stage in our relationship. We accepted our situation.

"Do you think you truly loved her," Jeff asked, "or was it mostly a sexual thing?"

"I admired her. Martha was strong, willing to work herself into the grave to keep that farm, and she was loyal to Thomas. And yes, I loved her." Then he surprised his boys by saying, "I always will."

When Jeff recovered from his dad's last comment, he asked, "How can you say she was loyal to Thomas when she cheated on him?"

"Technically, she did. But Thomas was gone long before he died."

"I guess divorce was out of the question," Brian said.

"Yes. For one thing, Martha would never have left Thomas. He needed her. And I wasn't willing to lose Jeff. And as disingenuous as it sounds, I didn't want to hurt your mother." Russ held up both hands. "I know how that sounds, but it's true. I never wanted to hurt her."

"You've kept this secret for years. Why are you telling us now?" Brian asked.

"I probably wouldn't be if Jeff and Sammy hadn't found pictures of Martha and me," Russ said. "They left us no choice."

"I'm surprised, Pops," Brian said. "This is a lot to take in. Especially after all the talks you've given us about treating women with respect." Almost shyly, he said, "You didn't treat Mom with respect, did you?"

"No, I didn't, and I have no excuse."

"Well," Brian said, "I think I also speak for Jeff when I say I hate that you hurt Mom, but you're our Pops. And I think it's the law that we have to love you." Then he turned to Jeff, "That's the law, isn't it?"

Jeff shook his head at his lovable younger brother. "Yeah, dufus, I think it's the law."

Brian stood, ready for the awkward testimony to end so he could join his friends. There was a party he wanted to attend.

"I'm not finished, Brian. You should sit back down." Giving his sons an apologetic glance, Russ added, "there's more to the story."

Brian's eyes got big. "Don't tell me there was another woman."

"Heaven forbid," Russ said. "Just sit back down, please."

Martha

Martha continued her explanation. "After Jeff was born, Stephanie resented Russ's time with me more than ever. Because she wasn't fond of small-town life, Russ knew she'd leave with Jeff if he divorced her. He didn't want to lose his son; so he stopped coming to the farm every day. When he didn't come, he sent one of his ranch hands to help with the chores. I understood."

Looking at her daughter apologetically, Martha said, "Now comes the hardest part of this conversation." She went to the kitchen for water, stalling for time. Sitting back down, she crossed her hands in her lap, raised her chin and began relating a secret she'd kept since before Samantha was born.

"On one of Russ's visits to the farm," Martha said, "he noticed a change in my body and asked if I was keeping something from him. I told him Thomas and I were expecting a baby, that on one of his good days, we made it happen. I said we'd always wanted a child, and this was our way of remembering the way things used to be.

"But he knew Thomas never had good days. He put his head in his hands and said, 'God help me. What

273

have I done?' But he loved you, Samantha. You've always been his Sammy."

Samantha knew it was possible she was Russ Windom's child, but to hear her suspicion verified was monumental—life changing. She'd always thought of Thomas Dubois as her biological dad, but since he died before she was born, she had no real attachment to him.

As far as Samantha was concerned, Martin was her dad, and she loved him. They had a strong father-daughter relationship despite the lack of a biological connection. He'd been her anchor as long as she could remember, and the discovery that Russ was her father was more than a little unsettling.

Martha told Samantha and Conner about Thomas's death. "When I woke one morning to find his lifeless body, I felt a tremendous sense of loss as well as relief. I was very pregnant at his funeral. Russ stood in line and expressed his condolences like everyone else. Stephanie wasn't with him. He came over that night, after everyone else left, and promised he'd take care of me. And he did. No one could have worked harder.

"You were born in the farmhouse, and Russ was here to welcome you into the world. We decided, that when the time came, I'd call and tell him I needed help with a calf. After Doc delivered you, Russ cut the cord, cleaned you up, wrapped you in a blanket, and handed you to me. We both cried. To have a tiny person that came from our love was amazing. You may have been born out of wedlock, but you were definitely conceived in love."

"So Doc has known all along," Samantha said.

Martha nodded. "Russ spent a lot of time with you until you were almost three. He was there when you took your first steps and when you began to talk."

"How did he manage to spend so much time here while he was still married?"

"Sometimes Stephanie would take Jeff and stay with her sister in Memphis for weeks at a time. When that happened, Russ would ride his horse through the pasture every afternoon, put her in the barn, and stay overnight. Then he'd ride home the next morning before the ranch hands arrived. He used to sing to you and rock you to sleep. He even got up with you through the night."

Samantha shifted positions. "So Uncle Russ was like a real dad to me until I was almost three?"

"He was."

"What happened after that?"

Martha's hand flew to her chest. "I did the hardest thing I've ever done in my life, but I did it out of love for Russ. He was killing himself taking care of two families, his ranch, and my farm. He was pulled every direction, wasn't getting enough sleep, and was always condemning himself for not doing enough. That pace of life was impossible to sustain.

"My parents kept trying to fix me up with Martin, who was a friend of theirs. I went out with him a few times when I visited them, and he proposed what amounted to a deal. I would be his wife and give him a farm, and he'd provide for us and be a dad to you.

"I know this is hard for you to hear, but it broke my heart to marry him, and Russ was crushed. But Russ couldn't keep going the way he was. He was exhausted all the time. He tried not to show it, but I knew.

"Russ has been the best dad he could possibly be in our complicated situation. When he discovered you liked the old piano the previous owners left, he paid for you to take lessons. And when his mom died, he made sure you got her baby grand. He also paid for much of your college.

"I know you remember him taking you and Jeff riding. I used to fix picnic lunches for the three of you when he took you swimming in that pretty swimming hole on his property."

Samantha remembered. "Jeff always liked to dunk me. One time he held me under so long Uncle Russ jumped in, clothes and all, to rescue me. Jeff's punishment was to get out of the water and sit on the bank. He was so mad at me. On the way back he repeated everything I said."

Martha smiled. "Every horse you ever had was a gift from Russ. It began with your pony, Pokey. His name was an indication of the pace he kept. I don't remember all the other names, but as your riding ability improved, another horse appeared. We fed them, but Russ gave them the required shots, trimmed their hooves, and brushed them until you were old enough to do it yourself."

"Even after he taught me, he'd come over to help," Samantha remembered.

"He enjoyed spending time with you. And he stuffed pillows in a Santa suit and brought you a gift every Christmas Eve."

"It was always something really nice," Sam remembered, "and he'd say it was from Santa. But I knew it was from him. He coached my softball team for years, like any other dad might do. That's really sad, Mama."

"It is. Russ was the best, most generous dad he could possibly be under the circumstances. Martin knew about him before we married and was understanding. To my knowledge, he was never jealous. We didn't have that kind of relationship. I married him for practical reasons, and he understood that."

"What do I do with all this, Mama? I don't know how to act around Uncle Russ, or Daddy, or even you."

Conner had been sitting quietly beside Samantha, holding her hand, offering support, listening with interest. He felt for Russ. Having his daughter right under his nose, unable to reveal their relationship, must have been agonizing.

Conner put his arm around Sam, pulling her close. "Well," he said, hoping to break the tension, "at least I can stop worrying that Jeff will make a move on you." It got a smile out of everyone.

"That's right," Sam realized. "I have two brothers. This is mind boggling. How do I make my brain accept the re-arrangement of so many relationships? Or do we pretend nothing has changed?"

Martha shrugged. "We'll have to discuss it. Russ asked me to call when we finish talking so he can come over."

When Sam began shaking her head, Conner said, "You'll have to deal with the awkwardness at some point. You might as well do it in the privacy of your home. And if it's now, you'll have less time to stress over it."

Martha picked up her phone and called Russ. Needing something to do, Samantha went to the kitchen and put slices of refrigerator cookies in the oven. Conner joined her.

"What should I do when Uncle Russ arrives?" she wondered aloud. "I don't even know what to call him."

CHAPTER SEVENTEEN

Samantha's anxiety peaked when she heard Russ's truck tires on the gravel.

"Don't hide in the kitchen," Martha said. "Come back in here and face Russ. And don't you hurt him. He loves you. He's loved you your whole life." Samantha did as her mother asked and watched Martha meet Russ at the door. He side-hugged her and kissed her on the cheek.

She blushed, Samantha screamed in her head. Had the two of them carried a torch for one another for over twenty years? Surely not. She would have known, wouldn't she?

Knowing he might be setting himself up for serious disappointment, Russ looked at his daughter, opened his arms, and hoped for the best. Samantha surprised herself by rushing into them.

Martha, Samantha, and Russ all cried. It was an intense, emotional scene. But it was Russ's reaction that caused Conner to blink back tears. The tough, big-hearted rancher, who'd never been free to openly love his daughter, physically shook with the effort to rein in his emotions. When Jeff and his brother, Brian, entered the room, everyone looked up.

"What's going on?" the younger boy asked. "Did somebody die?"

Jeff smacked him on the head. "Always the comedian."

But the comment gave everyone a well-needed chuckle. Wiping his eyes, Russ suggested they all sit. He took one of the upholstered chairs near Martha. Jeff sat on the sofa with Samantha and Conner, and Brian borrowed a chair from the dining room.

Conner smelled the aroma escaping from the forgotten oven, hurried to the kitchen, and returned with a plate of rescued cookies. After setting it on the coffee table, he took his seat next to Sam, and like everyone else, wondered what would happen next. Martha and Russ communicated with a look.

"Okay, I guess I'll get the ball rolling," Russ said, shifting in his chair. "Now that the gang's all here, we have a decision to make. The secret is in the open, as far as this group is concerned, but what about everyone else? What do we do with this information? Are we concerned enough about public opinion to keep it to ourselves? If so, we'll go on as usual. Nothing will change as far as the rest of the world is concerned.

"If we go public, we'll be the subject of gossip for a while—maybe our entire lives. Sammy, when you walk into Big Mama's, or even church, people will turn and whisper. Martha, there are people who'll enjoy feeling superior to you, because you broke one of society's rules and they didn't.

"I'll probably fare better than you simply because I'm a man. It's wrong, but that's the way it often is. If we make the decision to blow this secret open, we have to be ready for the fallout. This sort of thing isn't judged as harshly as it once was, but it's still gossip of the highest order. People won't forget. Your thoughts?" he said, looking around the room.

"I think I could handle it being in the open," Martha said, knowing that's what Russ wanted. "At least I don't live here anymore."

"But gossip doesn't honor county lines," Jeff reminded her.

"Mama, what about Daddy?" Samantha asked. "How would he feel about everyone knowing?"

"He'd be okay with it. He's known all along, and it happened before we married. It would have little effect on him."

"I have a question," Samantha said. "If you and Daddy are willing to be open about this now, why didn't you tell me before?"

"That's a fair question. At first, I was embarrassed to tell anyone, and Russ was married. Then, after waiting so long, I was afraid of how you'd react."

When Samantha only nodded, Russ asked, "Boys, what are you thinking?"

Brian spoke up. "The guys at school would hassle me, but I could take it."

Russ looked at Jeff, eyebrows raised. "Whatever," Jeff said. "I don't think it would have much impact on me, except people would know I have a sister," he said, winking at Samantha.

"Sammy, any thoughts?" Russ asked.

"Too many. I'm angry with you and Mama for keeping me in the dark all this time. We've lived a lie my whole life, and that doesn't give me a good feeling. Now that I know, it would be hard to pretend I don't. That knowledge changes things. It changes me. I don't know how the two of you did it all these years."

Russ leaned toward Samantha, gazing at her intently, fearing he was jumping to the wrong conclusion. "So you think we should tell people?"

"I don't know what to think."

"Russ," Martha said, looking at the father of her only child, "we haven't heard your feelings on the matter."

He shook his head. "I don't want to influence you. This decision is yours and Sammy's. Just remember, lettin' a cat out of a bag is a lot easier than puttin' it back in."

Samantha took a deep breath, closed her eyes, and said, "As far as I'm concerned, I guess we can tell people, but it's really up to Mama. I don't relish being the subject of gossip, but at least we wouldn't be living a lie. I vote yes if Mama does."

Martha could hardly believe what she was about to say. "All right. Let's do it."

Russ had the biggest smile on his face any of them had ever seen. "Since you've agreed to share our secret," he said, looking at Martha and then Sammy, "I'll tell you how I feel." He paused for dramatic effect. "I'm over the moon. Claiming Sammy as my daughter is a dream I thought would never come true."

"Congratulations, Pops," Brian said, "It's a girl." Jeff got up off the sofa just so he could knock Brian on the head again.

"Don't give him brain damage," Samantha said.

"Listen to our sister," Brian told Jeff.

"You know, Sammy," Russ said, "I was there when you were born."

"Mama told me. She said you cut the cord."

"I did. We were so happy, even though we knew the future would be difficult. Not telling you the truth has been hard, but I've watched you grow up, and I'm proud of the woman you've become."

"Before we stray too far from the subject of the big revelation," Conner said, "I'd like to suggest something. That is, if you don't mind." When everyone nodded their approval, he continued.

"I think you'd do well to agree on some unambiguous answers to questions that are sure to be asked.

"Un am... what?" Brian said.

"Unambiguous. Clear, precise," Conner explained.

"Conner can't help it," Sam teased. "Private school, you know." She said it as if it were something to be embarrassed about.

"Ohh," Brian said, as if that explained a shameful problem.

Conner cut his eyes sideways toward Samantha and grinned. "Back to what I was saying. You might want to agree on some standard answers."

"Thanks for dumbing it down," Brian said.

Jeff glared at him. "Will you shut up, Brian?"

Everyone grinned and Russ shook his head. "Please continue, Conner."

"What I'm trying to say is this. Well thought-out answers lessen the chance your words will be misstated or misunderstood. People are going to analyze what you say and form their own theories. But if everyone hears the same thing, there won't be as much to discuss. The gossip becomes less tantalizing."

"That's insightful," Russ said. "It makes sense."

"There's a correlation to a cross examination in front of a jury," Conner further explained. "On the stand, off the cuff answers invite distortions. A shrewd attorney can take a witness's careless words and manipulate them into a potentially damaging scenario. That's why attorneys help clients prepare their testimony."

"Okay," Russ said, "Let's think of some questions people might ask."

"For one thing," Conner said, "they'll want to know why you finally decided to admit the truth."

Martha spoke up. "Can't we simply say we thought it was time."

"And we felt the kids were old enough to understand," Russ added.

"That's good," Conner said. "And that's really all you need to say. Don't elaborate. Repeat what you just told me and then stop. You're not obligated to say anything else."

"What if they ask for details?" Brian asked. "I mean personal things."

"It's hard to believe anyone would be so bold," Conner said, "but people often surprise you. There are very few questions that you, Jeff, and Sam need to answer. If someone asks a personal question, just shrug. It's information you're not privy to."

"People will ask how we feel about it," Samantha said.

Conner nodded. "You're right. Each of you needs to think about that. Just make sure that what you say can't be easily misconstrued. Decide on your answer and don't let anyone goad you into saying more. I didn't mean to take the floor. You get the idea."

"Thanks, Conner," Russ said. "Great advice. I wouldn't have thought of that." Everyone nodded, murmuring their appreciation.

Jeff finally entered the conversation, "When do we do this?"

"I need more time," Samantha said. "I can't tell people how I feel about something when I'm not sure myself."

"Okay, we'll wait until everyone is ready," Russ said. "We'll get together again to make sure we're all on the same page."

"How will we go about telling it? Samantha asked.

"Shit. I mean shoot," Brian said. "In Tenacity, you just tell a few people, and it'll be all over town in hours."

Martha's phone rang. "I need to get this." With a sober look on her face, she listened. "I'll be right there." She ended the call, picked up her purse, and walked briskly to the closet for her coat.

Russ jumped up to help. "Is everything all right?" But he knew it wasn't. He'd seen that look on her face before. It was the indomitable one she got when facing a crisis. Russ stepped in front of her, wrapping his hands around her upper arms. "Is Martin all right?"

"No. He's had another attack." Martha turned to look at Samantha. "I'm heading to the emergency room."

"Give me your keys," Russ said.

"No. I'm going to the hospital."

"I know. I'm driving you."

Surprising Samantha, her mother did as he said. Russ threw his keys to Jeff. "Follow us in my truck. I'll need a ride home."

"Wait," Samantha said. "I'm coming to."

Conner took his keys from his pocket and grasped Sam's hand. "We'll meet them there."

Inside the hospital, Conner, Russ, Jeff, and Brian sat in the emergency ward waiting room, while Martha and Samantha hurried to Martin's side.

Looking up when his family walked in, he held out a hand, which Samantha eagerly took. "Daddy," she said, tears filling her eyes. He looked so much smaller lying in the hospital bed with tubes connecting his body to beeping machines.

"It's good to see you, baby girl. It's been a while. But now that all that terrible business with Hal is over, we can see more of one another."

"I've missed you, Daddy. You need to stop having these attacks. They're not good for you."

Martin smiled. "No joke." Looking at Martha, he said, "How did you get here so fast?"

"We left as soon as the nurse called. Conner drove Samantha, and Russ drove me. They were afraid we'd be too upset to drive. They're in the waiting room now, with Jeff and Brian."

"Did you get everything out in the open before you left?" he asked Martha.

"We did. The kids took it like champs."

"Good."

"Samantha," Martin said, "will you go out to the waiting room and ask Russ to come in. I have something to say to him. On second thought, tell them all to come in. We don't have secrets anymore. Your mother and I will have a few minutes alone while you're gone."

When Samantha and the men entered Martin's room in the emergency ward, Martin reached toward Russ. Clasping the man's hand in both of his, Russ said, "Hello friend. They said you were sick. You don't look so bad."

"I'm okay, but I have something to say to you, Russ, and I want all these good people to hear. It's going to sound like I'm planning on dying in the next few minutes, but I have every intention of going home. Still, I know I might not be in this world a whole lot longer, and this is an opportunity that may not present itself again.

"I want to thank you, Russ, in front of this whole group, for trusting me with Martha and Samantha." He stopped to cough. "You loved them before I came into the picture. Our marriage hurt you. I could see it in your eyes every time you looked at them. It had to be hard to bear. And every time Samantha called me Daddy, you must have been crushed. To add insult to injury, I adopted her."

Martin stopped to catch his breath. "I knew when I married Martha that she loved you. She told me she did. The main reason she married me was to keep you from killing yourself, trying to be everything to everyone. In spite of how you felt, you never tried to interfere in our marriage, even after your divorce. I thank you for that, and I admire you for being such an honorable man." Martin coughed, hesitating before continuing.

"I see your boys over there. They're good boys. You did a fine job raising them. Whenever they helped me on the farm, they worked hard and were always polite. You must be proud of them."

"I am," Russ said. "I need to thank you too. Knowing you treated Martha and Sammy with kindness and love helped me find peace with our situation. And you allowed me to remain in Sammy's life. You'll never know how grateful I am for that."

"It was the one thing," Martin said, "I could give you. Now, there's something I want to say to Martha, and I want everyone to hear." He turned to her and held her hand. "When I'm gone, dear, don't waste your life mourning me. I want you to love again. You're still a young woman, but time sprints by. Grab happiness while you can. And don't listen to anyone who says you didn't mourn long enough. Just get on with life."

"Daddy, stop talking like you're dying."

"I'm just getting a few things off my chest. I have some words for you too, Samantha. You've been the light of my life. I'm honored to have been one of your fathers. You know, you really had three parents. It's just that one of them was a silent partner. Russ was an active participant in your upbringing. Your mama and I always considered his opinions where you were concerned.

"I know you must feel at least a little betrayed," Martin said. "We lied to you for years, but I hope you can forgive us. Your parents, the three of us, did the best we could. And we all love you. I love you. And my wish for you is that one day you'll find the happiness you and your mother have given me."

Looking at the tall, blond man standing in the background, he said, "Conner, I recognize you from Samantha's description. I can't thank you enough for taking care of our girl during this latest ordeal. I don't know what we would have done without you. I appreciate all you've done. We all do. Well, I think that about covers it, and I'm talked out."

Russ, Jeff, and Brian said good-by and left for home. On his way out, Russ glanced back to see Martha and Samantha at Martin's bedside. He'd accepted them as a family years ago, but seeing them together still hurt, even after so much time had passed.

Conner and Samantha stayed at the hospital until Martin was settled in a room for overnight observation. Martha made a quick trip home for a few items so she could stay with her husband. "Sleep at the house tonight," she suggested to Samantha and Conner.

"Thanks, but we'll go back to Tenacity. Conner has to work tomorrow."

The following morning, after Conner left the farmhouse, Samantha reveled in accomplishing mundane, unexciting tasks. She washed the breakfast dishes, fed the animals, and made a few phone calls. Now that she was no longer in danger and the family secret was out in the open, at least to those concerned, she felt an enormous sense of relief. Maybe her life was getting back to some semblance of normal.

The doorbell rang, and for a fraction of a second she was filled with apprehension. Hal did that to her. He left her with a feeling of dread to remember him by. It was fleeting now, but still there, and she wondered if it would ever leave.

"Hi, Sammy," Russ said when she opened the door. "I came by to see if you're all right."

"I'm fine."

"May I come in?"

"Okay."

"Conner's not here?"

"He's at work."

"I like that boy."

"Me, too."

"Got any coffee?"

"I can make some," Samantha said, finding it hard to meet his eyes.

Russ followed her to the kitchen, sat down at the table, and watched his daughter. They continued their polite, succinct conversation until Sam set a hot cup of coffee in front of Russ.

After taking a sip, he asked, "What do you plan to do with yourself now that you're a free woman?"

"I've spoken with Principal Carter, and I'm getting my job back. Turns out the substitute didn't really want a full-time position."

"It'll be good for you to get back to your life." Then his expression turned grave, and he sounded troubled. "There's something I want to ask you."

"Okay," she said, dreading what he might have to say.

"How do you feel about last night's revelation?"

"I'm not sure how to feel." Then she blurted out the question foremost in her mind. "Do you still love my mother?"

"No beating around the bush, I see. Do I love your mother?" he repeated, stalling. Russ picked up his cup, took another drink, and hesitated a moment longer. Then, looking into his daughter's eyes, he said, "Yes, and she knows it. At least, I think she does. But she's married to Martin, and I'd never try to interfere. Is that what you're worried about?"

"I don't know. I saw the way you and Mama looked at one another and wondered. After you divorced, you could have gotten her back. I know you could. Why didn't you?"

Russ looked solemn. "Because of me, Jeff and Brian lost years with their mother. They chose to stay with me, but they shouldn't have had to make that decision. I wouldn't do that to you too. You love Martin—and you should. I couldn't take him away from you." Russ took a sip of coffee, and then said, "I answered your questions, now you can answer mine. How do you feel about all this?"

"You and Mama had an affair. I can't wish it hadn't happened, can I? If it hadn't, I wouldn't be here." Russ smiled, making him look younger. He was still handsome, lean, and strong, and she could imagine how irresistible he must have been to her mother all those years ago.

"Nothing has to change, Sammy," Russ said. "We're still the same people. Martin is still your daddy, Martha is still your mama, and I'm still Uncle Russ. You just know more about our past than you did before."

"It's more than that, and you know it."

"You're right, but there's no need for things to be awkward. You can still call me Uncle Russ. That doesn't have to change. But maybe you could come to the house for dinner, sometimes, with Jeff and Brian. I cook a mean steak."

"Okay. I'd like that."

Russ cocked his head and asked, "Does that smile mean you still love me?"

"You know I do," she said, rolling her eyes. Russ laughed aloud from pure happiness.

When Conner walked through the door that afternoon, Samantha waltzed into his arms and looked up at him. Seeing happiness in her sparkling eyes, he swung her around and kissed her. "You're in a good mood."

"I am. Uncle Russ came over. We talked, and I feel better about things. And I have my class back. I start on Monday."

"Anxious to get back to your kids?"

"I am. I've missed them. It'll take time to get back in the groove. Kids like routine. They like to know what to expect, and having a substitute has made school a little unpredictable. They'll test the boundaries for a while."

"Want to do something tonight?" Conner had stopped by his apartment for clothes again, hoping to stay through the weekend. Moving in was looking better all the time. He didn't want to leave Samantha, and he was tired of living out of the trunk of his car.

The pretty woman in his arms, who'd experienced far too much stress recently, looked up into his sky-blue eyes. "Can we just stay home and watch a movie? I need some peace and quiet in my life—

sweet, boring, peace and quiet. Did you bring extra clothes?"

Conner gave her a look that said, what do you think?

"Of course you did, Boy Scout."

The evening was low key, tranquil, and for the first time in a long time, Samantha felt completely relaxed. Just being with Conner made her happy. Her world was a thousand times brighter with him in it. Once again, she wondered what she'd do without him—in her life and in her bed. The thought of never touching him again was painful.

Saturday morning, while eating a leisurely breakfast, Conner asked Samantha, "If you had no time or money constraints, what changes would you make to the farm?"

"Why?"

"I just thought it would be fun to dream."

It was. One thought led to another, and before long they had a list.

Looking at all the projects they'd thought of, Sam said, "I hope you don't expect me to do all those things."

"No. But you could choose one project. It wouldn't have to be done all at once, and I can help you with it." After more discussion, they drove Samantha's truck to Cole's hardware and bought gallons of barn-red paint. After lunch, they'd start giving the old barn a facelift.

Conner and Samantha were making sandwiches in the kitchen when they heard a car drive up. Hal was no longer a threat, but they were so used to being on the look-out, it took a moment to relax. Soon a car horn drowned out the sound of barking dogs, and Conner walked out to see what was going on. The window on the driver's side of the car came down a few inches, and he heard his mother's voice. "We can't leave the car because of those dogs."

The smile he wore when he opened the door changed to a look of astonishment. He'd expected to see one of their Tenacity friends. Instead, it was his mother. What the hell was she doing at the farm? Stepping onto the porch, he yelled, "Hot Shot! Queenie! Come."

Obeying, the dogs trotted to his side and sat. Mrs. Wilmington and Kendall left the car, looking out of place with the barn behind them and chickens at their feet. Eyeing the dogs, Conner's mother asked, "Will they bite?"

"Not unless they see you as a danger." Initially, Conner assumed his mother had come to lure him home, but then he jumped to another conclusion. "Has something happened to Dad?"

"Your father is perfectly fine. I heard someone got killed because of that girl you're seeing. I had to find out if you're all right."

"You could have called."

"Why would I do that? You won't even talk to me. Besides, I needed to see for myself that you're all right. And I want to apologize," she added, seeing the stubborn look on his face. "Although I'm not sure for what," she said under her breath. "Are you going to invite us in?"

"I guess you can come in," Conner said to his mother. Nodding toward his sister, he added, "but not her."

"Conner! You can't talk to Kendall that way."

"I can. She's not welcome in this house. Not after what she did."

Kendall sighed. "It's okay, Mom. It's nice out. I'll sit on the porch in one of the rocking chairs." Frowning at Conner, she said dramatically, "If that's allowed."

Conner didn't back down. "Have at it."

"Will the dogs leave me alone?"

"No. They'll pester you to be petted."

Samantha, who'd been listening from the kitchen, walked to the entrance and welcomed Mrs. Wilmington to her home. "Have a seat, please. How about something to drink? I have sweet, iced tea in the fridge."

"That sounds nice, dear."

"I can make you a quick sandwich if you're hungry."

"No thank you. I just came to talk to Conner about a couple of issues. You don't mind if I do that, do you, dear?"

Okay, Samantha thought, no one could miss that cue. She was being dismissed.

"Samantha can hear anything you have to say to me," Conner said.

"That's okay, Conner. Talk to your mother. I'll be right back with that tea. Want a glass, Conner?" He thanked her but shook his head.

After she presented Mrs. Wilmington's tea, she poured two more glasses and announced she'd be sitting on the porch with Kendall.

"You sure about that?" Conner asked, concerned about her spending time with his sister.

"We'll be fine. You two have your talk." On the porch, Samantha handed a glass to Kendall, kept the other for herself, and sat in a nearby chair.

After a long silence, Kendall finally said, "I saw a big piece of furniture through the open door. Is that a gun cabinet by any chance?"

Samantha chuckled. "So Reagan told you what I said?"

"I think you scared her."

"I was just angry about my ruined dress."

"She shouldn't have done that. We should have been nicer to you. After the car stunt, Conner told me you'd been through a lot…"

"He said that?"

"Well, not exactly. I phoned him when I got home, and he yelled it at me. I've never seen him so angry. He's normally easy going. I didn't know we were bringing back a bad memory for you, but that's no excuse. What we did was mean and stupid, and we didn't think about how it might affect you or consider that it could be dangerous. I know it's not enough, but I'm sorry."

Samantha wouldn't tell her it was all right—because it wasn't. So she said, "Thank you for saying that."

"I don't see Reagan much anymore," Kendall admitted. "She found other friends. I think she mostly hung around me in hopes of getting close to Conner. Most of the girls I know are ga-ga over him, but she was the worst. You know how people have crushes on celebrities? It's like he's famous or something. Would you believe there's a group dedicated to him on the Internet?" Sam smiled. She'd seen it. Kendall rolled her eyes. "A couple of girls even made posters from pictures they found of him. Reagan was one of them."

"I'm not surprised."

"I suppose when he said he never wanted to see her again, she gave up." Kendall put her glass on the floor, walked to the porch banister, and peered at the pasture. "Are those your cows?"

"They are. They're the only ones I have left. Want to meet them?"

"I do."

Samantha wasn't sure if Kendall was really interested in the animals or if she just wanted to get away from the conversation in the living room. The windows were partially raised and the voices inside weren't exactly quiet.

Mrs. Wilmington was on a tirade. "I'm sure Samantha is a perfectly nice young woman, but she's not right for you. For heaven's sake, she lives in the middle of nowhere and has chickens in her yard. We let you go off on your own for a while. You've had your little adventure. Now it's time to grow up and start fulfilling your obligations."

Conner's head jerked back, as if he'd been struck, and he glared at his mother. When he finally spoke, his voice brimmed with anger and astonishment. "You let me go off on my own? I'm twenty-eight years old," Samantha heard Conner say as she and Kendall walked down the porch steps. "You can't tell me what to do anymore."

Kendall glanced back toward the door. "Conner grew up a long time ago, but Mom can't accept it. She's kind of a control freak." Kendall skipped toward the animals.

"If you run," Samantha warned, "you'll scare them away."

"Really? But they're so big. Especially that one," she said, pointing to Maynard. Samantha opened the gate, motioned the teen through, and closed it behind them. After watching Sam pet the huge animals, Kendall carefully edged closer.

"Maizie and Maynard like human attention," Samantha explained, "but you have to be careful around them because of their size. They could accidentally knock you over or step on your foot." Grinning, Kendall dared to reach out and touch the giant pets.

"Do you ride them?"

"No. I tried that when I was younger, but they weren't wild about the idea."

Walking back toward the barn, Kendall asked if Samantha had horses.

"Not anymore. I gave my last one to my neighbor. Since I take care of this place by myself, I don't have time to give her the care she deserves. I visit her sometimes and take her a treat."

"You have kittens!" Kendall exclaimed as she peeked inside the barn. Samantha was surprised to see the debutant plop herself on the ground to cuddle the furry babies. "The dogs don't bother the kittens? I thought they were natural enemies."

"Hot Shot and Queenie know not to. I believe they consider themselves the protectors of all the farm's residents, and that includes the cats. Sometimes they give in to temptation and chase the chickens, but they never hurt them. They just like to see them run."

Kendall dusted off the seat of her pants. "Did I get it all? Mom won't like it if I get dirty."

Samantha looked. "You're good. Your mom will never guess you've been crawling around on the barn floor."

Kendall flashed a smile and glanced out the wide door. Her mother was standing beside the rental car, alternately glancing at her watch and crossing her arms. Walking from the shadowed barn into the sunlight, Kendall thanked Samantha for showing her around.

"We need to go now," Mrs. Wilmington said when she spied her daughter, "or we'll miss our flight home."

She was opening the driver's door when Kendall held up a finger. "Just a minute, Mom." Seeing Conner on the porch, she ran up the steps and threw her arms around him. "I'm sorry," she said, before turning and running to the car. He wasn't sure whether she was apologizing for his mother or for her own earlier behavior. Whatever the reason, his feelings toward his sister softened a little.

CHAPTER EIGHTEEN

Skirting the real reason for his mother's unexpected visit, Conner used the excuse she'd given upon arrival: she'd heard about the shooting and was making sure he was all right. Ignoring the skepticism on Sam's face, he pretended all was well.

"Let's eat that lunch we didn't finish. I'm starving," Conner said. While they ate, he talked about painting the barn and anything else he could think of to avoid discussing his mother's visit. As he finished his second sandwich, he noticed Samantha had only eaten a few bites.

Since he'd returned the evening before, Samantha had been relaxed and cheerful. Their night together was tender and playful, and their morning was filled with optimistic plans for the future. Then his mother waltzed in and stomped on Sam's hard-earned, long-awaited serenity. Conner was doing everything he could to make Samantha happy, but his family kept interfering. How could he forgive them for that?

The look on Sam's face told him she wouldn't be distracted from the topic of his mother's visit. They were going to talk about it whether he wanted to or not.

"You heard what she said, didn't you?" Conner asked.

"Some of it."

"I'm sorry, Sam. Her priorities are distorted. It's not really about you. She has issues she's projecting onto us."

"But she's right," Sam said. "I'm not good for you. In her words, I'm not a proper choice. I live on a farm, just like she said, I'm divorced, I married a crazy person, and I put you and my friends in danger."

"There's nothing wrong with living on a farm, Sam. It's a good way to live. As for the rest of it, none of that was your fault, and you know it. What's this really about?"

"I should never have started anything with you. I just couldn't help myself. Then when Hal got out of prison, I took advantage of your kindness. But I'm not what you need."

Conner frowned, disliking the direction the conversation was headed. "I'm the one who gets to decide what I need."

"You deserve a family of your own," she told him, "even if you don't think so, and if we stay together, you'll never have that."

"Bullshit! For one thing, the doctor didn't say you couldn't have children, just that your chances weren't good. Medicine advances all the time. You still might be able to get pregnant. But you'd love an adopted child as much as one who came from your womb. And so would I." Whoa, he thought. That almost sounded like a proposal.

"But it would be a shame not to pass on your genes to some lucky child," Samantha said.

"Come on. That's ridiculous. I'm not so great and looks aren't what's important anyway. Besides, there's no guarantee my child would look anything like me. But if that's important to you, and our relationship ever got to that point, we could hire a surrogate. Just don't send me away because of some illogical misconception. It's not fair to either of us."

"My inability to conceive isn't our only issue. I refuse to cause a rift between you and your family. They expect you to find someone who fits into their world, like the society darlings I met at your parents' Christmas party."

"Those 'darlings,' as you call them, can't hold a candle to you. You wowed everyone at the party, outshined every woman in the room. All that aside, I'm in love with you."

He loved her? Unable to hold back tears, Samantha was dangerously close to losing her resolve. But she needed to do what was best for Conner. Sam always knew the day would come when she'd have to give him up, but she kept inventing excuses for her selfishness.

His confrontation with his mother was a wake-up call. Samantha was responsible for the gulf between Conner and his family, and she wouldn't widen it any farther. When Sam was a child, her mother let Russ go for his own sake. Now she had to find the courage to do the same for Conner.

Samantha wrapped her arms around herself to avoid throwing them around the man she adored. Longing to beg him to stay, she said, "Don't make this more difficult, Conner. It's time to face facts."

Looking at the floor, she said, almost to herself, "This is one of the hardest things I've ever done."

"Then don't do it, Sam. You're wrong about this."

"I don't think I could have lived through this ordeal without you," she continued, ignoring his words. "You probably saved my life, and I know you saved my sanity. I'll never forget you or what you did."

Taking a deep breath, Samantha focused on his face. "I love you, Conner. I need to tell you that, but what we have won't work. We're from different worlds."

Her hands flew to her face, and she released a pent-up sob. He reached for her, but she stepped away, shaking her head. It took every ounce of determination Sam could muster, but somehow, she resisted sinking into the comfort of his arms.

"Don't do this, Samantha. We love each other. We're good together. We'll work things out."

With a steadfast belief she was doing the right thing, Samantha wiped away tears and found the courage to speak the wretched words. "It's over, Conner. We're through. You'll never know how sorry I am. Don't make this any harder. Please."

"It should be hard—so hard that you can't do it."

"But I have to."

"You don't. We've talked about the baby issues. You know how I feel about that. And my family will come around. They will."

"I'll believe that when they come to beg for forgiveness. Now, please, Conner. Please just go. I'm dying here."

What could he do?

Leaving behind his shaving kit and extra clothes, he tenderly kissed Samantha's tear-drenched lips and walked out the door.

The minute he was out of sight, Samantha dropped to a sitting position on the hardwood floor. With her face in her hands, she listened as Conner started the Porsche and backed away. When silence replaced the sound of tires on gravel, she sat in the empty house, feeling more alone than she thought possible.

Then a mournful wail, from somewhere deep inside, forced its way past her lips, escaping between her tear-drenched fingers. She'd just made the biggest sacrifice of her life, and despair overwhelmed her. She'd done what was best for Conner, but the pain of losing him seemed almost too much to bear.

Samantha lay curled on the floor and sobbed. As tears fell on the cool wooden planks, something broke loose in her, and pent-up feelings poured out like dirty ditch water. She cried for the loss of Conner and the dreams that could never come true. She cried for the young woman who made the mistake of marrying the wrong man and for the baby she lost. She cried for the hurt she'd endured and the fear that remained. She even cried for Hal, for the way his disturbed mind erased the good in him and ended his life.

Her position on the floor revived the memory of the time, in almost the same spot, when she'd thought her life was over. Despite the fear she wouldn't survive the pain of that night, she'd eventually returned to the land of the living. The memory remained, but she managed to endure it. Could she also learn to live with this loneliness and yearning, or would the compounded pain be more than she could take?

Forcing her body to unfold, she stood, absently moving in the direction of the staircase. Collapsing onto the bottom step, she stared into space, a stream of tears cascading down her face and neck.

This situation was all her fault. She'd told herself she was only enjoying the company of a handsome, charming friend. He was sexy. There was no doubt about that. But she'd underestimated her ability to resist him. When she discovered how steadfast and truly unpretentious he was, despite his advantages, she didn't have a chance.

Sometimes, at her weakest moments, she'd even allowed herself to believe things could work out between them. Then she'd remember all the obstacles they faced, and reality would set in.

She and Conner had become so close, their lives so intertwined, it was hard to imagine living without him. Knowing she'd never again experience the happiness she felt with him was almost unbearable.

With Conner at her side, she felt stronger. He kept darkness at bay. Without him, grief threatened to bury her.

No stranger to emotional pain, Samantha knew the weeks, months, years to come would be difficult. Having experienced depression before, she knew she'd require more than willpower to cope. An appointment with her old psychiatrist was at the top of her to-do list. She knew what was coming, so why wait?

The way she saw it, she had only two choices— give up on life or accept the hand she'd been dealt and be as productive as possible. She'd just have to focus on family, friends, and the children in her classroom.

A woman didn't need a man in her life to be content, but Samantha greedily wanted more than contentment. She'd had a taste of real happiness, and it was hard to accept anything less. And Conner wasn't just any man. He was the person who owned her heart, and whether he knew it or not, it would be his as long as she lived.

With no way to turn off her feelings, she'd simply have to love him from afar. Then she thought about watching him fall for another woman. How would she bear it? But that's why she'd let him go, Samantha reminded herself. That's what was supposed to happen.

Falling in love with him was a mistake. On the other hand, look what she would have missed if she hadn't. At least she had memories. Maybe, after a while, they wouldn't hurt so much.

While the sun still shone outside the farmhouse, Samantha climbed the stairs to her bedroom and fell into bed. "Oh, dear God!" she wailed when she smelled his spicy scent on her sheets. "I desperately need your help."

Driving to his apartment, Conner's thoughts headed an entirely different direction. Sam loved him; so maybe he could convince her to reconsider. But if he managed to foist himself back into her life, he should be ready to stay the duration. She'd experienced enough hurt. He wouldn't be responsible for more.

He remembered telling Anna she should be with Max if he was the man she wanted. Then he'd stepped back to accept the role of friend, rather than lover. Conner had been willing to step out of the picture for Anna, but he could never willingly hand Samantha over to anyone else. He wanted her in a way he'd never wanted another woman. He had to think of a way to keep her in his life.

As soon as Conner arrived at his apartment, he phoned both Russ and Anna to tell them Sam might need their support. "She broke up with me," he said, "but she's upset." Instead of giving them details, he told them to ask her.

She'd sent him away, but her pain was obvious, and Conner was worried about her. If he couldn't be there to help, at least he could see that someone else was. Samantha was a strong woman, but she'd been through so much, and that much stress, for such a long period of time, would take a toll on anyone.

Monday morning, Samantha fed her animals, dressed in slacks and a bright blue sweater, and drove to school. On the way to their classrooms, fellow teachers hurriedly welcomed her back.

"I was so glad to see your truck in the parking lot when I drove in," another second-grade teacher exclaimed as they passed in the hallway. "Everyone has missed you. The kids are going to be thrilled."

The chatter of active children waiting outside for the bell to ring, contrasted with the teachers' quiet preparations inside the building. The school was a second home to Samantha, her fellow teachers and students a second family.

She looked around and smiled. Paper snowflakes hovered overhead, children's snowman drawings adorned the walls, and the winter theme graced every bulletin board. January in Mississippi might not bring the actual cold, white flakes, but the kids could dream.

The tagline on the bulletin board outside Samantha's room read "Keep warm with a good book." On poster-paper cups of hot chocolate, each student had written the name of a book and a couple of sentences describing it. Good job, Sam thought. She'd have to compliment the substitute on the display and find out how long it had been up.

The smell of textbooks, crayons, markers, chalk dust, and the residual aroma of small humans welcomed Samantha to the classroom. When the bell rang, excited children poured in. "Miss Lindsey, you're back!" One demonstrative little guy threw his arms around her, his head resting just above her waist. Other children took Samantha's smile as a cue to do the same, until she told them it was time to find their seats.

She might never have the life she dreamed of, but at least she had the love of her students. A classroom of active children was exactly what she needed to take her mind off Conner. If she focused on anything other than their needs and maintaining order, the natives would get restless.

Pleased to be back at work, Samantha wasted no time re-establishing the class's routines. The principal poked his head in the room to welcome her back, and fellow teachers passed by with a smile and friendly wave. She felt their support, even though they had no idea what she was going through.

At home, Sam re-discovered the piano as an outlet for her emotions. She felt a kinship with the melancholy chords of Beethoven's "Moonlight Sonata," Debussy's "Clair de Lune," and Chopin's "Prelude in E Minor." But it was the words of Dolly Parton's "I Will Always Love You," that best expressed her feelings and produced cascades of tears.

While Samantha was finding ways to cope with her loss, Conner was devising a way to get back into her life. Even if his plan didn't achieve the desired result, Sam would benefit, and she deserved everything he could give her and more.

Since flexible hours hadn't reduced Conner's productivity while Sam was in hiding, he convinced his boss to allow it a while longer. It would mean working nights and weekends, but he'd do it for Sam.

While Samantha reclaimed her role as a teacher, Conner drove to Tenacity and then down the little gravel road that led to the farm. In the barn, he assembled the painting supplies he and Sam bought the morning his mother showed up to manipulate his future. After positioning a tall aluminum ladder at the back of the barn, he climbed to the top and brushed barn-red paint onto the weather-worn wood.

It was hard work, but he gave the back side of the barn a new coat of paint before re-packing supplies, storing them inside, and returning to Clarkston. At his apartment, he showered quickly, donned slacks and a sports coat, and headed to the office for an afternoon appointment.

Tuesday, he painted half of the south side of the barn, which wasn't visible from the house. Wednesday, he completed it. After he painted half of the road-facing side, Samantha noticed.

First, she asked Russ, Jeff, and her parents if they were responsible. When their answer was no, she texted Conner.

Did you hire someone to paint my barn?

No.

Surely, you're not doing it. Are you?

She didn't receive an answer. Was he so angry he was refusing to text, or was he the guilty painter? Conner wanted to talk to Sam, but he had a long list of things to accomplish first.

He took great pains not to be discovered. Unless he was needed at the office, his mornings were spent working in Tenacity. If he had an early meeting, his farm chores were relegated to afternoon, which meant his work time was cut short.

Teachers stayed at school an hour or two after the children were dismissed, but Conner left the farm as soon as the afternoon bell sounded. He knew Sam wouldn't leave her class alone to uncover her interloper, but once the students left, she might try to catch him in the act.

Covered in a fresh coat of paint, the barn looked brand new. No, Samantha thought, it looked better than new. She loved it but couldn't help wanting to know the identity of her benefactor. She'd thought about rushing home to catch him in the act while her students were in music or art class. But since she suspected the mystery man might be Conner, she didn't.

Her heart raced at the mere thought of him. So what would happen if they actually faced one another? Afraid she'd run into his arms and beg forgiveness, she couldn't take the chance.

But how could the painter be Conner? Didn't he work five days a week? He might have hired someone. Deciding not to ponder the question any longer, she resolved to appreciate the gift and stop worrying about her altruistic intruder. He'd finished his project and that was that. Samantha couldn't know how wrong she was.

Returning home from a long day of teaching, she experienced the biggest surprise yet. On the side of the barn was a huge painting of a patchwork quilt square. Upon closer inspection, she saw that it was painted on a board attached to the wall. She'd discovered the idea in a magazine and had shown it to Conner. That eliminated any doubt about the identity of her benefactor, for she was sure she'd mentioned it to no one else.

The realization that Conner had done this for her moved her to tears. She sat on the ground, looking up at the colorful square on the newly painted barn, overwhelmed by the magnanimous gesture. "Not now," she told the dogs wanting her attention. "Why are you doing this, Conner?" she said aloud. "I'm trying to do the right thing."

Because Conner needed help getting started on his next project, he called Russ.

"Sure," the older man said. "What do you need?"

"Don't tell Sam, but I'm going to build her a fence. I know what I want it to look like. I just need help getting started."

Russ willingly offered his assistance. He liked Conner. He was good for Sammy. "I have to make a run to Clarkston sometime in the next few days," Russ said. "How about I drop by your apartment?"

When he visited, they discussed the fence, but not before Russ put Conner on the spot. "Why are you doing this, son? What's this all about?"

"The fence is something Samantha and I talked about before my mother showed up to ruin things, so I know it'll make her happy. But I have to admit, I'm hoping she'll realize I'm not going anywhere and consider taking me back."

"Do you mind telling me what happened? Samantha won't say much. And what does your mother have to do with anything?"

Conner told him about Mrs. Wilmington's unfortunate visit and explained why Samantha sent him away. "She thinks she's doing it for my own good."

Russ shook his head. "Just like her mother, trying to be noble. They've both hurt themselves and the people they love, doing what they mistakenly think is right. But it sounds like your mother may be a legitimate concern."

"Samantha comes first with me. Mom will have to change her tune if she wants me in her life."

"Do you mean that? Does Samantha really come first?"

"She does. She's the strongest, loveliest, most talented woman I've ever known, and I love her. I think about her all the time. I'm not even interested in other women. I mean, I like to look, like any other man. But that's as far as it goes."

Russ understood. He knew the feeling well. "It sounds like I don't have to say this, but I'll say it anyway. Be careful with her feelings. Sammy's had way too much hurt in her life. She doesn't need anymore."

After Conner purchased the necessary supplies, Russ helped him get started on a wooden post-and-rail fence. It was a huge project, but Conner was determined to complete it. Watching him work, Russ had to commend his daughter. Few women would turn down a man like Conner. She was misguided, but dang, his daughter had integrity.

Conner began the fence in an area Sam was less likely to notice, but it didn't take long for it to come into view. Because he couldn't wait to see the result, Conner stopped building long enough to paint the fence deep brown. It looked darn good. Russ and Jeff helped when they had time, but Conner did the lion's share of work. Sam texted Conner.

You have to stop. You can't keep doing this. It must be costing a fortune.

Not sure what you're talking about, Conner responded.

What am I going to do with you? She illustrated her text with a shrugging emoji.

There were a number of things he'd like to do with her. He'd dreamed of them, but he was smart enough to keep that to himself.

When he needed a change from building the fence, he focused on a new chicken house, since the old one had seen better days. The hens roamed freely during the day, but at night Sam locked them inside to protect them from foxes and coyotes.

Conner chose a design for the chicken coop that looked like a barn, planning to paint it the same shade of red as the real one. The appearance was important, but he was more concerned about safety. Sam told him snakes that dine on chicken eggs aren't usually poisonous, but he wasn't taking any chances. He would make that hen house so tight a slithery reptile couldn't possibly sneak in.

Having no building experience, other than the fence, he asked Max for advice. Because Max owned his own business and could re-arrange his schedule, he took time off to help Conner get started.

Aware of Samantha's misguided decision, Max was happy to do what he could to help Conner win her back. He not only thought they were good together, he also liked the idea of Conner being in a committed relationship. Max was confident in Anna's love, and he trusted her. He just had a problem with his wife having an unattached old lover as a close friend.

Once Conner completed the chicken coop, he went a step further, planting lemongrass, marigolds, rosemary, and thyme around the structure. Their pungent odors were reputed to repel snakes.

It's too much Conner. You have to stop, Sam texted again.

When he ignored the text, she e-mailed. That also went unanswered. She'd have to call. It took courage to pick up the phone and punch in his number, but she did. As there was no hope for their relationship, she couldn't let him continue spending money on the farm.

When Samantha heard the masculine voice at the other end of the phone, she felt as though someone had thrown hot water on her. Startled and abruptly warmed, it took a moment for her to speak. "Conner?"

"Sam," he said, "is everything all right?"

"Yes. I'm fine. But you have to…" Samantha heard a woman's voice in the background and her heart sank. What did she expect? She'd let him go so he could move on, but she wasn't ready. It was too soon.

The thought of him with another woman completely unbalanced her. Her heart raced, she felt sick and dizzy, and for a moment, she couldn't even remember why she called. The phone slipped from her fingers, but she caught it.

"It's right there in the folder on the dining table," Conner told the woman as he walked into the hallway. "I need to take this call."

"Sam," he said into the phone. Hearing nothing, he hoped she hadn't hung up. "Are you still there, Sam?"

"I'm....Yes, I'm here."

"Good. I'm glad to hear your voice."

"Who's there with you?" Sam couldn't help asking.

"Denise is here to go over a case with me," he explained.

Not her, Sam thought. The moment she'd seen Denise Graham at Conner's law office, she expected the attractive attorney to make a play for him. Sam knew Conner would eventually see other women but hoped he'd have the good sense not to get involved with that particular woman.

Forcing herself to focus, Sam remembered why she'd called. "Conner, you can't keep paying someone to do things for me at the farm."

"I'm not."

"Don't lie. It has to be you."

"All right," he admitted. "I'm checking items off our to-do list, but I'm doing the work myself and enjoying it. Who knew I was a farm boy at heart?"

"You're doing what? Did you quit your job?"

"No, I have flexible hours. Remember?"

She remembered too much. That was the problem. "You're obviously spending most of your time at the farm. How are you getting your law work done?"

"There are twenty-four hours in a day."

"You have to sleep sometimes."

"Don't worry about me, Sam. I'm doing what I want to."

Answering a muffled voice, Conner covered the mouth of the phone and yelled, "In a minute." He spoke to Sam in a soft, intimate voice. "I have to go and take care of that business you're so worried about. Call again and let's talk. Nothing heavy, unless that's what you want, I just like hearing your voice. I'd rather see you, but I'll take what I can get."

The following month at the farm, bluebird houses appeared in the yard, a large, insulated doghouse materialized at the end of the porch, and the fence line continued to grow. Between the farm projects and his regular job, Conner was working himself half to death. He lost weight and was routinely tired, but he'd never been more determined to do anything in his life.

Why are you doing this? Sam texted.

Because I love you, Conner answered honestly

The words played over and over in Samantha's mind. Despite her flaws and scandalous secrets, Conner loved her. She'd exposed him to the ugliest parts of her life, put him in danger, and thrown him out of her house. How could he still love her? Could she really be that lucky?

The next time Samantha had recess duty at school, one of the younger children ran to her, threw her arms around Sam's legs, and looked up at her with an adoring smile. Samantha smiled back, smoothed the child's hair, and experienced an epiphany that rocked her world.

She loved these children, and if the need arose, she could raise any one of them as her own. Could that be true of Conner as well? He'd said as much. Perhaps having his biological children really wasn't that important to him. Maybe she was no better than his mother, making a decision for him that should have been his to make.

He'd told her they could find another way to make a family if their relationship ever reached that point. She hadn't listened, and thanks to her unshakable belief that she was right, they were no longer together.

Had her realization come too late? Maybe not. Conner was still at the farm. She never saw him, but evidence of his presence was everywhere. Still, there was his family. They didn't approve of her, and that was no small thing.

Samantha's thoughts were jerked to the present by a commotion on the playground. Jogging toward two young boys, she called, "No pushing. Gregory, Mark, you know the rules."

Hoping to catch Conner at the farm, Samantha did something she'd never done before. Feigning illness, she left her second graders in the hands of a substitute and headed home. She wasn't sure why, but the need to see Conner that very moment was overwhelming.

Catching a glimpse of him, Samantha lost her breath. It had been months since he'd walked out her door, and she was hungry for the sight of him. The man of her dreams, tanned and shirtless, was working on the fence at the edge of the pasture.

Sam couldn't explain the intensity of her urge to reconnect with him, to touch him. As far as she knew, his family's opinion of her hadn't changed, but at the moment, none of that mattered. She was guided by pure instinct, and try as she might, she couldn't repress it.

Looking up when he heard the truck, Conner wiped sweat from his face and slowly walked toward Samantha. Unsure of what to expect, he kept his expression neutral. Was she glad to see him, or was she there to push him away again?

Meeting in the front yard, they stood only inches apart. They stared into one another's eyes, searching for a hint of what the other was thinking. When Conner saw longing on Sam's face, he wrapped his arms around her.

She didn't resist, so he leaned down and kissed her. The kiss was soft and sweet, but when she responded, it was all he could do to restrain himself from devouring her. He didn't ask why she was there or what she was thinking. She was in his arms, seeming to want him as much as he wanted her, and for the moment, that was enough.

They stood in the yard, kissing, grasping one another. Her hands clutched his back and shoulders, and he pulled her more tightly to his bare chest. With the smell of clean sweat permeating her nostrils and the taste of Conner thick on her lips, Samantha was besieged by pure, unadulterated emotion.

When her body molded to his, the impassioned man took a risk and asked, "Any chance we could take this inside?"

At the point where sensuality replaced logical thought, Samantha nodded.

Taking the familiar walk across the porch, a grain of conscious thought made its way into Conner's lust-laden brain. "Just so I know," he asked, "Is this reconciliation or a one-time thing?"

"How are your parents?" Sam asked a little breathlessly.

Conner frowned. "Really?"

"Just answer, please."

"I suppose they're all right. We don't talk much these days."

When Samantha sent him a pained look, the wrong-answer buzzer went off in his head. He was smarter than that. She was asking if he'd reconciled with his family. Conner kicked himself for ruining the moment. The last thing he wanted was a conversation about his family.

"All right," Conner said, "we'll call it a one-night stand, or more accurately, a one-afternoon stand. So let's make the most of it." If she wanted to think it would never happen again, he wouldn't argue. But if he had anything to do with it, this would be the beginning of a new chapter of their lives.

Scooping her into his arms, Conner practically sprinted up the stairs and fell on the bed. Thanks to the former basketball star's agility, they landed face to face, with Samantha on top.

"Just so you know," Conner said, "I'm not sticking around to see the regret on your face." That's what he said, but he planned to give her an experience she couldn't possibly regret.

The encounter had begun in a frenzied manner. Having been apart for months, they were hungry for one another. Conner strove to decelerate the experience, to make it memorable, although Sam's eagerness made that difficult.

Holding her in his arms, he slowly, soothingly rubbed her back. "Let's slow this down, babe. We have all afternoon, and I'm going to savor you." And he did just that. With no spot on her body left unkissed, Samantha writhed with want. When she was totally consumed with need, he gave her the sublime satisfaction she craved. In the moments after, they shared professions of love, which Conner knew would have little effect on Samantha's convictions.

As hard as it was, he was true to his word. When Samantha dozed off, he eased his arm out from under her and slipped away. If he wanted more than one afternoon, and he did, he had to keep his eye on the prize.

CHAPTER NINETEEN

With help from Russ and Jeff, Conner finally completed Samantha's fence, the last project on the list. Now it was time to visit his family. He hadn't seen them since the day Samantha broke up with him, and he'd spoken to his mother as little as possible. It was time for that to change. For his plan to work, he needed their cooperation.

Although he'd had little interaction with his mother, he'd talked with his father more than usual, and their conversations were enlightening. Conner had always loved the man who gave him life, but thanks to their discussions, he realized he liked him as well.

"You're a grown man," his father told him. "What you do and where you do it is your choice. I trust your judgment. Your mother is the one pressuring you to marry someone from our social circle, not me. But don't judge her too harshly. She's motivated by circumstances you don't yet understand."

In private, Mr. Wilmington let his wife know how displeased he was with her behavior. "I warned you he'd stay away if you pushed too hard. He loves you, but that won't keep him from fighting for the woman he wants in his life."

Mrs. Wilmington stood her ground. "He's blinded by that girl. We need to guide him in the right direction."

"You don't give our son enough credit. He's intelligent, levelheaded, and perfectly capable of selecting his own friends. And the woman he chooses to be with is none of our business, although I must say, I approve of his Samantha."

When Conner arrived at his parents' home, he greeted his mother coolly and then took his overnight bag to his room.

"I'll be back for dinner," he said, before leaving the house. "I want to talk with you and Dad afterward, and I'd like for Kendall to be here too. It's important."

Conner didn't have any particular place to go, but he wouldn't be drawn into a discussion before he was ready. Dinner was quiet, with Conner politely, but succinctly, responding to his mother's conversational attempts. After unsuccessfully trying to manipulate her son into revealing his after-dinner agenda, she finally relented.

In the living room, Will Wilmington made himself a drink, poured wine for his wife, and offered to get something for his son. Conner declined. He was on a mission, interested only in relating his story and stating his position.

"I'll have a glass of wine, Daddy," Kendall said, knowing the request would be denied.

"When you're twenty-one," Will said flatly. He looked at Conner. "We're all here, Son, ready to listen to what you have to say."

Conner's father retired to his favorite chair, while Mrs. Wilmington and Kendall settled on the nearby sofa. Conner stood, facing them, donning his attorney demeanor.

Unsure whether he was defending Samantha or prosecuting his family, he began. "I'm in love with Samantha, and she loves me. Despite our feelings, she ended our relationship, and I'm doing everything I can to get her back."

He explained what Hal did to her, told them about the trial, and related the events that occurred after the man's early prison release. The Wilmingtons knew part of it, but Conner wanted them to understand everything.

He told them about Sam's miscarriage and the doctor's prognosis. "She feels unworthy of a man because she might no longer be able to bear children. Believing I should have my own genetic offspring, she ended our relationship. I haven't proposed," he hurried to say. "She's just thinking ahead. I told her adoption is always an option, but she won't listen.

"We spoke recently, which I see as a big step forward, and she may be softening on the child issue. I believe we can clear that hurdle, but there's something else keeping us apart. That's what I'm here to talk about. You are the other reason she left me. Samantha adamantly refuses to come between us," he said, motioning between his family and himself."

Not pulling any punches, Conner told them exactly how he felt. "Mom, I know you and Kendall don't approve of Samantha. She knows it, too. You've done everything possible to make sure of that. You've been rude. No, more than that. You've been downright cruel to her—and to me. I never thought a member of my family would so blatantly disregard my wishes. I'm hurt, angry, and frankly, I'm ashamed of you."

Conner half expected his mother to walk out of the room, or at least argue her position. Instead, he was surprised to see her lip quiver and tears run down her face. He made no effort to comfort her, and neither did his father.

Conner assessed the reaction of each member of his family. His father was stoic, as usual. Kendall stared at the floor, and his mother hid her face in her hands.

Mrs. Wilmington turned her tear-stained face toward her son. "I'm so sorry," she stammered. "I didn't know that poor girl had been through so much. I did what I thought was right for everyone."

"Mom, I don't mean to be disrespectful, but whom I love is my business, not yours. I'm the one who gets to make that decision. If you want me in your life, you have to learn to respect my boundaries."

"Will keeps telling me that, and, of course, I want you in my life. I'm your mother. I just thought I knew best."

Fighting back a smile, Mr. Wilmington finally spoke. "You always think that, dear, and often you do. But not this time."

"So you don't want to come back to Savannah?" Mrs. Wilmington asked Conner.

"No, Mom. It's a wonderful town, and I enjoyed growing up here. But no. I'm not coming back."

"And you're not interested in any of the young ladies in our social circle?"

"No, Mom."

"Are you going to marry that girl—Samantha? I hope you're not planning to live out in the middle of nowhere on a farm."

"That will be my decision, but I'm not ready to talk about that now. I'm focused on getting her back in my life." When Conner told them about the work he'd done on the farm, his family finally understood how determined he was.

They talked for more than an hour, airing their concerns, and Mrs. Wilmington revealed the real reason for her reservations about Samantha. Her announcement would have shocked Conner if his father hadn't previously confided in him.

Most importantly, his mother promised to honor his choices. He went to sleep in his old room that night, feeling more hopeful about the future than he had in a long time.

Conner was working on a brief in his Clarkston apartment when Samantha texted that the Windoms and Lindseys had made an important decision.

We decided to reveal our secret. Everyone agreed on what to say, and each of us will tell one or more people. I thought you'd want to know. Keep your fingers crossed that this doesn't end badly.

If things feel awkward at first, don't let it get you down. People will talk for a while, but it'll blow over.

I hope so. Thanks, and good night.

I'm always here for you, Conner typed, heartened that Sam had initiated a conversation.

Samantha didn't tell him about the conversation she and her mother had had after the family meeting. "Mama," she'd said, "I know you loved Uncle Russ when you married Daddy. How did you get over him?"

"I didn't really," Martha said. "I just learned to live with the hurt."

"I don't know if I can do that. I miss Conner, and he misses me. I know he does. Look what he's done on the farm."

Martha smoothed her daughter's curls. "I had no choice. I had to give Russ up. He was married, he and Stephanie had a child, and he was trying to be everything to everyone. He couldn't keep going that way. It was too much for anyone. You have a choice, Samantha. That young man loves you. I see it in his eyes. And he stood by you through a lot of turmoil."

"But children?"

"We've talked about that. You know there are other ways to have a family. Your relationship might not even get to that point, but don't you think you should give yourself the opportunity to find out?"

Samantha sighed. "Maybe. But there's his family."

"They'll come around if they're decent people. And knowing what I know of their son, I can't imagine that they're not."

"Mama, I have something else to ask. I know I shouldn't, but I really want to know."

"Okay," she said slowly.

Samantha looked down, hesitating. When she returned her gaze to her mother, she asked, "Do you still love Uncle Russ?"

Martha didn't have to think about her answer. "Once you have a deep connection with a man, at least one like I had with Russ, I don't think you ever stop loving him—not completely. But love manifests itself in many forms."

"I know that. What I'm asking, I guess, is do you still have romantic feelings for him? You know, passion. I'm trying to wrap my mind around what happened with you and Uncle Russ. You love Daddy, don't you?"

Martha folded her hands together, pondering the question. "Yes, I love him, although I admit I didn't when we married. I liked him, there was affection, and after a while, there was more. We feel warmth and devotion to one another. It's hard to put into words." Answering the unspoken question she saw in her daughter's eyes, she said, "And yes, there is intimacy."

"And what about Uncle Russ?"

Martha sighed. "You're not going to give me a pass on this, are you?" She considered her answer. "With Russ, there was definitely passion, but more than that, there was need. He was part of me and his departure from my life left a hole no one else can fill. I hope that's enough of an answer because that's all I have for you. I've already told you more than a mother likes to tell a daughter."

Astonished by the implication of her mother's words, Samantha said, "You never got over him." Martha didn't deny it.

Samantha sighed. "I'll never get over Conner either, will I?" Martha pressed her lips together. She'd said enough. She wouldn't try to influence Samantha further. It wasn't her decision to make.

Conner answered his phone. "Russ, nice to hear from you."

The older man got to the point. "I thought you'd want to know that Martin Lindsey just died."

"You mean Samantha's…uh, Samantha's stepdad?"

"You can call him her dad. He adopted her. He had another attack, and this one got him."

"Is there anything I can do? Is Samantha all right?"

"Sammy's fine. I'm fixin' to go pick her up and drive her to her mother's. Don't worry. We'll take good care of her. I just thought you'd want to know."

"Thanks for calling, Russ. I appreciate it. Will you let me know about the funeral arrangements? I'd like to attend."

"Sure thing."

Conner stood in line with other mourners at the front of the Smokey Creek Baptist Sanctuary. Because Samantha was busy accepting condolences, she didn't see him until he was almost upon her.

When she did, her heart beat wildly. And when he leaned down to kiss her on the cheek, her knees buckled. Lack of sleep, grief, and the excitement of

329

seeing Conner combined to overwhelm her. He caught her before she fell and helped her to the front pew.

"I feel so stupid," Sam said, "fainting like some damsel in distress."

"You didn't faint. I bet you've been handling most of the funeral details and not getting enough rest."

"Some of that," she admitted.

"You're probably just tired out."

Samantha stared into clear blue eyes. "Thank you for being here, Conner. Will you come by Mama and Daddy's after the service? You can't imagine how many casseroles and cakes people have brought over. The table is piled with food. Come help us eat."

"I'll be glad to." He glanced at the long line of mourners. "Do you need to get back in line, or have you had enough for the day?"

"I'd better do my duty," she said, wishing she could stay right where she was. Sam returned to her mother's side, met Conner's eyes, and gave him a sad, appreciative smile.

Sam sensed the tall, handsome man's presence the moment he walked into her parents' Smokey Creek home. After hurrying to greet him, she escorted him to her mother, introduced him to a few friends, and steered him away from a group of ogling women.

Conner filled a plate from the abundance of food on the dining table while Sam poured him a glass of sweetened iced tea. Then she led him to an available spot at a table on the back deck. "Enjoy your meal," she said, "I need to mingle."

Through a picture-window, Conner watched her flit between the living room, dining room, and kitchen, greeting new arrivals, accepting condolences, and making sure everyone was fed.

He knew all the activity was helping her cope, but she'd be worn out by the end of the day. Once well-wishers returned home and nothing was left to distract her, she'd need someone to lean on.

As the crowd thinned, Russ approached Conner and Samantha, who were standing together talking. Pulling his daughter into a side hug, he said, "Since I drove you here, you're probably waiting for me to take you home. I know you're tired, but I think I should stay a while longer in case your mother needs something."

As Russ suspected, Conner immediately offered to take Samantha back to the farmhouse. When she agreed, Russ gave him a sly wink.

At first, the drive to Tenacity was quiet, except for occasional remarks about the funeral or the gathering afterward. But it didn't take long for Sam's comments to morph into a litany of memories.

She told Conner how Martin used to read stories to her at bedtime and how, in later years, he kept her truck's gas tank filled. With a sad smile, she shared how he would fall asleep in his chair, trying to wait up for her when she was a teen-ager.

Wiping tears away, Sam admitted mixed feelings about discovering Russ was her biological father. "The man in that casket, today, has always been my daddy. At least, that's how I thought of him. You understand, don't you? You were there with me when the truth came out." Samantha was in a pensive mood. "You've been with me through so much, Conner: evading Hal, discovering the truth about Russ and Mama, Daddy's wishes from his hospital bed, and now, his funeral. I know words aren't enough, but thank you."

"No problem. I'm always here for you."

That wasn't the first time he'd uttered those words. Sam remembered the way Russ ended his letters to her mother. "My heart will always be yours." Conner's words might be a little more pragmatic than Russ's, but the message was essentially the same.

"If you have time," Samantha said when they reached the house, "come inside and sit with me. I'm not quite ready to be alone." While Conner removed his suit jacket, Sam sat on the sofa, slipped off her high heels, and let out an audible sigh of relief.

Her reaction gave Conner an idea. "Wait here. I need to get a few things."

"What are you doing?" Sam asked when Conner bolted up the stairs.

"You'll see." He returned with a bottle of lotion, a washcloth, and two towels. Setting the items on the coffee table, he walked briskly to the kitchen and came back with a pan of warm water.

He carefully placed it on the floor, and then knelt beside it. "Now give me those feet." He wrapped his long fingers around Sam's ankles and pulled them toward him.

"That feels wonderful," she murmured when he placed her aching feet in the warm bath. After washing each foot and her ankles with the washcloth, he dried them with a soft towel and covered them with lavender-scented lotion. When he massaged her calves, her eyes closed, and her head fell against the sofa.

But Conner was just getting started. Sitting near her, he placed a towel over his suit pants, pulled her feet onto it, and began massaging the soreness away. When Sam's moans of delight brought sexual thoughts to mind, he recalled the step-by-step process of assembling the chicken coop. When that didn't help, he mentally reviewed a brief he'd worked on the night before.

"Mmm. Conner, will you come do this every day?" Saying nothing, he sent her a sexy, crooked smile.

After he massaged away her tension, he asked. "How about a drink?"

"Sounds good."

"Do you have any wine?"

"Um hum."

"Is that what you want?"

"Um hum."

When he returned with two glasses, Samantha was stretched out on the couch, sound asleep, doing an excellent imitation of a rag doll. Smiling at the exhausted woman, Conner carefully picked her up, climbed the stairs, and laid her on the bed.

She was still dressed in her funeral clothes. Should he remove them? It wouldn't be the first time, but that was different. Deciding to remove everything but her underwear, he dressed her in a soft sleepshirt and covered her with a thin blanket. Then he kissed her lips lightly and retired to an extra bedroom.

Hours later, a noise woke him. Something was wrong. He rushed into Samantha's room, and the sight of her stabbed at his heart. She was thrashing about, rolling her head from side to side. Among her unintelligible, distressed jumble of words, he distinctly heard her begging someone to stop.

Conner longed to comfort her, but if she was dreaming of being attacked, touching her was probably the worst thing he could do. So he spoke softly. "It's all right, Sam. It's me, Conner. You're safe. It's all right, sweetheart. I'm here." When she calmed down, he carefully pulled the cover over her shoulders, wishing he could lie next to her, knowing he shouldn't. Instead, he spent the night on the far side of the king-sized bed. The next morning, while Sam still slept, he silently erased any sign he'd been there.

Samantha awoke to the smell of coffee and bacon. Glancing at the other side of the bed, she saw that it was still made. She donned a robe and hurried downstairs, hoping to find Conner in the kitchen. And there he was, standing at the stove, barefooted, wearing a t-shirt and the suit pants he'd worn the day before.

When he saw Samantha, he smiled. Bless him, she thought, smiling back. Conner Wilmington must be the best man in the whole world. As if that wasn't enough, the good Lord gave him that fabulous face and body. His appearance was like…. She thought for a minute. It was like a shiny coat of paint on a steady, sea-worthy vessel. And someday, he'd take some lucky girl on the voyage of a lifetime.

She liked the analogy, except for the 'lucky girl' part. Thinking of him with another woman equated to self-torture.

"Smells good," Sam said.

Conner walked to her, pulled her body against his, and gave her a kiss that left her wanting more. Then he sauntered back to the stove and poured an egg mixture into a waiting frying pan, as if he hadn't just rocked her world.

"Get enough sleep, Strawberry Shortcake?"

"I did. And for your information, my hair may be strawberry blond, but I'm not short."

"That's a matter of perspective, sweetheart."

Sam wasn't sure whether he was trying to imitate Humphrey Bogart or John Wayne, but it was cute either way. "You're in a good mood this morning."

"Yes, I am," he said. "And how are you on this brand-new day?"

"Okay, considering. Thanks for last night. I assume you put me to bed and changed my clothes."

"I wasn't sure what to do about that," he admitted. "I knew you'd be more comfortable without your underwear, and it wouldn't have been the first time I removed those particular articles of clothing. But doing it while you were asleep seemed a little wicked."

"I appreciate your chivalry, gallant sir, but I thought you were comfortable with wicked."

"Oh, I am. I just wasn't sure you would be."

Samantha looked away, hoping Conner didn't see the flush that engulfed her body. His self-satisfied smile said that he did, and he knew what she was thinking.

She was flashing back to the pleasurable torture of slow, erotic undressing and Conner's wet kisses to her most sensitive body parts. Could he tell how much she wanted to drag him upstairs to bed?

Shaking away her thoughts, Sam watched Conner slide an omelet onto her plate and then stride to the sink to wash the pan. "Aren't you going to eat?" she asked.

"I grabbed toast earlier. I have to drive to my apartment, change clothes, and get to the office. Flexible work hours are over." He kissed her cheek. "Call me," he said, walking out the door.

Then he was gone, again. Having him back, even if it was only to console her, had been a gift, but the minute he left, Sam felt lonelier than ever.

It was a week before she heard from him, and that was only a quick call to check up on her. She was tempted to phone, as he'd asked her to, but she managed to avoid making that mistake.

Samantha didn't mean to play hooky, but after calling in sick in the morning, she began feeling fine. She must have had a short-lived case of whatever virus was making its way through the school. Since a substitute had already been called, Sam decided to use the time to attack a few projects around the farm.

Missing Conner and coming to grips with the death of the man she called daddy, Samantha took out her frustrations on the old chicken coop. She'd moved most of the hens to their new home, but a few refused to give up their old nests, so Sam decided to eliminate the choice.

She hadn't realized that knocking something down with a sledge hammer would be so satisfying. She'd hoped the work would extinguish thoughts of her dad and Conner, but images of both men surrounded her.

Samantha pictured Martin pulling the hay bailer behind the tractor, and then knocking the dust from his hat. He had a way of slapping it against his jeans before entering the house. It was a habit he probably wasn't even aware of, but it was a mental video Samantha treasured, something she'd always remember about the man who raised her. Knowing she'd never see him again or hear his laughter coaxed a tear down her cheek.

And she thought of Conner. She missed him so much her heart hurt. Evidence of his hard work dotted the farm: the red barn with the painted quilt square, a fence more beautiful than she could have imagined, the doghouse, the chicken coop, the bird houses.

Each project was evidence of his love, his way of staying connected, but now he seemed to be distancing himself. Why was it so hard? She should be glad he was backing off. She was the one who insisted on breaking up. Why couldn't she put her feelings for him behind her?

The following morning was a repeat of the previous one. The virus was rebounding, so she called in sick again. When it happened the third morning in a row, she went to Doc Waller's office at the end of his house.

After asking a few questions and checking her over, he asked, "Could you be pregnant?"

"I can't get pregnant."

"Who says?"

Samantha related what the doctor at the hospital said after the attack.

"He said probably?" Doc asked.

"I think his words were, 'It's not likely.' "

He raised his bushy eyebrows. "When was the last time you had sex?"

After she gave him an approximate date, Doc said, "We should do a pelvic, just to be sure."

Finishing the exam, he took off his gloves. "You can sit up now. It appears," Doc said, in his matter-of-fact way, "that your fancy hospital doctor was wrong."

Wide eyed, Sam asked, "What do you mean?"

Without commenting, he went to a drawer and pulled out a pregnancy test. "Go into that bathroom, young lady," he said, gesturing to a door, "and pee on this stick. Bring it back to me when you've finished."

In a daze, Samantha did as she was told. When she returned the test stick to Doc, she sat back on the exam table, and they both watched the clock. Looking at the wet stick, Doc said, "We'll do a blood test, as well, but the evidence, so far, says you're pregnant."

Unable to speak, Sam sat on Doc's exam table in her hospital gown, feet dangling, mouth agape.

"After you're dressed, come in the house and sit with me in the dining room. Margaret's at a meeting at the church; so she won't overhear."

They spoke, but Sam was too stunned to remember what was said. She walked to her truck in a stupor, drove home, and phoned Anna. "Can you come over? I'd come to you, but my truck is recognizable, and

I'm supposed to be in school. I hate to ask, since you have the kids, but I really need your advice."

"I just have Rex since Gracie's at school. She gets out at two, so I'm available until then. We'll be over in a few minutes."

When Anna arrived, Sam was pacing the front porch, waiting. "Come on in. I made a pallet for Rex on the kitchen floor, with blankets and a quilt. And I brewed coffee for us. Or just for you, I guess."

After dropping the diaper bag onto the quilt, Anna sat at the kitchen table with Rex in her arms. "You're a bundle of nerves. What's wrong, Sam?"

She didn't hesitate. "I'm pregnant. Doc just told me."

Anna was confused. "You said you couldn't get pregnant."

"I didn't think I could. I'm flabbergasted, excited, scared, and I don't know what to do next."

"How did this happen? I thought you and Conner broke up some time ago."

"He came by one afternoon for a visit," Sam said with a sheepish smile.

"I see. I take it you haven't told him."

"No. I'm pretty sure he's moved on like I asked him to. If I tell him, he'll offer to do the honorable thing, and then he'll feel trapped. But I know I have to tell him. How do you think he'll feel?"

"I'm not sure, but I do know he loves you. He may not be ready for a baby, at this point in life, but he'll adjust."

"I believe he loved me," Sam said. "He told me he did. But maybe not so much anymore. He stayed here the night of the funeral but slept in a guest room."

"Of course he did. You'd just buried Martin."

"That's true. I was pretty drained that night. But he's only phoned once, since, and we just talked a couple of minutes. What should I do?"

Anna's mind raced. Conner was her friend, too, and they kept in touch. She was probably more qualified than anyone to offer advice. "How far along are you?"

"Not very. Only about six weeks."

"Okay. Here's what I think you should do. Wait a while to tell Conner—maybe until after the first trimester. A lot of people do that, since there's less chance of miscarriage after the first three months. "That'll give you time to get used to the idea and think about what to say."

Sam nodded. "I like that. I feel less stressed already. At the moment, I don't know whether I'm coming or going. I thought I'd never have children. Finding out I'm pregnant with Conner's child is a miracle—a twisted, crazy, upside-down miracle."

"So you're happy about the pregnancy?"

"I am," Sam said, amazed at the turn of events. "Of course, I am. I just don't know how Conner fits into the scenario."

"Do you love him?"

"Desperately."

"Good. Then it'll all work out. You'll see."

"Do you know something I don't?"

"Just trust me. Everything's going to be fine."

Anna wanted to call Conner as soon as she returned home, but Rex had to be fed, changed, and put down for his nap. As soon as she laid the baby in his crib, she phoned her friend. "Conner, it's time. You need to do it now. I can't tell you why. You just have to trust me."

"Can't you tell me what prompted this, so I can judge for myself?"

"Afraid not. But I know the time is right," she said, praying her confidence was warranted.

"Okay. If you say so. Wow. This is really going to happen."

"Getting cold feet?"

"Let's say they're lukewarm. I'm nervous, but it's what I want. I'm doing this."

CHAPTER TWENTY

Conner immediately began making phone calls, taking care of details. Then he flew to Savannah to tell his family, face to face, what he expected from them. He spelled out his position on several fundamental issues and reminded them to respect his boundaries. His family's cooperation was crucial to the success of his plan, and failure wasn't an option. So he didn't mince words.

"Mom, when you left your family, they ceased being your priority. Instead, Dad and your children became your first concern. Am I right?" When she nodded, Conner continued.

"I appreciate everything you and Dad have done for me. You've given me the care and love I needed for a great start in life—a start many children aren't fortunate enough to have. But I'm an adult now, and Samantha is my priority. She's my future. I love you and hope you'll always be part of my life, but the time has come for me to put her first."

While Conner spoke to his family in Savannah, another piece of his plan unfolded in Tenacity. A truck, with an attached horse trailer, pulled up to the farmhouse, and the driver rang the doorbell. When Samantha opened the door, he shoved a receipt in her direction and asked where he should put the delivery.

"You're at the wrong house. I didn't order anything."

"Sorry, I forgot. I'm supposed to give you this." Curious, Samantha opened the envelope and read.

> *My dearest Sam, this gift may seem an odd way to show my love, but it's something you said you wanted. I bought the little guy for you, but when his mom objected to his leaving, I bought her too. It seemed wrong to separate them, just as it's wrong for people who love one another to be apart. Everyone needs someone who'll always have his back. I want us to be that for one another. The mom's name is Rosebud. You get to name the little guy. I love you, and I'm always here for you. Conner*

When her tears began falling, the driver said, "Lady, I'm sorry, but we need to move this along. I have to return this rig to a ranch in Louisiana before I can go home tonight." He walked to the back of the trailer, lowered the ramp, and led out a chestnut-colored horse and a mule colt.

"Aww. You're so cute." she said, hugging the colt. Feeling a firm nudge, she stood and rubbed the concerned mother's nose. "And you're beautiful,

Rosebud. You and…" She thought a minute. "You and Jasper will have a good home here."

"Where to?" the man asked.

She pointed to the corral and realized Conner had planned this all along. He understood that Rosebud and Jasper would need it while adapting to their new surroundings.

He'd thought of everything, even a water trough. After filling it with fresh water, she gave the new members of her animal family a clean bale of hay and closed the gate. Sitting on the fence, tears dampening her smiling face, she watched as the mom tried to wean her persistent offspring.

Inside the farmhouse, Samantha picked up the phone to call Conner. How could she thank him for such a magnanimous gift? And how should she respond to his note? When she finally punched in his number, he answered immediately. "Do you like them? I know it was presumptuous."

"I love them. I don't know what to say. I'm speechless."

"Then don't say anything. You like them. That's all I need to know. I do have one question. What did you name the colt?"

"Jasper. I don't know why. It just came to me."

"It's perfect."

"Conner, you're too good to me. Really. You shouldn't be doing all this."

"I like making you smile. I did make you smile, didn't I?"

"That you did. About the note…"

"Don't respond to the note until you're ready for us to move forward—together."

"I love you, Conner," Sam said softly, wishing she could ask him to come home, wanting to tell him he was going to be a father. But that wasn't news to give over the phone, and she agreed with Anna that it was best to wait.

She could cook him a good dinner though—to say thanks for Jasper and Rosebud. "Conner, would you like to…?"

"Wait. Don't say anything else. Not yet. I love you too, but I've been thinking about us and have come to a decision." He took a deep breath, hoping he wasn't making a mistake. "If you invite me to the farmhouse, give any kind of signal you want me back, I'll have my arms around you before you can blink. But the next time I come to you, I intend to stay—and not just for the night. I'm tired of leaving the next morning in what I wore the night before. I want my clothes in your closet and my toothbrush in your bathroom." Well, he'd said it. He laid it all on the line. He just hoped his strategy wouldn't backfire.

Samantha was stunned by his declaration. When she didn't speak, he said, "Maybe we should say good-night for now—talk again in a few days. In the meantime, I hope you'll think about what I said. And Sam…try to remember how good we are together."

Saturday afternoon, Anna arrived at the farm on the pretense of taking Samantha shopping.

"Shouldn't we go now?" Sam said. "It's getting a little late."

"The stores will be open until nine tonight," Anna stalled. "Max agreed to feed the kids and put them to bed. We'll have plenty of time to shop and then have a nice dinner. I've been looking forward to some no-stress girl time. Now sit down and tell me how you're doing. Are you feeling all right?"

They chatted a while before hearing cars on the gravel in front of the house. Samantha walked to the porch to see who her visitors were. Knowing what was about to happen, Anna hung back.

"Conner?" Sam said when the man's handsome blond head emerged from the Porsche. Then her attention moved to the other car. Surprised, she watched his entire family step out. "What's going on, Conner?"

"Hot Shot, Queenie, come with me," he said, walking across the yard to the porch. When he reached it, he wrapped his arms around Samantha and kissed her. Keeping one arm around her waist, he turned to face his approaching mother.

"What about the dogs?" Mrs. Wilmington asked.

"I won't let them bother you," Conner said. "Just ignore them."

"Why is your family here?" Samantha whispered.

"Mom has something to tell you."

"That's true," his mother said, reaching the porch. "It's time I own up to my mistakes."

"What? Why?"

"Because Conner loves you, and it's the right thing to do," Mrs. Wilmington answered. "Let's sit down, dear."

Conner arranged the rocking chairs so that he and Sam sat side by side facing his mother. Mr.

Wilmington and Kendall wandered toward the corral, leaving the three people on the porch to talk.

When Anna walked out of the house, Sam realized she'd forgotten all about the shopping trip. "I'm sorry. I..."

Anna didn't let her finish. "No problem. I need to get home. Max just called to say Rex is refusing his bottle." Later, she'd admit the shopping trip was a ruse. Now, she needed to make herself scarce.

Samantha watched Anna's car pull away from the farmhouse and wondered if she should have gone with her. Glancing at Mrs. Wilmington, and then staring at Conner, she silently begged him to save her from whatever was about to happen.

"My dear," Mrs. Wilmington began, "I want to apologize for disrespecting you when you were in our home. I was wrong and there's no excuse for my behavior. But I'd like to explain a few things, so maybe you'll understand what led me to behave so poorly."

Samantha slowly nodded, frowning slightly, and Conner's mother continued. "I suppose you think I consider you beneath our family. That's not true at all. I do believe our lifestyle would be an adjustment for you—one you might not want to make. I understand more about that than you think."

She took a deep breath before admitting her closely held secret. "Years ago, I had to face the daunting task of fitting into the Wilmington society scene. I didn't come from wealth. Far from it. My family lived on a discarded tugboat my father managed to make sea worthy. Because he didn't have a steady job, money was scarce, and we ate a lot of fish. He would load and unload commercial vessels whenever we docked at a port. When my brother and I were young, we played on a rusty swing set mounted to the boat's fenced-in deck, and my mother home-schooled us."

The scenario seemed so unlikely that Samantha looked to Conner for verification. "It's true," he said. "I only found out recently. She was ashamed of her background and hid it from everyone but Dad."

Samantha looked at Mrs. Wilmington, her eyebrows furrowed. "Where did you tell people you were from?"

"I said I was from a small town in Tennessee, and my dad was in the boat business. If people asked what kind of boat business, I lied and said he owned charter boats on the Tennessee-Tombigbee Waterway. It wasn't all a lie. I lived in rural Tennessee with my grandparents for high school. But when my dad discovered I'd gone on a couple of dates, he took me back to the tug. He said if I was old enough to date, I was old enough to work for a living." Mrs. Wilmington paused her story to ask for a glass of water.

"I'm sorry," Samantha said. "I should have offered."

When she started to get up, Conner stopped her. "I'll get it."

Sam wished he had let her go so she could escape the awkward situation, at least for a moment. She and Mrs. Wilmington sat in silence until Conner returned with three bottles of water.

After taking a few sips, Mrs. Wilmington continued. "Because I wasn't eighteen, I had no choice but to return to the boat. When I wasn't helping my mother with chores, I navigated the old tug, caught and cleaned fish, helped dock the boat, swabbed the deck, even learned to make some minor engine repairs. Needless to say, my hands weren't anywhere near soft, and my nails weren't manicured."

Conner's mother took a few more sips of water before returning to her story. "I wasn't allowed to return to high school, but managed to receive a GED diploma. After I married Will, I did take a few college courses."

Samantha was surprised at the revelation but didn't understand what it had to do with Mrs. Wilmington's treatment of her. If anything, it should have made her more sympathetic.

As if reading Sam's mind, the stylish woman said, "I'm sure you want to know what my story has to do with you. I'll get to that. But first, I'd like to tell you how Will and I met." Samantha sat spellbound, wondering what she would hear next.

"It was at a nautical service station," Mrs. Wilmington said with a tender smile. "Will was waiting for his family's recreational boat to be gassed up, while I waited for Daddy to fill the tug's tank. Will wandered to the hillside where I was sitting. We hit it off, and he asked if he could write to me."

"You could get mail on the boat?" Samantha asked. "Your dad didn't mind?"

"Daddy would have been furious if he'd known, and I was scared to death he'd find out," Mrs. Wilmington said. "Our family had a post office box in a small town in Georgia, which was our home base, and one of my jobs was to pick up the mail. As a precaution, Will always put a girl's name as the return address. If Daddy had seen the envelope, I was going to tell him one of my Tennessee friends moved to Durham, North Carolina, which is where Will attended school. Eventually, we plotted ways to see one another. That was harder."

Conner said, "It looks like your dad would have been happy for you to see someone who could support you."

"You'd think that, wouldn't you? But he would've been livid. Will's parents wouldn't have been pleased either. He was a college boy with a trust fund, and I was a high school dropout living on a tugboat. We didn't let that stop us. I would tell Will which port the tug was docking in, and he'd meet me when he could. We managed to see each other secretly—a few minutes here, an hour there, at least when Will wasn't away at school."

"How long did you sneak around like that?" Conner asked.

"A couple of years. We were still evading my dad after Will graduated from Duke. On one of our secret meetings, he proposed, and we married that day."

"What about your family?" Sam asked.

"I called Daddy on his ship to shore radio and told him I was married and wouldn't be coming back. I explained that Will was a college graduate, and his family was well-off, thinking that might lessen his anger. You know what he said? He told me I'd never fit in, that one day I'd crawl back and beg to live on the boat. I made the decision, then and there, that I'd do whatever was necessary to fit in. I was in love with Will and never wanted to go back to that rusty old boat."

The story was a contemporary fairy tale, but Sam wondered why Cinderella had become the mean stepmother.

"Will's parents wanted to get the marriage annulled," Mrs. Wilmington said, "but of course they couldn't. We were old enough to make that decision ourselves. So Will's mother determined to make me into a refined woman who could traverse her son's world. She had her work cut out for her. Not only was I from another socio-economic level, I'd had very little social interaction, except for that brief time living with my grandparents. I'll never know what Will saw in me that allowed him to overlook so many significant differences."

Mrs. Wilmington shook her head, remembering. "Talk about a tough mother-in-law. Will's mother was relentless. But when she got through with me, I knew my responsibilities and how to behave. It was hard, and many nights I cried myself to sleep."

Thank goodness, Sam thought, anxious to end the awkward interaction, Conner's mother finally seemed to be getting to the crux of the conversation.

"When you came to Savannah," she told Samantha, "I saw the way Conner looked at you. When I learned of your background, I got worried. At first, I feared you couldn't fit in. Later, I was afraid you wouldn't want to. Since Conner hadn't yet realized he was in love with you, I thought I could nip the relationship in the bud."

Mrs. Wilmington hesitated before continuing, as if what she was about to say was difficult. "I want what's best for my son and know from experience how hard it is to fit into a world that's foreign to you.

I didn't want you and Conner to have to go through what we did. And, I have to admit, for selfish reasons, I feared he'd realize he was in love with you and refuse to return to Savannah. Can you understand?"

"What changed?" Samantha asked. "Why are you telling me this now?"

"Now, he knows he loves you." Sam looked up at Conner, who smiled and winked.

Mrs. Wilmington touched Samantha's arm. "The two of you are in love, just as Will and I were—and still are. There's no fighting that. Fitting into my husband's world was hard, but definitely worth the effort. I now realize you're more than capable of doing the same, but Conner tells me that's not what he wants. Finally, after a lot of soul searching, I'm able to accept that."

Conner's mother looked past Sam to search her son's face, seeming to ask if she'd said enough, if she'd done all right.

Thinking she saw approval in his eyes, Mrs. Wilmington spoke her closing words. "I won't ask for forgiveness. I don't deserve it. Not now. Maybe one day I will." Then she rose and walked toward the corral, to her daughter and husband.

Conner stood, held out his hand, and helped Sam from her chair. Pulling her close, but not so close he couldn't look into her eyes, he said, "That eliminates one objection to us being together. I believe we can handle the other."

Tears flowed down Sam's cheeks as she nodded.

"Does that mean I can move in?" he said with a smirk.

Sam almost told him that depended on how he felt about becoming a daddy. But she said, "You're moving a little fast, aren't you?"

"Sometimes you like that," he teased.

Samantha liked everything about Conner Wilmington. When she raised up to kiss him, he clutched her possessively, hoping he once again had the right. With one hand in her hair, he kissed her with fervor.

Kendall cleared her throat, and Conner looked up to see his sister's smug face. Irritated by the interruption, his tone was clipped. "What is it, Kendall?"

"Mom apologized to Samantha. I want to do the same."

"That's not necessary," she said. "We had that talk the last time you were here."

"I know, but I want you to know how truly sorry I am. The pranks Reagan and I pulled were mean and dangerous. I hope you can forgive me. I'd like to be your friend."

With one arm still around Conner, Samantha held the other out to Kendall.

"Got room for two more?" Mr. Wilmington asked.

When Kendall released one arm from around Samantha, her father eagerly moved in, and her mother hesitantly followed. It was obvious that Mrs. Wilmington felt awkward with the display of emotion, but Sam gave her credit for making the effort.

Conner's father patted him on the back. "This is good, Son. This feels right." When the hug ended, the older man grasped Samantha's shoulders and looked into her eyes. "I hope you'll give this family another chance. We can do better." Then he kissed her on the cheek and gave her a bear hug.

Stepping back, the large man rubbed his ample belly. "Anyone else hungry? Where's this Lucky place my son's been talking about?"

"Lucky's Catfish House," Conner corrected. "Deep-Southern flair with a touch of Cajun for good measure."

Thanks to Anna's foresight, Samantha was dressed for the occasion. She and Conner traveled in the Porsche, while the Wilmingtons rode in the rented sedan. Conner was all smiles on the way to Lucky's, although he'd never been more nervous.

Samantha's emotions matched Conner's, but for a different reason. She had a secret to reveal, one that shouldn't be shared in a moving vehicle. How would she say it? Should she just blurt it out? How would he react?

After deciding to end the suspense as soon as they arrived at Lucky's, the Wilmingtons pulled into the parking space beside them. Samantha sighed, unsure whether to feel disappointed or relieved. The revelation would have to wait.

Conner led Sam into a private room filled with familiar, expectant faces. Samantha's mother sat at a long, rectangular table with Anna and Max to her right and Russ, Jeff, and Brian to her left. The Wilmington family quickly took seats across from them and then turned to watch Conner and Samantha.

Standing in the middle of the room with all eyes on them, Sam asked, "What's going on?" Conner didn't make her wait.

When he dropped to one knee, her hand flew to her mouth, tears ran down her face, and her knees almost buckled.

"Samantha Suzanna Lindsey," Conner began, "you are the loveliest, bravest, most talented person I know. When I asked you to dance at Max and Anna's reception, I knew you were sweet and beautiful, but I had no idea how important you'd become to me. I think of you when I wake up, when I go to sleep at night, and every moment in-between. I love you with the kind of love that supports, understands, and forgives—the kind that lasts. I want us to be a team, to face whatever life throws at us—together. Will you please share the rest of your life with me? I'll do my best to make you happy. Marry me?"

Samantha took a minute to control her feelings, before leaning over and whispering something in Conner's ear. Worried, he took her outstretched hand and followed her through the door that led outside. On the pier overlooking the murky water, Conner grasped her arm. "Careful. Don't trip over that," he said, gesturing to the resin reptile next to the "Do not feed the gator" sign.

The guests inside murmured until someone shushed them. Then they all strained to hear what was happening outside. They heard Conner laugh, but couldn't tell if it was happy laughter, or "I can't believe you said that" laughter—or something else.

When the door burst open, Conner yelled, "She said yes, and she's pregnant!"

Samantha laughed. "Looks like we won't be saying the baby came early."

"But I thought she couldn't get pregnant," someone said.

"What?" another exclaimed.

"How?" came a confused response, to which Brian quipped, "The usual way, I'm guessing."

Sam and Conner's smiles verified the declaration. Everyone stood and applauded. Then the hugging and crying commenced.

Anna breathed a sigh of relief. After assuring Conner the time was right, she'd prayed events would occur as planned. She knew her childhood friend well. If Conner had proposed after learning about the baby, she would've questioned his motivation. She might even have turned him down, thinking it was the noble thing to do. Thrilled with how the plan materialized, Anna couldn't wipe the smile off her face

Samantha introduced the Wilmingtons to her friends and family. "This is my mother," she said, with her arm around Martha's waist. "We lost Daddy recently." Once condolences were extended, she continued. "And these are my good friends, Anna and Max."

Russ saved her the embarrassment of deciding how to introduce him. "I'm Russ Windom. I live on the farm next to Sammy. These are my boys, Jeff and Brian."

Conner spoke up. "They know the story. I thought it best to tell them."

Looking for something to say, Russ settled on, "Good. That's good."

With her arm around Conner's waist, Samantha looked at the smiling people she loved most. Her world had righted itself, and she thought about the wish she made on that glittering night in Mill Village Park.

Unconvinced that the corridor possessed mystical powers, she'd nevertheless turned her face heavenward and wished to be whole again. When she'd opened her eyes, Conner Wilmington, her wish incarnate, was making his way toward her.

Was the corridor of old oaks, at the entrance to town, truly responsible for Tenacity's mystical occurrences? Sam had no idea, but her plea had been granted, and she was whole again. Getting to spend her life with Conner was a bonus she would never have thought possible.

Desperately needing to hold one another, Samantha and Conner stole a private moment on the pier. Between eager kisses, they managed to sneak in a little marriage talk and easily agree upon a plan.

Inside, Conner tapped a drinking glass with a spoon. When he had everyone's attention, he said, "I have another announcement to make."

"You're having twins," Brian guessed, loudly enough for everyone to hear.

Jeff smacked his head. "Shut up, dufus."

"Hey, Pops told you to stop doing that. You're going to give me a concussion."

Conner smiled. "No, it's not twins." Then his eyes widened, and he glanced at Sam. When she shook her head, his shoulders relaxed, and he returned to his announcement. "We've decided to get married right away if my family can stay a few days. This is Saturday. We'll plan the wedding tomorrow, get the license on Monday, and get married Monday night."

"Or Tuesday," Sam said.

"Okay. Tuesday. That'll give Miss Emma plenty of time to get here."

Conner saw his dad put a hand on his mother's arm, a silent warning not to protest. He breathed a sigh of relief when she sat back in her chair and pressed her lips together.

"What about a wedding dress?" Kendall asked.

Sam said, "I'm sure I have something in my closet."

Conner grinned at his practical fiancé.

"Where will the wedding be held?" Martha asked.

"We have an idea," Conner said, "but we have to make sure it's possible. We'll let you know."

Mr. Wilmington couldn't hold back a smile. "I hope so."

After the announcement and dessert, discussions centered around sleeping arrangements for the night. Conner was surprised to discover his parents were already planning to stay in Max and Anna's guest house.

Russ wanted to escort Martha back to Smokey Creek that night. "I'll follow you home, make sure you get there all right."

Martha smiled, knowingly. "It's too soon, Russ."

"I know," he said. "I've waited twenty years. I can wait longer."

"Besides," Martha said, "I'm not driving to Smokey Creek tonight."

When she explained her plan, Russ rubbed the back of his neck. "You sure about that? It won't get you any mother-in-law points."

Russ and Martha approached the future bride and groom. Because Jeff had overheard their conversation, he followed. He couldn't wait to see Sam and Conner's reaction to Martha's plan.

"What are you smirking about?" Conner asked Jeff.

"Looks like you're staying with me tonight, bro."

Conner chuckled. "Not on your life."

Jeff looked at Martha. "Tell him."

"I'm staying at the farmhouse with Samantha tonight," she announced. "You two shouldn't sleep together until the wedding."

"What?" Samantha blurted.

Russ shrugged when Conner looked to him for help. "Martha says that's the way it's done."

"In the nineteenth century," Sam said, annoyed with her mother's interference.

"Come on," Martha coaxed. "It's only two or three nights. You can wait that long."

Samantha wanted to ask when her mother had become the poster child for propriety, but she restrained herself.

Conner tugged his fiancé to a corner where they came to an agreement. Returning with resigned, but unhappy faces, they agreed to Martha's plan. "But Conner's driving me home," Sam said. "Take the key, Mama, and go on in. We'll hang around here for a while, have a couple of drinks."

"Okay," Martha said. "I'll leave the porch light on."

As the group walked toward the door, Jeff doubled back. "I'll be glad to follow you home," he said, his smirk returning. "I wouldn't want the two of you to get lost on the way." Samantha reached up and smacked his head.

Rubbing the spot, he spoke to Conner. "My front door will be unlocked in case you need to stay at my place."

"Anna also doubled back. "Here," she said, slyly handing Sam a key to their cabin. "This opens the front door. The place is yours as long as you need it. Use it for the honeymoon if you like. We'll keep your whereabouts a secret."

CHAPTER TWENTY-ONE

The newly engaged couple headed for the Porsche the minute their entourage left the parking lot. "I have an idea," Conner said, wiggling his eyebrows. "Let's think of our honeymoon as a series, with the first episode beginning tonight. But it'll make you late getting back to the farmhouse."

"Oh, dear. Whatever will Mama think?" Sam said with an exaggerated Southern accent. In her normal voice, she asked, "Why in the world would my mother suggest such a thing? I'm already pregnant for heaven's sake. A honeymoon series sounds perfect. I take that back. Mama returning to Smokey Creek sounds perfect, but a series will do just fine."

Unable to wait until they got to the car, they shared a scorching kiss in the middle of the parking lot. When someone yelled for them to get a room, Conner yelled back, "We plan to."

On the trip to the cabin, the groom-to-be pulled off the road to kiss Sam. "You're right about this car being too small," he said. "Right now, I'm wishing for a van."

"A van just may be in your near future," Sam said, with a sympathetic smile, "but you can always drive the Porsche to work. Then she pushed him away. "Drive. Fast. I have the cabin key in my hand."

They jumped from the car the minute it stopped. Conner scooped Sam into his arms and reached the entrance in record time. After unlocking the door, without putting her down, Conner carried his fiancé over the threshold.

"That way," she instructed, pointing to the bedroom. "Let episode one commence."

Conner grinned. As soon as Sam's feet hit the floor, they disrobed, threw back the cover, and jumped into bed. Episode one was all action with no discernible dialog. There was a reconciliation scene, a celebration scene, and, of course, the climax.

Samantha could hardly believe what was happening. She was in Conner's arms, again. They were really together, and they always would be. Cuddling close to the man she loved, his warm skin next to hers, she dreaded leaving his arms.

Wishing they could entwine their naked limbs and fall asleep, they sighed and reluctantly forced themselves from bed. Sam considered defying her mother by staying at the cabin, but Conner wouldn't begin their marriage by disrespecting his future mother-in-law. Desperately wanting more time together, they, nevertheless, dressed and drove the short distance to the farmhouse.

"Damn those floodlights," Conner complained when they stepped onto the porch. "Your mother's going to catch you sneaking into the house looking deliciously debauched."

"Deliciously?"

"Definitely."

Reluctant to part, they stood outside the front door. "I should go in," Sam said.

"I suppose so," Conner said, giving her a dream-worthy kiss. "I'll see you tomorrow, and we'll find time for episode two."

"Do we really get to spend our lives together, Conner? Are we really getting married?"

"We are. Are we really having a baby?"

"We are. Good-night, husband-to-be," Sam said, leaning toward the man she'd just made love with. Their last kiss was soft and sweet, full of love and the promise of much more.

Conner opened the front door at nine the following morning after spending the night in Max and Anna's cabin. "Anybody home?" he yelled.

When Sam came from the kitchen to give him a good-morning kiss, Conner looked down at the woman in his arms, overjoyed at the prospect of spending his life with her.

"Come on in the kitchen," Martha called. "We have a lot of decisions to make."

"Sorry about Mama," Samantha whispered.

Conner smiled. "Whatever it takes, my dear. Whatever it takes."

Once Conner helped himself to a cup of coffee and sat down at the kitchen table, the front door opened again. "It's me," Anna called, carrying a foil-covered casserole dish.

"Me, too," Gracie yelled. "I'm skipping Sunday School 'cause we have to plan."

"Come on in. We're in the kitchen," Sam said, standing to greet them.

Anna hugged everyone. "I may only get to stay until Rex gets hungry. Lately, he's been refusing his bottle. Max is good with him, but when it's time to eat he wants his Mama."

Gracie didn't jump into Conner's lap the way she used to. As a six-year-old, she was getting too sophisticated for that. Still, she sidled close, silently asking him to pick her up. He obliged. "How's my girl?"

"Good. Can I...I mean may I be your flower girl? I already know how."

Conner glanced at Samantha, who nodded.

"Of course," he said. "We'd never consider anyone else."

When the adults began talking about arrangements, Gracie wandered from the room. After a while, Anna went to check on her and heard the child's voice upstairs.

"Who are you talking to, Gracie?"

"Billy."

Anna peaked into the kitchen to ask who else was in the house.

"No one," Sam said.

Anna frowned. "Are you pretending, Gracie?"

"No, ma'am. I'm talking to Billy."

Anna told Gracie to come downstairs. When the child was safely within reach, she asked, "Who is Billy?"

"The boy I play with when I come to Aunt Sam's."

That brought Sam and Conner from the kitchen.

"I played with a boy named Billy when I was a little girl," Samantha said matter-of-factly.

"Oh," Anna said, her eyes widening. "Your imaginary playmate?"

"I'm beginning to wonder if he's as imaginary as I once thought." Stroking Gracie's dark curls, Samantha said, "Gracie, we heard you talking to Billy. Did he talk to you?"

"Sort of."

"What do you mean?"

"Well, words don't come from his mouth. He sort of thinks them, and I kinda know what he's thinking."

"It's because of the corridor," Anna announced.

Conner wanted clarification. "What's because of the corridor?"

"Billy. He's another of their miracles. The old oaks are at it again."

"Or," Martha said, "the fact that Gracie's imaginary playmate has the same name as Samantha's is a coincidence."

The group returned to the task at hand, abandoning the unanswerable question. Since Sam and Conner wanted nothing more than to get married and begin their lives together, they readily agreed to Martha's and Anna's suggestions.

When it came time to feed Rex, Anna left with a list of calls to make from home. Conner and Sam were in such a state of ecstasy, they weren't a lot of help. That left Anna and Martha to see that things got done. Mrs. Wilmington was dying to get into the act but listened to her husband when he said it wasn't her place.

Martha worked with the bride and groom through the afternoon, getting their approval on various issues and making calls. For the first time, Conner realized they could never pull a wedding off so quickly if they lived anywhere else. But in Tenacity, because everyone was so willing to help, things fell into place.

Conner and Samantha hoped Martha would drive to Smokey Creek that night, but she showed no signs of leaving. When she put Anna's casserole in the oven and prepared a salad for supper, they exchanged disappointed glances.

After they ate, Sam and Conner excused themselves, saying they were going for a drive. "Don't wait up, Mama. We might be late."

Pulling up to the cabin, they saw twinkling fairy lights strung across the porch ceiling. More of the same was inside, giving the cabin a dreamy, romantic atmosphere. "Wow," Sam said, impressed by the ambiance.

"Wow," Conner repeated. And they both remembered the night, about a year earlier, when they had turned lights on for Anna and Max's honeymoon. This time, it was Anna who provided the ambience for them.

As they gazed around the room, Conner pulled Samantha close, her back against his chest. "Tonight the romance is for us, and I plan to take full advantage of it."

Sam leaned her head back and looked up at the man she loved, amazed that the last few turbulent years had led to such happiness. Turning in his embrace, she wrapped her arms around his neck, molding her body to his. "Let episode two commence."

"First, I have something to give you.

"You certainly do," she cooed close to his ear.

"No, not that. Not yet. I hate to suggest this, since I'm really enjoying our present position, but we should sit on the sofa."

Once they sat, he pulled a small box from his pocket, put it in one of Sam's hands, and covered it with his own. "I bought this to commemorate our engagement."

"I think this commemorates it just fine," Sam said, wiggling the diamond on her left hand.

"It's nothing like that. When I gave you the bracelet at Christmas, I told you I'd add charms as we made more memories, and last night was one of the most memorable events of our lives."

Conner removed his hand and Sam opened the box. "It's a fish."

"Not just any fish. It's a catfish—because you said yes at Lucky's," he explained unnecessarily. "And here's one to commemorate tomorrow."

"It's a tree." Sam said. "It's perfect."

"I like to think it's an old oak. What charm should I get when the baby comes?" Conner wondered aloud.

"Maybe something simple, with the name and birthdate on it."

"That's right. We have to think of names. I could buy you a separate bracelet for children's charms."

"Just how many children do you think we'll have?"

"As many as you want," Conner said. "If we run out of bedrooms, we'll add a wing."

"So we'll live at the farm?"

"Of course. I'd never ask you to leave your home. Besides, I love the farm."

Samantha breathed a sigh of relief. She'd assumed that's what they'd do, but they hadn't talked about it.

He showed up with his family, swooped her off to Lucky's, and proposed. It had all happened so quickly.

Samantha looked at Conner with concern in her eyes. "Do you think you'll get bored on the farm? This isn't exactly the environment you're used to?"

"With you, I could never be bored. Besides, I've been compiling a mental list of things to do in Tenacity. I want to float the Tanakbi, eat seafood nachos at Bar None, help Jeff deliver a calf. And there are lots of things about farming I'll need to learn."

"So we're going to be farmers?"

"Maybe."

Conner took the charms from Sam, put them on the coffee table, and took her hands in his. "Speaking of our future, I haven't had a chance to tell you. I've made a career decision. I'd like to build my own practice and specialize in family law. It's not as lucrative as other law fields, but it calls to me.

"I learned a lot about investing while working for Dad, and I'm good at it; so we'll be all right financially. That'll be important with kids to raise. Ponies cost money."

"We're buying ponies?"

"Of course. Kids have to have ponies."

⁕⸛⸙⸛⸗

Monday morning, while Sam was looking through her closet for a dress to get married in, Anna swooped in to spirit her away to a boutique in Clarkston. Because she knew Conner was planning to propose, she'd already looked for a dress that might suit her friend.

Instead, she found an entire shop specializing in the bohemian style she thought Samantha would like.

"I just know you'll find something here," Anna said as they walked into the store. "The dresses in this place look like you."

And she was right. Sam found a long, flowing, bohemian-style dress, with shoes and a floral headpiece to match. Had Sam looked for months, she couldn't have found anything more ideal than the champagne-colored ensemble.

After purchasing a dress for Anna, Sam's matron of honor, they traveled to a children's boutique and found a long flowing dress for the flower girl.

The Wilmingtons made arrangements to stay through Tuesday. They let Kendall's school know she was out of town, cancelled Mrs. Wilmington's committee meetings, and Will Wilmington negotiated his business remotely. Miss Emma would arrive Tuesday afternoon in plenty of time for the ceremony.

Conner and Samantha became engaged Saturday evening and made plans on Sunday. That left two days for their friends and family to prepare the corridor for the wedding.

Barring the bride and groom from the area, they worked tirelessly to surprise them with a setting they'd never forget. Monday, they blocked off one side of the corridor, allowing traffic to travel through. Tuesday, after commuters left for work, Scott and deputy Garret blocked the corridor entrance for the final preparations. Tenacity residents had no problem using the town's other entrance for the remainder of the day.

Kendall and Mrs. Wilmington helped Luanne, the local florist, adorn an arched trellis with white and champagne blossoms. To avoid wilted flowers, they waited until the afternoon of the wedding to begin and had to work quickly. After filling the gaps with a few realistic-looking silk flowers, the arbor was ready in time.

With the help of a cherry picker from Anderson Architecture and Construction, Russ, Jeff, Brian, and Max worked most of Monday and Tuesday attaching lights to the branches of the old oaks. The tiny bulbs would mimic thousands of twinkling stars peeking through the leaves, making an already ethereal-looking setting appear even more otherworldly.

Jeff and Brian stopped working with the lights long enough to help Scott and Conner's dad haul folding chairs from the church. Once they were positioned and the flowered arch was in place, the workers stood back to admire their handiwork.

There was only one thing left to do. It was Russ's idea, and Martha and Samantha loved him for it. At the end of the first row, on a small table, they placed a long-stemmed rose and a framed photograph of Martin.

When the time came, strings of tiny lights and flickering candles illuminated the corridor, soft recorded music filled the air, and excited guests waited impatiently for the proceedings to begin. Conner stood, straight and unwavering, in front of the flower-covered arch, looking classically handsome in a cream-colored, linen-blend suit.

When a recorded piano version of "Make Believe Land" began, Anna said, "Now," and Gracie began her walk. Wearing a delicately flowered dress, she scattered daisy petals down the middle of the road.

The little girl stopped at the altar, gestured for Conner to lean down to her level, and kissed him on the cheek. "I love you, Uncle Conner," she said, before rushing to sit by her father.

With a tender grin on his face, Conner said, "I love you too, Gracie." Every guest wore a smile at the impromptu display of affection. Before the wedding, Anna had explained that marriages were about expressing love in front of friends and relatives. Gracie took the explanation to heart.

The melodious voice of Nat King Cole was Anna's cue to begin. She walked down the aisle to the tune of "When I Fall in Love," and Max's heart swelled with devotion and pride.

As Anna passed Conner, she whispered, "I'm not going to kiss you."

"That's probably best," he whispered back, and they shared an understanding smile.

As a piano version of Joe Cocker's "You Are So Beautiful" began playing, the guests stood and turned to watch the bride walk down the corridor on Russ's arm. A bouquet of pale apricot roses and white hydrangeas complimented the champagne-toned dress.

"Ahh," Gracie cooed to her father. "Aunt Samantha looks like a fairy princess. And this," she said, gesturing to the glittering corridor, "looks like her palace. Uncle Conner must be the prince."

Conner and Samantha locked eyes as she walked down the aisle, absorbing the monumental significance of the moment. When Russ delivered

Sammy to the altar, he kissed her cheek. She released his arm, kissed him back and said, "I love you, Pops."

He made it to his chair before burying his face in his hands. After so many years of loving Samantha from afar, Russ had just walked his daughter down the aisle—and she'd called him Pops. Understanding how that impacted the strong, steady man, Martha gently rubbed his back as they both fought to silence sobs.

Sam signaled for the recording to continue. Without prior planning, she sang to the man she loved, and when she got to the part that spoke of him being everything she ever wanted or needed, Conner quietly joined in. They finished the short verse together, and there wasn't a dry eye in the corridor.

Mrs. Wilmington's tears fell for a number of reasons, but regret topped the list. She'd hurt her son and the woman he loved by trying to keep them apart. She had to start listening to her husband's advice and accept her children's decisions.

If not for Will's insistence, she would have tried pushing Conner and Samantha into a big elaborate wedding, but this casual, intimate moment in the middle of a tree-surrounded highway was an emotional experience beyond anything she could have imagined.

She felt love all around her, not only between the bride and groom, but among the guests. The residents of Tenacity took care of one another, and she was beginning to understand the pull the community had on her son. She was jealous of it but also understood and appreciated it.

In front of friends and relatives, Samantha and Conner exchanged the traditional marriage vows, leaving out the obey part, of course. At the very moment the minister gave Conner permission to kiss the bride, a strong breeze blew through the corridor.

"Wish, wish," the rustling leaves seemed to whisper, and Samantha wondered if her heartfelt wish could possibly be responsible for so much happiness. A recording of "The Prayer," began to play, and Conner artfully twirled his wife into a dance.

When the next tune began, the groom signaled for everyone to join in. It wasn't long before guests brought folding tables from the beds of their trucks, food and drinks seemed to appear from nowhere, and the first-ever corridor party began.

Jeff was touched by the intimate ceremony, as well as Sammy and Conner's love for one another. He wasn't ready to settle down just yet but hoped he'd experience that with someone one day. His dad and Martha would probably make it to the altar before he did. When Jeff saw Conner and Samantha slipping away, he turned off the music and yelled, "They're leaving!"

Everyone called out their congratulations, and Conner and Samantha headed to their chosen honeymoon destination—the farmhouse.

Conner had offered to take Samantha anywhere she wanted to go for their honeymoon, but the farmhouse was her choice. They would honeymoon at home for the rest of the week and return to work on Monday. Why waste precious time traveling to some distant destination? Maybe they'd go on a trip sometime in the future, but for now, they just wanted to be alone.

Walking up the porch steps to the farmhouse, Samantha said, "We did it, didn't we?"

"We did."

"Thank you, Conner."

"For what?"

"For loving and saving me. I can't forget the past, but it doesn't hurt anymore. Everything that's happened has led me to this moment, and I'm happier than I ever thought possible."

Conner kissed her. Pulling back, he gazed into her eyes. "So am I. I love you, Sam. You're my life now—you and the baby you're carrying. You're my priority. Never question that. Scooping her into his arms, he said, "And so it begins," and he carried her into the house.

Curtains fluttered at the wavy-paned windows that opened to the deep front porch. Muffled chimes resonated from the antique grandfather clock, standing proudly in the front room. And the distinct aroma of the gracious old farmhouse welcomed the bride and groom home.

Conner looked into his wife's beautiful face, whose smile mirrored his own. Samantha was the love of his life. He was exactly where he wanted to be. And he had no doubt that he'd made the proper choice.

Acknowledgements

Thanks to my husband, **Buff Blount,** for his patience and his help in publishing *The Proper Choice.* He is my partner in every sense of the word.

A special thanks to the following ladies who lent their valuable time and expertise out of the goodness of their hearts. This is a better book due to their input.

Melaney Myers, for taking time away from her own writing to critique *The Proper Choice*. Her advice and encouragement were invaluable.

Barbara Tims Minter for her support, her comments, and for finding my spelling and punctuation mistakes.

Many thanks to my volunteer first readers for your corrections and suggestions.

Gigi Blount
Delma Simms
Jim Siders
Susan Guilbert Thayer

Anita Blount is a Mississippi native who spent thirty-three years as an Army spouse before returning home with her husband, Buff.

After seeing much of the world, she appreciates the charm of the Deep South and the idiosyncrasies of its people. Her writing epitomizes that appreciation.

Anita is a mother, a grandmother, and a former elementary school teacher.

The Proper Choice, Anita's second novel in the Tenacity series, follows *A Lovely Condition*. Although each book stands alone, the author suggests reading them in order for the most enjoyment. Watch for book three of the Tenacity series as Jeff Windom's love interest surprises him as much as it does everyone else.

If you enjoyed this book, please leave a brief review on Amazon and Goodreads.

You can visit Anita's website at
www.anitablountbooks.com.

56114549R00210